Best of ...ers

Dilly Court g...up ...e return this... London and began her ...er in te... or, ...he da... ripts for commercials. She is married with two g...wn-up ...hildren and four grandchildren, and now lives in Dorset on the beautiful Jurassic Coast with her husband. She is the bestselling author of twenty-four novels.

A Mother's Promise
Hetty Huggins made a promise to her dying mother that she would look after her younger sister and brothers. Little did she know how difficult it would be.

The Cockney Angel
Eighteen-year-old Irene Angel lives with her parents above the shop where her mother ekes out a living, whilst her father gambles this little money away.

A Mother's Wish
Since the untimely death of her husband, young mother Effie Grey has been forced to live on a narrowboat owned by her tyrannical father-in-law Jacob.

The Ragged Heiress
On a bitter winter's day, an unnamed girl lies danger-ously ill in hospital. When two coarse, rough-speaking individuals come to claim her, she can remember nothing.

A Mother's Secret
When seventeen-year-old Belinda Phillips discovers that she is pregnant, she has no option other than to accept an arranged marriage, and give up her child forever.

Cinderella Sister
With their father dead and their mother a stranger to them, Lily Larkin must stay at home and keep house whilst her brothers and sisters go out to work.

A Mother's Trust
When her feckless mother falls dangerously ill, Phoebe Giamatti is forced to turn to the man she holds responsible for all her family's troubles.

The Lady's Maid
Despite the differences in their circumstances, Kate and Josie have been friends since childhood. But their past binds them together in ways they must never know.

The Best of Daughters
Daisy Lennox is drawn to the suffragette movement, but when her father faces ruin they are forced to move to the country and Daisy's first duty is to her family.

The Workhouse Girl
Young Sarah Scrase's life changes forever when she and her widowed mother are forced to enter the notorious St Giles and St George's Workhouse.

A Loving Family
Eleven-year-old Stella Barry is forced into service when her family find themselves living hand-to-mouth.

The Beggar Maid
Must Charity Crosse give up her dream of running a bookshop and be forced to return to begging on the streets?

A Place Called Home
Despite her difficult childhood, Lucy Pocket is determined to create the family and home she has always longed for.

The Orphan's Dream
Motherless since she was five, Mirabel Cutler was raised by her father. But when he dies suddenly, Mirabel is cast out on the street by her ruthless stepmother.

The
Best of Sisters
Dilly Court

arrow books

9 10

Arrow Books
20 Vauxhall Bridge Road
London SW1V 2SA

Arrow Books is part of the Penguin Random House group of companies
whose addresses can be found at global.penguinrandomhouse.com

Copyright © Dilly Court 2007

Dilly Court has asserted her right to be identified as the author of this
Work in accordance with the Copyright, Designs and Patents Act 1988.

First published in Great Britain by Century in 2007
This edition reissued by Arrow Books in 2017

www.penguin.co.uk

A CIP catalogue record for this book is available from the British Library

ISBN 9781784752545

Printed and bound in Great Britain by Clays Ltd, Elcograf S.p.A.

Penguin Random House is committed to a sustainable future
for our business, our readers and our planet. This book is made
from Forest Stewardship Council® certified paper.

Acknowledgements

I would like to thank David Clarke of the Lakes District Museum and Gallery, Queenstown, New Zealand for his invaluable help in my research concerning the larger than life character Captain William (Bully) Hayes, and the fascinating history of the Otago goldfields.

I would also like to thank Matt Brown for giving me an insight into sail making and life aboard nineteenth-century sailing ships.

Thanks too, to my friends Kate, Georgina, Ellie and everyone at Random House for their support and encouragement, and last, but certainly not least, my splendid agent, Teresa Chris.

Chapter One

Wapping, East London,
summer 1862

A shaft of moonlight struggling through the grimy panes of the skylight sketched the pattern of the window on the bare floorboards of the sailmaker's loft. Huge rolls of canvas, wooden spars, spools of twine, sailmaker's palms and needles were set out with workmanlike precision, in readiness for the next morning when the sailmaker and his apprentices would arrive for an early start. It was hardly a comfortable dwelling place, but orphaned, twelve-year-old Eliza Bragg had only vague memories of living in a proper house. She was used to the smell of hemp, tar and beeswax and the eerie shadows, like ghosts of long-dead mariners, that lurked in the corners of the sail loft above Uncle Enoch's chandlery.

Eliza had never known her mother, who had died giving birth to her, and, although she could remember her dad's gruff voice, his infectious chuckle and the smell of the river mud that had clung to his clothes, mingling with the faint aroma of pipe tobacco, his craggy face was rapidly fading into a misty blur. He had been a waterman, working the dark and sometimes sinister waters of the Thames. In the end it was the river that had taken his life when, in thick fog, his boat had been rammed by a larger vessel. His body had never been found. Eliza, who had been just seven at the time, had comforted herself with the fancy that he slept beneath the glassy surface of the great river, rocking gently in a cradle of green waterweed, and one day might simply wake up and come home.

Her elder brother, Bart, had followed the family tradition and was now in his last year as an apprentice waterman. She was waiting, a little impatiently as she was hungry, for his return from a hard day's work on the river. Straining her eyes in the light of a guttering stub of a candle stuck in an empty beer bottle, Eliza sat on a stool at one of the trestles, reading a history book that she had won for being a diligent student at the church school for which Uncle Enoch had grudgingly paid a small annual fee. To her chagrin, he had tried his hardest to get her into one of the non-fee-paying ragged schools, but her entry had been refused on the grounds that Enoch Bragg was a comparatively well-off man. Her schooldays had ended when she was ten years old. Enoch did not approve of educated women and Eliza suspected that he did not like women at all. He had made it clear that, in his opinion, she had had enough book learning and she must now earn her living by working in the chandlery.

At one end of the table, she had set out supper for herself and Bart: half a loaf of bread, a heel of cheddar cheese, from which she had scraped most of the green mould, and a pitcher of small beer. Outside the sail loft, the familiar sounds of the Thames were muted by the night, but Eliza knew that the river never slept. Working with the tides, there was the constant movement of sailing ships, barges, lighters and wherries, docking and unloading with the banging of hatch covers, shouts of the stevedores and clanking of anchor chains. Then the whole process would continue in reverse as the empty holds were loaded with cargo. There was the seemingly endless tramp of feet on gangplanks, the rumble of cartwheels over cobblestones, the creaking of cranes, and finally the setting of sails, with the flapping sound of canvas taking up the wind.

By day there was hustle and bustle, noise and colour, but by night the soot-blackened buildings and the inky water took on a more sinister aspect. Eliza had read in her history book that the pre-Celtic name for the Thames was tamasa, meaning dark river, and she could see how the swirling water had earned its reputation. Slithering its way through London, the river was life and death to the folk who eked out a living on its banks. Sometimes the water was thick and oily-brown, the colour of stewed tea, and sometimes it was grey-green and scaly with flotsam like a half-submerged crocodile. At night, living up to its name, the dark river slunk through the city, black and sticky as tar; the last resort for the desperate and suicidal. In all its moods, the river was both awesome and dangerous. But then, Eliza reasoned, the whole of London was dangerous and the East End particularly so: Bart had forbidden her to go out alone at night and never, never to venture up Old Gravel Lane to the Ratcliff Highway, where every other building was a cheap lodging house for seamen, a drinking place or a brothel, and deep in the alleyways there were gaming hells and opium dens. By day there was drunkenness, violence, vice and robbery and, by night, even the police were afraid to venture into that particular area.

Eliza cocked her head, listening to the throbbing of a steam engine and the hoot of its whistle as the ship prepared to sail. She could hear the rhythmic chant of the seamen as they hauled in the anchor, and the even louder voice of the mate bellowing orders to the crew. Glancing at the clock on the wall, Eliza chewed the tip of her finger, wondering where her brother had got to; he was late for his supper and that wasn't like him. She closed her book and she blew out the candle to save it for when Bart came home, dirty, tired and hungry. It was stiflingly hot in the loft as it always was in summer, and correspondingly cold in the winter, but she had grown used to the extremes, having lived here since her father's untimely death five years ago. Uncle Enoch had begrudgingly taken them in, or rather he had allowed them to live in his sail loft, given them just enough food to keep body and soul together, and had insisted that they attend the mission church of St Peter's in Dock Street, at the end of Old Gravel Lane, three times on a Sunday. Bart had complied with this at first, but now at twenty he was a full-grown man, strong and muscular from years of rowing and working on the river, and his fiery temperament often clashed with that of their domineering uncle. Eliza admired and adored Bart, who was not only her elder brother but also her protector and her friend.

Waiting anxiously, she went to the top of the ladder that led down into the chandlery where Uncle Enoch spent his days making a tidy profit, though what he did with it was a mystery. Eliza imagined that he had a brassbound chest hidden in the cellar of his house just a few streets away, where he lived alone; too miserable and mean to share his life with a housekeeper, let alone a wife.

Straining her ears, she leaned through the

opening and peered down the wooden stepladder. She shivered suddenly, in spite of the heat, and her heart began to thud; there was no reason to be frightened, but a dreadful feeling of apprehension enveloped her like a London particular. Sliding down the ladder with the nimbleness of long practice, she made her way between the shelves stacked with every conceivable item that a shipmaster might want or need. Alone in the darkness, she hesitated, pricking her ears and listening to the pounding of booted feet on the cobblestones. As they came nearer, Eliza knew by some sixth sense that Bart was in trouble and she ran to the street door. She had barely reached it when someone began hammering on it with their fists. She could hear Bart shouting urgently for her to let him in and she tugged at the iron bolts with both hands. Before she had got the door half open, Bart pushed in past her. 'Lock it, for God's sake. Bolt it, Liza, and don't open it for no one.'

Even as she shot the last bolt, Eliza could hear the sharp blasts of police whistles and men shouting. 'Whatever is it, Bart? What's happened?'

Leaning against the wall, Bart bent double, fighting to catch his breath. 'I killed a man, Liza. I killed him dead.'

'No, no, you couldn't have, not you.' Eliza peered into his face. Even in the gloom, she could see that he was deathly pale and a pulse was throbbing at his temple. 'Speak to me, tell me it ain't true.'

'Shhh!' Bart clamped his hand over her mouth as the footsteps stopped outside.

Someone tried the door. 'It's locked. He can't have gone in there.'

As the sound of trampling feet grew fainter, Bart released her with a long, shuddering sigh. 'They've gone, but they'll be back. I've got to get away, Liza. If they catch me I'll hang and that's for sure.'

'Tell me what happened,' Eliza cried, running after him as he made his way through the shop, his boots barely seeming to touch the rungs of the ladder as he climbed up to the sail loft.

Hampered by her long skirts, Eliza got there to find Bart throwing his few possessions into a ditty bag. 'Bart, for the love of God, tell me what's going on.'

He paused, staring at her, his face ghostlike in the moonlight. 'I never meant to do it, Liza, but I lost me temper. The cove was drunk and he wouldn't pay what he owed me. I threatened to toss him in the river if he wouldn't cough up the money. He took a swing at me, caught me on the nose and I was mad with pain. I picked him up and chucked him over the quay wall.'

'That's not so bad, is it? I'd say he deserved a ducking for trying to cheat you.'

Bart's face contorted with anguish as he shook his head. 'If only it were just that. He was stone dead when we pulled him out. He must have hit his head on something and his neck was broke.'

'Oh, Bart!' Eliza wrapped her arms around his waist in an attempt to comfort him. 'You never meant to hurt him, I'm sure. The coppers will understand that it was an accident.'

'I won't stand a chance if they get me. There's no justice for those what can't afford a mouth-piece. If I go up before the beak, it'll be the gallows for me.'

'No, no!' She hugged him with all her might. 'Don't say that.'

Gently, Bart disentangled himself from her grasp. 'Don't be scared, Liza. I just need to get away from London for a while.'

'But what will we do, where will we go?' Eliza struggled against the tears that burned the back of her eyes. She must not cry; she was a big girl now and not a baby.

Bart shook his head. 'Not you, poppet. You're only a kid, and a girl at that. I've got to make a run for it and I can't take you with me.'

'But you can't leave me here on my own. You can't.'

'Listen to me, Liza. There's a ship sailing for Australia on the tide and I aim to be on it.'

'Then take me with you.'

'I can't.' Bart's voice cracked with suppressed

emotion. 'I'll have to work me passage. Uncle Enoch will look after you, and I'll send for you when I've made me fortune in the goldfields.'

Her tears were flowing now, pouring down her cheeks in an unstoppable stream. Hiccuping and sobbing, Eliza clutched Bart's hand to her wet cheek. 'Please take me, I'll work me passage too. I'm stronger than I look.'

'You wouldn't last the voyage, sweetheart. Now let me go, don't make it harder for me than it is.'

'You said you promised our mum on her deathbed that you'd look after me,' Eliza cried, dashing the tears from her eyes on the back of her hand. 'You can't leave me. I won't let you.'

Before Bart could answer, there was a loud hammering on the door downstairs. 'We know you're in there, Bartholomew Bragg. Give yourself up or it'll be the worse for you.'

Fear for his safety surmounted Eliza's dread of losing him. She pointed to the skylight. 'Get up on the roof and you can shin down the drainpipe, just like we used to do when Uncle Enoch locked us in with no supper.'

Bart stared at her for a moment and then he wrapped his arms around her, holding her close and rubbing his cheek against her hair. 'Be brave, Liza. I swear I'll send for you as soon as I can.' With one last hug, he let her go, and hitching the ditty bag over his shoulder he leapt onto the table beneath the skylight. He pushed it open and climbed out. Eliza could just make out his silhouette crouched against the purple night sky. A cloud had passed across the moon giving him a fleeting chance of escape. With a wave of his hand, Bart disappeared into the darkness.

Composing herself, she went back down the ladder and made her way slowly through the shop. 'All right, no need to beat the door down. I'm coming.'

The thudding on the door persisted, accompanied by threats bellowed through the keyhole. Slowly, to give Bart more time, Eliza pulled back the bolts, one by one.

'Open up, I say.'

She opened the door and was pushed back against the wall as two policemen barged in, their truncheons held at the ready. Outside, she could see a group of sailors, most of them the worse for drink, and she slammed the door.

One constable raced up the ladder and the other came towards Eliza, his black brows drawn together in a menacing frown. 'We know he come in here, so where is he?'

'I dunno what you're on about,' Eliza said, shrugging. 'There's been no one through that door since the shop closed.'

He caught hold of her ear, giving it a vicious tweak. 'You're lying, girl. He was seen heading this way.'

Before she could answer, the other man slid down the ladder. 'There's supper set for two up there, Reg.'

She could smell onions on the breath of her tormentor. His black walrus moustache and mutton chop whiskers quivered as he spoke. 'Tell me the truth now.'

'I am telling you the truth. Me brother is due home for his supper and that's all I know.'

'Leave her, Reg. Ten to one he's given us the slip down one of the alleys. We're wasting valuable time here.'

He released her with an exclamation of annoyance and Eliza staggered against a stand of shelves. They left the shop, banging the door behind them and she shot the bolts across, leaning against the wall and stuffing her hand in her mouth so that they would not hear her anguished sobbing. Without Bart her whole world felt as though it was crumbling into dust. He had been mother, father and brother to her since they were orphaned and now, suddenly he was gone; accused of a terrible crime and set on leaving the country for a far-off land. Somehow, Eliza managed to climb the ladder to the sail loft. She threw herself down on the straw palliasse that served as a bed and cried herself to sleep.

Next morning, she found that the rats had polished off the bread and cheese and there was nothing left to eat, but she was not hungry.

Downstairs she could hear Uncle Enoch hammering on the shop door and demanding to be let in. Climbing stiffly off the thin mattress, she made her way slowly down the ladder. She pulled back the bolts with a heavy heart, dreading Uncle Enoch's reaction when he found out what had happened last night.

'Lazy little good-for-nothing,' Enoch said, pushing her out of the way. 'I expect the shop to be opened and cleaned ready for business and I catch you sleeping. Just look at the state of you.'

'Sorry, Uncle.' Eliza bent her head, staring down at her bare feet.

'And I've had the police round knocking on my door in the middle of the night. Where is he? Where's that bastard brother of yours?'

So he knew; her heart sank. 'I – I don't know.'

Enoch glowered at her. His eyes narrowed into slits beneath beetling brows. 'Don't lie to me, girl. Unless you want your mouth washed out with soap. Where is he?'

'Gone.' Raising her chin defiantly, Eliza looked him in the eye. 'He never done it. It were an accident and Bart's gone off on a ship. They'll never catch him.'

He caught her a blow across her cheek that knocked her to the ground. 'I've raised a nest of vipers. Is this all the thanks I get for my Christian charity? I never wanted to take you in, but I did it for the sake of my dead brother. Is this how you repay me?'

Eliza bit her lip so that she would not cry. She scrambled to her feet, clutching her cheek. 'It were an accident and I don't know where he's gone to.'

'You're lying.'

'No, I ain't. I'm telling you the truth.'

'Don't answer back. Haven't you learnt anything in church on Sunday?'

'I done nothing wrong, Uncle.'

'Nothing wrong?' Enoch's voice rose to a roar. He went to search behind the counter, scrabbling around amongst the ledgers and receipts until he found a piece of card and a pencil. He wrote something on it and beckoned to Eliza. 'You've helped a murderer to escape and you won't say where he has gone. You are a liar and everyone shall know it. Come here.'

Reluctantly, Eliza went to him.

'Turn round.'

Eliza turned her back to him and she could feel him pinning the card to her thin cotton blouse. The pin scraped her flesh but she did not cry out.

'You'll wear that until you've learnt your lesson. Now get about your business and clean the shop before the customers arrive.' Enoch looked up as the door opened, and a ruddy-cheeked, bald-headed man strode in followed by four boys. 'You're late, Peck,' Enoch said, scowling. 'Don't expect me to lower the rent on the premises if you can't fulfil your orders.'

Ted Peck, the sailmaker, strode past Enoch, heading for the ladder. 'Don't worry, old man, you'll get your rent as usual.'

Eliza kept her head bowed so that she did not have to look at the youths as they filed past her. She did not know what Uncle Enoch had written on the placard but she could guess, and it wouldn't be flattering. Ted stopped at the bottom of the ladder, waiting until the last apprentice had scampered up into the loft before following them at a more orderly pace. When he reached the top, he looked back over his shoulder. 'Miserable old bugger,' he said, scowling at Enoch. He closed the hatch with a bang.

Enoch looked up, frowning. 'I'll double his rent if he's not careful. And you,' he added, pointing his quill pen at Eliza, 'get to your work or I'll take you across the road to the workhouse and leave you there.'

The threat of the workhouse was enough to make Eliza run out to the back yard where she filled a bucket with water from the pump. She carried it back inside, walking slowly so that she did not spill water on the tiled floor. Having fetched a mop, scrubbing brush and a cake of lye soap from the store cupboard, she was about to start work when Ted wrenched the hatch open and slid down the ladder. 'How many times have I told you to clean up your mess before we start work?'

Enoch looked up from the ledger. 'What's this?'

Ted approached him with a belligerent out-thrusting of his chin. 'You may own the place, mister, but that don't give your relations the right to leave my sail loft like a midden. There's been food left out and that's brought in the bleeding rats. They've had a go at the spanker we've been working on, and eaten half a pound of beeswax to boot. I tell you, Enoch, I ain't running a home for waifs and strays up there and that's a fact.'

Enoch turned on Eliza with a face like thunder. 'You, girl. Go up there and sort it out. From now on you sleep under the counter. Don't never bring food into the chandlery again.'

'Come now, that's a bit harsh.' Ted cast an anxious glance at Eliza. 'Maybe I spoke up a bit too hasty.'

'You did not. I've been a sight too lenient with the girl and her feckless brother. Get up that ladder, Eliza.'

There was no point in arguing, and she climbed up into the loft where the apprentices were sitting cross-legged on the floor, working on the large piece of canvas that Eliza knew would eventually become a fore-and-aft sail, called a spanker. Stepping carefully, and ignoring the taunts from the Tonks brothers, two of the older apprentices, she went over to the table to clear away the debris left by the rats. She was not in the mood to be picked on by anyone, least of all two cheeky boys only a few years her senior. Mostly the apprentices treated her with casual indifference, like a younger sister or an amusing puppy-dog, and the copper-headed Tonks brothers were all right if you kept them in their place. Dippy Dan Bullen was a bit simple and laughed a lot even when things weren't funny. Only Davy Little was her real friend, and then he had to make certain that the other lads were not looking when he chatted to her, or gave her a fluff-covered humbug from his pocket. They would have teased him mercilessly had they seen him taking notice of a mere girl.

Ginger Tonks looked up and grinned. 'What's this we hear about your Bart then, young 'un?'

Carrots nudged Davy. 'Your little friend's brother is a murderer, Davy. Did you know that?'

'He ain't,' Eliza cried, balling her hands into fists. 'Don't you dare say that. It were an accident and that's the truth.'

'Is that why you got LIAR written on your back?' demanded Ginger, chuckling.

Davy leapt to his feet. 'That's enough. Leave her alone, can't you? Whatever Bart's done it ain't Liza's fault.'

'Ooer!' Dippy Dan jumped up and did a jig, giggling and chanting. 'Davy's sweet on Liza, Davy's sweet on Liza. Bart's going to have his neck stretched. Bart's going to have—'

'Shut up!' Davy turned on him. 'You ain't funny, Dippy.'

'Leave him alone,' Ginger said, shoving the needle through the canvas with the aid of a sailmaker's palm. 'Best get on, Davy, or Peck will give you what for.'

'Be quiet, all of you,' Eliza said, piling the palliasses one on top of the other and shoving them in a far corner. 'And don't let me hear one bad word about Bart or I'll . . .'

'Or what, young Liza?' Carrots got to his feet and struck a pose. 'Want to take a big feller on then?'

'She can't, but I can,' Davy said, squaring up to him. 'Pick on someone your own size.'

'Stop it.' Eliza swept the remains of the supper into her apron. 'I'll tell you this once and for all: my brother never killed no one, at least not intentionally. He's gone off on a ship to the other side of the world and . . .' Choking on a sob, Eliza bunched up her apron and made for the ladder.

Davy followed her to the open hatch. 'Don't pay no heed to them idiots.' Thrusting his hand in his pocket, he pulled out an apple and handed it to Eliza. 'Here, take this. The rats ate your supper and I bet you ain't had nothing to eat this morning.'

Eliza hesitated, certain that this was Davy's dinner, but she didn't want to hurt his feelings and she was extremely hungry. She took it with a smile and a nod. 'Ta, Davy.'

At ten o'clock that evening, just as it was getting dark, Enoch emptied the till and put the takings into a leather pouch. 'Don't forget,' he said, scowling at Eliza, 'you sleep under the counter and I want the shop floor cleaned and everything nice and tidy when I arrive in the morning.'

'Yes, Uncle.' Dog-tired and fraught with worry about Bart, Eliza stood with her hands behind her back, digging her fingernails into her palms and biting back tears. Apart from the apple that Davy had given her, she had eaten nothing all day and now she was light-headed with hunger.

Enoch was about to leave, but he paused in the doorway, delving his hand into his pocket. He produced two pennies, tossing them onto the floor at Eliza's feet. 'Get yourself something to eat in the pie shop. I won't have anyone say I neglect my duty. And make sure you lock up after me.'

After he had gone, Eliza bolted the door. Left alone in the gloom, she felt suddenly nervous. The stands of shelves seemed menacing as they loomed over her in the half-light; there were creaks and scuffling sounds coming at her from all directions. It could have been the floorboards contracting in the cool of the evening, or it might be rats coming out to look for food. She had been forbidden to go upstairs to the familiar surroundings of the sail loft, but the shop at night was a frightening place. Even if Bart had been late home, at least she had always known that he would come eventually. How would she manage without Bart to comfort and protect her? All day, she had worried about him, wondering if he had managed to get a berth on a ship and praying that he had got away. Surely she would have heard if the police had caught him? The light was fading fast now and Eliza went behind the counter to look for a box of vestas, and having found one she lit a candle. Its flickering flame cast ghostly shadows on the walls and ceiling. Something brushed past Eliza's cheek and she let out a scream, but it was only a moth attracted by the candlelight.

By now, she was trembling with fear, as well as hunger, and shielding the flame with her hand she went through to the back of the shop. She stuck the candle on the lid of a paint tin with a bit of melted wax, and unlocking the door to the back yard she went outside into the velvet warmth of the July night. The stench from privies, overflowing sewers, rotting detritus in the streets and the stinking mud from the river made Eliza cover her nose with her hand, but within a few seconds she had accustomed herself to the noxious smell. She felt her way through the packing crates and other items that Uncle Enoch stored outside, to the heavily locked gate. She turned the iron mortice key in the lock and shot back the three strategically placed bolts. It would, she thought, be easier to escape from the Tower of London than Uncle Enoch's back yard. As she stepped outside into the alley, something large and black ran across her feet. An unseen hand touched her arm and she screamed.

'It's only me, Liza.'

Spinning round to face him, Eliza slapped Davy on the shoulder. 'You idiot, you frightened me half to death.'

'Sorry, I never meant to. I was waiting for you.'

She took a deep breath, struggling to control her erratic heartbeats. She had thought for an instant that it was the police, who had been lying in wait to trap her into telling them where Bart had gone. 'How did you know I'd come out this way?'

'I knew you'd have to get some grub and the old skinflint wouldn't be asking you round to dine at his place.'

Even in the darkness, Eliza sensed that Davy was grinning and suddenly her own mood lifted. 'I got tuppence,' she said, jingling the coins in her pocket. 'Let's go to the pie shop.'

'I wouldn't say no to a plate of pie and mash. The old man's drunk his wages again this week. We're on bread and scrape until Pete brings his wages home from the brewery.'

'Come on then,' Eliza said, breaking into a trot. 'I'll race you to the pie shop.'

Later, having enjoyed a plate of steak pie, mash and gravy washed down with mugs of sweet tea, Eliza and Davy walked down Old Gravel Lane to Execution Dock, where pirates had once been hanged and left in cages to rot, as a warning to those who might consider following their bloodthirsty profession. Despite its grim history, or maybe because of it, Eliza and Davy often walked this way; deliberately ignoring Bart's stern warning never to venture there, especially at night. Drunken sailors of all nationalities were weaving their way back to their ships, some with equally intoxicated women hanging on their arms, singing, laughing and taking swigs of jigger gin from crusty bottles. Eliza cast a pitying glance at an old woman bent double, skimming the pavements for dog faeces, which she would sell as pure to be used in the tanneries. Turning her head away, Eliza held her nose. 'I don't know how she can do that.'

'I don't expect she's got much choice,' Davy said, guiding Eliza away from a particularly putrid pile of turds. 'Hey, lady, there's a tuppenny-worth of pure here.'

The old woman raised her head. 'Ta, ducks.' Shuffling up behind them she scooped the revolting mess into her bucket.

Eliza walked quickly on. 'Poor soul! I don't suppose she was always like that.'

Davy fell into step beside her. 'It's easy to fall on hard times.'

Coming to a halt on the edge of the quay wall, Eliza stared down at the oily black water slithering out to sea on the high tide. The reflections of the gaslights shimmered in fractured pools on the surface. 'It looks like dead people holding flaming torches beneath the water,' Eliza said, shuddering.

Davy looked over her shoulder. 'It's just your imagination, Liza. It looks like reflections of the street lights to me.'

She gave him a sideways glance, unsure whether or not he was laughing at her; he wasn't. 'That bloke died in the river; the one that Bart pushed off the quay wall. He never meant to kill him.'

'Did he drown then?'

'He was dead when they fished him out. Bart thought his neck was broke.'

Davy hooked his thumbs into his belt with a careless shrug. 'There's plenty of corpses dragged from the river every night. The dead houses is stacked high with suicides and them what's met a sticky end. Me dad says that poor sods chuck themselves off bloody bridge in New Gravel Lane, sometimes two or three a night. They ends up floating in the East London Dock or else they gets carried out through the basin into the river. He drags them out all bloated and swollen – that's when he's sober enough to know what he's about.'

Eliza had seen the odd dead cow or dog floating downstream but never a human body; she quickly put the image out of her mind. 'Don't let's talk about it.'

A noise from across the street put a stop to the conversation as two drunken men lurched out of a pub, falling into the gutter. Punching and kicking, they rolled over and over on the thick carpet of straw, mud and horse dung. Men and women staggered out of the pub door, forming a small crowd and egging them on. Then the fight seemed to escalate as minor scraps broke out, and soon there was a tangle of flailing limbs, shouting, swearing and grunts of pain.

'Come on,' David said, grabbing Eliza by the hand. 'Let's get out of here.' They ran along the quay wall in the direction of home. Davy slowed down a little as they reached the workhouse at the end of Old Gravel Lane. They were out of range of the brawling drunks now, but he would not allow Eliza to rest until they reached the alley behind the chandlery.

Breathless, and with a stitch in her side, Eliza leaned against the gate. 'You'd best get home, Davy; it's late and you got to get up early.'

'Will you be all right on your own, Liza?'

'Of course I will.' She tossed her head, but inside she was quaking at the thought of going back inside the empty building.

'I'll see you in the morning then. Ta-ta.' Davy loped off in the direction of Farmer Street, where his large family dwelt in a damp, overcrowded cellar.

Eliza crept into the yard. In the distance she could still hear the blasts of police whistles and men shouting. A pair of eyes glowing in the dark made her stifle a scream, but it was only a cat out hunting: she could have cried with relief when it leapt on top of the wall with an angry miaow.

Having locked and bolted the gate, Eliza was fumbling for the key to the back door when someone grabbed her from behind and a hand clamped over her mouth.

Chapter Two

'It's me, Liza. I'm taking me hand away. For God's sake don't scream.'

'Bart!' Sobbing with relief, Eliza turned, flinging her arms around his neck. 'Bart, you've come home.'

'I can't stay, poppet. I just come to make sure you was all right.' Cocking his head on one side, Bart was silent for a moment, listening. He laid his finger on Eliza's lips. 'I can hear the cops' whistles. Was you followed?'

'No, there's a fight going on outside the Blue Anchor.'

'What was you doing on Execution Dock?' Bart gave her a shake, and then he hugged her in a grip that almost robbed her of breath. 'I told you never to go there.'

Eliza pushed him away, half laughing, half crying at the relief of seeing him when she thought he had left her for good. 'Don't scold me, Bart. I'm so happy to see you.'

'I ain't stopping. Let's get inside.' Bart stood back while Eliza unlocked the door. Once inside, he leaned against the wall, closing his eyes. 'I don't never want to live through another twenty-four hours like the last.'

Eliza felt along the shelf for the vestas and lit the candle. Holding it high, she could see that Bart was both dirty and dishevelled, with dark stubble sprouting from his chin. 'Where've you been all this time, Bartie? Why didn't you go on the ship to Australia like you said?'

'Missed the boat, didn't I? But I went round the docks until I found a ship bound for New Zealand. I've heard stories about goldfields where you can pick up nuggets the size of a baby's head and get rich overnight. That's where I'm bound, Liza. I'll come home a rich man or not at all.'

'Don't say that, you're scaring me.'

He patted her cheek. 'You mustn't worry about me, love. I'm as tough as the next man, and I've got the will to succeed. I'll not let you down, little sister.'

'Oh, Bartie!' Eliza wrapped her arms around his waist and laid her head against his chest. 'I wish I could come with you. It's horrible here without you.'

'Has he been cruel to you?' Bart's voice cracked with concern.

'No.' She did not dare look him in the face. He would know for sure that she was lying. 'Not particularly.'

'What do you mean, not particularly? What's the old bastard done since I left?'

'Ted Peck complained because I'd left food on the table and the rats had made a mess of things. Uncle Enoch said I can't sleep up there no more.'

'What?'

'It don't matter, honest. I don't mind sleeping under the counter.'

'That's it!' Bart's voice rose to a roar. 'I'll not have me sister treated like a common counter-jumper. We're Braggs, you and me, Liza, and the old man's got to take heed of that once and for all.'

'What are you going to do?'

'We're going round to his house in Bird Street, and I'm having it out with him.'

'But the police?'

'Damn the cops, I say, damn them all. I ain't leaving London until I'm sure you're fixed up proper.'

Storm clouds had blotted out the moon and a steady drizzle was falling as Bart dragged Eliza along Green Bank to Bird Street. Uncle Enoch's tall, narrow house was wedged between a tobacco warehouse and a seamen's mission. Although it was close on eleven o'clock at night, and in spite of the rain, the street was teeming with people. Ragged children stood in the gutter, soaked to the skin and ankle-deep in filth, begging for money from passers-by. Prostitutes solicited from gloomy doorways and drunks lurched out of the many public houses and gambling dens. Pickpockets, petermen, stevedores, lightermen and sailors crowded the street and, after the heat of the day, steam rose from the pavements. The damp night air was filled with the stench of unwashed bodies, tobacco and the fumes of alcohol. In the midst of all this hustle and bustle, Bart and Eliza were able to mingle unnoticed and they made their way to Enoch's house.

Bart hammered on the door knocker and, eventually, Enoch stuck his head out of an upstairs window, his nightcap askew and his face contorted with rage. 'Who's that there, pounding on my door at this time of night?'

'Let us in, old man.'

'Get away from here, you bastard. I don't want to know you.'

'If you don't open the door, I'll kick it in.'

'No need for that.' Enoch disappeared into the room, slamming the sash so that the glass windowpanes rattled. Seconds later he opened the door. 'Come inside before someone recognises you.'

The entrance hall was little more than a narrow passage. Enoch led the way to the kitchen at the back of the house. Eliza had been in the dingy room just once before, five years ago, on the day that her father had been buried beside her mother in St George's churchyard. She saw now that nothing had changed, from the rusting range to the unwashed flagstone floor and the grimy, small-paned window that looked out onto the back yard.

'I ought to turn you over to the police,' Enoch said, scowling at Bart. 'What are you doing here, you villain?'

'I may be a villain in the eyes of the law, but I wouldn't treat a dog like you treated me little sister. I won't have it no longer, old man.' Bart took a threatening step towards Enoch, who backed away seizing a wooden chair and holding it in front of him.

'Lay a finger on me and I'll see you hanged. You'll end up in Newgate, Bartholomew Bragg. You see if you don't.'

Despite his harsh words, Eliza could see by the way his eyes rolled, exposing the whites, and his mouth worked constantly, even when he was not speaking, that Uncle Enoch was terrified.

'That's right,' Bart said, snatching the chair from Enoch and hurling it across the room. 'I'll probably end up on the gallows, so I've got nothing to lose, and wringing your skinny old neck ain't going to make a scrap of difference.'

'Leave me be.' Enoch sank to his knees, clasping his hands in front of him and closing his eyes, as if he were in church, praying.

'You leave Eliza be.' Grabbing Enoch by the throat, Bart dragged him to his feet. 'I'm dead serious. I'll be gone by daybreak, far away from England and far from you, old man. But I got to be certain that my Eliza is being looked after.'

'She will be, I promise.' Enoch's face had turned grey-white, matching the colour of his nightshirt.

'She's to be fed and housed decent. She's to be clothed and shod like a young lady and I don't want her treated like a skivvy. Do you understand me?'

'I – I do.'

'I want you to swear on the Bible that you're so fond of thrusting down our throats. Come on, old man, where is it? You must have one.'

'Over there.' Enoch pointed to a wooden shelf in the alcove at the side of the chimneybreast.

'Fetch it, Liza, and put it in his hand.'

Eliza did as she was told, eyeing her uncle warily, half expecting him to leap up and throttle Bart, but seemingly he was genuinely fearful, and he clutched the Bible to his chest.

'Swear on it. Swear that you'll care for Eliza just as though she was your own daughter. Promise me you'll let her live here, in your house, and that you'll make the place decent.'

'I – I swear it.'

'Bart.' Eliza tugged at his sleeve. 'Don't make me live here with him.'

Enoch scrambled to his feet, still clutching the Bible. 'No, she wouldn't be comfortable here.

This isn't a good place for a little girl to live.'

'You'd best see to it then. Find her some lodgings with a respectable family. If you don't, I swear I'll come back and cut out your black heart and feed it to the crows.' Bart held his hand out to Eliza. 'Come on, Liza, we're going back to the shop just for tonight. Tomorrow you'll be housed like a young lady. Ain't that right, Uncle?'

'That's right,' Enoch mumbled through chattering teeth. 'That's right. Now get out of here and don't let anyone see you leave.'

Bart left before daybreak. Eliza managed to see him off with a smile and only broke down into floods of tears when he had disappeared from sight. She had never felt so lost and alone and, if it were possible for a twelve-year-old heart to break, then she was certain hers had shattered into smithereens. As the first grey shards of dawn filtered through the skylight, she set about tidying the sail loft before Ted and the apprentices arrived. Bart had refused to sleep in the shop and had laid the palliasses side by side, just as they had always been. In spite of this, Eliza knew that he had not slept much at all; she had awakened several times to hear him pacing the floor, but each time she had drifted back into a sleep of sheer exhaustion. Having left the sail loft clean and without a trace of having been used, Eliza set about cleaning the shop floor, dusting and tidying the counter ready for opening.

Enoch arrived on the stroke of seven and, as she let him into the shop, Eliza glanced up at him nervously, wondering what sort of mood he was in this morning. As he strode past her, his face was pale and tight with anger. At first he did not speak and she found his silence more frightening than a tirade of words. She stood, shifting from one foot to the other, while he went behind the counter and took down the stock book.

She licked her dry lips. 'Wh-what do you want me to do next, Uncle?'

Enoch looked at her for the first time, his brows knotted together over the bridge of his nose. 'Come here, girl.'

She hesitated, eyeing him warily.

'You set Bart on me by telling lies, I know very well you did.' Unbuckling his leather belt, he doubled it up, slapping it against the palm of his hand. 'You need a lesson in respect for your elders. I can't have you turning out bad like your brother. Come here.'

'No! I won't. You can't beat me for nothing. You promised Bart you'd look after me. You swore on the Bible.'

'Insolent child!' Before she had a chance to escape, Enoch caught Eliza by the scruff of her neck, forcing her to bend over a pile of coiled rope. He brought the belt down across her back-side with such force that the air exploded from her lungs in a howl of pain. Again and again he thrashed her until she fell, half-fainting, to the floor. Dimly, she heard the door open and the sound of chattering voices that ceased abruptly.

'Gawd's strewth, man. You've half killed the poor little sod.' Ted's voice was harsh with rage as he lifted Eliza up in his arms. 'Fetch some water, Davy.'

'Leave her be,' Enoch snarled. 'She's a limb of Satan and she deserved every last lash of my belt.'

'I've never even beaten me apprentices with such viciousness, and some of them deserved a lot worse. Why, Eliza's nothing more than a child and a girl at that. Call yourself a good Christian man, Enoch Bragg. I'd say it was Satan that had got into you.'

'Her brother is a murderer. Bartholomew Bragg is a cold-blooded killer who attacked an innocent man and sent him to his grave. He is a bastard in the true sense of the word and they've both got tainted blood. It'll be the workhouse for her before the day is over.'

'You'd do that to your own kith and kin?' Ted set Eliza gently down on her feet, supporting her with his arm around her waist.

'She's no kin of mine. I'm washing my hands of her as from today.'

Eliza leaned against Ted, too bruised and sore to take in the enormity of Uncle Enoch's words. This was a nightmare: it couldn't be happening. She felt Ted's arm tighten around her and he shook his fist in Enoch's face. 'You're an evil old codger, and no mistake.'

'Bah! You're a soft-hearted old fool.' Enoch spat the words as he retreated behind the counter.

Davy came running in from the yard, carrying a mug of water. 'Here, Liza, take a sip of this.'

Wetting her dry lips, Eliza managed to drink some of the cool water. 'Ta, Davy.'

'He's a brute,' Davy whispered. 'My old man ain't as bad as that, even when he's boozed up.'

'Get to your work.' Enoch pointed a shaking finger at Ginger, Carrots and Dippy Dan who were standing in the doorway open-mouthed. 'Get up that ladder, you're cluttering up my shop. And that goes for you too, Peck. I'll thank you to mind your own business.'

Ted squared up to Enoch, sticking out his chin. 'I'm making it my business, Enoch Bragg. You're not fit to look after a dog, let alone a child. Never mind what her brother has done.' He turned to Davy. 'You know where I live, boy?'

'Yes, sir.'

'Then I'm trusting you to take Eliza to my house. Tell my wife that she'll be staying with us for a while. Mrs Peck will take care of her.'

'Come on, Liza,' Davy said, ignoring Enoch's

protests and taking her by the hand. 'It ain't too far to walk.'

She cast an anxious glance at her uncle, waiting for him to say something, but he turned his head away and opened the ledger. Too stunned to speak, Eliza allowed Davy to lead her out of the shop into the sunshine.

The Pecks lived in a terraced, red-brick cottage in Hemp Yard, a small court off Green Bank, built in the shadow of the huge warehouses that surrounded the London Dock and its basin. Davy hammered on the door until Mrs Peck opened it, peering out from beneath a starched, white cotton mobcap and blinking like a dormouse awakened from its long winter sleep. 'Who's there?'

'It's me, Davy Little, and I've brought Eliza Bragg with me. The boss says she's to stay with you awhile and you'll know what to do for her. Old bugger Bragg has beaten her something cruel.'

'Watch your language, my boy.' Dolly Peck squinted short-sightedly at Eliza. 'Are you Tom Bragg's daughter?'

Eliza nodded. The sun was beating down on her sore back and she was beginning to feel sick. Her knees were trembling so that she could hardly stand, and she clutched at the doorpost for support.

'Bring her in, boy. Don't keep her standing on the pavement.'

'I'd best get back, missis,' Davy said, helping Eliza into the living room. 'You'll be all right here, Liza. I'll come and see you when I've finished work.'

For a moment, Eliza clung to his hand, but she knew he would get into trouble if he took too long. She managed a wobbly smile. 'Ta, Davy. I'm all right, I am really.'

'That's the ticket.' He gave her a cheery wink as he went out into the street, closing the door behind him.

'Well then, Miss Eliza, let's have a look at you.' Dolly picked up a pair of steel-rimmed spectacles and put them on. Her eyes looked enormous through the thick lenses and her jaw dropped as she peered at Eliza. 'That man ought to be horsewhipped. Take off your blouse while I go out and get some water and clean linen.'

Eliza had to bite her lip so that she did not cry out as Dolly bathed her back with warm water from the kettle. 'Wicked, wicked man,' she said, tut-tutting and shaking her head. 'You poor little thing. You must stay here with us for as long as you like.'

'I don't want to be no trouble, missis.'

Taking off her specs, Dolly blinked and wiped her eyes. 'If my Ted says you're to stay here, then stay you shall.' She put the bowl aside and picked up Eliza's torn, bloodstained blouse. 'This is past repair. I'll find you something to wear and Ted can send Davy round with the rest of your things later.'

'That's all I have,' Eliza whispered. 'I ain't got nothing but what I stand up in. Uncle Enoch says no one needs more than one set of clothes; anything else is greed and vanity.'

'Well, I'd like to say a few choice words to Mr Enoch Bragg, the old skinflint. Never you mind that, dearie. I was feeling quite poorly this morning; could hardly drag meself from me bed, but now I'm so downright cross with your uncle that all me aches and pains has quite disappeared. Come upstairs to the bedroom, my dear. I'm sure I can find something that will fit you.' Getting to her feet, Dolly went towards the staircase, bumping into a chair on the way. 'Drat, who moved that chair?'

'Why don't you keep your spectacles on, Mrs Peck?' Eliza stared curiously at Dolly, momentarily forgetting her pain and discomfort.

'I don't need them, dear. Just for close work. My Ted always said I had a fine pair of eyes, the colour of the sky in summer,' Dolly said, tripping over the bottom step. 'I really don't need to wear specs.'

At the top of the narrow staircase there were two bedrooms, of which Dolly's was the larger, looking down onto the street. Eliza gazed round the room with a gasp of pleasure. She had lived in the sail loft for so long that she had almost forgotten what it was like to be in a proper house. The scent of lavender and clean linen brought back distant memories of the home she had once shared with her dad and Bart, and a lump to her throat. One day, Eliza thought, clasping her hands together, I will have a bedroom just like this and all to meself. She made an effort to memorise every detail, from the iron bedstead draped with a patchwork quilt, to the pine wash-stand with its china jug and bowl, patterned with red cabbage roses. Above the bed there was a framed picture of Queen Victoria, looking rather bored but extremely regal. Floral print curtains hung at the windows and a rag rug made a pool of bright colour on floorboards that had been scrubbed white, like boiled beef bone.

Seemingly unaware of the emotions that her simply furnished room had stirred in Eliza's heart, Dolly opened a wall cupboard and had begun sorting through the garments. She selected a cotton blouse that must have once been white, but was now yellowed with age. It was several sizes too large for Eliza, but tied in at the waist with a piece of coloured ribbon, it did not look too bad; at least that was what Dolly said and Eliza was happy to believe her. Having tut-tutted again at the state of Eliza's bare feet, Dolly said they would have to buy her a proper pair of boots. Mr Peck would have to cough up the money, whether he liked it or not.

'Now this will be your room,' Dolly said, as she squeezed past Eliza. She went out onto the landing and opened a door that led into a boxroom, empty except for a truckle bed. She heaved a sigh. 'This was to be the room for our babies when they come, but the Lord never saw fit to bless us with children.'

A wave of dizziness swept over Eliza and she leaned against the lintel, wincing as the wood pressed on her sore back.

'Perhaps you'd better lie down for a bit,' Dolly said, pointing to the bed. 'Lie on your tummy, dear, and it won't hurt so much.' She felt her way along the wall to the top of the stairs and went slowly down, hanging on to the banister for dear life. Eliza sat on the bed watching her. She couldn't help feeling that Mrs Peck really ought to wear her specs, or one day she would have a terrible fall.

'Well, what are we to do with you?' Ted drained his glass of small beer and wiped his mouth on the back of his hand. Having finished his supper of boiled bacon and pease pudding, he pushed his chair back from the table. 'How old are you, Eliza, my dear?'

'Twelve, sir.'

'She's just a baby,' Dolly said, reaching out to

clasp Ted's hand. 'Let me keep her by me for a while? It gets lonely with you out at work and me being a poor invalid, and not able to go out.'

Ted patted her hand. 'I know, ducks, but Eliza's old enough to work and I'm not a rich man. Bragg says he don't want her back and I can't afford to keep her if she don't pay her way.'

'I'm used to working,' Eliza said stoutly. She had eaten a whole plateful of bacon and pease pudding and, although her back was still smarting and the bruises were sore, she was already feeling much better. 'I'm used to hard work. I done me bit ever since I left school two years ago, and I studies me books of a night, when it's light enough for me to see the print.'

'Please, Ted. At least let her stay at home until the cuts on her back heal. I can teach her to sew and together we can make her a new frock; she'll need some proper clothes if she's to get a job.'

'It was sewing that ruined your eyes, Dolly.' Rising to his feet, Ted took a tobacco pouch and a pipe from the mantelshelf. 'You was the best seamstress in Wapping until your sight failed.'

'I can see perfectly well,' Dolly said, pouting. 'If Eliza has a talent for sewing, maybe we could get her apprenticed to a seamstress. It's a nice clean job and she could work from home.'

Ted sat down again and began filling his pipe with tobacco. 'Sewing shirts for twopence-halfpenny a time and weakening her eyes working by candlelight? I think we can do better for our new daughter, Dolly, for that's how I shall think of Eliza from this day onwards.'

Why they were being so kind to her, Eliza did not know. She looked from one smiling face to the other, and her heart felt as though it would burst with gratitude at such unaccustomed and warm-hearted treatment. She was barely able to hold back the tears that stung her eyes. She had always thought that Ted Peck was a stern old man, not much better than Uncle Enoch, but now seeing him at home, relaxed and smoking his pipe, talking kindly to his wife, Eliza thought he must be the nicest man in the world, apart from Bart of course.

She must do all she could to help these wonderful people. She jumped up and began clearing the supper dishes from the table. In the scullery there was a bench with a wooden tub for washing the dishes, and wall shelves on which to stack the clean crockery. As she worked, Eliza thought once more how nice it would be to have a home just like this. Maybe, when Bart had made his fortune in the goldfields, they could afford a house in Anchor Street or Red Lion Street. She could imagine Bart sitting at his own table, smoking a pipe of tobacco just like Ted, having eaten a splendid meal that she had cooked for them on their own range. If Bart found a lot of gold, they might even be able to afford gaslight instead of candles.

'Eliza,' Ted called from the living room. 'There's someone to see you.'

Wiping her hands on her apron, Eliza went through and found Davy standing outside the front door. He smiled when he saw her. 'Hello, there. I promised I'd come and see how you was getting on.'

She went out into the street with him, so as not to interrupt Ted or awaken Dolly, who had dozed off in her chair by the range and was snoring gently.

'How are you, girl?' Davy asked anxiously.

'I'm much better now, thanks to your gaffer.'

He leaned against the wall, hands in pockets. 'Yeah, he's not a bad old stick, though he can be a bit of a tartar at times.'

'Well, he's been very kind to me.'

Davy gave her a straight look. 'And you ain't had much of that from old Enoch, have you?'

'No, but I'm wondering if he'll take me back just to clean and tidy the shop, like I've always done. Ted says I got to pay me way, and I don't know nothing else but scrubbing and cleaning.'

Davy shook his head. 'He's made Dippy Dan do it, given him a penny a day for his pains. Poor old Dippy, he ain't the sharpest knife in the box, but then his old man knocks him about regular. I reckon he's beaten out most of the brains that the poor chap was born with.'

'Then I'll just have to find me a paying job somewhere else. There must be someone who wants a strong girl, willing to work hard.'

Dolly did her best to keep Eliza at home; she pleaded with Ted, and when that didn't work she cried until she made herself ill, and had to be put to bed with a cold compress on her forehead. In the days that followed, Eliza gradually took over the running of the household; it wasn't difficult to keep such a tiny house clean and, when she was feeling up to it, Dolly showed her how to cook simple meals. Eliza found that she liked cooking and she learned quickly; soon she could boil and mash potatoes or set them round a piece of meat to roast in the oven. She could fry bacon and eggs, make a stew, and Dolly promised to show her how to make a suet pudding when the weather cooled down a bit.

She had been living in Hemp Yard for three weeks when Ted came home one day looking very pleased with himself. He announced with pride that he had found just the job for her. Next morning, shortly before seven o'clock, Ted walked Eliza to the lodging house in Old Gravel Lane where he introduced her to the landlady, Mrs Tubbs.

'I hear you're good at housekeeping, Eliza,'

Mrs Tubbs said, looking Eliza up and down.

'I'm a good worker, missis.'

Poking Eliza's arm with her fat forefinger, Mrs Tubbs shook her head. 'Looks a bit on the scrawny side to me, Mr Peck. Are you sure she's up to a day's hard work?'

'Eliza's a good girl and very willing. I'm sure she'll give satisfaction, ma'am. But I want her to be treated fair.'

Mrs Tubbs bristled and all her chins wobbled. 'I'm as fair an employer as you'll find in the whole of Wapping, not to mention Shadwell and Limehouse. You won't hear nobody round hear speak ill of me. I'm willing to give the girl a chance, so I'll say good day to you then, Mr Peck. Follow me, young Eliza, and I'll show you what to do.'

Without waiting for an answer, Mrs Tubbs waddled down the dark passage to the back stairs. Casting an anxious glance at Ted, who nodded and gave her an encouraging grin, Eliza followed her new employer down to the basement kitchen.

The smell assailed Eliza's nostrils even before Mrs Tubbs opened the door: rancid food, cabbage water, mouse droppings and bad drains. It was all Eliza could do not to retch, but Mrs Tubbs didn't seem to notice anything out of the ordinary. Situated as it was, half below street level, the kitchen was lit by a window leading out into an area that was piled high with rubbish, allowing just a glimmer of daylight into the room. A slatternly woman with a mobcap pulled down over her eyes was dozing in a chair by the range. Judging by the sour smell of gin that hung about her in a damp cloud, she was sleeping off the excesses of the night before. Mrs Tubbs went over and kicked the leg of the chair so that the woman awakened with a start and a loud snort.

'Wake up, you lazy bitch. There's breakfasts to get for me gents.' Mrs Tubbs shook her by the shoulders. 'Maisie Carter, you'll be out on the street where you belong if you don't stir your lazy arse and start work.'

With a grunt, Maisie got to her feet. 'All right, all right, keep your hair on, missis. I hears you.' Blinking and wiping the dribble off her chin with the back of her hand, Maisie stared at Eliza. 'Who's that?'

'This here is Eliza, and she's going to do the cleaning. Show her where to find things and don't let me catch you clipping her round the ear, that's my job.' Having said that, Mrs Tubbs heaved her large frame back up the stairs and disappeared through the baize door.

As soon as the door closed, Maisie sat down again. 'You heard her, get the breakfasts ready for the gents.'

The table was piled high with pots, pans and stale food. Something, nasty had dripped from an upended jug and pooled on the flagstone floor. Eliza had a terrible feeling that this was not going to be a good day. 'I'm here to clean, miss. I dunno how to do breakfasts.'

'Trust her to hire a stupid, lazy slut.' Maisie reached into her pocket and pulled out a stone bottle. She clenched the cork between teeth long and yellow like those of an ageing horse, and pulled it out. She spat the cork onto the floor and took a swig of the liquid.

Eliza had smelled spirit often enough on the breath of drunken sailors to know the difference between gin, brandy and rum. This was definitely gin. She backed away from Maisie, well out of arm's reach. 'I ain't stupid nor lazy and I'll make the breakfasts if you'll tell me what to do.'

Maisie grunted and took another swig of gin. 'There's joints in the larder,' she said, waving her hand in the direction of a cupboard, 'and they can eat yesterday's bread, that's in there too. There's small beer in the pitcher and tankards on the shelf. Gawd's strewth, do I have to do everything round here? Get to it or you'll feel the back of me hand across your chops.'

Tempted to run, Eliza knew she must do her best, if only to prove to Ted that she was worthy of his trust. Keeping a wary eye on Maisie, who was knocking back gin as if her life depended on it, Eliza began methodically to clear the table, piling the dirty crocks in the stone sink and filling an empty flour sack with the stale food. She bit back a scream as a startled mouse scuttled out of a half-eaten pork pie, and a lamb chop seemed to move on its own, alive with maggots.

As she opened the larder door, a cloud of blowflies flew out, buzzing angrily around her head; the stench of rotten meat and mouldy potatoes made her want to vomit.

'Get a move on.' Maisie let out a loud burp followed by a hiccup. 'Take the grub upstairs to the dining room afore they starts banging on the floor and creating.'

The shelves were alive with cockroaches and silverfish and Eliza had to force herself to pick up the platter of roast beef, shaking the insects off onto the floor. She set the beef joint down on the table, returning to the larder to collect the roast pork that might have looked appetising had not the crackling been blackened with an army of ants. The bread was sprouting blue-green mould and a mouse had drowned in the pitcher of small beer. She fished it out with a wooden spoon, comforting herself with the thought that it had died drunk and happy. She did what she could to make the food look edible, loaded it onto a wooden tray and was searching for some tankards when the ceiling began to reverberate, and flakes of whitewash fell all around them, like a snowstorm. The sound of feet drumming rhythmically on the floorboards upstairs rolled around the kitchen like thunder.

'Get your backside up them stairs,' Maisie mumbled in a slurred voice, half raising herself from her chair. 'Stop dawdling, you bleeding, stupid mare.'

Eliza didn't need a second bidding: the memory of Uncle Enoch's last beating was still fresh in her mind. She hefted the tray upstairs to the dining room, following the sound of feet stamping, hands pounding on a table and raised men's voices. The lodgers stopped chanting as Eliza entered the room, staring at her in a brief moment of silence, and then one of them, a fat man with half a dozen chins bulging over the top of his collar, began to laugh.

'No wonder we've had to wait, boys, they've got this one from the workhouse I don't doubt. What's your name, skinny little monkey?'

Setting the tray down on the table, Eliza looked the portly gentleman in the face. 'I may be a skinny monkey but that's better than being a fat pig.'

The fat man puffed out his reddening cheeks as hoots of laughter rippled around the table.

'Got you there, Tully, old chap.'

'Serve yourselves, gents,' Eliza said, with as much dignity as she could muster. She left the room, closing the door behind her and almost colliding with Mrs Tubbs.

'What are you doing up here, girl? I thought I told you to start cleaning in the kitchen?' Without waiting for an answer, Mrs Tubbs caught hold of Eliza by the ear and marched her back to the stairs.

Maisie slid off her chair as they entered the room, grinning sheepishly at Mrs Tubbs. 'I told her to start with the pots and pans, missis. But she would insist on taking the food up to the gents. I know her sort and I'd watch that one if I was you.'

Mrs Tubbs sniffed the air. 'Have you been at the Hollands again, Maisie?'

'Just a medicinal drop to settle me poorly stomach.'

'You'd better not let me catch you drunk, madam. I won't give you no second chance this time.' Mrs Tubbs gave Eliza's ear a spiteful tweak. 'And you girl, get on with your work. I've got Stinger on the wall there and you'll feel the sting of his tail if you don't do your job.' She pointed her finger at a cane hanging on the wall. 'Do we have an understanding, Eliza?'

Chapter Three

In the hellish working conditions of the lodging house, Eliza kept sane by focusing her mind on returning home at the end of a hard day's toil. Ted was so convinced that he had found her a suitable position with a kind employer that Eliza did not want to disappoint him. The Pecks were so good to her, so kind and loving, just like real parents: she would have cut off her right arm rather than upset them. And so she said nothing about the reality of working for Mrs Tubbs, keeping the bullying and beatings with Stinger to herself. At least, when she handed over her wages at the end of the week, she felt she was contributing to her keep.

Although Eliza went off cheerfully each morning, putting a brave face on things, she slowed her pace as soon as she left Hemp Yard. She had to force her bare feet to walk in the direction of Old Gravel Lane. Each day, she suffered the taunts and bullying of Maisie Carter, who was usually drunk and always vicious. Mrs Tubbs was a sadistic slattern who cheated her gentlemen lodgers, gave them rotten food, watered-down small beer, and kept them sweet by giving them free access to the favours of her chambermaids. Eliza got to know Gertrude, Flossie and Meg when they came down to the kitchen for their meals. They were all workhouse girls, taken on by Mrs Tubbs when they were ten or twelve, ostensibly as chambermaids but, as Eliza soon realised, making the beds and emptying the chamber pots were the least of their duties. Mrs Tubbs picked only the best-looking girls and then she groomed them, feeding them up and dressing them in a manner that accentuated their physical charms; painting their faces until they looked like wax dolls and forcing them to submit to the lodgers' demands. Eliza wondered why they put up with such treatment, but Meg told her in confidence that to go against Mrs Tubbs was a one-way ticket back to the workhouse or, even worse, ending up on the streets with the myriads of other forlorn prostitutes risking disease and sudden death.

Eliza was truly thankful that she was too young and skinny to qualify for Mrs Tubbs's attention and she did her best to fulfil the almost impossible task of keeping the establishment clean. At night, when she went home, she hid her chapped and work-worn hands beneath her skirts and, although she was always exhausted to the point of dropping, she somehow managed to keep awake long enough to satisfy Dolly's close questioning about her duties and the people she met during the day.

In the privacy of her bedroom and by the light of a single candle, Eliza wrote long letters to Bart giving thumbnail descriptions of the lodgers: portly Mr Tully, who could eat two dozen oysters at a sitting and, no doubt as a result, suffered from dreadful wind. He had not forgiven her for calling him a pig and had complained bitterly to Mrs Tubbs, telling her that Eliza was rude, clumsy and in need of severe chastisement, but she left that bit out of her letters. She went on to describe Mr Benson, a clerk in a law firm who had a habit of saying 'Ah, dearie me' for no apparent reason, and whose black suits were shiny at the elbows and frayed at the cuffs. Then there was noisy Mr Jack, who styled himself as a dealer in fancy ware and went round with a barrow, door to door, selling cheap jewellery, cufflinks, studs, lockets and combs for the back hair, for a penny apiece. Mr Jack, who was young and cheerful, always wore a cherry-red velvet waistcoat and nankeen trousers, and was quite Eliza's favourite – until Freddie Prince arrived, and then her whole life seemed to change.

The other lodgers came and went, most of them being commercial travellers who stayed for just a night or two and then moved on, but Freddie Prince was different from anyone she had ever met. He insisted on being addressed as 'doctor', although Mr Jack said that he was a crocusser, a phoney medical man who plied his trade from a suitcase, selling pills, potions and nostrums in the streets. Eliza suspected that this was sour grapes as Mr Jack's nose was put out of joint by the dashing doctor, whose smile could brighten the dullest day. Dr Prince was loud and flamboyant, a larger than life character with a line in patter that, in the end, silenced even Mr Jack. Eliza was rather shy of him at first, but he always had a kind word for her, and always said 'thank you' when she served him with his food. He never laughed at her discomfort as the other men did when their coarse jokes brought a blush to her cheeks. Dr Prince told them to hush, and to watch their tongues in front of a young lady. He even gave her a pot of salve to rub on her work-roughened hands, and he made it seem as though she was doing him a favour by testing out his new ointment before he tried it on the general public. He was all right, was Dr Prince – and quite good-looking for an old man of twenty-three or twenty-four.

Eliza wrote about all these people, never once mentioning the beatings with Stinger doled out almost daily by Mrs Tubbs for the slightest mistake or, more often than not, for something of which Maisie had falsely accused her. The only good thing she could have said in Mrs Tubbs's defence was that she was not as strong as Uncle Enoch, so the thrashings were painful but less severe. The letters could not be posted until Eliza had an address for Bart, but she was certain that he would contact her one day soon, and, until that time, she kept them hidden beneath her mattress.

August was a month of sweltering weather when the whole of London baked beneath a relentless sun. Even the Thames seemed to flow slowly and more sluggishly towards the sea. East Enders, desperate to get cool, plunged into the turgid, filthy waters to obtain some relief and some died of shock, others drowned and were carried off downriver and the less fortunate ended up with cholera, dysentery or typhus.

It was over a month since Eliza had started working for Mrs Tubbs, and she came downstairs one morning at the end of August, wondering how she could face another day in that hateful establishment. Ted and Dolly had been sitting quietly at the table and they leapt to their feet as she entered the living room, rushing over to hug her and wishing her a happy birthday.

'H-how did you know?' Stunned and suddenly choked with tears, Eliza could only stare at them. Uncle Enoch had never wished her happy birthday; he thought such treatment only spoilt a child.

'Davy told us,' Dolly said, wrapping her arms around Eliza in a motherly hug.

'Let your dad give you a birthday kiss, Liza,' Ted said, opening his arms.

'Dad?' Eliza was crying now, she couldn't stop herself. 'I wish you was me dad, Ted. And you, Dolly, you're just like a real mum to me. Th-thank you both.'

Dolly sniffed and wiped her eyes on her apron. 'I love you like a daughter, Eliza. If you could bring yourself to call me Mum, I'd like it above all things.'

Eliza nodded, unable to speak.

Ted hugged her and kissed her on the tip of her nose. 'You're a good girl, Liza. Dolly and me got you a birthday present to show how much we care for our little daughter.'

Clapping her hands like an excited child, Dolly pointed to the table, on which were set out a brand new pair of leather boots, and a blue bonnet adorned with silk roses and an ostrich feather.

'New boots. I never had a pair of new boots in me life, and a bonnet too. Oh! It's beautiful,' Eliza gasped, picking up the bonnet and fingering the blue silk. 'It's the most beautiful thing I've ever seen.'

Dolly clasped her hands to her bosom, beaming with pleasure. 'It ain't new, Eliza. I have to be honest with you, but the pawnbroker said it had belonged to a real lady.'

'Put it on, Liza,' Ted said. 'Let's see how you look in it.'

Eliza put the bonnet on her head, fumbling with the long blue ribbons. Dolly snatched them from her hands and tied them in a bow at the side of her cheek. 'There now, you're as pretty as a picture.'

'You're thirteen,' Ted said smiling. 'A young lady now, Liza. You'll do us proud.'

A shaft of fear stabbed through Eliza's heart, and she would have ripped the bonnet off her head if Dolly and Ted had not been standing there, smiling so proudly. Turning thirteen meant one thing in Mrs Tubbs's establishment, and looking pretty, if that were true, was a definite disadvantage; Eliza had no intention of ending up like Gertrude, Meg and Flossie.

'Is anything wrong, dearie?' Dolly's face crumpled into lines of distress.

'No! No, of course not.' Eliza sat down, thrusting her feet into the boots, concentrating on doing up the buttons so that she did not have to look Dolly in the eye. 'I dunno what to say, that's all. I never had such wonderful presents in me whole life.'

Ted cleared his throat with a loud harrumph. 'Well you deserve them, ducks. Now get along to your place of work. You don't want to upset that nice Mrs Tubbs, now do you?'

'No, I don't.' Nice Mrs Tubbs indeed! Eliza

managed to smile but it was not easy. She longed to tell them the truth, but she must not spoil the day. She stood up, wriggling her toes inside the boots; if she was being honest her feet were not too comfortable. It was so long since she had worn shoes that it felt very strange. 'I'd best be on me way or I'll be late for work.'

'You must wear your bonnet as well,' Dolly said, thrusting the dreamy confection of silk and feathers into her hands.

'No, really, I'd rather keep it for Sunday best.'

'Don't be daft, girl,' Ted said, pulling on his cloth cap. 'We bought it for you to wear every day like a proper young lady. I'll walk you to the corner, Liza. And enjoy seeing folks admiring my pretty daughter.' He offered her his arm and Eliza took it with a smile. Dolly gave her one last hug and, standing in the doorway, she waved enthusiastically. As they turned the corner, Eliza saw that she was still waving, although she suspected that without her specs Dolly could see no further than the end of her nose.

Her new boots that creaked with every step and her blue bonnet certainly did attract stares from passers-by. Ted puffed out his chest with pride as they said goodbye on the corner of Old Gravel Lane. He strolled across the road to the chandlery and Eliza walked on to Mrs Tubbs's establishment with a heavy heart. She had already decided that she was going to hide the bonnet as soon as she got to work, but she was not quick enough: Maisie spotted her as soon as she entered the kitchen. Lurching up from her chair, Maisie stumbled over a stool and only saved herself from falling by clutching at the edge of the table, sending a pile of dirty plates crashing to the floor.

'Look at you,' she jeered, pointing drunkenly at Eliza's bonnet, 'all dolled up like a Whitechapel doxy.'

Eliza tugged at the ribbons but she only succeeded in tying them into a tighter knot. 'Leave me be.'

'Think yourself all la-di-da don't you?' Staggering crabwise with her boots crunching on shards of broken china, Maisie followed Eliza to the broom cupboard. 'Look at you in new boots as well. Some bloke must have paid you well for your services, you little whore.'

'Shut up!' Turning on Maisie, Eliza faced up to her, too angry to feel frightened. 'Leave me alone.'

Maisie's face contorted with rage and she raised her arm as if to strike Eliza, but, losing her balance, she fell flat on her back shrieking for help and with her legs waving in the air, like an upturned beetle. Eliza snatched up a broom, brandishing it in Maisie's face. 'Serves you right for drinking all that gin. You leave me alone or I'll bop you one with this broom.'

'What's going on in here? I could hear the noise upstairs in the dining room.' Mrs Tubbs's stentorian voice echoed round the kitchen.

Reluctantly, Eliza lowered the broom; it was no use trying to explain. She glanced anxiously at Stinger hanging on the wall, and her backside was already tingling in anticipation of the next assault.

Maisie scrambled to her feet, pointing at Eliza. 'She done it, missis. She come in flaunting herself and she broke them plates on purpose, just to spite me.'

'Shut up, you drunken fool. You've been at the jigger gin again, Maisie. I've warned you a hundred times what'll happen if you pour that foul stuff down your throat.'

Muttering and whining, Maisie crawled over to her chair and sat upon it, shivering. 'I only takes a drop of two to ease me twinges, missis. When the miseries get into me bones there's nothing to ease them but a drop or two of gin.'

While attention was diverted away from herself, Eliza struggled with the knot in the ribbon. Then Mrs Tubbs turned to stare at her and Eliza's hands shook as she noted the appraising look in her employer's eyes.

'That colour brings out the blue in your eyes, Eliza.' Mrs Tubbs stood with arms akimbo, smiling and looking Eliza up and down until she felt like a prime beef animal in Smithfield Market. 'How old are you, Eliza?'

She was tempted to lie, but attending church three times a day on Sunday had left its mark on Eliza and she had to tell the truth. 'Thirteen today, missis.'

'Ah! Thirteen, you're almost a woman and you ain't half bad-looking now I take a proper look-see. How do you fancy training to be a chambermaid then, Eliza?'

Shaking her head, Eliza finally managed to undo the ribbon and she yanked the bonnet off her head, stowing it at the back of the broom cupboard. 'If it's all the same to you, missis, I'd rather stick to the job I've got.'

Mrs Tubbs waddled across the floor towards her, hooking her arm around Eliza's shoulders. 'Come now, dearie. Wouldn't you like three square meals a day and a pretty new dress to match that fine bonnet?' She cast a meaningful look at Stinger.

Eliza shook her head. 'No ma'am, I'd rather keep to what I know.'

'Then it's time we had a chat with Stinger,' Mrs Tubbs said, snatching the cane from the wall. 'Bend over, Eliza. Maybe a taste of Stinger's medicine will help you change your mind.'

Stiff and sore, Eliza was cleaning out the grate in the upstairs parlour when the door opened and Dr Prince came in. She was not supposed to be in the public rooms when the lodgers were about, but it was mid-morning and she had not expected any of the gents to be in residence. Clambering to her feet, she muttered an apology.

'Don't mind me, Eliza. I was just looking for a lost collar stud.' Dr Prince grinned ruefully. 'Can't find the damn thing anywhere. I'm always losing the little devils, and it don't do for a professional gent to turn up at someone's front door with his collar half undone.'

He looked so pleasant and friendly that Eliza found herself smiling back at him. 'I suppose not, sir.'

'Help me look, there's a good girl. If you find it, I'll give you a farthing.' He began rummaging around on the sofa, sending cushions flying onto the floor.

Eliza set the bucket back in the hearth and immediately spotted an ivory collar stud lying in the grate. She bent to pick it up, uttering an involuntary grunt of pain as her sore muscles went into spasm. Mrs Tubbs had meant business this morning when she used Stinger. Eliza had not given in, but she knew that this was the first of many beatings to come if she didn't accept her terms.

'Is anything wrong, Eliza?'

She looked up to find Dr Prince eyeing her with a concerned look in his startlingly blue eyes. 'No, sir. I mean yes, I'm a bit stiff.'

He put his head on one side. 'Have you been horse riding, young lady?'

Responding to the twinkle in his eyes, Eliza found herself chuckling at the ridiculous thought that she might be rich enough to own a horse, or even hire one from a livery stable. 'No, sir.'

'Then my guess is that someone has seen fit to tan your hide. Am I right?'

Eliza held out her hand with the collar stud resting on her palm. 'I found it in the grate, sir.'

Dr Prince took it but his eyes never left her face and he ran his hand through his wavy bronze hair. 'Thank you, Eliza.'

'You're welcome, sir.'

'Now answer me truthfully. Did Mrs Tubbs beat you?'

Eliza stared down at her new boots.

'I guessed as much. Now a hiding from Mrs Tubbs, with all that considerable weight behind her, would be rather painful. I have a special ointment in my medicine case that will alleviate all the soreness. Come to my room, Eliza, and I'll give you some to take home with you.'

Going to a gentleman's room meant only one thing, according to the other girls. Startled and ready to run out of the door, Eliza shook her head. 'No, ta for the offer, but it's better already.'

'You needn't be afraid of me, Eliza. I'm a medical man.'

She snatched up the bucket filled with ashes,

clutching it in front of her like a shield. 'I ain't allowed in the gents' rooms.'

'Wait.' He caught hold of Eliza's hand as she went past him. 'Has that woman been threatening you? You can trust me. I know exactly what goes on in this establishment. If it wasn't so cheap, I wouldn't stop here another night. Come, child. You can tell me.'

'Please leave me be, sir. I'm all right, really I am.' Glancing up at Dr Prince, Eliza saw that he was frowning: she could tell by the expression in his eyes that he did not believe her.

'I'm not convinced, but I won't say anything more on the subject, for now.'

Eliza bobbed a curtsey and hurried back to the kitchen where she found Maisie sprawled on the floor, face down, with an empty bottle clutched in her hand. Stepping over her, Eliza set about clearing up the broken china and washing the pots and pans from last night's dinner. She had just finished when Mrs Tubbs sailed into the room, stopping short to stare down at Maisie's prostrate figure with an exclamation of annoyance. 'Get up, Carter.'

Maisie groaned, but did not move.

'Get up this instant or you're sacked.' Mrs Tubbs prodded Maisie in the ribs with the toe of her shoe. 'Do you hear me?'

Maisie rolled over onto her side and opened one bleary eye. 'Is it morning yet?'

'You're drunk and you're sacked.' Aiming a savage kick at Maisie's ribs, Mrs Tubbs staggered and almost came down on top of her.

'You can't sack me,' Maisie said thickly. 'I'm your sister.'

'Sister or no, you're a drunkard and I'm sick of carrying you. Either get up and start cooking them joints of meat before they walk out of the larder on their own, or get out of my house for good.'

Eliza stared, open-mouthed. She had often wondered why Mrs Tubbs kept Maisie on, and now she had the answer. Surely two sisters could never have been so unalike in appearance? Although, now she came to think of it, they were identical when it came to nastiness.

'And you, girl.' Mrs Tubbs turned her fierce gaze on Eliza. 'What are you staring at?'

'Nothing, missis.'

'Get on up them stairs to the dining room; you're starting your new job as chambermaid today. I've got your replacement all ready to take over cleaning the kitchen.' She turned to point her finger at a small girl cowering in the door-way. 'Come here, child, don't stand there snivelling.'

Maisie got to her feet, lurched sideways and landed on her chair with a grunt. 'Throw that one back, sister, she's too small to be of any use.'

Mrs Tubbs caught the unfortunate child by the

ear and dragged her into the kitchen. 'This here is Millie, and she's the new scullery maid. You, Eliza, you show her what to do and then get up them stairs, double-quick.'

Staring at the terrified girl, Eliza felt anger boil up inside her. Millie was puny and undersized; she was probably seven or eight, Eliza thought, but she only looked five or six. Her brown eyes were underlined with smudged shadows and appeared to be far too large for her oval face; her lips quivered as though she was trying hard not to cry.

'She's too little,' Eliza said, placing her arm around Millie's shoulders. 'She won't have the strength to do my work.'

Mrs Tubbs seized Stinger from the wall, swishing it through the air. 'Fancy another taste of Stinger then do you, Eliza?'

'No, I don't and I don't want to work above stairs neither.'

'Ho, don't you? We'll have to see about that. Bend over, girl. You watch this, Millie Turner, because this is what bad servant girls gets.' Brandishing the cane, Mrs Tubbs advanced on Eliza.

'Beat me again and I'll call a copper.'

Mrs Tubbs let out a roar of laughter that made the saucepans clang together on their hooks in a carillon. 'And who'd take any notice of a scrap of a girl like you? I'm within me rights to whip you whenever I feels like it, ain't that right, Maisie?'

Maisie lifted her head, opening one eye. 'Give her what for, that's what I say.'

'Bend over. I won't tell you again.' Mrs Tubbs took a step nearer to Eliza.

She stood her ground. 'I won't.'

Mrs Tubbs's fat arm shot out, grabbing Eliza by the scruff of the neck, and bending her double over a stool she held her down with one hand, using the other to lift Eliza's skirts and expose her bare buttocks. She brought the cane down hard, again and again. Millie's terrified keening and Maisie's drunken laughter drowned Eliza's screams. Mrs Tubbs seemed to have lost all self-control and, for a moment, Eliza was certain that she was going to die. Then, suddenly, the beating stopped and a man's voice was raging at Mrs Tubbs. Raising her head, Eliza saw Dr Prince snatch Stinger from her and break it across his knee.

'That's what I think of you, madam. You are nothing more than a sadistic bully and you should be reported to the magistrate for child cruelty.'

Sick with pain, Eliza slipped to the floor. As she tugged her skirts over her bare backside she felt something warm and sticky on her hand. It was blood. Stifling an anguished cry, she was convinced that she was dying; bleeding to death after that savage beating.

Mrs Tubbs glared at Dr Prince with narrowed eyes. 'That's no child. She was bleeding before I took Stinger to her. She's begun her courses and that means she's full grown. Do you fancy being the first to have her, Dr Prince? I'll do you a cheap deal if you like.'

He tossed the broken pieces of the cane onto the flagstones and stamped on them. 'Madam, you disgust me. I'm taking this child away from here and if you try to stop me, I'll have you closed down for running a brothel.'

Mrs Tubbs recoiled as if Dr Prince has slapped her across the face, but she appeared to recover quickly. 'One word from you, Freddie Prince, and I'll have you arrested for peddling quack medicines.'

'Touché!' He clicked his heels together in a mock salute and his generous mouth curved into a wry grin. 'It takes one scoundrel to recognise another. But,' he added, his smiling fading, 'I meant what I said about child cruelty. I'm taking Eliza back to her family, and if I hear you've been ill-treating that other poor, unfortunate little creature, then I promise you I'll have the law on you.'

Trembling and still not fully understanding why she was bleeding and what Mrs Tubbs had meant by her 'courses', Eliza was more concerned about Millie than herself. She wrapped her arms around the terrified child. 'There, there, don't cry little Millie.'

'Take Eliza then,' Mrs Tubbs stormed, 'and you can take that one as well, she's too weak and puny to be of any use to me. You can leave her at the workhouse door on your way to finding a new lodging. I don't want the likes of you upsetting my gentlemen clients.'

'And I wouldn't stay in this filthy hovel one night longer, madam.' Dr Prince held his hands out to Eliza and Millie. 'Come, my dears, the sooner we're out of here, the better.'

'Good riddance, that's what I say.' Turning on her heel, Mrs Tubbs stalked out of the kitchen, pausing at the door to shoot a malevolent glance at Maisie. 'And you, you drunken slut, get cooking them joints or I'll have your guts for garters.'

Outside on the pavement, he paused to set his bowler hat at a rakish angle on his head and, having peered at his reflection in the grimy window, he picked up his portmanteau and the case containing his medicines. 'All right, Eliza. Show me where you live.'

Eliza looked at him doubtfully. 'You won't really leave poor Millie at the workhouse will you, doctor?'

'I can't see any other course open to me, I'm afraid.'

'Dolly and Ted will look after her,' Eliza said stoutly. 'They took me in and treated me like their own. I even think of them as me mum and dad.' A twinge of pain in her lower back made Eliza grimace and clutch her stomach. She could feel the warm, stickiness between her legs and once again panic seized her.

'What's the matter?' cried Millie, clutching her hand. She cast Dr Prince an anguished glance. 'If you're a doctor, sir, then you'd best help her.'

Freddie started walking. 'This isn't in my field of expertise. You'll be fine, Eliza, just lead the way home.'

Dolly opened the door just far enough to peer outside. 'Who is it?' Her voice was tremulous and the tips of her fingers white as she held tightly to the door.

'It's me, Eliza, I'm not well.'

The door opened but Dolly's expression changed subtly as she squinted at Dr Prince. 'Heavens above, what's going on?'

Doffing his hat, he executed a nifty bow. 'Dr Frederick Prince at your service, ma'am. But my friends call me Freddie, which I much prefer.'

'A doctor!' Dolly's eyes opened wide. 'What's wrong with Eliza?'

'If I may come in for a moment?' Freddie put one foot over the threshold.

'I'm really sick,' Eliza said, unable to prevent her bottom lip from wobbling, although she was trying hard to be brave so as not to frighten Millie.

'A woman's condition, ma'am,' Freddie said, dumping his cases on the floor. 'Not within my powers to advise.' He tapped the side of his nose, winking.

'Oh! Yes, I understand.' Dolly put her arm around Eliza's shoulders. 'Come into the scullery with me, Eliza. And you, doctor, please take a seat and your little girl too.'

'Not my child,' Freddie said, clearing his throat. 'Another matter for discussion between yourself and Eliza.'

Suddenly businesslike and seemingly forgetting her invalid status, Dolly took Eliza into the scullery and, while she tore an old cotton sheet into strips, she told Eliza that she must expect this situation to occur monthly, although she was a bit vague as to the cause and became flustered when Eliza tried to ask questions.

'We mustn't keep the good doctor waiting,' Dolly said, making a pad from the rags with a quick demonstration as to how to fasten it. 'There's nothing wrong with you, dear. It's just one of the torments that we women have to suffer. It will go away in a day or so. You can clean yourself up at the pump and fill the kettle when you've done. We must offer our guest a cup of tea. Oh dear, I think my palpitations are returning; perhaps the doctor can give me something for them. Hurry up, dear. Don't just stand there.'

Still not much the wiser, but feeling relieved that her condition was not going to prove fatal, Eliza went out into the yard and drew water from the pump. Having completed her ablutions, she filled the kettle and took it back into the house. She found Freddie sprawled in Ted's chair by the range and Dolly perched on the edge of her seat listening enthralled to the medical jargon that tripped off his lips. Millie was huddled on a stool with her arms wrapped around her knees, eyeing them warily.

'Of course,' Freddie continued, puffing out his chest, 'I'm not one to boast, but I have excellent qualifications from the University of Paris where I studied medicine.'

'So why don't you set up in practice, doctor? Or work in one of the London hospitals?' Dolly asked, wide-eyed with interest.

'Because, ma'am, I prefer to spread my talents amongst the poor and needy. I am a free spirit and a free thinker. I work to benefit mankind and bring my knowledge to those most in need.'

Dolly leaned forward, her eyes shining. 'Can you give me something for my nerves, doctor? I'm a martyr to my nerves and palpitations have kept me confined to the house for many long years.'

Eliza set the kettle on the hob and drew up

another stool to sit beside Millie. 'Don't be scared, dear,' she whispered. 'No one is going to hurt you.'

'My dear lady, I shall give you some of my blood purifier, Sanguis purus, which will do the trick nicely. We'll soon have you dancing in the street like the pretty young woman that you are.'

Covering her face with her pinafore, Dolly burst into a fit of giggles. 'Oh, doctor, you are a one.'

Eliza stared at Freddie, and, seeming to feel her glance, he looked up with a benign smile. She was certain that he winked at her, but it was done so quickly that she thought she might have been mistaken. Surely the doctor was not having Dolly on? Eliza set about making a pot of tea and, as instructed by Dolly, she fetched a packet of broken biscuits from the cupboard in the scullery.

Freddie took a bottle of medicine from his suitcase, and Eliza was sent to fetch a teaspoon. He administered a dose with the aplomb of a fairground magician: Eliza half expected him to produce a rabbit from his bowler hat, but he merely put the cork back in the bottle, placing it on the mantelshelf.

Dolly smacked her lips, smiling happily. 'I can feel it doing me good already.'

'So it will, Mrs Peck,' Freddie said, resuming his seat by the fire. 'Eliza will see that you only take one teaspoonful at a time. It's unwise to overdose on medication.'

Eliza poured the tea into Dolly's best china cups. 'Can Millie stay here with us, Mum?'

'Oh, Lord. Don't ask me such awkward questions, Eliza. Not in front of the good doctor. I don't know what to say.'

'Say yes, please say yes. Otherwise she'll have to go back to the workhouse.'

'I don't understand why you brought the workhouse child here in the first place,' Dolly said, frowning. 'And shouldn't you being going back to your place of work, dear?

Eliza stared helplessly at Freddie; she couldn't bring herself to tell Dolly the truth. The dire facts about Mrs Tubbs's activities might bring on a severe attack of the vapours and undo all the good that Dr Prince's medicine had done.

Freddie seemed to understand Eliza's unspoken plea for help. He reached out to pat Dolly's hand. 'My dear lady, there is something that I should discuss with your husband when he returns home, the facts being too harsh for the ears of a delicate person such as yourself.'

'Oh, Lord above us.' Dolly's mouth turned down at the corners and her lips wobbled ominously.

'You must not distress yourself, ma'am. As my patient, I advise you strongly to calm yourself.'

'Yes, doctor. Anything you say.' Dolly sank

back in her chair, fanning herself with her hand.

Freddie pulled a pocket watch from his waistcoat pocket and, taking Dolly's wrist gently between his fingers, he took her pulse. 'As I thought, ma'am, your pulse is racing. I strongly advocate a rest in bed until your husband returns from work and, if I may, I will call upon him or, better still, I'll visit him at his place of work.'

'Of course, I'll go to my bed immediately.' Dolly rose unsteadily to her feet. 'Eliza will see you out and you, little girl, whatever your name is, you can help me upstairs.' Beckoning to Millie, Dolly took her by the hand. 'Can you see the way, dear?'

Millie shot a puzzled look at Eliza, who gave her an encouraging nod.

'Yes'm. I can see fine.' Millie led Dolly to the stairs, guiding her between the furniture.

'Eliza,' Freddie said, when they were out of earshot. 'I have a proposition to put before you.'

Chapter Four

'How would you like to work for me?' Freddie's eyes twinkled, although his face was set in a serious expression.

'Doing what, sir?'

He set his hat on his head, and struck a pose with his thumbs tucked in his waistcoat pockets. 'I am a professional man, although some ignorant people call my profession crocussing, which is blatantly as unfair as it is untrue. I peddle hope and comfort to the unfortunate poor and in doing so I make myself a reasonable living, which is only right and proper. Now I could do a lot better with an assistant, or maybe two, if that little scrap upstairs is not to return to the workhouse. She's suitably pale and thin and, with a bit of coaching, would make an excellent ailing child, who can be seen to benefit miraculously from my nostrums. What do you say, Eliza? I could pay you the same as Mrs Tubbs, maybe more if we did well together.'

Eliza stared at him, dazed. 'Work for you, sir? As a doctor's assistant?'

'An assistant, certainly. How about it?'

'I think I'd like to, but you would have to ask Dad, I mean Mr Peck.'

'And that's exactly what I intend to do.' Freddie picked up his bags. 'We'll go to Mr Peck's place of work right away. Where is it, by the way?'

'Eliza, don't leave me.' Millie's voice rose in an anxious wail as she came running down the stairs.

'Come along then, Millie.' Eliza held out her hand.

'You ain't taking me back to the workhouse.'

'There's no fear of that,' Eliza said firmly. 'You and me is going to be the doctor's assistants.'

Enoch was hunched over his ledgers like a carrion crow huddled over the remains of a dead rat. He scowled ominously when he saw Eliza as she followed Freddie into the chandlery. 'What's this then? And who are you, mister?'

'Doctor,' Freddie said, setting down his bags. 'Dr Frederick Prince and I've come to see the sailmaker.'

'What's she doing with you?' Enoch pointed his pen at Eliza.

'I don't think that's any of your business, sir.' Freddie marched to the bottom of the ladder that led up to the sail loft. 'Ahoy, there, Mr Peck. Permission to come aboard, sir.'

The hatch opened and Ginger's freckled face

appeared through the hole. 'Who's asking?'

'Dr Frederick Prince, late of the University of Paris.' Freddie mounted the ladder with Eliza and Millie close on his heels. 'I've come to speak to your employer, lad. Make way there.'

Ted climbed off his stool, approaching Freddie with a curious stare. 'Who wants me then?'

Eliza moved closer to Davy, who was sitting cross-legged on the floor, working on a lateen sail. He looked up and grinned. 'Who's that, Liza?'

She laid her finger on her lips. 'Shhh! I'm trying to hear what they're saying.' But it was impossible. Ted had taken Freddie to a far corner of the loft where he conducted his business, out of earshot of the apprentices. Eliza watched them, wishing she could hear what they were saying, but struck by the difference in the two men. Ted was much older, of course, and stooped from a life spent bent double working on canvas. He had seemed big and strong to her, but standing beside Freddie he looked quite small and insignificant. Freddie was not much taller, but he held himself straight, like the guardsmen that Eliza had once seen standing outside Buckingham Palace. Although he was slim, he had wide shoulders and a solid look about him that might make men think twice before they challenged him to a bout of fisticuffs. There was something about that him reminded

Eliza of Bart, or maybe it was simply being back in her old home that had made her think of him at this particular moment. Her heart contracted with the pain of missing her brother. He had promised to send for her and she knew that he would keep that promise, if he could; but there were terrible dangers at sea, she knew all about those from the mariners who came into the chandlery. She had grown up listening to seamen's tales of storms, typhoons, ships lost and men drowned. Her throat constricted painfully and it was only when Millie tugged at her hand that she came back to earth. For a moment her imagination had taken her into wild seas, storm-tossed ships and Bart in peril of his life.

'How do I know it's all above board?' Ted's raised voice echoed around the sail loft as he stood glaring at Freddie.

'I can assure you that I am an honest man dedicated to helping those less fortunate than myself.'

'You can't soap me, mister. I know all about you crocussers. Quacks and charlatans, the lot of you.'

Eliza opened her mouth to protest and then thought better of it; this was not going at all to plan. She glanced anxiously at Freddie, but he was looking unperturbed.

'Mr Peck, I understand your feelings, sir. And I agree that there are many unscrupulous men in my profession but I am not one of them.'

Ted frowned, shaking his head. 'I don't know about that. From what you've just told me about Mrs Tubbs, who I thought was a good, respectable woman, I'll have to think hard before I trust Eliza to someone else.'

'I can assure you—' began Freddie but was cut short by Ted holding up his hand.

'I need time to think it over.'

The boys had stopped working and were listening to this exchange, open-mouthed.

Davy scrambled to his feet and came to stand by Eliza. 'What's going on, Liza?'

'Get back to work, all of you.' Ted turned on the apprentices with a fierce frown. 'And you, Davy Little. This is none of your business.'

'I'll call round this evening,' Davy whispered out of the corner of his mouth. He scuttled back to his place, sitting on the floor beside Dippy Dan, who as usual was chortling and mumbling to himself as he coated lengths of yarn with beeswax.

'Of course you must talk it over with your good lady,' Freddie said equably. 'And, if I may, I will call upon you this evening to hear your decision. Good day to you, Mr Peck.' As he walked past her, Freddie bent down with his lips close to Eliza's ear. 'Don't worry, my dear, Freddie Prince always gets his own way in the end.'

'We'd best be going too then,' Eliza said,

eyeing Ted nervously, unsure whether he was cross with her or merely put out by the strange turn of events.

'Yes, yes,' he said impatiently. 'Get on home then, Liza. We'll sort this out later.'

With Millie following her like a shadow, Eliza shinned down the ladder into the shop below. She hesitated when she saw that Uncle Enoch was standing with his back to the door, arms folded across his chest, barring Freddie's exit.

'Let me pass, my good fellow. I have business to do.'

'And how does it concern my niece?'

'Your niece?' Eyebrows raised, Freddie turned to Eliza. 'Is this true?'

Eliza nodded. 'It's true, but he threw me out on the street. Ted and Dolly took me into their home.'

'That's a lie!' Enoch's brows knotted over the top of his nose and his nostrils flared. 'This child is a daughter of Satan and she lies. She ran away from me when I chastised her for being untruthful. I'll say it again, mister, what is your business with my niece?'

'He's lying,' Eliza cried. 'Don't believe him, Dr Prince.'

'A doctor!' Enoch's lip curled. 'A crocusser more like.'

'I could show you my diploma from the University of Paris, but I don't feel the need to prove myself to you, sir.' Freddie held his hand out to Eliza. 'I've heard enough and I know who I believe. Come, Eliza and Millie, we're finished here.'

Flinging his arms out across the door, Enoch glared at Freddie. 'Take this child from me and I'll have you charged with kidnapping. Eliza is my dead brother's daughter and I am her legal guardian.'

'How much?' Freddie demanded, putting his hand in his pocket. 'How much do you want for her, you old villain?'

'You insult me, insinuating that I would sell my own flesh and blood.' Enoch's eyes gleamed with greed. 'But I will take a nominal sum to compensate me for all the expenses involved in her upbringing and education. Four pounds.'

'That seems a rather large nominal sum.'

'Two pound ten.'

'Two guineas and that's my last offer.'

'Done!' Enoch held out his hand.

Freddie produced two golden sovereigns and two shilling pieces, dropping them into Enoch's outstretched hand. 'Now move aside, sir. Our business is concluded.'

Enoch sidled past Freddie, casting a scornful glance at Eliza. 'Good riddance.'

Dizzy with relief and barely able to believe that she was really and truly free of Uncle Enoch, Eliza tossed her head. 'Same to you, you old skinflint.' Holding tightly to Millie's hand, she followed Freddie out into the street. 'Did you really buy me?'

'I bought your freedom, Eliza. Now you go on home to Dolly, and I'll find myself some new lodgings.'

'You will come round tonight, like you said?'

'I will indeed. Freddie Prince always keeps his word.' With a cheery wink and a smile, Freddie strolled off carrying his cases and whistling.

Millie tugged at Eliza's hand. 'What about me, Liza? You won't let them send me back to the workhouse, will you?'

'Of course not,' Eliza replied staunchly. 'We'll go and talk to Dolly; she'll make Ted see sense.'

They arrived home to find Dolly had come downstairs and was sitting in her usual seat by the range. 'That medicine is truly wonderful,' she said happily. 'Your Dr Prince is a miracle worker.' Reaching for her spectacles, Dolly set them on the bridge of her nose, peering at Millie who was loitering in the doorway. 'Come in, dear. There's nothing to be scared of in my house.'

'Can she stay, Mum?' Eliza pleaded. 'I'll look after her and Dr Prince has offered us both a job helping him to peddle his cures, only . . .'

'Only what, ducks?'

'Dad wouldn't give him a direct answer. Said

he has to come back after supper and he'll think about it.'

'We'll see about that,' Dolly said, getting slowly to her feet. 'Fetch me my bonnet and shawl, Eliza. We're going to market and I'm going to buy some material to make dresses for both of you. My own little girls.'

Eliza stared at her in amazement. 'But you never go out.'

'That was before I had my blood purifying medicine. I'm a new woman, Eliza. A new woman and a mother.'

When Ted returned home that evening, Eliza and Millie were seated on the floor surrounded by scraps of cotton print and calico. Eliza had mastered backstitch and, with her tongue held between her teeth, was concentrating on sewing a straight seam, but Millie was having difficulty with simple tacking and was sucking her finger where she had pricked it on her needle.

'Hello, what's going on here?' Taking off his peaked cap, Ted shot a questioning look at Dolly.

Dolly smiled up at him as she plied her needle. 'I've been out to market, Ted. Me and the girls went together, and we bought some material to make them clothes suitable for their new employment.'

'But Dolly, you haven't been out of the house for years unless I was there to go with you, let alone go to market.' Ted's eyes rounded in surprise and he sat down on his chair beside the range. 'And you ain't touched a pair of scissors since you had to give up sewing because of your eyes.'

'Well, it's a miracle and that's for certain. And, Ted Peck, I owe it all to that Dr Prince. He give me this tonic for my blood and it's worked a treat. I feel well for the first time in years, and it's all thanks to him.'

Ted stared at her in disbelief. 'And you're wearing your spectacles!'

'Just for the close work, my dear. You know very well that I don't need them the rest of the time.'

'I forgot for a moment.'

'And you must allow these girls to work for the good doctor. Think of the people he can help, just like me.'

'But the child, Dolly.' Lowering his voice, Ted jerked his head in Millie's direction. 'Think of the responsibility. We can't take on another mouth to feed.'

Eliza had kept her head bent over her sewing, but she looked up now, casting an appealing look at Dolly. 'Please, let Millie stay. I'll help look after her and Dr Freddie said she can earn some money as the ailing child.'

'Then that's settled.' Dolly fastened off her piece of sewing and snipped the thread, pointing her scissors at Ted. 'It's up to you, Mr Peck, you being the head of the household, but for myself, I say yes.'

Freddie had rented a room in a house in Anchor Street, just around the corner from Hemp Yard. It was not much of a place, as Eliza discovered when she went round to his lodgings for her first lesson in her new trade. The house was a modest two-up and two-down, very similar to Ted and Dolly's dwelling, but in a much less salubrious neighbourhood. In Hemp Yard, the terraced houses were tenanted by workingmen and their families, but the dwellings in Anchor Street were crammed from attic to cellar with unfortunates who had nowhere else to go. The buildings were unsanitary and run-down to the point of dereliction. Whereas the inhabitants of Hemp Yard considered themselves to be respectable, hard-working people, and took a pride in keeping their street clean, tidy and relatively vermin-free, the denizens of Anchor Street seemed to be content to live in squalor. Feral children roamed the street day and night, begging or stealing off unwary passers-by. Horse dung and dog excrement carpeted the road and clogged the drains. Rotting vegetable matter filled the gutters; the air was thick with flies and their squirming grubs thrived on the corpses of dead cats and rats.

Although she was used to the rough areas

around the docks, Eliza had never had cause to venture into this particular slum. The buzzing of bluebottles in the summer heat provided a constant humming background to the whining of beggars, the shrieks of the street urchins and the cacophony of voices shouting in many different languages. The people who hurried past without giving her so much as a casual glance were a colourful mix of all nationalities and occupations: dock workers, sailors, prostitutes, bootblacks and match sellers. A chimney sweep emerged from one house followed by his stunted apprentice boys: skinny little fellows with soot engrained into their flesh and their stick-like extremities burnt and scarred. It seemed to Eliza that the dregs of London's poor lived in this street; many of them would end their days at the bottom of the river, driven by drink, opium and relentless poverty. If Dr Prince had not offered to teach her an honest trade and one that would benefit the poor and underprivileged, she might have turned tail and run home. But she was determined to work hard, if only to repay Ted and Dolly for their unstinting kindness. Stepping over a body that lay slumped in a doorway, Eliza continued up the street, searching for number seventeen.

The first time was the worst, and gradually she grew accustomed to the sights, sounds and disgusting smells that were part of life in Anchor

Street. Eliza went to Freddie's lodgings early each morning to begin a day of work and study. The main tenant was the widow of a seaman, who had been left to raise four children with no income but that which she could make from subletting rooms. Beattie Larkin was old, at least twenty-five, Eliza thought, and she had disliked her on sight. Beattie lived in the back room with her four little boys, aged from five down to the six-month-old baby, and it seemed to Eliza that she was always hanging round Freddie, fluttering her sandy eyelashes and making sheep's-eyes at him. He was unfailingly charming in response to these clumsy attempts to seduce him, but Eliza did not believe that he could be interested in such a slatternly trollop of a woman. He was, she thought, too much of a gent to hurt Beattie's feelings, if she had any. For two pins she would tell her to lay off pestering a professional gentleman and go and practise her charms on Basher Harris, the stevedore who lived in the upstairs back bedroom with his aged mother, who was very deaf.

In the front bedroom there was a whole family of Italians who made ice cream, calling it hokey-pokey and selling it for a halfpenny a lump. The Donatiellos were numerous, noisy and excitable and there seemed to be dozens of them all living in one room, laughing, quarrelling, singing and gabbling away in Italian. There was the momma and poppa, nonna and six children: how they all fitted into one small room Eliza could not begin to imagine, but they did, and all seemed none the worse for it. The two eldest sons, Carlo and Guido, were big, dark and handsome young men; Eliza thought that Beattie would do better with one of them than casting her eye in Freddie's direction. At least if she hooked one of the Italians, she would have plenty of pasta and ice cream with which to feed her scrawny little nippers.

In the beginning, Freddie instructed Eliza in how to make up some of the potions that he sold from his suitcase. First there was the blood purifier that had worked such wonders for Dolly, and this was made by steeping dried sassafras leaves in water, then sweetening the strained liquid with burnt sugar and pear juice. There was salve, concocted from goose grease and turpentine and fragranced with lavender oil, which could be used for treating anything from chapped hands to burns. There were cough drops made from boiled sugar, honey and lemon juice, and pills recommended for anything from gout to dropsy that were simply pellets of chalk coated with sugar. Flowers of sulphur were packed into small boxes and sold with cardboard tubes so that the yellow powder could be blown into the open mouth of those afflicted with sore throats. There was quinine for fevers and laudanum to soothe pain.

Eliza was well aware that some of the medicines were sheer hocus-pocus and that it was Freddie's convincing patter that sold them, but she had witnessed Dolly's miraculous cure brought about by taking the blood purifier. She could not be certain whether this was as magical at it had seemed, or whether it had worked simply because Dolly had believed that it would.

When they started out on the streets Eliza was nervous and unsure of herself, simply handing out the bottles, phials and pillboxes, but as her confidence grew, she became bolder and was ready to supplement Freddie's sales patter with confirmatory remarks as to the efficacy of his nostrums. They usually worked alone, leaving Millie in the care of Dolly, who had really taken to the child and took pleasure in her company. Dolly's cure, if it were such, had led to her taking in a few orders for sewing as well as renewing her interest in all things domestic. Freddie only brought Millie in as the ailing child, to be miraculously cured by a single sip of his patent medicine, the Cure-All, when they worked the markets. He would set up his suitcase on a wooden stand with Eliza at his side and Millie mingling with the crowd. Then, if things were not selling well, he would pick Millie out of the audience, seemingly at random, and bring her to the front. Her cheeks, which had filled out a little and become rosy with good food and Dolly's loving care, had been whitened with flour and her eyes underlined with smudges of soot. Freddie had procured small crutches from one of his shady contacts and Millie would lean on these until given a dose of the mixture by Eliza, when she would throw away the crutches with an exultant cry and do a little dance. This always went down very well, but they had to be careful not to repeat it too often in case someone had seen the act on a previous occasion.

Eliza enjoyed working for Freddie: in fact, she hero-worshipped him. Despite the fact that most of his patent cures were simple placebos, she admired him for being an educated man dedicated to helping the poor and sick. She did not think of what they did as being dishonest. After all, she reasoned, if something made other people feel better, what harm was there in charging them a halfpenny or even a penny for a bottle of medicine or a poke of pills? Above all, Freddie's medications gave poor people a little hope and that, thought Eliza, was worth more than money in a world where disease carried off young and old alike, rich and poor, but mostly the poor.

Apart from being clever, Freddie was also funny, and when they were making up potions in his room, he would have Eliza in fits of laughter as he regaled her with stories of his adventures and amours. He was, he said, the youngest son of a country squire, and, with no hope of an inheritance, he had been packed off to London to study medicine at Bart's. But an unfortunate incident involving a wild party and a young woman with the colourful name of Spitalfields Sal, had led to his expulsion before he had qualified. When questioned, he admitted that a law writer who had fallen on hard times had drawn up the diploma from the University of Paris. It was not really a fake, just a slight bending of the truth. Had it not been for Spitalfields Sal he would in all probability have qualified as doctor of medicine, and would now be bored to death in a country practice with a dull wife and a quiverful of children. Eliza had wanted to know more about his family but Freddie had shrugged his shoulders. Father and mother deceased; one sister married to a local landowner and four brothers who considered him to be the black sheep of the family and wanted nothing to do with him. 'So you see, Eliza,' Freddie had said, with his customary charming smile, 'you and I are both orphans. We have much in common and so we face the harsh world together.' He had taken her hand and kissed it: at that moment, Eliza had fallen in love. Of course, he could not be compared to Bart who was all things wonderful to her, but he came a close second in her affections.

Although Eliza kept well away from the

chandlery, she saw Davy every evening when their day's work was done and he came to call at the house in Hemp Yard. She always asked him the same question and he gave her the same answer: there had been no letter from Bart. She clung stubbornly to the belief that he was alive and continued to write letters to him, hoping that one day she would have a forwarding address. Every night, she mentioned him in her prayers.

The summer faded into autumn and Ted decided that Millie, who could neither read nor write, ought to go to school. Dolly was tearful at the thought of being parted from her, but she had to agree that getting an education was important, even for a poor girl. She put on her specs and spent many evenings sewing a school dress and a pinafore. On her first day, Eliza took Millie to the Board School in Communion Street. The schoolyard was filled with children, the girls skipping and playing with hoops; the boys were either scrapping or racing round energetically, whipping tops and shouting.

Millie hung back, clutching Eliza's hand. 'I'd rather go with you and Freddie,' she whispered, biting her lip.

Eliza brushed her cheek with a kiss and gave her a gentle push towards the gate. 'You'll be fine. Look, there's Mary Little, Davy's sister. She's the same age as you. Hey, Mary.' Eliza put two fingers in her mouth and whistled, beckoning to

Mary as she looked around to see who was calling her.

Mary ran up to them, smiling shyly. 'Hello, Liza.'

'This is Millie Turner and it's her first day at school. I want you to look after her, and see that no one bullies her.'

With a gap-toothed grin, Mary held her hand out to Millie. 'Come with me then, Millie.'

They went off hand in hand and Eliza swallowed a lump in her throat as she watched them disappear into the crowd of whooping, giggling children. With Bart so far away, Millie had become as dear to her as a real sister and Dolly was like a mother to them both. Eliza was still a bit in awe of Ted, who was inclined to be brusque and strict at times, although he was never unkind. Brushing a tear from her eyes, Eliza turned on her heel and hurried off to Anchor Street where she was to help Freddie make up a batch of cough mixture and cold cures, ready for the start of the winter ailments.

She knocked on the door, expecting that Beattie would open it, but no one came and she knocked a second time. The door opened but it was Carlo Donatiello who brushed past her without a second glance. She managed to slip inside before it closed and she went straight to Freddie's room. She knocked but there was no answer and, assuming that he must have overslept, she tried the handle. The door was unlocked and she and walked in, ready to tease Freddie for being a lazybones. The curtains were drawn but the pale morning sunlight filtered through the moth holes; it was the noise from the bed that made Eliza peer into the dim corner. Her hand flew to her mouth, stifling a gasp of shock and dismay as she saw two figures writhing about on the narrow bed. Completely naked, with her brassy blonde hair tumbling over her shoulders and full breasts, Beattie was astride Freddie, moving rhythmically up and down as though she were riding a pony. Horrified but also fascinated, Eliza saw Freddie's hands move up Beattie's glistening body to cup her breasts; his back was arched and his eyes closed and, to Eliza's horror, he too was naked. She had heard the chambermaids at Mrs Tubbs's house describe the act of love, but she had never before witnessed anything like this. If she had not known better she would have thought they were both in agony, judging by the grunts and moans that issued from their lips. Freddie was groaning, moving faster and faster and squeezing Beattie's plump breasts until they resembled a couple of pounds of chitterlings. Beattie's bare buttocks bumped and slapped on his thighs and her knuckles showed white as she clutched the bedrail. With her head thrown back, Beattie's throaty gurgling rose to a crescendo and, almost without knowing she was doing it, Eliza screamed with her.

Beattie collapsed onto Freddie's chest and they turned their heads to stare at her with startled, unfocused eyes. Then, as if stung by a wasp, Beattie let out a screech and leapt off Freddie with one bound, taking the bed sheet with her and wrapping it round her naked, sweating body.

'Little bitch,' Beattie screamed. 'Bleeding peeping Tom.'

Covering his naked lower half with his pillow, Freddie sat up in bed, his face and torso slicked with beads of sweat. He managed a feeble grin. 'Hello, Eliza. You're early.'

Swaying dizzily on her feet, Eliza clamped her hand over her mouth. She was going to be sick, her heart felt as though it had swollen up and was going to burst; she couldn't breathe.

'Get out,' Beattie cried, advancing on Eliza with her hand raised. 'Get out before I fetch you a clout round the lughole.'

Eliza needed no second bidding; somehow her feet seemed to work independently of her brain. They carried her out of the room, out of the house and along the street, regardless of anything or anyone in her way. She had no clear idea where she was going and she ran, sobbing and gulping air into her lungs. How could Freddie do that with Beattie? How could he make love to a brassy, foul-mouthed trollop? How could he be so – dirty? In her head, Eliza could hear echoes of the sermons that she had been forced to endure three times a day on Sundays. It was Sodom and Gomorrah all over again. Freddie, her idol, had tumbled from his pedestal and Eliza felt nothing but horror, disgust and contempt. She had thought he was so perfect and now she found that he was just a man – a weak and stupid man who had allowed himself to be led astray by a tart.

Without realising it, Eliza had run towards Execution Dock. She fell to her knees on the quay wall, leaning over the edge and staring into the hypnotic swirl of the chocolate-coloured water. The stench of raw sewage hit her in the stomach and she vomited. Clutching her belly and sobbing, Eliza rocked herself backwards and forwards. All around her there was the hustle and bustle of the docks, people going about their business and taking no notice of a young girl even though she was in an obvious state of distress.

'Ah, there you are, Eliza.'

Freddie's matter-of-fact voice behind her made Eliza turn her head slowly to peer up at him through a mist of tears.

'Go away. Leave me alone.'

Gently, Freddie lifted her to her feet. 'There are some things that you just don't understand, my dear.'

'Go away. I hate you.' Flailing her fists against his chest, Eliza broke down in a fresh bout of sobbing. 'You're a wicked, wicked man. I never want to see you again.'

'You're right, I'm just a man, and I make mistakes – lots of them. But right now we need to have a chat about grown-up things, Eliza.'

Chapter Five

For a brief moment, when Bart opened his eyes, he could not remember where he was. He had been dreaming of home; London in winter, with fingers of fog creeping through the skylight of the sail loft and Eliza's rhythmic breathing, soft as a whisper, coming from the straw palliasse by his side. It was Christmas morning, and in his dream he had been about to wake Eliza and give her the cowrie-shell necklace that he had purchased from a sailor in Wellington. Blinking against the bright morning light and swatting off the cloud of sandflies that had invaded his rough shelter, Bart realised that the necklace was still clutched in his hand: he was in New Zealand's South Island, and Eliza was half a world away. He sat up and stretched his cramped muscles before tucking the necklace safely away in his pack. He scratched his chin where a beard had grown during his four-month voyage from London to Wellington, and licked his dry lips. Thoughts of Eliza, left to the not very tender mercies of Uncle Enoch, had brought tears to his eyes and he dashed them away, cursing his own weakness. But, for all his efforts to harden his heart, her oval face, with its sweet but serious expression, blotted all other thoughts from his mind. The stiffness in his muscles, the creeping damp that was eating into the marrow of his bones and the hunger growling away in his belly, all counted for nothing as he pictured his little sister, so young and innocent, unprotected and alone in the unforgiving tumult of London's dockland. During the whole of his long journey Bart had been haunted by fears that Enoch would break his word; that he would not find a kind and respectable family to look after Liza and that he would continue to treat her with callous indifference, or worse, and there was nothing that Bart could do about it.

A spasm of cramp caused him to stretch out his legs, rubbing his tortured calf muscles. The trek through incredible country that ranged from rolling plains, untamed bush, jagged mountains and deep gorges through which rivers tumbled their way to the coast had been a severe test of his courage and stamina. With a reflex action, he slapped at a sandfly that had just stung his wrist. He couldn't tell if the spot of dark red blood was his own, or had belonged to the squashed insect. He flexed his hands, staring down at his short, square-tipped fingers with nails bitten to the quick and sunburnt skin, cracked and bleeding from the hard work he had endured during the sea voyage from England.

Closing his eyes against the glare of the rising sun, Bart clenched his teeth. The feelings of guilt that had racked his soul since he had sailed away from London had grown worse with the passing of time. If he could have turned back the clock he would gladly have done so: he would have walked away from the cove who had cheated him. But he knew in his heart that it was his own quick temper that had brought him here. He had come this far, working his passage and suffering almost intolerable hardship and privation on board the brigantine *London*, the overcrowded immigrant ship carrying eight hundred passengers bound for New Zealand.

The wooden vessel had stunk with the odour of unwashed bodies, vomit and excrement, and was permanently damp both above and below decks. Summer storms in the Bay of Biscay had caused the ship to heel on its beam-ends. Bart had muttered the prayers that he had learned in church, this time with genuine feeling, begging God to look after Eliza when he met his watery end. There had been a temporary lull until they reached the Cape of Good Hope, where they encountered huge seas and howling gales. The brigantine had battled its way valiantly against unrelenting tempests. There was neither rest nor sleep for the crew as they struggled to keep the vessel on course in mountainous seas. With the ship's timbers creaking and groaning in protest, it had plunged into troughs so deep that Bart had seen green water rising higher than the topmast. Then, when it seemed that the ship would be smashed like matchwood in the ferocious conditions, the sturdy vessel had miraculously, or so it had seemed to him, fought its way to the crest of the wave, taking on water, breaking spars and slicing canvas, but still afloat.

During this terrifying time there had been neither respite nor hot food and all hands were permanently on deck or down below pumping the bilges. The ship had carried two sailmakers, but one of them had been injured during a particularly bad storm, when, thrown against the bulkhead, he had broken his arm. With one of the mainsails badly ripped, Bart had offered his services; he had not lived in the sail loft for five years without learning a bit about the process of making and repairing sails. The captain had been only too pleased to allow him to relinquish his duties on deck in order to help the sailmaker. With the mainsail mended, they were able to limp into Capetown where the ship took on fresh water and supplies.

On the last leg of the voyage, the ship had been becalmed in the doldrums and encountered cyclones in the Indian Ocean: a vast expanse of water that seemed to stretch into infinity. At night there was inky blackness all around them, punctuated with sparkling diamonds of stars and, on a clear night, a silvery pathway that led across the water to the moon. Bart was not a scholar, but now he wished that he had the mastery of words so that he could write to Eliza and recount the amazing things that he had seen: the schools of dolphins playing in the bow waves and the whales, huge leviathans that rose from the sea sending plumes of water from their breathing holes before plunging into the aquamarine depths, with the majestic flip of their enormous tailfins. But as he had had no writing materials, he had stored up all these things in his memory, intent on putting them down on paper when they made landfall.

They had reached New Zealand and the port of Wellington in North Island at the end of October and, to Bart's surprise, he found that he had entered a world where it was springtime, even though he had left London in midsummer. With little money, he had to find work and somewhere to stay while he made provision for his assault on the goldfields. Eventually, after footslogging around Wellington for a day, he had seen a sign in a taproom window advertising for a potman. He had been hired on the spot, without any request for references, but it did not take him long to realise that he had been taken on mainly for his burly physique and uncompromising attitude. His main job had been breaking up the fights that had frequently occurred between customers who were the worse for drink, and tossing them bodily out onto the street.

He had slept beneath the counter, washed himself at the pump in the yard and hoarded every penny that he had earned, hiding it in a leather pouch under a loose floorboard. It was in the taproom that he had met Tate, a young man from Bermondsey, south of the river, who had spent most of his life since leaving the orphanage dodging the law and earning his living by bare-knuckle fighting; his broken nose, half-closed left eye and cauliflower ears were a testament to his prowess or lack of it. On the day in question, Tate had been involved in a brawl, although for once it appeared to Bart that it had been none of his making. Tate had been sitting at a table, drinking a pint of beer and minding his own business, when a couple of Irish miners had started an argument that had escalated into a fight, with punches flying in all directions. Bart had waded in to drag them apart and had received a blow on the nose for his pains that had brought blood gushing from his nostrils. Tate had leapt to his feet and, with the skill learned in the back streets of Bermondsey, he had laid out the two Irishmen and a few more besides. When the bleeding from his nose had been staunched, Bart had bought Tate a pint and they had started talking about London and home. With neither close friends nor family, Tate only seemed to miss his local pub and a plate of jellied eels. He had, he said, arrived in Wellington more than six months ago, and had found himself work labouring on the docks. He had been endeavouring to save stake money, intending to get a passage to Port Chalmers in South Island where he would hire a bullock team and cart and head for the goldfields of Otago. But, he had said, grinning ruefully, there had been distractions: drinking, gambling, and a man had certain needs. He had winked, tapped the side of his nose and gone on to extol the virtue, or rather lack of it, of a certain barmaid in a hotel in Cable Street. He had even offered to introduce Bart to her or one of her equally accommodating friends. Bart had been tempted, but he had shaken his head and stuck to his decision to save every penny towards his stake.

During the next few weeks they had become firm friends, and eventually, in the second week of December, they had scraped together enough money to buy a passage on a vessel bound for Port Chalmers. When they had arrived in Dunedin, they had come across many men similarly inclined, all intent on heading for the goldfields. Determined not to waste any more time, they had used most of their stake money to buy provisions and canvas to provide a shelter against the elements. Tate was all for buying a couple of old nags from a livery stable, but Bart had argued that it would cost too much; they would need digging tools, tents and food when they reached their destination. Although Tate grumbled, he had eventually given in, and they had set out on foot to make the long and arduous trek to Queenstown, Fox Camp and fortune.

It was now nine days since they had left Dunedin and, by Bart's reckoning and the rough map that he had purchased in Port Chalmers, they were very close to Fox Camp. Swatting at the sandflies with his cap, Bart scrambled to his feet, looking about him and taking stock of their position. Last night, having followed the course of the Kawarau River for many miles, they had turned away from its tumbling turquoise waters and had entered a wide gorge dissected by shallow, bubbling creeks that merged into another body of water that Bart reasoned must be the Arrow River. Now it was light, Bart caught his breath as he gazed up at the steep-sided gorge, clad with dense, green, native forest, and above that, like some sleeping prehistoric creature, the saw-toothed mountains of the Crown Range, tipped with snow, white and sparkling in the sunlight. Who could have imagined any country like this, he thought, breathing in the wine-cold air, so fresh, sweet and clean that it made him light-headed. What stories he would have to tell Eliza when eventually he had the time to put pen to paper.

Bart's empty stomach contracted in a loud rumble and he licked his dry lips; it was time to eat, then they must break camp and set off, taking advantage of the early morning cool. He glanced down at Tate's booted feet sticking out of his canvas cover; there were gaping holes in the soles that were stuffed with leaves to keep out the damp. Looking down at his own boots, Bart pulled a grim face as he saw his bare toes sticking out where the uppers had parted with the soles. If they had to trudge much further, they would end up barefoot as well as starving.

'Ho, Tate, rouse yourself, you lazy bastard.' Bart picked up a pebble and tossed it at the canvas shelter.

'Hey, what?' Tate's tousled head popped out from beneath his covers. 'What's up?'

'It's morning and we'd better get going if we're to reach Fox Camp by nightfall. I don't fancy another night being bitten to death by bloody sandflies.'

'Well, don't just stand there, you lazy sod, get a fire going and make us a brew. I'm parched and me belly's empty.' Tate got to his feet and stretched. 'Here, give us the billycan and I'll fetch the water.'

Bart reached down, picked up the can and tossed it to Tate, who stumbled off towards the river. With the aid of a handful of tussock grass, his tinderbox and the kindling that he had kept dry in his shelter, Bart soon had a fire snapping and crackling, sending plumes of smoke into the azure sky. He sat back on his haunches. The majestic scenery that surrounded them was eerily silent; it felt as though he and Tate were the only two living beings left on the planet. He could feel the sun's rays gaining in strength as it rose higher in the sky and his clothes had begun to steam. It might be Christmas Day, but everything was so different here compared to the grey streets of London, the turgid waters of the Thames and the teeming populace that he had to pinch himself in order to make sure he was not dreaming. It hurt! He was wide awake and, once again, his throat constricted as he thought of Eliza. This was the first Christmas that they had spent apart; he could only hope and pray that the old bugger was being kind to her. He scrambled to his feet, sniffing. He was a grown man and he would not cry, even though his heart was hurting like a bellyache after eating green apples. He could hear Tate's heavy footsteps crunching on the stones as he trudged up from the riverbank.

'It's your turn next time, mate,' Tate said, hooking the handle of the billycan on the forked tree branch over the fire. 'What's up with you then?'

'Bleeding smoke,' Bart said, rubbing his sleeve across his eyes. 'I stink like a dead rat that's been flung on a bonfire. The first thing I'm going to do when we get to Fox Camp is to find a hotel and have a hot bath.'

'Me, I want a nice hot barmaid with big titties and thighs like pillows.' Tate grinned and pointed to the river. 'There's plenty of cold water down there if you want a bath.'

'Seems like you need it more than me. It would cool you down a bit.' Bart reached for the flour sack. 'Be serious for a moment, Tate. There's just enough flour to make some damper for breakfast and that's it. There's enough tea for one brew and no sugar left. I'm telling you, we've got to get there today or we'll starve.'

'You worry too much,' Tate said, squatting down on his haunches by the fire. 'We've come this far, ain't we?'

As the sun plummeted in a fireball behind the mountains to the west, Bart and Tate finally arrived on the outskirts of Fox Camp, exhausted, footsore and weak with hunger. They trudged between ranks of canvas tents and wooden shacks. The billowing smoke from hundreds of campfires hung in an aromatic cloud above them. Bart sniffed appreciatively at the tempting aroma of frying bacon, damper baking on hot stones and the scent of freshly made tea. As they made their way towards the main town, they attracted little or no attention other than a casual, impersonal glance from the bearded, mud-covered figures intent on preparing their supper. Mongrel dogs wandered in and out between the shelters, more intent on scavenging for food than barking at strangers.

Having reached the main street, Bart and Tate paused for a moment, taking in the scene. Fronted by wooden boardwalks, shaded and protected from the elements by canopies and awnings, the street was lined almost entirely by single-storey buildings. What struck Bart forcibly was the noise and bustling activity. He had grown accustomed to the silence of the wilderness and it was something of a shock to hear raucous laughter, raised voices and music emanating from the open doors of hotels and bars. The rumbling of cartwheels and thudding of horses' hooves on the packed mud road throbbed painfully in his head. The street was crowded with miners, seemingly intent on having a good time as they lurched in and out of the bars. Lamps burned in shop windows, the stores being open to all comers even though it was Christmas night. He studied a board outside the Provincial Hotel advertising the cost of dinner and a bed for the night. He put his hand in his pocket and his fingers closed round a few pennies, all that was left of his savings. 'How much money have you got, Tate?' Bart counted the coins in his palm. Not enough there for dinner, let alone a bed and a much needed bath.

Tate shook his head. 'Bloody hell, they must have struck it rich here if they can get away with these prices.'

'I've got enough for a bag of flour, some tea and maybe a bit of bacon, but that's all.' Bart pocketed the coins. 'We'll have to pitch camp outside the town.'

'Maybe not.' Tate held out his hand. 'Give us your money, old chap. I feel lucky tonight.'

Bart hesitated, following Tate's gaze as he peered into the hotel lobby. 'You ain't going to gamble away my money.'

'Have you got a better idea?'

The coins were heavy and cold in Bart's pocket and his fingers touched the cowrie-shell necklace that he had bought for Eliza. He wouldn't be much use to her if he died of cold and hunger; reluctantly, he parted with all but three of his pennies, dropping them into Tate's outstretched palm.

Tate dropped his pack at Bart's feet and strolled into the hotel lobby. 'Meet me here later.'

This could be the worst decision of my life, Bart thought, as he hefted the two packs onto his back. If he loses, then we're done for. There wasn't much he could do about it now – their lives depended on the turn of a card or the toss of a dice. Bart walked to the nearest store and bought a pound of flour, a poke of tea and a half-pound bag of sugar: at least they would have some sort of meal. Not much, but something to keep body and soul together. He walked slowly back to the hotel. Tobacco smoke wafted out of the open door, together with the malty smell of beer. His mouth was parched – a pint would go down well at this moment, but he hadn't even a farthing left in his pocket. He dropped his packs on the boardwalk and squatted down beside them with his head in his hands.

'Hello, dearie, down on your luck are you?'

Looking up, Bart saw a shapely ankle peeping out beneath the hem of a scarlet taffeta skirt and a waist corseted so tightly that he was certain he could span it with his hands. As he jumped to his feet, his eyes rested momentarily on milk-white, twin globes protruding above a low-cut bodice. He had to drag his gaze upwards and found himself looking into a pair of mischievous blue eyes beneath sandy brows. He pulled off his cap, clutching it to his chest. 'How do, ma'am.'

A chuckle bubbled up from her throat so that her breasts shook, seeming to be in imminent danger of popping out of her bodice. She cocked her head, smiling. 'It's Daisy, love. Daisy Dawkins.'

'Bart, Bartholomew Bragg from London.'

'Well, Bart Bragg from London, you look as though you could do with a drink.' Daisy tucked her hand into the crook of his arm.

'I'd like nothing better,' Bart said, shaking his head. 'But you was right the first time. I'm broke, Daisy.'

She eyed him up and down. 'Just arrived, have you?'

'That's about it.'

'Then I'll buy you a beer, my lad. And when you've struck it rich you can remember Daisy Dawkins was the first to lend you a helping hand.' Giving his arm a companionable squeeze, she led him into the lobby of the Provincial Hotel and through to the bar room where she perched on the edge of a barstool, signalling to the barman. 'Two pints of your best, Jim.'

'Right you are, Daisy.'

Bart pulled up a stool, eyeing Daisy curiously. She was obviously very much at home in these surroundings. Back home he would have called her a loose woman, but despite her worldly air, he sensed a touching, underlying innocence in her that reminded him forcibly of Eliza. Her silver-blonde hair was piled up on her head in a halo of curls, and to him she looked like an angel.

'Well then, love, tell us your story,' Daisy said, taking a swig of her beer.

Bart drank deeply. He didn't want to tell this beautiful creature that he had killed a man. He hesitated. In the far corner of the room, he could just make out Tate's dark head bent over a hand of cards. From the hunch of his shoulders, Bart guessed that his lucky streak was not proving so good after all.

Daisy laid her hand on his knee. 'Is he a mate of yours, dearie?'

'We travelled together from Wellington.'

'Gambling and prospecting don't go well together. I seen whole fortunes change hands in a night.'

'We need stake money,' Bart said, trying not to stare at Daisy's breasts. He could feel the alcohol going straight to his head, and a stirring in his loins that was almost impossible to ignore. It was months since he'd had a woman and then it had only been a quick coupling with a prostitute in a back alley off Ratcliff Highway. It had satisfied a need, but had been a simple business transaction. Although his spirit yearned for a deep emotional attachment, he was only too aware that he would not find what he was seeking in the back streets and brothels. His work on the river and caring for Eliza had left little time to go looking for a respectable young woman with a view to courting her. Raising his eyes, Bart saw that Daisy was sipping her beer and smiling at him in a knowing way. He felt his cheeks flame beneath his whiskers and he looked away quickly.

'It's all right, love,' Daisy said softly. 'I ain't no angel. You don't have to be shy with me.'

He finished his drink, wiping his mouth on the

back of his hand. 'You've been good to me, Daisy. I ain't one to take advantage of a woman.'

'Glory be to God, a gent.' Daisy's laughter echoed round the bar, causing a few heads to turn. 'I tell you what you need, love.' She leaned closer so that her breasts grazed Bart's bare forearm. 'A bath, a shave and a bit of food.'

He closed his eyes, inhaling the intoxicating smell of woman laced with beer and cheap cologne. 'I never had a more tempting offer, but I can't leave Tate on his own.'

'He's a big boy, just like you,' Daisy said, running her hand up Bart's leg to his thigh. 'Here, Jim,' she called to the barman. 'If that fellow over there wants to find his mate, tell him where I live and he's to wait outside. Me and this big fellow have got a bit of business to do.' She slid off the stool, taking Bart by the hand and chuckling at Jim's crude response.

Unable to believe his luck, Bart snatched up his pack and leaving Tate's belongings in the care of the barman, he followed Daisy out of the hotel, along the crowded boardwalk and through a narrow doorway into a wooden building just a little way down the street. As she opened a door at the end of a dark passage, Bart felt the steam hit him in the face together with the smell of carbolic soap.

She walked in ahead of him, taking no notice of a naked man sitting in a zinc bathtub, or the man towelling himself down in the corner. She tossed a coin to a red-faced woman with muscular fore-arms, whose job appeared to be filling the tubs with hot water from a bubbling copper. 'Here, Flo, give this one some clean water and a razor.' Daisy patted Bart on the cheek. 'Me room's next door, love. See you in ten minutes or so.' She sashayed to the door and blew him a kiss as she left the room.

'Get in then, what are you waiting for?' demanded Flo, tipping a pitcher of water into the tub. 'You're lucky, fellah. Daisy don't usually take to strangers.'

'Is that so?' Bart stripped off his clothes, hesitating when he got down to his breeches and glancing warily at Flo.

'Get them off then, love. You ain't got nothing that I ain't seen a dozen or more times a day.' She stood, arms akimbo, watching him with a wide grin.

Acutely conscious that his close encounter with Daisy, and the promise of more to come, had left him with an erection that would have done justice to a stallion, Bart dropped his pants and leapt into the hot water, but not before Flo had given him an admiring nod of approval. He ducked his head beneath the scalding water, praying that his manhood was not going to end up braised like a plateful of sweetbreads.

Fifteen minutes later, clean-shaven and glowing all over, Bart felt almost shy as he went into Daisy's room.

'So I was right,' Daisy said, eyeing him appreciatively. 'I knew there was a good-looking chap beneath all that dirt and fuzz.'

As he set his pack down on the earth floor, Bart was only dimly aware of his surroundings as his eyes feasted on Daisy, voluptuous in her state of undress. Her shapely body was clearly visible beneath a diaphanous wrap made of some thin, gauzy material, leaving little to the imagination. She came towards him, moving slowly with her arms outstretched and her pale hair hanging loose about her shoulders. She smiled up at him as she twined her arms around his neck. 'We'll have supper afterwards.' With her lips parted and her eyes half closed, Daisy pulled his head down so that their lips met.

Her mouth tasted sweeter than honey and Bart slid his hands beneath her robe. Her skin was smooth, soft and cool as silk and he cupped her heavy breasts in his hands with a feeling of awe. Her lips opened beneath his and she returned his kiss with a ferocity and hunger that took him by surprise. He forgot everything except his need to take this woman who was offering herself to him with such unashamed enthusiasm. Lifting her off her feet, he carried her across the floor and laid her on the crude wooden bed. Her hands were expertly stripping him of his clothes even as her mouth devoured his lips. She arched her body beneath him, guiding him into her and wrapping her legs around him. Bart gave in to sheer physical pleasure and abandoned himself to the expertise of a woman well versed in the art of lovemaking.

As they lay together in the satiated afterglow, Bart stroked Daisy's cheek and was shocked to find it wet with tears. He raised himself on his elbow, peering into her face as he attempted to read her expression in the flickering candlelight.

'What's up, Daisy. I didn't hurt you, did I?'

Daisy sniffed and hiccuped. 'No, of course you never. You was wonderful, Bart. And you was such a gent. I ain't used to being treated like a lady. It's usually just a grunt and a fumble and then it's over. They does up their breeches and stomps off without even a thank you.'

'I thank you, Daisy. I thanks you from the bottom of me heart,' Bart whispered, nuzzling her neck. 'You saved me life tonight, girl. And I won't forget it.'

'Get on with you,' Daisy said, snuggling into the curve of Bart's body. 'You'll forget all about me when you find that big gold nugget.'

He stroked her hair, closing his eyes and luxuriating in the sensual delight of holding a naked woman in his arms, the softness of her flesh and the weight of her breasts against his chest. 'I'll never forget this, ducks. You're a star, Daisy, a shining star.'

Halfway between crying and laughing, Daisy traced the outline of Bart's jaw with her tongue. 'I been called a lot of things in my time, but never a star.'

He inhaled the scent of her, tasting her sweetness and feeling himself hardening against her plump thighs. Bart let out a sigh. 'You're too good for this sort of life, sweetheart. Much too good.'

'I'm good at being bad,' Daisy said, nipping Bart's lips with a mischievous chuckle and moving as swiftly as an eel to straddle him.

'Hey, wake up in there.' Tate's voice outside the door awakened Bart, bringing him abruptly back to reality. The candle had burnt out and the room was in darkness except for a shaft of moonlight coming from a small window high up in the wall. A fist was hammering on the door, making the thin panels shake.

'Bart, are you in there?'

Daisy raised her tousled head, blinking drowsily. 'Who the bleeding hell is that banging on me door?'

Bart raised himself to a sitting position and kissed her damp forehead. 'Shut up, Tate. I'll be with you in a minute.'

Outside the door, Bart could hear Tate mumbling. He swung his legs over the side of the bed, turning to kiss Daisy once more but this time on her full lips. 'Ta for everything, Daisy, love. I'll pay you back one day, I swear I will.'

She stretched and smiled up at him, taking his hand and holding it to her breast. 'Forget the money, darling, it ain't everything. Just promise that you'll not forget me.'

He kissed her again, removing his hand reluctantly as he felt her nipple harden beneath his touch. He tucked the patchwork quilt up around her neck. 'Never. I'll never forget you, ducks. Take care of yourself.'

He went outside to face Tate, who was leaning against the wall smoking a cheroot. 'Had a good time, mate?'

Even in the darkness, Bart knew that Tate was grinning. 'Let's go,' he said, shouldering his pack. 'I bet you lost the lot.'

'That's where you're wrong. I lost a bit and then I won.' Tate pressed a bag of coins into Bart's hand. 'There's enough cash to stake us for a month and a bit more besides.'

The leather pouch felt reassuringly heavy in Bart's hand. Now he would be able to repay Daisy for her generosity. He could still taste her and her fragrance clung to his body, filling his senses with delight. 'Let's go then, and get some food. I'm bleeding starving.'

'Not so fast,' Tate said, snatching the pouch from Bart's hand. 'You've had the best of it as far as I can see. I want a woman and the whore's free now.'

A red mist blotted out Tate's shadowy figure: vicious, blood-curdling rage seized Bart as his temper flared white-hot. Daisy was his woman. She belonged to him now, and just as Eliza was his little sister to be loved and protected from the evils of the world, it had become so with Daisy. He grabbed Tate by the throat and smashed him against the wall. 'Leave her alone. If you go anywhere near her, I'll kill you.'

Chapter Six

It had been a strange Christmas without Bart. Although Eliza had Dolly and Ted to care for her, there was always a painful void that only Bart could fill. It was too soon to expect to hear from him, but not knowing whether he was safe and well, or even if he had survived the perils of the voyage, made her anxious and unsettled. She had bought him a present in Spitalfields Market, a woollen scarf that she tucked under her mattress to await his return. No matter what anyone said, and Ted had tried to warn her that Bart might never be able to come home, she was certain that God would not be so cruel as to part her for ever from her beloved brother. She prayed every night for his safe homecoming.

Despite missing Bart, Eliza was not unhappy; she had a real family with Dolly, Ted and Millie. Then there was Davy, dear, faithful Davy, who came round almost every evening when he had finished work. Sometimes they would sit on the wall of the workhouse in New Gravel Lane, swinging their feet and chatting about what they had done that day; at other times they would go for walks along the dockside, looking at the vessels and making up stories about their voyages to exotic parts of the world. Occasionally Millie went with them, but Dolly was strict with her, sending her to bed early saying that she was a growing girl and needed her sleep.

And, of course, there was Freddie, who was now her employer and her mentor. Eliza admired Freddie for his medical knowledge, his undoubted charm, and his ability to convince the public that he had the magic nostrum that would cure all ills. She loved him for his sense of humour and boundless good nature. But she was also aware that he was all dash and panache, and his brashness had in it an element of childish naivety: sometimes Eliza felt that she was the adult and Freddie was her wayward offspring. Since the episode when she had caught him *in flagrante* with Beattie Larkin, Eliza had learnt that his weakness was women. Catching them in the compromising position had shocked and temporarily sickened her, and she might never have gone back to that hateful house if Freddie had not followed her that fateful day.

Now, with the passing of several months, when winter had reluctantly given way to a faltering spring, Eliza could look back on that time with a rueful grin. Freddie had found her in despair on Execution Dock and he had been the soul of kindness and contrition. He had taken her by the hand, and had led her to a quiet place in the churchyard where he sat down beside her on a lichen-encrusted tombstone. He had explained the facts of life in such a calm and matter-of-fact manner that Dolly's previous, embarrassed explanation about Eliza's monthly courses had seemed, by comparison, quite comical. He had gone on to give her a paternal lecture on the general untrustworthiness of young men, who had but one thing on their minds. When he was satisfied that she had listened and understood, he had confessed that sometimes his own carnal desires overcame common sense, but that he was just a man and subject to human frailty. He hoped that she would think none the worse of him. He had assured her that Beattie meant nothing to him other than a release for his physical needs, and that he would make sure that Eliza was not subjected to a similar circumstance in the future. They had walked back to Anchor Street, hand in hand and with harmony restored.

Since then, Eliza had been an apt pupil, and she had absorbed everything that Freddie had to teach her with regard to the crocussing trade. After a few weeks he had been satisfied to leave her to work on her own while he went out selling door to door. She was proud that he trusted her to make up the cough mixtures, throat tablets and liniments unsupervised. With the usual epidemic of winter colds, chills and inflammation of the lungs, business had been booming and, even with spring on the way, had shown no signs of slowing down.

Eliza had left Millie at the school gates and she wrapped her shawl more tightly around her shoulders as the March wind brought with it a smattering of snow, and a temporary return of winter weather. She trudged, slipping and sliding on the slushy pavements, to Freddie's lodgings. She knocked on the door and waited, cupping her numbed hands to her lips and warming them with her breath. These days, she never entered unannounced, even though Freddie promised her that he had tired of Beattie's demanding ways and their relationship was strictly platonic. Eliza knew very well that Beattie blamed her for the waning of his desire, but it seemed a small price to pay for saving Freddie from a predatory female with a vulgar tongue and loose morals.

Beattie's eldest boy opened the door, squinting at Eliza with dumb insolence. 'You can't come in,' he said, scratching his skinny body in a way that made Eliza feel unclean and itchy.

'Don't be daft,' Eliza said, pushing past him and heading for Freddie's room. The door was open and she could hear raised voices.

Inside, Beattie stood with her hands clutched to her belly, sobbing hysterically and screaming at Freddie.

'Calm down, Beattie.' Freddie caught sight of Eliza and his worried frown gave way to a relieved smile. 'Thank goodness you've come.'

'It's all her fault,' Beattie screeched. 'You've been cool to me ever since that snooty little bitch caught us in the act, and she's to blame. I give you everything, I did, and look what I gets in return. Coldness, neglect and me in the family way again.' She turned on Eliza with her fingers hooked into claws.

Freddie caught her by the wrists. 'Beattie, be reasonable. You know it can't be mine. We haven't – er – you know what, for months. Anyway, I'm a doctor and I wouldn't have allowed it to happen.'

'You're a man and you don't bloody care.' Beattie clawed ineffectually at his face. 'It's your little bastard what's in me belly and don't you go saying it ain't.'

Eliza edged towards the door. 'Perhaps I should go.'

'No, please wait.' Freddie helped Beattie to a chair and made her sit down. He patted her hand. 'I know you're upset, but you're talking nonsense.'

'You bastard,' Beattie hissed. 'You know it's yours.'

Freddie backed towards the door, shaking his head. 'I know nothing of the sort. Fetch my things, Eliza, we're leaving.'

'Leaving!' Beattie's voice rose to a scream. 'You can't leave me, you vile blackguard. I'll report you to the magistrate for crocussing. I'll ruin you, you swine.'

'Do as you please, but I swear that the child is not mine.' Freddie delved in his pocket and pulled out a handful of coins. He tossed them onto the bed. 'That will keep you and your boys until you are fit to go back to your old profession, my dear.'

'Libertine!' Beattie took off her shoe and pitched it at Freddie's head. 'I won't let you get away with this. I'll make you pay.'

Freddie pushed Eliza unceremoniously out of the door as he attempted to deal with Beattie's eldest son, who had run to his mother's aid, and was kicking him in the shins and using swear words that were hitherto unknown to Eliza. 'Here,' Freddie said, taking a threepeny bit from his pocket and pressing it into the boy's hand. 'Take this and bugger off.'

Outside in the street, he leaned against the door with a sigh of relief. 'That was not something I would have wanted you to witness, Eliza. And I'm sorry for it.'

'Actually,' Eliza said, grinning, 'I wouldn't have missed it for the world.'

His relieved expression changed to one of alarm as the noises within the house grew louder. Beattie's caterwauling appeared to have reached the ears of the Donatiello family upstairs. The sound of booted feet thudding down the bare stair treads, and the deep baritone voices of Carlo and Guido trumpeting like angry bulls, made Freddie snatch up his bags.

'Leg it, Eliza,' he said, breaking into a run.

She needed no second bidding. She had heard the Donatiello family's verbal battles often enough. She had seen Carlo and Guido using their fists one minute and then, having blackened each other's eyes or bloodied a nose, flinging their arms around one another and hugging. As all their quarrels were conducted in mellifluous Italian, Eliza had never understood a word that was said, but she knew one thing and that was that the brothers used their fists first and asked questions later. She ran.

Breathless, red in the face and sweating, despite the extreme cold, Freddie stopped, setting his bags down and leaning against a wall. He had come to a halt outside Uncle Enoch's chandlery and Eliza tugged at his sleeve. 'This is my uncle's shop, Freddie. Best move on a bit.'

He took a silk handkerchief from his breast pocket and mopped his brow. 'Let me get my breath back. Look round the corner, Eliza. Make sure those mad Italians haven't followed us.'

Before Eliza could move, the door to the chandlery opened and Enoch stepped out onto the pavement. He stopped, glaring at Eliza over the top of his woollen muffler. 'What d'you want, girl?'

'Nothing, Uncle, we was just – passing by.' Eliza glanced anxiously at Freddie.

'Passing by!' Enoch spat the words at her. 'Come to importune me for money, I expect. Well, I've washed my hands of you and that worthless brother of yours. You'll not get another penny from me.'

'As I see it, Mr Bragg,' Freddie said, drawing himself upright, and hooking his arm around Eliza's shoulders. 'As I see it, sir, whichever way you care to look at it, you sold this girl to me for a couple of pounds just months ago. She is nothing to you and she wants nothing from you.'

'No doubt she's your whore, you damn crocusser.' Enoch spat on the ground at Eliza's feet. 'I always knew you'd end up on the street, you bitch. You're a harlot, just like your mother.'

Freddie lunged at Enoch; his aim was not scientific but he landed a blow on Enoch's beaky nose with a resounding crack of bone and a spurt of blood. Squaring up, Freddie danced about on his toes, fisting his hands. 'Take that for a start. Come on, Bragg. Fight like a man.'

Enoch backed into his shop doorway,

clutching his bleeding nose. 'I'll have the law on you – you quack. Common assault is what this is. You've broke me nose, you bugger.'

Eliza caught Freddie by the arm, pulling him away. 'Leave him be. Come away.'

But Freddie seemed to be elated by his prowess as a boxer and he continued to dodge backwards and forwards, dancing on his toes, daring Enoch to fight. 'Come on, Bragg. You're very brave when it comes to hurting little girls. Let's see you take on someone your own size.'

'Hooligan!' Enoch muttered, and disappeared into the shop, slamming the door behind him.

Freddie stood still, a look of disappointment clouding his face. 'Damn it, I was just beginning to enjoy myself.'

'Stop it.' Eliza grabbed him by the arm and shook him. 'You'll end up in jail if you carry on like this.'

He straightened his hat and picked up his bags. 'Did you see that punch? Landed right on his conk and drew claret. I wonder if I should give up medicine and consider pugilism instead?'

Eliza glanced up at the window of the sail loft where she caught a glimpse of two ginger heads. 'We got to get away from here.'

'You're absolutely right, of course. Come, Eliza. We have our work to do, healing the sick.'

Just as they were about to move off, the window above them opened and Davy stuck his head out. 'Best get away quick, Liza. The old bugger has sent Dippy Dan out the back way to fetch a constable.'

In spite of her agitation, she managed a smile. 'Ta, Davy.'

'Ted's out,' Davy said, leaning dangerously over the windowsill. 'He won't know nothing about it if you move on quick.'

She nodded. 'See you later then.'

'I think we might try Shadwell Market,' Freddie said, striding off as if nothing had happened. 'Come on, Eliza. Don't dawdle.'

Really, Freddie was the most exasperating man at times, she thought, as she trotted after him. He was homeless, and now the police would be looking for him as well as the Donatiello brothers, who had plenty of time on their hands until the beginning of the ice-cream season. She knew that they both had a soft spot for Beattie, and probably enjoyed her favours. In fact, either one of them could have fathered her little mistake. But Eliza did not fancy Freddie's chances if the brothers caught up with him. It was just as well, she thought, that Basher Harris, the stevedore who lived in the upstairs back bedroom with his aged mother, was doing his day shift in the docks. One punch from him would knock Freddie into next week.

They had reached the bridge in New Gravel Lane that crossed the polluted water oozing from the docks and emptying into the Pool of London. As they came to the middle of the bridge, Eliza looked down into the oily, tobacco-coloured water, and shuddered. The bloody bridge, as it was known locally, was a magnet to the poor desperate souls who threw themselves off the parapet seeking oblivion; their bloated corpses fished out nightly in the drag, a grim harvest of human detritus.

A ragged woman slumped on the cobblestones held out her claw-like hand, begging for money. 'For pity's sake, mister, give us twopence,' she cried, grabbing Freddie's coat-tail. 'A penny then, just a penny, for the love of God.'

He hesitated, looking down at her raddled face and the empty bottle lying by her side.

'Don't stop, Freddie,' Eliza said, glancing anxiously over her shoulder. 'There's two coppers coming down the street. Best move on quick.'

'Save a poor soul, your worship,' the woman cried, scrambling to her knees and steepling her fingers as if in prayer. 'The water is cold but they say as how you don't feel nothing much when it closes over your head for the third time.'

Freddie gave her twopence. On an instant, seeming to recover miraculously, she leapt to her feet and headed towards the nearest pub, her bare, purple feet slipping and slithering on the icy pavement.

'Hurry, Freddie,' Eliza hissed in his ear. 'Maybe they ain't looking for us.'

'I'm an innocent man, they have no cause to arrest me,' Freddie said, hefting his cases beneath his arms. 'Keep close to me, Eliza.'

Before they had gone two steps, there was a shout from behind. 'That's him, constable. The one you're looking for. Tried to bribe me to keep quiet, he did.'

Eliza turned her head and saw to her dismay that the drunken woman was being supported between two policemen, and she was pointing at Freddie.

'Run,' Eliza screamed. 'Oh, Freddie, run.'

'Dr Frederick Prince does not run from the law.' Freddie turned to face the constables as they strode towards him, swinging their truncheons. 'I'll sort this out, my dear. You must go home. Go now.' Lifting the case that contained his pills and potions onto the top of the parapet, Freddie leaned back giving it an almost imperceptible shove with his shoulders so that it hurtled downwards, hitting the water with a loud splash. 'Oops,' Freddie said, folding his arms across his chest.

'Why did you do that?' Eliza demanded, horrified to see the life-saving medicines sinking to the bottom of the cut.

'That's the evidence gone. It's my word against Enoch's now, Eliza.'

'Let me speak for you, Freddie. Let me tell them what a good man you are,' she cried, clasping his hand.

'Good man?' Freddie's smile wavered. 'Oh Eliza, my dear girl. I'll miss you terribly. Now run away while I keep them talking, or do I have to throw you in the cut with the medicine chest?'

He was smiling down at her with genuine tenderness in his eyes and she simply could not run away and leave him to his fate. Eliza faced the constables. 'You got the wrong man, officers. This here is Dr Frederick Prince, a physician with a genuine diploma from the Paris Conserve – conservative. He done nothing but heal the sick and I won't let you take him away. My uncle got what he deserved – you can't blame Freddie for punching him on the nose.'

Freddie shook his head, prising her fingers from his hand. 'Go, Eliza. I insist you go now.'

The elder and more senior of the two constables placed his burly body between them, turning to Eliza with a stern look. 'Move on, missy, or we'll have to take you in too.'

'Come on, miss.' The younger man took Eliza by the arm. 'You'd best do as he says.'

His superior officer took a pair of handcuffs from his belt. 'Dr Prince, I'm arresting you in the name of the law.'

Freddie offered his wrists for cuffing. 'I'm sure

we can sort this out, officer. I'll come quietly, but I insist that you let this young person go. She has nothing to do with me.'

'Oh, Freddie, how can you say such a thing?' Eliza cried, struggling to get free. 'You can't arrest Dr Prince. I'm telling you, he ain't done nothing wrong.' She lashed out with her foot at the constable who had arrested Freddie, but he moved out of reach.

'Send her on her way,' he said, seizing Freddie by the scruff of his neck. 'We got our man.'

The young constable guided Eliza to the edge of the bridge, where an interested crowd had turned out of the pubs to enjoy the spectacle. 'Go home, little girl. You shouldn't mix with men like him; they'll only get you into trouble.'

She stood on the pavement, watching helplessly as the constables marched Freddie away. The crowd was jeering and there was nothing she could do to help him. She felt lost and alone. Blind panic, despair and anger raged within her breast. She turned in the direction of home, and, blinded by tears, Eliza broke into a run. A cold, sleety rain was falling from a solid sky as she reached Hemp Yard. Winter had reclaimed its territory, and she felt as though her heart had frozen into a block of ice. She came to a halt outside the house, shivering as much from shock as the chill that was seeping into her bones. Her first instinct had been to rush into the house, but a small voice in her head warned her to stop and think. Dolly had been so much better for taking the medicine that Freddie had made up for her. She was a changed woman from the sickly, housebound invalid that Eliza had known when she first came to Hemp Yard. Dolly thought the world of Freddie and to tell her that he had been arrested might cause her to relapse, and Ted would be furious. He would be angry with Freddie and he would be vexed because she had lost her job.

Eliza stood on the pavement trying to decide what to do for the best. Then she caught sight of her reflection in a muddy puddle. Her beautiful blue bonnet was soaked and almost certainly ruined. The ostrich feather hung limply over her forehead and, as she brushed a salty mix of tears and sleet from her cheeks, she found that there was blue dye dripping down her face. She could not go into the house in this state; she must compose herself and think what to do next. But it was hard to think straight when she was shivering uncontrollably. She began to walk, wrapping her arms tightly around her body in an effort to keep warm. She must keep walking or she would freeze to death and she must find alternative work, at least until the police discovered that Freddie was innocent of any crime, other than punching Uncle Enoch on the nose. They would release him, she told herself, forcing her feet to move one in front of the other at a smart pace. Freddie was a healer, a doctor who gave hope to hundreds of poor people. He was a kind and wonderful man and she loved him.

Eliza stopped at the bottom of New Gravel Lane, close to the workhouse where Millie had spent her first few miserable years. The realisation that she loved Freddie hit her in the stomach like a punch from a prizefighter. No, it was impossible: she was only thirteen – Freddie was a grown man who thought of her as a child. Uncle Enoch had accused her of being Freddie's whore, a dreadful word that made Eliza feel sick with shame. As if Freddie would do anything as dishonourable as to take her in the way that he had taken the slut Beattie Larkin.

If only Bart were here. Hot tears trickled down her cheeks in an unstoppable flow, as if a dam had burst within her. She was grieving for Bart all over again and now she had also lost Freddie. Sniffing and gulping, Eliza found her way into the churchyard and huddled on the tombstone where she had once sat with Freddie. He had explained the ways of love so gently and kindly, freely admitting his own weaknesses. In spite of the cold, she felt her cheeks burning with shame; her love for Freddie was pure and unsullied by the lusts of the flesh. She would have walked through fire for him. She would willingly devote her life to helping him in his crusade to bring health to the poor and needy. She did not want to do the vile things that Beattie had done with him, naked and brazen, making noises like beasts in the marketplace. Wrapping her arms around her knees, Eliza crouched on the stone slab and sobbed.

Someone was shaking her by the shoulder and calling her name. Eliza opened her eyes. 'Oh, Davy, it's you.'

'It's me all right and a good thing I come looking for you,' Davy said, taking off his ragged jacket and wrapping it around her shoulders. 'Another hour and they'd have been digging a hole to plant you in, Liza. What was you thinking of? It's freezing cold and you're soaked to the skin.'

'They've arrested Freddie,' she said, choking on a sob. 'T-took him away like a common criminal and all because he punched Uncle Enoch.'

Davy grinned. 'I know, I saw it. We all saw it and we cheered. That were one of the best punches I've ever seen. Broke his nose it did.'

'It was Uncle Enoch's fault. He said horrible things and Freddie bashed him.'

'I know. And I'd have had done the same.'

She shivered, wrapping his jacket closer around her shoulders. 'How did you find me? And why aren't you at work?'

'Ted sent me out on an errand when he come back to the sail loft. I was worried sick about you. I thought the cops might have got you too, and so I went to your house, but you wasn't there. I was just on me way back to work when I seen you huddled on the tombstone. Fair give me a turn you did, I thought you was frozen stiff.'

'I can't feel me feet. Help me up, Davy.'

He put his arm around her waist and helped her to her feet. 'Lean on me, Liza. Take one step at a time.'

Very slowly, Davy guided Eliza's steps until the feeling began to return to her limbs. 'I'm all right now,' she said, biting her lip as her lower limbs burned and tingled. 'I can walk on me own.'

'I'll take you home.'

'No! Not yet. I can't tell them what's happened.'

'You're frozen to the marrow, girl. At least let me take you to me mum, she'll look after you until you feel a bit better.'

'I d-don't want to be no b-bother,' Eliza said, through chattering teeth.

'Don't talk soft. You know me mum's always pleased to see you. Come on, Liza, or you'll get me into trouble with old Peck for being late back.'

Too cold and wet to put up an argument, Eliza

allowed Davy to link his arm in hers and they made their way to the cellar room in Farmer Street where the Little family lived. Ada was sitting on an upturned orange crate with the youngest child, Sammy, suckling at her breast. Toddlers Eddie and Artie were on the floor at her feet attacking a bowl of bread sops and growling at each other like hungry puppies.

Ada looked up with a tired smile. 'What are you two doing home at this time of day?'

'I brought Liza here to get dry, Mum. She's had a bit of a to-do as you might say. Anyway, I got to get back to work or I'll be in trouble. I'll see you later.' With a cheery wink in Eliza's direction, Davy left the room, closing the door behind him.

'Well, ducks, you'd best take them wet things off,' Ada said, shifting the baby from one breast to the other. 'It's lucky we got a bit of a fire today. Go and get warm, while I finish feeding Sammy. Then I'll make us a nice cup of tea and you can tell me all about it.'

Huddling closer to the fire where two lumps of coal were feebly hissing out a modicum of heat, Eliza took off her wet shawl and spread it across the hearth. 'Things must be looking up then, Mrs Little.' She hesitated, realising that it was a bit rude to make a reference to Arthur Little's habitual condition of being too drunk to go to work. 'I mean, is Davy's dad well enough to ...?'

Eliza stopped, biting her lip. She was just making matters worse.

Ada shook her head, sighing. 'No, ducks. My Alf is a martyr to his bad back. The only thing what helps him is a few beers down the pub. I can't begrudge him that, now can I?'

Eliza shook her head, wishing she had never raised the subject. But Ada did not seem at all put out.

'My Davy went down the docks last night and he found a pile of coal what must have fallen off a collier while they was unloading. He keeps an eye on the wharves to see when a coal boat comes in. He's a good boy, is Davy.' As if in agreement, baby Sammy unlatched his mouth from his mother's nipple, made a satisfied mewing sound, hiccuped and spewed milk from his mouth. Ada covered her bare breast and hitched him over her shoulder, rubbing his back until he let out a loud burp. 'That's better out than in. You hold him for me, ducks. I'll make a brew. It'll help warm you up and keep you from going down with a chill.' Ada rose to her feet, handing the baby to Eliza.

She watched in silence as Ada scooped up some of the used tea leaves that had been left to dry on a piece of newspaper close to the fire and tipped them into a cracked china teapot with half its handle missing. Using her skirt as a potholder, she lifted a soot-blackened kettle from the trivet and poured boiling water onto the leaves. While she waited for the tea to brew, Ada took two tin mugs from a shelf and wiped them on her apron. 'Sorry, love, we ain't got no sugar or milk. I give the last of it to the little 'uns,' she said, filling a mug and handing it to Eliza. She bent down to separate the boys who were squabbling over who was going to lick out the bowl. 'Behave yourselves. We got company.'

Mercifully, Ada did not seem at all curious as to the reason for Eliza's bedraggled state and, although the fire did little to dry her wet clothes, the weak tea warmed her stomach. She sat on an upturned beer crate, sipping her tea and listening to Ada, who seemed delighted to talk about her family. She was so proud of Davy and his prowess as Ted's apprentice. Then there was Janet, his younger sister, who had been taken on as a scullery maid in a big house in Golders Green and was doing quite nicely, thank you. Pete was just twelve, and he had got a job in the brewery sticking labels on bottles, although to be truthful the pay was very poor. Nine-year-old Ruth was also working, and had found employment in a sweatshop in Leman Street where she picked up fluff, cotton and pins for a few pence a day.

As she nursed the sleeping baby and listened to Ada recounting her children's exploits with such love and pride, Eliza looked round the gloomy cellar, wondering how she managed to keep so cheerful and positive in these dank, vermin-infested surroundings. It was not pity that she felt, but deep admiration for Ada's courage in the face of such abject poverty. She thought about her comfortable, although by no means luxurious, home with Dolly and Ted, and suddenly all her problems seemed as nothing when compared with Ada's daily struggle for existence. One day, Eliza thought, when she was grown-up and had made her way in the world, she would do something to help Davy's family.

'And Mary's really clever,' Ada said, continuing the one-sided conversation. 'Mary can read and write and she's not yet eight.' She took the baby from Eliza and held him close to her sagging bosom. 'Maybe one day she'll be a schoolteacher and we'll be ever so proud of her. My nippers will amount to something in this world, just you see if they don't.'

Eliza stayed with Ada until Millie and Mary returned from school. By that time she had calmed down enough to face going home, and even managed to keep up the pretence that all was well. During a sleepless night, with Millie curled up at her side, snoring softly, Eliza thought hard about what Bart would advise in this situation. In the cold, early hours of the morning, she decided that he would tell her not to give in and to take positive action.

Next morning, she went out as usual, as if going to work. It took her the best part of the morning to walk to the City Police Office in Old Jewry Street. At first the sergeant at the desk refused to give her any information. Eliza allowed her bottom lip to tremble and just thinking of Freddie in a prison cell brought tears to her eyes. Eventually, after telling a downright lie, and saying that Freddie was her brother, she discovered that his case was being heard next day at the court in East Arbour Street, Stepney. In spite of her pleas to be allowed to see him, the sergeant was adamant in his refusal, and there was nothing Eliza could do except start out on the long walk home.

Next day, leaving at the usual time with her faded, water-stained bonnet on her head, minus the feather that had suffered irreparable damage, she set out for Stepney. She took a seat in the public gallery and waited nervously for Freddie's case to be heard. When he walked into the dock, looking tired and strained but holding his head high, she had to bite her lip to prevent herself from calling out to him. Perhaps he would be bound over to keep the peace, she thought, clasping her hands tightly in her lap. At first, after the charge of public disorder was read out, she thought that the proceedings would be over quickly, but to her dismay the clerk of the court summoned Uncle Enoch to the witness stand. She listened in horror as Enoch Bragg denounced Freddie as a charlatan and a mountebank who sold fake medicines to an unsuspecting public. Then, as if that was not bad enough, he accused Freddie of abducting an innocent young girl, his orphaned nice, Eliza Bragg. That blackguard, he said, had stolen a mere child away from her legal guardian and now he was using her for his own sinful purposes. He was guilty of corrupting morals and despoiling innocence, and he had assaulted her legal guardian into the bargain. 'He is a sinner,' Enoch roared, pointing his finger at Freddie. 'A vile rogue who uses women for his own pleasure and then abandons them.'

Stuffing her hand into her mouth, Eliza stifled a scream.

'And you need not take my word for it. For here, in this very courtroom, is a young woman seduced and then abandoned by this libertine.' Waving his arm, Enoch turned to point at Beattie Larkin, who rose from her seat, clutching her swollen belly.

'It's true, m'lud. He got me in the family way and then he scarpered.' Raising her hanky to her face, Beattie glanced up and spotted Eliza. Her eyes narrowed and she let out a howl of rage.

'And there she is. That's the trollop that he left me for.'

'No!' Jumping to her feet, Eliza leaned over the railing. 'It's a pack of lies. None of it's true. You got to believe me, milord. It's all lies.'

Chapter Seven

Rain and more rain: cold downpours that drenched the land, turning the Arrow River into a roaring torrent and its steep banks into mud slides. Clouds of black sandflies tormented Bart's flesh with stinging bites that itched relentlessly for days and almost drove him mad at night. The low ground that was neither river nor scrub was covered, knee-deep, with thick, primeval mud and it would have been easy to imagine pre-historic beasts roaming the bush. That's what Eliza would have said, Bart thought, grinning to himself. She was keen on book learning, bless her little heart! He'd never had much time for that sort of thing himself, but he could picture her now, reading to him from the one and only book in her possession. With a lump in his throat, he remembered evenings in the sail loft when he had come home from work wet, dirty and tired. Eliza would have his meal ready for him, and after supper, while he enjoyed a pipe of baccy, she would read to him. For the most part he hadn't paid much attention, but one story had stuck in his mind and it came back to him now.

With her small face alight with enthusiasm, Eliza had told him about a humble woman from Dorset, a certain Mary Anning, who had discovered the bones of great monsters, millions of years old. Personally, he'd never been able to understand why anyone could get excited over a pile of old fossils, but Eliza had been interested in that sort of thing. She was a clever girl, that little sister of his. He wasn't much of a praying man, but dear God, he thought, casting his eyes heavenwards: look after my Eliza. Keep her safe and well until I can go home.

Bart sighed, emptied rainwater from the brim of his oiled-canvas hat and then rammed it back on his head. Nothing could keep a fellow dry in this deluge, but at least the wide brim kept the water from his eyes. Even when the rain ceased, he would still be wet, soaked by the spray from the rushing waters of the Arrow as he panned the gravel for those tiny gold specks of dust, or hopefully a large nugget that would make his fortune. His limbs ached with cold and fatigue but Bart kept working with single-minded determination. Life here in the Otago goldfields was even harsher than he could have imagined, but he had one purpose and one purpose only: to make enough money to return home and give Eliza the life that she deserved. Only a few weeks ago, a man had waded into the river to rescue his dog which was in danger of being swept away and, in doing so, had stumbled across a gold nugget the size of a house brick. In an instant he was a rich man, and his life had been changed for ever.

Bart had heard these stories on the infrequent evenings when he had sat in the bar of the Provincial Hotel, listening to the seasoned prospectors telling of huge finds in the Shotover and Kawarau rivers: two hundred pounds of gold had been found in a matter of months. Just a bit of luck, that was all he needed to make it big and then he would return to London, a gentleman of fortune. Slapping at the sandflies with his hat, Bart heaved one foot out of the mud at a time, stamping his boots on the slime-covered rocks and watching with grim satisfaction as the cloying mass flaked into the waters, disintegrating and dispersing in the torrent. Trudging to firmer ground, he stopped and cocked his head, listening for sounds of Tate who had been panning the river a bit further downstream. They had made their claim upriver, at a safe distance from the other prospectors who were ready to come at a man with a shovel, a knife or a rock if he dared to trespass on their workings.

'Tate.' Bart paused, waiting for a reply. When there was none, he cupped his hands around his mouth and shouted again. 'Tate, where are you?'

Still no answer: he cursed beneath his breath. Tate was a good mate, but he was bone idle when it came to the backbreaking work of panning for gold. At the beginning, they had agreed to share the cost of the bare necessities, such as food and kerosene, but Bart had to be quick to get the money off Tate before he headed for the gaming tables. Drink was not Tate's besetting sin, but gambling was a fever in his blood and, once he had begun a card game, there was nothing that would get him from the table until the bitter end. Sometimes he won, but more often he lost. When he won, he bought drinks for everyone and lavished presents on his woman of the moment; when he lost, he returned to camp full of contrition, flat broke, but ready to start all over again. On these occasions, and there had been many during the four months they had been in Fox Camp, Bart had to curb his violent temper. Berating Tate verbally or flattening him with a punch might have made Bart feel better in the short term, but he was well aware that working together they had more chance of surviving and striking it rich than if trying to exist alone. Winter was already on its way and he had paid attention when the older miners spoke of terrible storms, ice, snow and the torrential waters of the Arrow that, in full spate, had claimed hundreds of lives.

He called again as he trudged up the gorge towards their canvas tent, but he did not really expect a reply. Tate had found a couple of raisin-sized nuggets last evening, just before dark, and although he had agreed to spend the money on fresh provisions, Bart did not hold out much hope. Tate, with his easy-going, cheerful charm, was a born liar and if he had a conscience, then he was able to put it aside when it suited him. As Bart followed the narrow path they had cut through the bush, the sun's feeble rays slanted down, barely penetrating the gorge. It was April and already cold, particularly at night and early in the morning. As he entered the crude shelter, Bart found that it was barely drier inside than out. His clothes were sodden and he needed to get them off quickly before the chill entered his bones. Disease killed as many diggers as knife or shotgun wounds, and many died of pneumonia, typhoid, scarlet fever and measles, or were crippled by frostbite and rheumatism. Many simply died of starvation. With their store of flour and lard used up and only a spoonful of tea left in the battered tin, Bart could only hope that Tate had fulfilled his promise, and purchased fresh provisions before he took to the gaming tables.

With his teeth chattering, Bart stripped off his wet garments. His one change of clothing lay on the relatively dry patch of earth beneath his wooden cot. He put them on, shivering and cursing his numbed fingers that made the simplest task difficult. His empty belly growled with hunger. He had to tighten his belt a notch to prevent his trousers from falling down. He shrugged on his jacket, which, despite his weight loss, was tight across the shoulders. Hard physical work had developed his muscles until they were knotted and sinewy like the trunk of an aged tree. He tipped river water from his boots and slipped his bare feet back into them, grimacing at the feel of cold, wet leather. When he had enough money, the first thing he would buy would be a pair of good, tough boots. They would be new ones that fitted properly, not second-hand ones that rubbed his toes and heels into blisters that burst and turned into running sores. Ramming his hat on his head, Bart tucked his leather pouch into his belt and set off for Fox Camp.

First he would eat and then he would seek out Daisy; his Daisy, the girl he loved almost as much as he loved little Eliza. Daisy had been his one comfort in this hostile place. For some reason that Bart found impossible to explain, she had taken to him and had welcomed him into her arms and into her bed with never a mention of payment for her favours. She was warm, generous and beautiful and to Bart she seemed untouched and untainted by her sordid pro-fession. He couldn't wait to see her; to hold her and to lose himself in those precious intimate moments when she belonged to him, and him alone. He quickened his pace, slithering and slipping on the rough ground as he followed the course of the river down to the flats and Fox Camp.

A line of packhorses waited patiently outside the general stores while men loaded them with supplies for the diggers in Macetown, a settlement some ten miles up the track. Even at this time of the day, a little after noon so Bart guessed by the angle of the pale sun peeping out from behind a cloud, the grog shanties, bars and pubs were full of drinkers. The sound of piano music, laughter and loud voices could be heard as the doors to the establishments opened and closed on a constant stream of men.

Suddenly Bart was more anxious to see Daisy than to eat. The mere thought of her made his heart beat faster and ignited a raging fire in his loins. He headed straight for the Provincial Hotel, but was forced to sidestep to avoid a bellman as he marched along the boardwalk, ringing his bell and extolling the merits of the Provincial Hotel at the top of his voice. On the far side of the street, another bellman had set up a rival action advertising the newly opened Prince of Wales Hotel. They were shouting each other down, bawling out their slogans and trading insults. Bart had a vague idea of the rivalry between the two establishments, but he was not interested in idle gossip. He had more important things on his mind. 'Damn fools,' he muttered to himself, hurrying towards the hotel. He was about to enter when the door burst open and he was almost bowled over by a tall, powerfully built man.

'Hold on, fellow.' The man's voice rang out in a deep baritone laced with a strong American accent. 'You must have worked up a darn good thirst to be in such a hurry.'

'I beg your pardon, guv,' Bart said, steadying himself against the wall. He was not in a mood to pick a fight, and even if he were so inclined, this bearded man with his fine head of auburn hair had a leonine appearance. He looked like a formidable opponent.

'An Englishman, if I'm not mistaken.'

'From London.' Encouraged, Bart held out his hand. 'Bart Bragg.'

'Captain William Hayes. I own the Prince of Wales Hotel across the road. You should drink there, sir. It's a much superior hotel to the old Provincial here, and we have first-class entertainments every night. It would be my pleasure to buy you a drink, if you would like to come and see for yourself.'

'I thank you kindly, guv. Maybe I will.'

'Good day to you then, sir.' With a slight inclination of his head, Hayes strolled across the street, lighting a cigar.

Bart hesitated, watching Hayes until he

disappeared into the hotel on the opposite side of the road. Although it seemed churlish to ignore the invitation to follow him, he was more eager to find Daisy than to care much whether or not he offended anyone, even an important-looking cove like Captain Hayes. Daisy spotted him as soon as Bart entered the bar, and she came towards him smiling and swaying her hips. He felt his heart lurch against his ribs, and his mouth went dry at the sight of her; she looked good enough to eat. Her blue dress exactly matched her eyes and it was cut low to expose an appetising swell of white breasts.

'I didn't know you was acquainted with Bully Hayes,' Daisy said, wrapping her arms around Bart's neck and kissing him on the mouth. 'I'd steer clear of him, Bartie. They say as how he was a pirate and a slaver. He's trouble.'

'Never mind him. It's you I come to see, Daisy.' Holding her close, he could feel her heart beating against his chest. Her lips tasted sweeter than cherries and the scent of her was making him dizzy. 'Let's go to your place.'

She pulled away from him, pinching his cheek with a mischievous sparkle in her eyes. 'Ain't you going to buy a girl a drink first?'

He knew she was teasing, but the allusion to her way of living drove a shaft of jealousy straight into his heart. 'Don't talk like that. I can't stand it.'

Daisy's eyes clouded and her mouth drooped at the corners. 'Don't be mean, Bartie.'

Hating himself, Bart brushed her lips with butterfly kisses until they curved into the smile that sent his senses spiralling. 'Let's go.' He heard his voice come out thick with desire, but he could wait no longer. He took her by the hand and strode out onto the street, pulling her behind him.

'Not so fast, you'll have me over.' Daisy stopped, refusing to move.

'That was me intention, girl.' Bart scooped her up in his arms and carried her down the street towards her lodgings, much to the amusement and ribald comments from the passers-by. As soon as they were inside Daisy's room, Bart kicked the door shut. He set her on her feet, pressing her against the wall and devouring her lips with kisses. He loved her, and he wanted her as he had never wanted any woman in his life. Fear, frustration, anger and desire whirled around in his head, blotting out everything except his need to take her then and there against the wall like a common prostitute. Except that she was not a common prostitute, she was Daisy, the young woman he loved with a passion that he could never have imagined. When he was done and his desperate need temporarily sated, Bart buried his face in her neck, ashamed and contrite.

'I'm sorry, Daisy. I never meant to be disrespectful and rough with you.'

She held him tight, rocking him like a baby. 'You wasn't either of them, love. You're my man, Bart. I know as how you'd never do me harm.'

He raised his head and looked into her eyes. Tears sparkled on the tips of her long lashes but she was smiling.

'My God, I love you, Daisy. I don't want no other man to lay a hand on you ever again. I wants you to be mine for ever.' He lifted her off her feet, crossed the floor in two strides and set her down gently on the bed.

'I knows you mean it, Bart,' Daisy whispered, pulling him down beside her. 'But it ain't possible. A girl's got to live.'

'Not like that.' He stared into her eyes, drowning in their blue depths. He had not the words to tell her just how much he loved her; he could only express himself in one way. He kissed her slowly, teasing her lips until they opened with a sigh, running his hand down her neck to the swell of her breasts, cupping them and kissing them until she moaned with pleasure. He took her again, slowly this time, savouring every moment, his eyes intent on her face and his soul delighting in her ecstatic sighs as he drove her to a climax. Spent and happy, Bart held her in his arms and she lay with her head on his shoulder.

It seemed to him that they were lost in time and space; the only two people in the world. 'I love you, Daisy,' he whispered, twisting a lock of her hair around his finger and marvelling at its silky softness. 'I want us to be together always, girl. I want to marry you, if you'll have me.' He felt her body stiffen and she turned her head away. Cold fingers of fear clutched at Bart's heart. 'Daisy me love. Say something.'

She snapped to a sitting position and swung her legs off the bed. 'It ain't possible, Bart.'

'What?' Unable to believe what she had just said, he sat up slowly, staring at her hunched shoulders. 'Why not? I loves you and I want to take care of you and keep you safe.'

She gave him a long, pitying look. 'It don't work like that out here. I'm a whore and that's how I make me living. Don't pretend I'm something that I'm not, Bart. We'll both get hurt if you do.'

'Don't say that.' He slipped his arm around her shoulders. 'You're not a whore, you're a wonderful, warm person and I loves you with all me heart. Leave all this behind, Daisy. Come away with me and we'll manage somehow.'

She shook her head, brushing angry tears from her eyes. 'You live in a dream world. Where would we go? How would we live? Can you imagine us living in a prospector's hut on damper and a bit of bacon every now and again?

You haven't lived through a bad winter here. You don't know what it's like.'

'I don't care. I'll build a stone cabin with a chimney and a fireplace. I'll pan for gold and I'll dig a mine. We'll be rich one day, Daisy. You and me, together.'

She rose to her feet, shaking out her crumpled skirts. She smiled down at him as she buttoned her bodice. 'It's a lovely dream, my dear. But it ain't real. Now, I got work to do.'

He sprang to his feet, grabbing her by the shoulders and shaking her so that her blonde curls tumbled about her face. 'I won't have you sell yourself. I won't stand for it. D'you hear me?'

Daisy gave him a cold look. 'The whole of Fox Camp can hear you. Let me go, Bart. Let me go this instant.'

'No. I'll never let you go. I tell you I loves you, Daisy, and I'll kill any man what lays his hands on you.'

Her eyes were blue ice as she met his anguished stare. 'You're hurting me. Let me go.'

He had not meant to hurt her. Once again he had allowed his evil temper to take hold. Bart dropped his arms to his sides, shaking his head. 'I'm sorry. I wouldn't harm a hair off your head, but I meant what I said. I wants you to give up this filthy business. I'll not stand by and let them bastards have their way with you.'

Daisy's eyes narrowed and her soft cheeks

hardened into a stubborn jaw. 'Don't you dare talk to me like that. You can't tell me what to do, Bart Bragg. No one tells me what I can and can't do. If you don't like things the way they are then you can get out. Get out now.'

Bart stared at her dumbly, unable to put his deepest feelings into words. She was so heart-breakingly beautiful, so available and yet so unattainable. Her tumbled curls shone like a halo around her head. She was his angel – coarse men might have corrupted her body, but in her heart and soul he knew she was as untouched and innocent as his Eliza. He was lost in a maze of conflicting emotions. He couldn't lose her, but neither could he bear the thought of other men having her. Anger, frustration and fear welled up inside Bart, threatening to choke the life from him. He seized the one and only chair in the room and smashed it on the ground. Daisy screamed and backed away from him, her eyes wide with fear.

He looked down at his hands clenched on the broken chair back and saw blood trickling from a cut. He could not meet Daisy's eyes – she must hate him now for the coarse creature that he was. Choked with shame, he hurled the shattered wood at the wall and stomped out of the room.

Outside in the street, Bart found his way barred by a large crowd of onlookers who had gathered to watch the escalating contest between the two bellmen. When he had taken Daisy back to her room, the competition had seemed good-humoured, but now, with voices hoarse from shouting, it was a battle of words. The crowd seemed to be enjoying this spectacle, and they were joining in, encouraging the two men to even greater heights. Stupid fools! What did he care for the senseless rivalry between two hotels? He had just ruined his chances with Daisy. She had seen the worst of him and she would probably never speak to him again.

He was just about to move away when he caught sight of Tate's coppery head. Bart pushed through the crowd towards him.

Tate saw him and grinned. 'You're just in time to see the fun. There'll be a fist fight in a moment.'

'What do I bloody care?' Bart said, through clenched teeth.

'What's up with you? Didn't she give you a good time?'

It was all he could do not to throttle Tate, but the crowd pressed round, hemming them in and making it almost impossible to move. The noise was deafening, but the violence around him seemed to counteract his own aggression. Bart shook his head. 'It's me. I'm always the one in the wrong.'

'Women,' Tate said, shrugging. 'They do that to a bloke. Forget her for a moment and watch the spectacle.' He pointed to the far side of the street. 'See that bloke over the road, outside the Prince of Wales, that's the barber. He's shouting for Bully Hayes and the other bloke is Jimmy Lungs. He's on the Buckinghams' side.'

'What's it all about anyway?'

'Shut up, it's just getting interesting.'

'And I tell you, ladies and gentlemen,' roared Jimmy Lungs, 'that the entertainment put on by the illustrious Buckingham family is not a half-crown swindle. Need I say more?'

'Take that back you lying villain,' shouted the barber, his voice cracking. 'You can't get away with saying that Captain Hayes is a swindler.'

'I never said that, you horse's arse. But what d'you expect from a bloke what's had his ear chopped off for cheating at cards?'

A ripple of consternation mixed with amusement went round the crowd, followed by a buzz of excited chatter.

'He's done it now,' Tate said out of the corner of his mouth. 'You can't accuse a fellow of cheating at cards and expect to get away with it.'

'You'll pay for that,' the barber croaked, shaking his fist at Jimmy Lungs. He turned to the crowd, bellowing for their support, and then collapsed, falling to the ground.

The crowd roared, catcalled, cheered and some of them clapped their hands. Tate turned to Bart, shaking his head. 'All this started with a woman, my lad. Young Rosie Buckingham from the Provincial Hotel went and married Bully Hayes. Her brothers don't think much of the match, especially since she was their star turn. It's going to turn nasty, mark my words.'

'I don't give a tinker's cuss for the bloody Buckinghams,' Bart said wearily. 'I've had enough for one day, Tate. You can buy me a drink, that's if you ain't gambled away every last penny.'

'As a matter of fact, I won.' Tate slapped his breast pocket, grinning. 'And what's more I'll buy you a steak dinner over at the Prince of Wales. I want to see what Bully makes of all this to-do.'

Separated from Tate by the rapidly dispersing crowd, Bart had no option but to make his way across the street to Hayes's establishment. Tate went straight to the bar and Bart was about to follow him when Bully Hayes came striding into the room. There was an expectant silence as all eyes turned towards him.

Bully came to a halt, an impressive figure, bristling with rage but speaking in a well-controlled voice. 'For your information, gentlemen, what you have just heard is nothing but a pack of lies put about by the Buckingham family in order to discredit me. I will see their bellman, Jimmy Lungs, in court. I want it further known that my wife and I are holding a private ball in this establishment on Friday evening, and I hereby invite all present here to attend.' With a stiff bow, he strutted towards the door, pausing when he saw Bart. 'We meet again, Mr Bragg.'

Bart inclined his head in a nod.

'The invitation is open to you as well, sir. I've no doubt a handsome young fellow such as yourself has a lady that he would like to bring with him. Mrs Buckingham would be pleased to meet her, I'm sure.'

Bereft of speech, Bart nodded again, but Hayes had already left the building, no doubt, Bart thought, to demand the arrest of Jimmy Lungs. Slowly he made his way to the bar. Tate pushed a foaming pint of beer along the bar counter towards him.

'Here, you look as though you could do with this. What's up?'

'Nothing,' Bart said, taking a long draught of cool beer. He couldn't bring himself to speak of what had passed between him and Daisy, but he had already made up his mind to seek her out and apologise. He would go down on his knees if he had to and beg her forgiveness for his display of temper. He would ask her, humbly – he would beg her if necessary – to accompany him to the ball.

'You look bloody down in the dumps about nothing, mate,' Tate said, giving Bart a knowing look. 'Forget the little trollop. There's dozens more like her to be had round here.'

White-hot light flashed in front of Bart's eyes and he grabbed Tate by the throat. 'Take that back, you bastard. Take that back.'

Tate's eyes bulged from their sockets and he nodded. Bart released him, but with murder still in his heart. No one could talk about his Daisy in that way. There was a sudden silence as the other customers turned their heads to stare at them. Bart picked up his glass with a shaking hand and swallowed a long draught of beer.

Tate eyed him warily, rubbing his throat. 'You're a mad bugger, Bart Bragg. Best get some victuals inside you afore you do someone a mischief.'

Bart pushed his glass towards the barman. 'Same again.'

'Make that two, mate, and we'll order two steak dinners as well.' Tate turned to Bart, frowning. 'Keep that temper of yours under control or you'll get us chucked out.'

'I'll not eat with you. You insulted my Daisy.'

'She's a fine woman – no insult intended.'

Staring moodily into his glass, Bart shrugged his shoulders.

Tate perched on a bar stool next to him. 'Listen to me, mate. You need to be careful of Hayes. He's got a reputation as an all-in fist and boot fighter. You don't want to get mixed up in his family squabbles. Best watch your step, or you'll end up with more than an ear missing.'

Bart shrugged his shoulders and stared moodily into his glass. 'What do I care about the Buckinghams, or Hayes come to that, when I've lost me girl?'

Tate produced a leather pouch from his pocket and tipped some of its contents on the bar counter in front of Bart. 'I can see as how you don't know much about women, mate. Hire yourself a fancy suit and take Daisy to the ball on Friday. She'll be eating out of your hand.'

'Where did you get that gold?' Bart demanded, staring at the coins. 'You never stole it, did you?'

'I told you, you daft bugger. I won it fair and square at poker. Take it.'

'But we need it for our stake money.'

'You can't shag a sack of flour. If she's the one you want, get in there, fellah.'

On the night of the ball, Bart stood outside the door to Daisy's room. In spite of the fact that she had generously accepted his apologies for his outburst of temper, he was a little nervous about taking her to such a public function. He knew he was a clumsy fellow, with few social graces, but he desperately wanted to prove to her that he could behave like a proper gent. He ran his finger round the inside of his starched collar. The hired evening suit had been made for a shorter but fatter man; the trousers were too short and the crutch was uncomfortably tight, but at least the jacket fitted properly over his well-muscled shoulders. He was about to knock again when Daisy opened the door. He caught his breath at the sight of her. In her flame-coloured dress, with her waist corseted in to a hand's span and her fine bosom accentuated, but tantalisingly concealed beneath a waterfall of lace, Daisy slanted him a wicked look beneath her thick, doll-like eyelashes. 'My, you do look smart, Bartie.'

Horribly conscious of his shabby boots and inwardly cursing the store for not stocking proper shoes in his size, Bart prayed that Daisy would not look down at his feet. 'You look beautiful, Daisy. Good enough to eat.'

She tucked her hand through the crook of his arm. 'Just you behave yourself tonight, Bartie. The other girls are mad with jealousy that my fellah is taking me to Bully Hayes's ball.'

As he led her down the dark corridor and out into the street, Bart felt his heart swell with pride. No other man would have a partner half as lovely as his Daisy. 'We're going up in the world,' he said, his voice breaking with emotion. 'You and me together, girl.'

She tossed her head so that her gold earrings jiggled and flashed in the light of the naphtha flares that pooled on the boardwalk. 'It's going to be the do of the century and it won't half put the Buckinghams' noses out of joint.'

Bart could hardly believe his luck. Here he was, a penniless prospector, going to the social event of the year with the most beautiful woman in the world. As they reached Bully's establishment, Daisy paused, staring across the street at a sign placed on the boardwalk outside the Provincial Hotel, advertising a one-act farce, entitled 'The Barbarous Barber of the Lather and the Shave'.

'Look, Bartie. Bully won't like them making fun of him like that. I wonder how it's all going to end.'

'Badly,' Bart said, taking her by the arm. 'But it don't concern us, ducks. We're going to have the time of our lives tonight.'

Inside the hotel lobby, Bully Hayes, resplendent in a black tailcoat and gold-embroidered waistcoat, stood beside his heavily pregnant wife. 'Rosie, my love, this is Mr Bart Bragg from London,' Bully said, shaking Bart's hand.

'And this is my fiancée, ma'am,' Bart said proudly. 'Miss Daisy Dawkins.'

Rosie held out her hand to Daisy, smiling. 'Pleased to meet you, Miss Dawkins. But I think we've already met at my brothers' hotel across the road.'

'We won't mention them tonight, my dear,' Bully said, frowning. 'Take your lady into the ballroom, Mr Bragg. Feel free to enjoy the Hayes's hospitality.'

'Maybe we'll have time to chat later, Daisy?' Rosie said, casting a sidelong glance at her husband. 'If you don't mind, William.'

'Anything that makes you happy, my bird.' Bully leaned down to kiss her on the cheek and then turned to the next couple. 'Good evening and welcome to the ball of the century. May I compliment you on your good taste in boycotting that farce across the street.'

Bart led Daisy into the ballroom that was bright with the light of hundreds of candles and filled with the sound of music and laughter. 'There's just one thing, Daisy,' he whispered.

'What's that, dear?'

'I can't dance.'

Daisy's laughter, that sounded to Bart's ears like the tinkling of fairy bells, made the people in their vicinity turn around and smile. Standing on her tiptoes, she kissed Bart's cheek. 'Never mind, neither can most of these great galumphing miners. Just put your arms around me and hold me tight, Bartie. Pretend we're making love and it'll all come natural-like.'

By the end of the evening, with many cups of punch inside him and intoxicated with love for Daisy, Bart was as good a mover as any man in the room except perhaps for Bully himself, who was exceptionally light on his feet. The ball went on into the early hours of the morning and became very lively and quite rowdy by the end. When at last they left the hotel, emerging into the frosty night air, Bart felt that he was the happiest man in the universe as he walked Daisy back to her room.

'I could have died laughing when you said I was your fiancée,' Daisy said, chuckling. 'But I have to say it made me feel a bit grand.'

'I meant it, Daisy. I'd give you the world all wrapped up in a satin ribbon if I could.'

'You are a love, Bartie. I really believe you would.'

'Will you, Daisy? Will you be my wife?' Hesitating in the doorway, Bart hardly dared put the question for fear of being turned down again. They had not made love since the day they had fallen out, and although he wanted her quite desperately, he was afraid to make the first move.

'Yes, I think I will after all.' Daisy danced into the middle of the floor and stood in the shaft of moonlight, holding out her arms and swaying as if to the music of a hidden orchestra. 'Well, what are you waiting for, Bartie? Come in and close the door.'

Next morning it was raining; cold sleety rain that soaked through Bart's clothes before he was halfway to the camp. The tops of the mountains were already tipped with snow and the cold air went down into his lungs like shards of ice. He hoped that Tate would have a fire going and a billycan of boiling water to make a brew of tea. The unaccustomed amount of alcohol that he had drunk had left him with a headache as well as a parched throat and mouth, but it had been a most wonderful night and it was not only the ball that he remembered. Making love with Daisy had taken them both to new heights of passion and delight. His last sight of her was indelibly imprinted on his memory: he had left her sleeping soundly, with her flaxen hair spilling over the pillow like spun silk and her red lips swollen from kissing and parted slightly, as though she was smiling.

'Hey, Tate,' Bart called as he neared the shack that they had constructed with canvas and stones to withstand the winter storms. 'Wake up, you lazy sod.' There was no sign of life and no sign of smoke from a campfire. He was cursing Tate for being a lazy bugger when it occurred to Bart that something was wrong. It was quiet, too quiet, with just the sound of the rushing waters of the Arrow River but no obvious movement inside the shack. As he lifted the flap of canvas that served as a door, Bart stifled a cry of horror. Tate was lying on the floor with a dark stain of blood, already congealing, from a knife wound in his chest. His eyes were open but glazed and his skin had a bluish tinge. Bart had pulled enough corpses out of the Thames to know that he was dead.

Chapter Eight

Working in the pie and eel shop for fourteen hours a day was not Eliza's idea of bliss, but she had to earn her keep. With Freddie gone, there was no one to give her a reference and, unless she wanted to pick oakum for a few pence a day or work in one of the manufactories, there was little choice. She had come upon this job by chance, at the end of the dreadful day in the courtroom when Uncle Enoch had denounced Freddie as a kidnapper and an evil seducer of young girls. His accusations had been backed up by Beattie Larkin's hysterical outburst, and after that it had been obvious that the judge was not going to be lenient. Freddie had been sentenced to seven years' deportation to the penal colony in Australia. Eliza could barely remember what had followed, apart from the fact that she had leapt to her feet, screaming that the verdict was unjust and unfair. Freddie had turned his head and smiled directly at her, a special smile with a hint of sadness, and he had shaken his head, putting his finger to his lips, as if he were asking her to hold her peace. But she had not kept silent.

She remembered raving at Uncle Enoch, Beattie and the judge, until two court ushers carried her bodily out of the courtroom and deposited her on the pavement.

Later that day, Ted had gone to the City Police Office to find out where they had taken Freddie. When he had returned home Eliza had sensed that it was not good news and Ted had confirmed her worst fears: Freddie had been taken to one of the prison hulks downriver, to await deportation. If only she could have visited him in prison, at least she would have been able to say goodbye properly. She would have told him that she would be waiting for his return, whether it was seven years or seventy. At that moment, Eliza had felt her heart turn into a lump of stone inside her breast. She could not weep and she could not confide her deepest feelings to anyone; Millie had been sympathetic but she was only a child and could not possibly understand what it was to love someone, as Eliza loved Freddie, and to lose him in such a cruel and barbaric fashion. After receiving the dreadful news, Eliza had run from the house and had come to her senses hours later, walking aimlessly on Execution Dock. But this time there was no Freddie to come and comfort her, and no Davy to take her home to his mother. The mewling cries of the seagulls overhead had exactly matched the misery in Eliza's soul and she wished that she could fly away with them; fly to the hulk where Freddie was chained like a common criminal and follow him into exile. In the end, it had been Millie who had come to find her. She might not have understood fully, but she had seemed to sense Eliza's distress. She had tugged at her sleeve, complaining that she was hungry and there was no food in the house. Dolly had been so upset that she had retired to her bed and Ted had gone back to the sail loft to make up the work he had lost during the day. The fire had gone out – it was cold at home – and she was scared. That had brought Eliza abruptly back to the present and she had taken Millie to the pie and eel shop. There was a sign in the window – HELP WANTED, APPLY WITHIN.

The pieman had taken her on with no questions asked. Since then, Eliza had arrived each morning at seven o'clock to start peeling sackfuls of potatoes ready for boiling. After the potatoes were done there were pounds of onions to be peeled and chopped, which she did shedding tears and sniffing as the pungent juice burned and stung her eyes. After a week or two she was called upon to do the job that made her shiver with disgust – skinning eels. Gritting her teeth and swallowing the bile that rose in her throat, somehow Eliza managed to get on with this horrible task, but she vowed never to eat a plate of eels ever again.

The small scullery where she worked was behind the main kitchen. It was dark, damp and running with cockroaches, silverfish and ants. Outside in the yard, there was a huge barrel in which she had to deposit the potato peelings, onion skins, the remains of the eels and butchered bones. The whole odorous mess hummed with blowflies and was soon heaving with maggots. Rats lurked behind the barrel, even in daytime, and the stench made Eliza's stomach churn so that she could not eat, even when it was time for her dinner of bread and jam or dripping.

It was high summer now, a hot and heavy early July when the river was as foul-smelling as the yard behind the pie shop. She ended her shift at nine o'clock in the evening and it was still daylight when Eliza left the humidity and heat of the kitchen. She had just finished the seemingly endless task of washing pots and pans, and she walked out into the equally hot, humid and stinking streets. Her back and legs ached, and the skin on her hands was cracked and raw from being constantly in water, but it was good to get out of that hateful place. Walking down to the quay, she had hoped to get a breath of fresh air, but there was not even the slightest breeze to waft away the fishy smell of the eels and the pungent odour of onions that clung to her hands, hair and clothes. Her stomach rumbled and Eliza realised that she had not eaten since a slice of bread at breakfast.

All around her there was the usual hustle and bustle of the river; a brigantine had docked and was being unloaded of its cargo of timber. She stood watching the men working and she wondered if the ship had come from Australia or New Zealand. If only she were a man, she would sign on as a deck hand and then she could go out to those far-flung countries and find the two men whom she loved with all her heart and soul. Oh, Bart, Eliza thought, fighting back tears, and Freddie. Why did you both have to leave me? But she wasn't a man, she was a girl, not quite fourteen, penniless and with a doubtful future ahead of her. A slight breeze ruffled her hair, bringing with it just a faint scent of pine from the planked wood piled up on the dockside. It was clean and fresh and the cool wind fanned her hot cheeks. The dying rays of the sun turned the Thames into a river of molten gold, flowing endlessly towards the sea. On this fine evening, its waters looked tranquil and benign. In all its moods the river was part of her life, sometimes the instrument of death and at others the bringer of good fortune. The Thames had carried Bart and Freddie away from her, but it would also bring them home. There was always hope. A renewed spirit of determination entered her soul; Eliza lifted her chin and turned in the direction of home. She would not be beaten down by cruel fate or the unfortunate circumstances of her life. There was something better just around the corner and she would find it, or die in the attempt.

The door to the house in Hemp Yard was wide open and Eliza could hear raised voices even before she had set her foot on the threshold. Ted was standing by the range, his arms folded across his chest, and he was scowling at Uncle Enoch, who, with his black suit and top hat, filled the small room with his malevolent presence.

'Keep your voice down, Enoch.' Ted's voice shook with anger. 'I won't have you come here and upset Dolly. You know that she's a sick woman.'

'Bah, she uses her ill health as a stick to beat you over the head, you simpleton.'

'Get out of my house. We'll talk about this matter like rational men in the chandlery, tomorrow morning.'

'Dad?' Eliza paused in the doorway, suddenly frightened. 'What's going on?'

'Nothing for you to worry about, ducks. Your uncle was just leaving.'

'Not without her,' Enoch said, turning his fierce gaze on Eliza. 'This farce has gone on long enough. I'm taking you home with me.'

Backing away from him, Eliza was ready to run. 'No! No, you can't do that. I won't go with you.'

'It's all right, Liza.' Ted held out his hand. 'Come here, love. Stand by me. This is your home, and I'll not let him take you from it.'

'I have the law on my side, Peck. I'm her legal guardian and I want her back. Now that she's bigger and stronger, I can find plenty of work for her in the shop.'

'I won't leave Ted and Dolly,' Eliza cried, running to Ted and flinging her arms around him. 'They're my parents now. Not you.'

A cry from the stairs made them all look round as Millie came hurtling down, jumping the last two steps. 'You shan't take Liza away. I won't let you.'

Enoch raised his arm to strike her, but realising his intention Eliza rushed forward and dragged her out of harm's way. 'Don't you dare touch Millie.'

'Ted, what's going on down there?' Dolly's wavering voice came from the bedroom above them.

'Get out of my house this minute, Enoch Bragg.' Ted made a move towards him, fists clenched as if he meant business.

'You don't want me, Uncle,' Eliza cried, cuddling Millie who had burst into tears. 'I'm no use to you. You said as much when you threw me out.'

'I'm a sick man.' Suddenly, Enoch changed his tone; his neck seemed to shrink into his shoulders like a tortoise retiring into its shell. His eyes shifted furtively from Ted to Eliza. 'I can't manage the chandlery on my own. God knows I'm a good Christian and I forgive you for your lapse from virtue, Eliza. I'm prepared to take you back home where you belong.'

'She belongs here with us,' Ted roared. 'You threw her out, you bastard. And then you as good as sold her to Freddie Prince. I know, because I was there to witness the wicked deed. You just want her unpaid labour. You want a slave.'

Enoch clutched his chest. 'My heart is weak; the doctor said so. I tell you I'm a sick man and I need my family round me.'

'You're a liar.' Standing at the top of the stairs, pale-faced and trembling, Dolly clutched the banister rail for support. 'You shan't take my girl from me. I love Eliza. We love Eliza and she's our child now, along with little Millie.' Holding out her arms to Eliza and Millie, she collapsed onto the top step and burst into tears.

Millie raced up the stairs to fling her arms around Dolly, but Eliza turned on Enoch in a fury. 'Look what you've done. You're an evil man and if your heart is sick it's because it's been eaten up by meanness and cruelty.'

'If you don't go now I'll throw you out.' Ted strode to the door and opened it wide. 'I'm not a violent man, but you've tried me too far, Bragg.'

'And if you don't give Eliza back to me, I'll cancel your lease on the sail loft,' Enoch said, through clenched teeth. 'And what's more I'll keep your tools and your materials in lieu of outstanding rent. I'll ruin you, Ted Peck. Take your choice.'

'Get out.' Ted jerked his head in the direction of the street.

'I knew you'd act stubborn.' Enoch produced a roll of parchment from his pocket. 'I've got the necessary legal documents here. They prove that I'm Eliza's legal guardian. Do you still refuse to let her go?'

Ted stuck out his chin. 'I do.'

'Constable. Do your duty.'

A shadow fell across the doorway and a police constable entered the room, truncheon at the ready.

Enoch opened the door to the chandlery and, cuffing Eliza round the ear, he sent her sprawling onto the flagstones. 'That's to show you who's master here, Eliza. I'll see you in the morning, and I want this place swept and dusted before I arrive. Don't think you can escape because I've locked the back door, the windows are barred, including the skylight up above, and I'm taking the keys with me.'

'You can't keep me here against my will.'

'I can do anything I like, my girl. Until

you're twenty-one and of age, you'll do as I say.'

Even in the gathering gloom, Eliza could see that he was sneering at her as he slammed the door, shutting out the world and leaving her in darkness. She scrambled to her feet, rubbing her wrist that she had jarred in the fall. The stands of shelves towered above her head, casting sinister shadows; piles of rope coiled on the floor looked like snakes ready to strike, and barrels of pitch were lined up like short, fat soldiers on parade. A year ago this would have terrified her but now, she realised, she had grown up enough to put these fancies out of her mind. Inanimate objects could not hurt her; only people could do that. She climbed the ladder to the sail loft where she felt closer to Bart, Ted and Davy, and she set about making a bed from folded canvas. It was not very comfortable but she was exhausted after a long day's toiling in the pie shop and the emotional upheaval of being wrested from her loving home. Her eyelids were growing heavy and, in spite of her physical discomfort and the ache in her heart, she was drifting slowly towards the sweet haven of sleep. Murmuring a prayer for Bart and for Freddie, Eliza curled up with her cheek resting on her hand, just as she had done since she was a small child.

A shaft of sunlight tickled her nose. Eliza opened her eyes, sat up and stretched her cramped limbs. Oddly enough it did not seem strange to be back in the sail loft. Everything looked, smelled and felt exactly the same and there was comfort in familiarity. Last night she had been determined to disobey Uncle Enoch's orders to see that the place was clean and tidy before he arrived to open the shop, but with the clock on the wall showing that it was already a quarter to seven, she decided that things would go easier for Ted if she allowed Uncle Enoch to think he had won. She tidied her bedding away and went down into the chandlery. It was not so hard, after all, to do the chores that she had been used to doing since she was a child, and by the time Enoch arrived she had the floor swept and the stock sorted and dusted.

'Hmmph!' Enoch growled, looking round as if he wanted to find something to complain about. 'At least you haven't forgotten how to do your job. You can clear up the back yard and after that you can polish the brass. Don't forget our bargain, Eliza. You work for me and Peck keeps his business. Put one foot wrong and he'll be out on his ear together with all his apprentices. Do you understand me?'

Eliza nodded.

'Speak out, girl. Do you understand what I've just said?'

'Yes.'

'Yes, what?'

Although she knew perfectly well that he wanted her to call him sir, Eliza was not going to give him the satisfaction. With a defiant lift of her chin, she looked him in the eye. 'Yes, I do.'

The clout around her ear made bells ring in Eliza's head and she stumbled backwards, falling against a warm body.

'Crikey, Liza,' Davy said, setting her back on her feet. 'What's going on?'

'Put her down and get up that ladder, boy.' Enoch shook his fist at Davy and the other apprentices who had crowded into the chandlery behind him. 'Get to work, all of you.'

'You're a rotten bully,' Davy cried, hooking his arm around Eliza's shoulders and glowering at Enoch. 'Picking on a girl half your size. I don't see you taking on one of us big fellows.'

Ted had followed them in and he pushed his way past the gaping Tonks brothers and Dippy Dan. 'What's up, Davy?'

'He clipped Eliza round the ear,' Davy said, his voice shaking with anger. 'That old goat almost knocked her senseless.'

'No.' Eliza pulled free from Davy's protective arm. 'It was nothing, Ted.'

'All right, Davy. I'll deal with this. You boys get up that ladder and start work.' Ted waited until the last one had disappeared through the hatch and then he turned on Enoch, white lines of fury etched from his nose to his chin. 'Now see here, Bragg. You may have got the upper hand at the moment, but I'm warning you, if you lay a finger on Eliza again I won't answer for the consequences.'

'You can't threaten me, mister. You owe me two months' rent. I've half a mind to throw you and your damn sail-making business out anyway.'

'Please, Dad.' Eliza stepped in between them. She knew Ted well enough to sense that his temper was close to breaking point. Uncle Enoch was deliberately goading him.

'You are an evil man, Enoch Bragg,' Ted hissed through clenched teeth. 'You're a sanctimonious hypocrite.'

'I'll not stand for that.' Enoch took a swing at Ted.

Eliza leapt out of the way, just managing to dodge his fist.

'I'll kill you, you bastard.' Ted grabbed Enoch by the throat. 'You've torn my family apart and you've broke poor Dolly's heart. You'll give us back Eliza or, so help me God, I'll choke the life out of you.'

Enoch's eyes bulged from their sockets and his face turned from a deep shade of purple to blue as Ted forced him down on his knees. A cheer rang out from the apprentices who were hanging through the opening to the sail loft, but neither Ted nor Enoch took any notice of them.

'Stop, stop, you're killing him,' cried Eliza, tugging at Ted's arm. 'He's not worth it, Dad. Please leave him be.'

'You're right, Eliza.' With a hefty shove, Ted sent Enoch sprawling onto the ground. 'I wouldn't risk the gallows for a scurvy knave like you, Bragg.'

Enoch clutched his throat, rolling his eyes and coughing. 'You'll suffer for this, Ted Peck.'

'I should have finished you off when I had the chance.' Ted brushed off Eliza's restraining hand. 'Go home, Eliza. Go home and look after Dolly. She needs you.'

Above all she wanted to be free, but Eliza hesitated, watching Enoch warily as he got to his feet. He had it in his power to ruin Ted and the expression on his face terrified her. She opened her mouth to try to reason with him, but he pushed her aside.

'You're finished, Peck. Get out and take those hooligans with you.'

'Make me.'

'Stop it, both of you,' Eliza cried, grabbing Ted's sleeve.

He wrenched free from her grasp and took a swing at Enoch, catching him a blow on the jaw.

'Bastard!' Enoch's face paled to an alarming shade of grey and he clutched his chest, doubling up as if in agony and falling to his knees.

'Uncle!' Eliza rushed to his side but he fell

backwards, writhing and kicking. Then he was still. There was a moment of shocked silence when even the apprentices were quiet. Eliza knelt by his side. Enoch's eyes were open but staring in a glassy, fish-like fashion that terrified her more than his violent outburst of temper. She looked up at Ted, who was standing transfixed, breathing heavily and staring at the prostrate body. 'I think he's dead. We've killed him, Dad.'

'Good riddance, I say,' Davy shouted from above, followed by a muted cheer from Ginger and Carrots.

'Hear, hear,' added Dippy Dan, and was immediately elbowed in the ribs by Carrots.

Ted glanced up, frowning. 'Get to work, boys. All of you that is except Davy; you'd best go for the doctor.'

Sliding down the ladder, Davy pushed his cap to the back of his head, staring at Enoch. 'Looks to me like he needs the undertaker, guvner.'

'Fetch the doctor and the undertaker,' Ted said wearily. 'And find a man with a cart so that we can take the body back to his house. We can't leave him here on the floor.'

Ginger and Carrots were peering through the hatch, their faces alight with curiosity. 'Is he dead, guv?'

Ted shook his fist at them. 'I said, get back to

work.' He helped Eliza to her feet. 'Are you all right, ducks?'

'He said he had a bad heart and I didn't believe him. We killed him.'

'His own badness killed him, love.' Ted wrapped his arms around her in a comforting hug.

The soot-blackened graveyard of St Peter's in Old Gravel Lane was cheerless even in mid-summer. Eliza could hardly believe that there were so many people who claimed to have known Enoch, and who had come to pay their last respects at his funeral. Black-clad mourners, most of them unknown to her, had expressed their sorrow at the passing of a good, Christian man. As she stood between Ted and Davy, Eliza had nodded her head in acknowledgement of their sentiments, but had been unable to share them. She could not imagine what good Uncle Enoch had ever done for any one person, but he had certainly managed to convince these church-going folk that he was a worthy citizen and a kind benefactor.

The sun was high in the sky, the heat was stifling and many of the tightly corseted women in the congregation appeared to be close to fainting in their black-bombazine mourning clothes; the men in their starched white collars and green-tinged black frock coats were hardly faring better. Holding their top hats respectfully in one hand, many of them surreptitiously took out their handkerchiefs and mopped their brows as sweat trickled down their faces. There was a loud clump of wood on wood as the pall-bearers lowered the coffin into the grave and it came to rest abruptly on the top of another interment, just a few feet beneath the ground. The stench of corrupting flesh was almost unbearable, and the air in the overcrowded graveyard was thick with buzzing flies. Due to lack of space, the departed were piled in graves one on top of the other, and after a particularly heavy rainstorm, newly planted coffins would often pop up like corks from ginger beer bottles and float on the surface.

The vicar gabbled a few words and, covering their noses with their hands, the congregation filed quickly past the grave, tossing handfuls of soil on top of the coffin that was so near the surface as to be level with the ground.

For a moment, Eliza felt that she was going to be sick, but Ted had taken her by the hand.

'Come along, ducks. We've laid the old scoundrel to rest. Let's go home.'

Even as they moved away, the gravediggers had begun piling earth on top of the coffin and the vicar had disappeared into the relative cool of the church.

'Buried that close to the surface, I wouldn't

trust the old bugger not to climb out of his coffin and walk home,' Davy whispered in Eliza's ear.

She covered her mouth with her hand to stifle a giggle, and received several reproachful glances from the mourners who had clustered in the street to chat. She had to curb a sudden and childish desire to stick her tongue out at them and run away. It was an effort to walk sedately beside Ted, but she managed it somehow. He stopped at the corner of the street, turning to Davy. 'Take her home, there's a good lad.'

Eliza shook her head. 'No, ta. I need to know where I stand and I'm going to see Uncle Enoch's solicitor at Worboys, Worboys and Grimstone in Sun Tavern Fields. It's only a short walk away.'

Ted looked doubtful. 'Are you sure, Eliza? It's been a hard time for you.'

'Quite sure.'

'I should go with you, but I've got to get back to the sail loft or God knows what them boys will get up to on their own.'

'If you'll let him, Dad, Davy can come with me. If I'm to run the chandlery until Bart gets back, then I need to know it's all legal and proper.'

'Now, Liza, my dear. You're just a girl – you can't hope to run a business on your own.'

'I'm fourteen next month and I've spent half

my life in the chandlery. I can do it, I know I can.'

It had taken all Eliza's powers of persuasion to make the solicitor's clerk take her seriously. At first he had tried to send her on her way, advising her to come again and bring her father with her next time. Then he had said Mr Grimstone was occupied with a client and could not see anyone. Finally, after Eliza and Davy had sat in the office for over an hour, refusing to leave, the clerk had reluctantly gone into the inner sanctum to speak to the elusive Mr Grimstone. When he had reappeared, he had somewhat grudgingly admitted that his employer would see them now.

'Well then,' Mr Grimstone said, sitting back in his chair and eyeing Eliza with a curious stare. 'So you are Enoch Bragg's niece.'

Folding her hands in front of her, Eliza nodded. 'Yes, sir.'

'And you are?' Mr Grimstone turned to Davy.

'Davy is my friend, sir,' Eliza said quickly, before Davy had a chance to answer for himself. 'We've just come from my uncle's funeral and I need to know who owns the chandlery and the house in Bird Street.'

'Ah, you're direct, I like that,' Mr Grimstone said, with a nod of approval. 'I drew up the legal documents after your father's untimely demise, when Enoch became your guardian. That was a good few years ago now.'

'If you please, sir,' Eliza said, refusing to be deflected from her purpose. 'I just need to know if Uncle left a will.'

'She needs to know, mister.' Davy leaned across the desk, scowling at the solicitor.

'Sit down, young man, and you too, Miss Eliza. As it happens, your uncle changed his will a week ago leaving everything to the church, but the document remained unsigned and therefore is not legal.' Mr Grimstone opened a drawer in his desk and rifled through some papers. 'Ah, I have it.' He pulled out a scroll of parchment and laid it on the desk in front of him. 'This is definitely the last will and testament of Enoch James Bragg.' He lit a cheroot, and with it clamped between his teeth he untied the red tape.

Eliza sat still, hardly daring to breathe, while he scanned through the document with his lips moving silently, and smoke from the small, black cigar spiralling into the air above his head. After what seemed like an age, Mr Grimstone took the cheroot from his mouth and balanced it on the edge of his desk. Eliza couldn't help noticing burn marks all along the edge of the desk. It was a wonder, she thought, that he hadn't burnt the place to the ground.

He cleared his throat. 'If you wish, I'll make it simple, Miss Eliza.'

She nodded. 'Thank you, sir.'

'The long and the short of it is, and cutting out the legal jargon, everything now belongs to your brother, Bartholomew Bragg.'

'I see,' Eliza said slowly, barely surprised that Uncle Enoch had not thought to include her in his will. He had told her often enough that she was a mere female and not much use for anything except menial tasks and childbearing. She looked Mr Grimstone in the eyes, and found to her surprise that he was smiling at her quite sympathetically. 'My brother is—' Eliza stopped short. She could hardly admit to a man of the law that Bart was on the run from the police.

'Quite so.' He nodded his head and tapped the side of his nose. 'Say no more on that subject. I am well acquainted with Mr Bartholomew's urgent desire to see the world.'

She could no longer keep up the pretence of being disinterested. 'So what happens now? What happens to the chandlery and to me?'

'Well now, if there are no other male relatives who could run the business until Mr Bragg returns, then I see no reason why you, as next of kin, should not be in locum tenens.'

'I don't quite understand, sir.'

'It means, in common parlance, Miss Eliza . . .' Mr Grimstone picked up his cheroot and finding that it had gone out he struck a vesta and puffed at it until the end of the cigar glowed red. He exhaled with a contented sigh, sending smoke rings up to the ceiling. 'It means, my dear, that at a very tender age, you've been left holding the baby.'

Chapter Nine

Immediately after her meeting with the solicitor, Eliza went to the sail loft to find Ted. As she suspected, he had returned to work rather than go home. She knew that he still loved Dolly, but in a moment of extreme stress, he had admitted that the person who now inhabited the body of his dear wife was almost a stranger to him. Dolly's increasing dependence on her medication, her frequent lapses of memory and her obsession with illness were causing him much distress. The saddest part was that no one seemed able to help. Ted had called in the doctor, but he had shaken his head, prescribed laudanum and charged a large fee for his advice. Eliza did what she could, but she had seen Ted age visibly; his business had suffered and money worries only added to his burden. She said little to Davy on the walk back to Old Gravel Lane. In her mind she was rehearsing what she would say to persuade Ted to let her manage the store.

At first he was doubtful about her ability to run the chandlery, but she pointed out that he would be there to help and advise her. She was perfectly capable of ordering stock and serving customers, and she would hire a man to do the heavy work. After all, she had practically grown up in the chandlery and she was well versed in the day-to-day running of the business. In the end, after a great deal of persuasion, Ted agreed that she should have a chance to prove herself. Eliza set to work there and then, fired by the will to succeed. She was doing this for all of them, but it was mainly for Bart. When he came home he would find a thriving business and he would be proud of her.

The shop had been closed until after the funeral, both out of necessity and as a mark of respect, but now Eliza wanted to reopen as soon as possible. First and foremost there was the matter of obtaining credit from the suppliers. She would not be able to trade unless they agreed to extend the arrangements they had made with Enoch. Without a reliable guarantor, she knew she would have difficulty in gaining their trust, but Ted was well respected in and around the London docks. With a great deal of trepidation she asked him and, to her surprise, Ted agreed to accompany her when she paid courtesy calls on the wholesalers.

Four days after her meeting with Mr Grimstone, Eliza reopened the chandlery. The odd thing was that no one seemed to notice any difference. It was almost as if Enoch was still around: she kept looking over her shoulder, half expecting to see him hunched over his ledgers. She served in the shop all day, staying on late each evening to take stock and to go through the accounts. She would have been quite content to work alone, but Davy insisted on staying with her, helping where he could and walking her home after dark. At the end of her first week of trading, Eliza had balanced the books and made out orders for their usual suppliers. For the first time, she was grateful to Uncle Enoch for having forced her to learn every aspect of the business. On Saturday evening, she closed the ledger with a satisfied sigh and went to fetch her shawl from the back room. She found Davy fast asleep, squatting against a row of shelves with his head in his arms. He woke up with a start as she took her bonnet and shawl off a wooden peg.

'Is it that time already?'

'You don't have to do this every evening, Davy. I'm very grateful, but I can take care of meself.'

He scrambled to his feet. 'Ted don't like you walking home in the dark and I don't mind doing it.'

'At least it's a bit earlier tonight. Let's go.'

Outside the summer evening was fading into dusk and flocks of starlings filled the air with their noisy chatter as they came in to roost on the tall buildings.

'It's not quite dark,' Eliza said, glancing up at the sky. 'I'll be all right on me own. You could go straight home if you wanted to.'

'That's just it – I don't want to. The old man will be dead drunk as usual and the nippers will be grizzling because they're hungry. Mum will be trying to make things right and the blooming cellar stinks like a midden. The later I gets home the better.'

'I'm sorry.'

'It ain't your problem, Liza. It's his fault that we live like sewer rats. But one day I'll make it up to Mum. When I'm a qualified sailmaker I'll have me own business and get the family out of that place.'

'I know how you feel,' Eliza said, quickening her pace to keep up with his long strides. 'I worry about Dolly and Millie. I've hardly seen them all week. They'll be thinking I've deserted them.'

'You desert them? Never!' Davy broke into a jogging run. 'Come on, Liza. I'll beat you to Hemp Yard.'

Try as she might, Eliza couldn't quite keep up with him. Davy reached the house first and Eliza caught up with him, panting and holding her side. 'That weren't fair. I've got a stitch.'

Davy tweaked the ribbons of her bonnet. 'You was beat fair and square, admit it.'

She held up her hands. 'I do. But you don't have to wear petticoats and a long skirt.

'I should think not. I'd look pretty damn silly.'

'You're a clown,' Eliza said, giggling. She opened the door and stepped inside.

Millie had been sitting at the table with her head bent over a schoolbook, but she jumped to her feet when she saw Eliza. 'Wake up, Mum. Liza's come home.'

Waking with a start, Dolly peered at Eliza. 'Is that you, dear?'

'Yes. I'm home early for once.'

'We've hardly seen you for days,' Millie said, rushing up to Eliza and wrapping her arms around her waist. 'I've missed you – we've both missed you.'

Eliza gave her a hug. 'I had to sort things out at the shop.'

'I've been really poorly,' Dolly complained, huddling beneath her shawl. 'You and Ted are always too busy for a poor invalid.'

'I'm sorry, Mum. I'll do better now, I promise.'

Davy had been hovering in the doorway; he gave an embarrassed cough. 'Er, I'd best be getting home.'

'Thanks for all your help.' Eliza shot him a grateful smile.

He shrugged his shoulders, blushing. 'It weren't nothing. Anyway, I got to go. Goodbye, Mrs Peck.' He hurried off, the hobnails on his boots clattering over the cobbles.

'Little Millie has done her best,' Dolly said,

wiping her eyes on the corner of her apron. 'But she ain't much of a one for cooking and she don't know how to make my medicine.'

'I tried, Liza.' Millie's bottom lip wobbled ominously. 'I done me best but I couldn't remember exactly what you put into the mixture and it turned out all wrong.'

'Never mind, I'm here now.' Taking off her bonnet, Eliza held it for a moment before setting it down on the table. It had once been such a heavenly shade of blue, that is until the rain ruined it, but as custom dictated, she had attempted to dye it black and the result was a rather streaky shade of grey-green. Uncle Enoch would have said that her pride in it had been sinful vanity, and its ruin was her just punishment. She stifled a sigh, and picked up the kettle that was warming on the hob over a few bits of smouldering driftwood. 'I'll soon make up your medicine, Mum. Just as Freddie showed me.'

'The dear doctor,' Dolly said, sniffing. 'I can't believe the judge was so cruel and unfair as to have him transported to Australia, not when he done so much good for the poor and sick.'

The mention of Freddie's name brought tears to Eliza's eyes and she hurried into the scullery so that neither Millie nor Dolly would see that she was upset. When she opened the food cupboard all she found there was a small bag of sugar, a poke of tea and a dried-up piece of sassafras root. The laudanum bottle had been full when she had last looked but it was now empty. She bit her lip as feelings of guilt assailed her. She had left too much for young Millie to do on her own. Looking after Dolly was a job in itself and she shouldn't have expected a mere child to cope with the shopping and cooking. Eliza took the piece of sassafras and began grating it into a bowl. When Ted got home from his business in the docks, she would ask him for some money to buy supper.

Millie came hurrying into the scullery. 'Dolly says she's going to fall off her chair in a swoon if she don't get her medicine right now.'

'It's nearly ready,' Eliza called, hastily adding sugar and hot water to the grated root.

'It smells horrible,' Millie said, wrinkling her nose. 'I'm glad I don't have to take that stuff.'

'Then it's lucky that you're not sick, isn't it?' Eliza said, smiling.

Millie rubbed her belly. 'I'm awful hungry, Liza. We ate the last of the bread and dripping at dinnertime. There weren't no money left in the tin so I couldn't go to the market.'

'I'll go out to the shop when Dad gets home. We'll have pie and mash, pease pudding too.' Eliza strained the mixture into a medicine bottle. 'And I'll get a pennyworth of laudanum for Mum. I'll look after you better from now on, love. Things are going to change round here, you'll see.'

On Monday morning, Eliza went in person to take the orders to the suppliers. She was determined to establish good working relationships and most of them had known her since she was a child. They treated her with respect and a good deal of sympathy but she knew in her heart that their confidence in her was mainly due to Ted's backing. If that was so, then she did not care: she might be just a girl, working in a man's world – but she would prove her worth, or die in the attempt. It was well into the afternoon when she returned to the chandlery, where she had left Davy in charge. He was serving a ship's quartermaster with a barrel of pitch and a pair of sea boots. The man paid for his goods, hefted the barrel on his shoulder as if it weighed little more than a pennyweight, and left the shop. As the doorbell jangled, Ted appeared at the top of the ladder.

'If that's Eliza back, you come up here, Davy. I only give you leave to mind the shop while she was out, so don't take advantage.'

'Coming, guvner,' Davy said, shinning up the ladder with the agility of a monkey.

Eliza went behind the counter and settled down on Enoch's old stool to study the books. It did not take her long to realise that, although

Uncle Enoch had been ruthless in collecting most of the outstanding debts, there were mysterious instances where he had allowed almost unlimited credit to certain people. Tickling her nose with the feathery end of her quill pen, Eliza made a note of the names and addresses. Gradually, a picture began to emerge: some of these names she recognised as being the businessmen who had attended Enoch's funeral, and almost all these men were considered to be pillars of the church. It would seem, she thought, staring at the copperplate entries in the ledger, that Uncle Enoch had bought the good opinion of his peers. No wonder they had flocked to the church to pay their last respects to such a generous benefactor. 'We'll see about that,' Eliza said out loud as she underlined the total sum of the unpaid debts. 'They won't find me so eager to buy their good opinion.'

'Who are you talking to, Liza?'

Startled, Eliza looked down from her high perch and saw Millie standing by the counter. 'I didn't hear you come in.'

'You was too busy talking to yourself,' Millie said, giggling. 'I come on me way home from school. I thought I could give you a hand.'

'And so you shall. I'm sure the shelves could do with a bit of dusting.' Eliza slid off the stool and, as she rounded the counter, she stopped, staring down at Millie's bare feet. 'Where are your boots?'

'I dunno.'

Eliza took her by the shoulders and gave her a gentle shake. 'Of course you know. Tell me. I promise not to be cross.'

'I give them to Mary.' Millie's violet-blue eyes filled with tears. 'Don't be angry, Liza. I done it to stop the big boys teasing her. They said as how she'd got nits in her hair and called her a fleabag. They said her dad spent his money on booze and couldn't afford to buy her a pair of boots.'

'Don't cry,' Eliza said, giving her a hug. 'I know you meant it kindly, but now you haven't got any boots. Won't the big boys tease you?'

'I don't care if they do. I was used to worse than that in the workhouse.'

'You poor little soul.' Eliza stroked Millie's hair back from her forehead. 'I can only imagine what you must have gone through in that place. But you shouldn't have given your boots to Mary. What will Ted say?'

'It's summer and I don't need nothing on me feet.'

Unable to argue with the logic of this, Eliza dropped a kiss on top of Millie's head. 'Never mind the boots for now. Find a duster and we'll sort something out later.'

Millie trotted off to find a piece of rag and Eliza went back to writing a list of addresses from the ledger. She glanced up as the door opened and a broad-shouldered, bearded man with a shock of black curly hair came storming into the shop. His bushy eyebrows were drawn together over the bridge of his nose in a frown and he was holding Millie's boots in his hand. Eliza's heart sank. It was Arthur Little, and, by the looks of him, he was ready for a fight.

'I gets home and finds my Mary parading round in these here boots.' Arthur leaned over the counter, shoving his face close to Eliza's. 'I don't ask for charity and I'll thank you not to interfere in my business, young woman.'

She recoiled, choked by a waft of stale beer on his breath. 'Don't you shout at me, Mr Little. It was an act of kindness from Millie, not charity.'

'Call it what you like, it's all the same thing and I won't have it.'

'Keep your voice down,' Eliza hissed, as two prospective customers walked into the store.

'I don't take orders from a chit of a girl.'

His raised voice attracted curious looks from the two men, one in first mate's uniform, the other obviously a seaman. Arthur shook his fist at them. 'Mind your own business, mates.'

They shrugged and strolled off behind one of the stands.

Arthur flung the boots on the floor. 'I can look after me own family.'

'What's all the fuss about?' Ted stuck his head through the open hatch. 'What's going on, Liza?'

'It's between me and her.' Arthur jerked his thumb at Eliza. 'Interfering little mare.'

'Oh, Gawd! It's me dad, out for trouble,' Davy said, peering over Ted's shoulder.

'Keep out of this, boy.' Ted pushed him aside and slid down the ladder. He faced up to Arthur. 'Don't you take that tone with me, mister.'

'I said all I got to say.' Turning on his heel, Arthur staggered unsteadily out of the chandlery.

Ted turned to Eliza. 'What's up with him?'

'It was nothing, just a misunderstanding.'

'Look, ducks. I don't mean to be unkind, but there's always going to be men what will try to bully a young girl on her own. I got me own work to do. If you can't cope alone then we'll have to get a man in to manage the store.'

Eliza knew that he had her best interests at heart, but even if there was some truth in what he said, she was not going to give in so easily. 'I can manage, Dad. I promise you I can and I'll sort it out meself.'

When the shop was closed for the night and Millie had gone home with Ted, Eliza made the excuse of wanting to walk by the river with Davy, saying she needed some air and time to think.

'What's it all about then?' Davy asked, as Eliza turned the mortice key in the lock. 'Why do you want to walk along the river? It's hot as hell and the stench is really bad tonight.'

'I don't want to walk by the river; it was just an excuse to keep Dad and Millie happy. I'm going to Anchor Street to call on Basher Harris. You needn't come with me if you don't want to. I can go alone.'

'Not in that quarter and at this time of night you don't,' Davy said, taking her by the hand. 'I dunno what you want with this fellah, but you ain't going on your own and that's that.'

She smiled and gave his fingers a squeeze. She wasn't going to admit it, but she was quite glad to have Davy's company. Anchor Street and the surrounding area was no place for a young girl to be out alone at night. Eliza had been aware for some time now that she was attracting unwanted attention from men as they passed her in the street. They made suggestive remarks, openly propositioning her and offering money for her services, and she felt much safer with Davy at her side. At fifteen, he was as tall as most full-grown men: lifting heavy spars and rolls of canvas had broadened his shoulders and developed his arm muscles. He might have inherited his father's gypsy-like appearance but his good looks were unmarred by the ravages of drink and ill temper. As they walked, she gave him a sideways glance and she realised, with a jolt of surprise, that Davy was fast approaching manhood. As if sensing that she was looking at him, he turned his head and grinned. Suddenly he was a boy again and Eliza chuckled with relief.

Even this late in the evening, Anchor Street was seething with people: sailors of all nationalities looking for lodgings or a woman of easy virtue; malnourished, ragged children playing in the gutter while their mothers entertained their clients; a knife-grinder just finishing off his day's work; stevedores and watermen either returning home from work or setting out on the night shift. The air was thick with tobacco smoke, the stench of drains, unwashed bodies and cheap grog. Eliza clutched Davy's hand a little tighter as they approached Beattie Larkin's house. Bart would have been furious if he had known what she was about to do and Freddie would never have allowed her to venture into Anchor Street at night, not even if he were to accompany her. Taking a deep breath, she knocked on Beattie's door.

There was silence and then someone threw up the sash above their heads. Mrs Donatiello stuck her head out of the window, shouting something in rapid Italian before slamming it shut. This time, Davy hammered on the knocker and after a bit they heard a baby crying and approaching footsteps echoing on the bare boards. It was Beattie herself who opened the door with a baby slung haphazardly over her shoulder. 'Oh, it's you. What d'you want?'

'Not you, that's for sure,' Eliza said, putting her foot in the door so that Beattie couldn't slam it in her face. 'I come to see Basher Harris.'

The baby began to cry and Beattie shifted it to the crook of her arm. 'Well he don't want to see you.'

'And you'd know what he wants, would you?' Pushing past Beattie, Eliza stepped over the threshold closely followed by Davy.

'Here, you can't barge your way into my house,' Beattie protested.

Eliza stopped, staring down at the sleeping baby. 'Is this supposed to be Freddie's nipper?'

'Course it is. Didn't I swear in court that he was the father?'

Looking over Eliza's shoulder, Davy chuckled. 'I didn't know your doctor pal was a Chinaman, Liza.'

A bubble of laughter rose up in Eliza's throat together with a dizzying feeling of relief as the baby opened its dark, almond-shaped eyes, staring at her in an unfocused way. With its olive skin and jet-black hair, there was no possibility that Freddie could have been the father.

'It's a wicked lie,' Beattie said, covering the baby's head with a tattered piece of shawl. 'I never went with a Chinaman. I never even been in the Chinese laundry. Freddie is the father and the bastard's gone off to Australia leaving me to cope all on me own.'

'Not exactly on your own, though,' Eliza said, heading for the staircase. 'You've got five other little bastards to keep you company, Beattie. I'm glad that Freddie is safe from your clutches, you wicked, lying cheat.'

'Why, you little bitch! I'll have you up for slander, I will.' Beattie stamped into her room and slammed the door.

'Come on, Davy,' Eliza said, lifting her skirts and taking the stairs two at a time. 'Let's get this over quickly so we can get out of this horrible place.'

Basher Harris was at home in the back bedroom eating his supper of bread and cheese, while his elderly mother slept on an iron bedstead in the corner of the room. He chewed impassively as he listened to Eliza's proposition.

'I know you got a job in the docks, Mr Basher,' Eliza said, standing as close to the door as possible in case he took umbrage at being disturbed whilst eating. 'But I come to offer you different work, if you've a mind to it.'

'Like what?'

'Like working hours that would suit better with caring for your poor, sick mother. It would be daytime work, Mr Basher. No working nights in the docks. Clean work too and not dangerous.'

'Go on.' Basher sat munching his food, his

heavy brows lowering as if in a permanent state of frowning. 'Speak up.'

'I need someone to do the heavy work for me in the chandlery,' Eliza said, picking her words with care. What she wanted to say was that she needed someone big and tough-looking, like the gorilla she had seen once in a picture book; but maybe that would not be very tactful. Taking a deep breath, she tried again. 'I need a man of business what can collect debts for me.'

Basher looked up from his plate, his beady eyes gleaming. 'You mean a bloke what could bend an arm or leg the wrong way if required.'

Eliza managed a smile, although her lips felt numb. 'Not exactly, but I do need someone who looks as though he means business, er – without actually breaking bones. And I need someone to stand by me in the shop when I get a difficult customer. I need someone strong to do the heavy lifting and delivering goods to the ships. Might you be interested, Mr Basher?'

Mrs Harris groaned and stirred. Basher leapt to his feet and hurried over to the bed. He tucked the grimy coverlet up around his mother's chin with a degree of gentleness that both surprised and touched Eliza.

'There, there, old girl,' he said softly. 'Go back to sleep. There's nothing to worry about.' He turned, staring at them: a tall tower of a man who could have picked them up, one in each hand,

and dangled them like cherries on a branch. For a moment, Eliza thought he was going to throw them out of the window, but his stern features melted into a shy grin and he held his hand out. 'Me name's Arnold, miss. Although most folks calls me Basher.'

She put her hand into his big paw and tried not to wince as he squeezed it, pumping her arm up and down. 'Do we have an agreement then, Mr – er – Arnold?'

'That might depend on me wages, miss.'

'I'll match what you was getting in the docks. And, if we suit, then maybe I can do a bit better, Mr Arnold.'

He slapped his thigh with his hand. 'It's just Arnold, miss. When do I start?'

When they were outside in the street, Davy turned to Eliza, his brow creased in a worried frown. 'I know as how you needed a chap with a strong arm, Liza. But can you afford to pay him that much?'

'I can't afford not to,' Eliza said, with a confident air that she was far from feeling. 'But hopefully one look at Basher, I mean Arnold, and the debtors will pay up.'

'It's your business,' Davy said doubtfully. 'Anyway, let's get away from here. I'll see you home.'

'No, Davy. I want to see your mum. I've been doing a lot of thinking since Uncle Enoch passed away. I got a suggestion to make.'

She refused to say more, even though Davy was bursting with curiosity. Although it was still daylight when they reached Farmer Street, the cellar was in almost complete darkness. Despite the summer heat, the dank chill struck Eliza to the bone; the stench of bad drains, human effluent and sour milk made her want to retch. Eddie and Artie had been put down to sleep on a palliasse in the corner, but were still wide awake, nudging, pinching each other and giggling. Pete had come home from the brewery and was sitting on the earth floor, eating a bowl of sops, and after a long day in the sweatshop nine-year-old Ruth was perched on an upturned tea chest, rocking Sammy in her arms.

Ada looked up from hacking slices off a stale loaf of bread. 'Hello, love.' Her smile faded when she saw Eliza. 'Oh, Liza. I'm so sorry about them boots. I begged Arthur not to make a fuss but he's hot-headed at times.'

Eliza bit back a cry of dismay as a rat darted across the floor and disappeared down a hole in the brickwork. She looked round at the unwashed, underfed children and her resolve hardened. 'Mrs Little, I got a proposition for you, so I'll come straight out with it.'

Ada wiped her hands on her apron. 'Best be quick, ducks. It wouldn't do for Arthur to come home and find you here.'

'Uncle Enoch left everything to Bart. But until

he comes home, I've got the running of the shop and the use of the house in Bird Street.'

'I'm not quite with you.' Ada shot a puzzled look at Davy, who shook his head, shrugging.

'I can't sell the house because it don't belong to me, but I can let it out. I want you and your nippers to take it. You can have it for the same rent as you pays for this one room. I don't want to make a profit from friends.'

Ada slumped down on a rickety chair, staring at Eliza. 'I – I dunno what to say.'

Pete leapt up from the floor. 'Say yes, Ma. Say yes.'

'A proper house?' Ruth jiggled Sammy until he was sick over her shoulder. She didn't seem to notice. 'Oh, Ma. A real home.'

'You can't do it, Liza.' Davy shook his head. 'What will Ted say?'

'It's up to me. The solicitor said as much. You was there, Davy.'

'I couldn't take advantage of you. It wouldn't be fair.' Ada's mouth worked as if she wanted to cry.

Eliza thought quickly. 'Maybe you could help out a bit with Mum. Sometimes she just needs company in the daytime when we're all out. Or someone to give her a bit of dinner. You see, she's not very well.'

'I'd do that anyway if you was to ask. But my Arthur would never agree to it.' Ada buried her face in her apron, rocking herself backwards and forwards. 'Oh, it's not fair. We could have a proper home, but for his blooming pride.'

'Oh, Mum,' Davy said, his voice breaking with emotion. 'It's an offer you can't refuse. Never mind the old bugger.'

'Yes, Ma. Oh, do say yes.' Ruth tugged the apron from Ada's face. 'Say yes.'

'We'll all die of lung fever if we stays here,' Pete said, jerking his head in the direction of Eddie and Artie, who were suddenly quiet and staring wide-eyed, as if they understood that something important was being said.

'I dunno . . .' Ada looked from one to the other. 'I dunno what to say.'

Eliza shivered. She couldn't wait to get out of this dreadful pit of darkness. 'Don't say nothing now. Why don't you come along and see the house tomorrow evening, after I shut the shop. Mr Little might have a change of heart if he sees it.'

'I said it before, I've never taken charity from no one, and I'll not start now.'

'It's not charity, Mr Little,' Eliza said, setting Artie down on the flagstone floor of the kitchen in Bird Street. 'You would be paying the same rent as you are now. That's not charity.'

'I can support me own family, ta very much, young woman. So don't you go putting grand ideas into my Ada's head. We don't need you and your pity.'

'Please, Dad.' Davy cleared his throat with a nervous cough. 'Won't you think about it?'

Arthur turned on him, glowering and shaking his fist. 'When I wants your opinion, I'll ask for it. I dunno why I let you drag me here, Ada. Get on home, the lot of you.'

The smaller children began to howl and the older ones huddled together in a corner of the room, but Ada drew herself up to her full height. Eliza could see that she was trembling from head to foot and she didn't blame her for being afraid. Despite his years of toping, Arthur was a large man with a resounding voice and fists like hams. The position seemed hopeless, but she had reckoned without Ada's maternal instinct.

'Now you listen to me for once, Arthur Little.' Ada pushed Davy aside and wagged her finger in front of her husband's face. 'I've borne you ten children, two of them stillborn, but I've never complained, even when you've drunk yourself stupid and beat me. Now I've got the chance to better our lives and to get out of that stinking hole in Farmer Street. You can stay there if you wants to, but I'm bringing the nippers to live in this little palace, and no one's going to stop me. D'you hear me, Arthur? No one is going to stop me.'

It was as if a mouse had roared at a lion. Arthur

had seemed to crumble in the face of Ada's ferocious attack. He had given in without another word.

Although Ted questioned the wisdom of Eliza's decision to let the property at a peppercorn rent, he welcomed the news that Ada was going to help care for Dolly, and he did not oppose the scheme. He even allowed Davy a couple of hours off next day to help his mother pack up their few belongings and move them to their new home. As usual, Arthur took himself off to the pub.

Eliza would have liked to help with the removal, but she had to look after the store. True to his word, Arnold turned up for work, looking strangely clean and tidy in a black suit that might have belonged to his father or even his grandfather. The jacket was stretched so tightly across his broad shoulders that the seams were in danger of bursting open like an overripe peapod. The sleeves were too short, revealing a large expanse of frayed cuff, below which his wrists and hands dangled, giving him such a comical appearance that Eliza had to stifle a giggle. She sent him out into the yard to stack the crates, boxes and barrels in some sort of order, but with strict instructions to come inside if she called him.

After just a week, Eliza was amazed at the difference that Arnold's presence made to the attitude of the men who had previously tried to take advantage of her youth and gender. With Arnold lowering in the background like a volcano that might erupt at any moment, they had paid up and left without haggling about price, or attempting to bully her into giving them credit. She had completed her list of outstanding debtors and she was eager to send Arnold out to collect the money owed, but he would need something decent to wear. Uncle Enoch had been a big man, not muscular, but large-boned and slightly corpulent. Eliza decided that Enoch's clothes would be ideal for Arnold and, although the thought was repugnant to her, she must clear out his possessions in order to give the Littles more space.

That evening, after work, Eliza walked home with Davy. She was both surprised and gratified to see the changes that Ada had wrought in such a short period of time, turning the house in Bird Street into a real home. The odours of damp and dry rot, vermin, must and mothballs had been replaced by the clean smell of carbolic soap and beeswax polish. The rusty kitchen range had been scoured and treated with black lead, and a pan of thick soup simmered on the hob, giving off a tempting aroma of mutton stew. Arthur was slumped in Enoch's old chair by the range, snoring loudly, and the youngest children, looking surprisingly clean, played on the floor with a set of wooden bricks. At the table, Mary and Millie sat with their heads together over a reading book.

'Millie, you should be at home with Mum,' Eliza said, attempting to sound stern but unable to suppress a chuckle as Millie hurtled off the stool to hug her.

'We was just practising our reading, Liza. I give Mum her tea afore I come round here. She said it was all right.'

'I said I'd see her home any night she wanted to pay us a visit,' Davy said, ruffling Millie's hair. 'She's a good little kid, but she shouldn't have given her boots to Mary. I think the old man was right to give them back.'

Millie's smile faded. 'I wanted Mary to have me boots. Now I got to beat up them boys what teases her.'

Davy lifted her back onto the stool. 'Any beating up to be done, you leave that to me, poppet. I been saving from me wages and I got almost enough to buy Mary a pair of good second-hand boots, so don't you fret.'

At that moment Ada came in from the back yard carrying a pitcher of water. She stopped when she saw Eliza, uttering a cry of surprise. 'Well now, this is a pleasure.'

'I just come to relieve you of some of Uncle's things,' Eliza said, keeping her voice low for fear of waking Arthur. 'I thought they would do for

Arnold.'

Ada set the jug down on the table. 'Come into the front parlour, Eliza. I've put all your uncle's things in there, laid out so as you could take what you wanted.'

Eliza followed her out of the warm kitchen into the front room. 'You've done wonders, Ada. And in such a short space of time.'

'I can't tell you how much it means to me to have a proper home.' Ada's voice cracked and she blinked away a tear. 'Don't take no notice of me, Eliza. It's tears of happiness that I'm shedding. Silly old me.'

'I'm glad I could help. Uncle Enoch never appreciated his home. He never appreciated nothing.'

'Well, he's dead and gone, and can't hurt you no more. There's his things, such as they are. He wasn't what you call a big spender, was he?'

Enoch's clothes had been neatly laid out on the horsehair sofa. Eliza couldn't bring herself to touch them. 'Perhaps Davy could bring them to the chandlery tomorrow?'

'Of course he can. And there's this as well, I found it in a cupboard in the old man's bedroom.' Ada reached up to the mantelshelf and took down a small, wooden box and passed it to Eliza.

Inside she found a daguerreotype of a young woman, faded but still clear enough to reveal an oval face framed with ringlets of light hair and large eyes that held a hauntingly sad expression. Ada cleared her throat. 'I thought perhaps it was your mother, Eliza. You look just like her. And there's a mourning brooch too. The hair in it is flaxen just like yours. I reckon your dad must have had it made up.'

As she held the likeness in one hand and the brooch in the other, Eliza felt hot tears flooding down her cheeks. 'I'm sure it's my mum; she's just as I imagined her. But I don't understand why Uncle Enoch kept it hidden. Bart would have liked to have it, I know he would, but it's too late now. He might be dead too for all I know.'

'Now, now, don't give way to morbid thoughts. Your Bart is a big, strong fellow and he's well able to take care of himself. He'll turn up on your doorstep one day, large as life. I'm certain of it.'

Wiping her eyes, Eliza pinned the brooch to the neck of her black dress. 'You're right, Ada. He'll come home and I'll be waiting for him. I'll build the business up bigger and better than Uncle Enoch ever done. I swear to God, I will.'

Chapter Ten

Bart peered into a shard of mirror balanced precariously on a table made out of planks salvaged from the ruins of Fox Camp after the great storm. He scraped at his beard with a somewhat rusty cut-throat razor, swearing loudly as he nicked his cheek. It was bitterly cold inside the stone hut that he had built with his own hands after his first shelter had been swept away in the floods of that dreadful winter. Despite temperatures well below freezing, he had hefted the stones from the riverbed, piling them together without the advantage of mortar. He had not had the necessary skill to build a chimney, and in desperation had lit a fire just outside the door to take the bitter chill from the single room, half choked by the smoke, but glad of the smallest degree of warmth to keep himself from freezing to death. Somehow, against all odds, he had survived and the winter was over now, with the hint of spring softening the air even though the mountaintops were still iced with snow.

Bart dabbed at the cut with a piece of rag. What he wouldn't give for a jug of hot water and some shaving soap, but these were luxuries that he had learned to do without. Life had been hard enough before Tate's murder and afterwards had become almost unbearable. The police had never found the culprit and, due to his reputation for being quick-tempered, Bart himself had come under suspicion for a while. It had been Captain Hayes who had spoken out for him and, with no evidence or motive, the police had come to the obvious conclusion that Tate had been murdered for the bag of gold he had won at cards. He had been buried in the cemetery along with hundreds of other unfortunate souls who had died violent deaths or been taken by pneumonia, typhoid or scarlet fever. A wooden cross, simply inscribed 'Tate' in pokerwork, marked his grave. It was then that Bart realised that he had never known him by any other name; he did not even know if Tate was his surname or his Christian name. Neither did he know whether there was anyone in England who would mourn his passing: it seemed that Tate had left this world as he had come into it, unwanted and unloved.

Drying his face on a scrap of cloth, Bart put on his one good shirt, a waistcoat and his jacket that was showing signs of wear and tear but would have to do until he could afford a replacement. Feeling under the straw palliasse on his wooden bunk, his fingers curled around a pouch containing the small amount of gold that had taken him two weeks to pan from the river. Today was his day for going down into Fox Camp, now rebuilt and renamed Arrowtown. His need for fresh supplies was only a little greater than his need for Daisy. Sometimes in the dead of night, huddled in his straw bed too cold to sleep, he was tormented by fears that Daisy would get tired of waiting for him to strike it rich; that one of the handsome, younger bucks who had come upon their fortune in gold nuggets would steal her away from him. In his heart, Bart knew that Daisy was faithful and that she loved him, although he could not think why she would give herself so completely to a rough, penniless, ill-tempered fellow such as himself. He had not even had the money to buy her an engagement ring, and marriage was out of the question until he had found that crock of gold that was at the end of the elusive rainbow.

With one last look around his hut, he went outside and dragged the ill-fitting door across the entrance. There was no lock, nor even a bolt, but it would keep some of the cold out and there was nothing of value for anyone to steal. Making his way through the wet scrub, slipping on the frosty surface of the mud, he began the trek down the mountainside towards Arrowtown. As he neared the settlement he could smell woodsmoke from the campfires of the tented community, the scent of boiling hops from the brewery and the mouth-watering aroma of freshly baked bread. New buildings had popped up like a field of mushrooms and the town had lost none of its robust bustle and vitality. Bart entered the town with a spring in his step. Soon he would be with Daisy; he would take her in his arms and taste the sweetness of her lips, bury his face in her scented hair and feel the softness of her voluptuous body against his.

Her old lodgings had been destroyed in the storm that had wiped out half the town, taking with it the roof of the Provincial Hotel and damaging the Prince of Wales into the bargain. But Bully Hayes and Rosie had already left, suddenly and with no warning, in the middle of June, having sold the hotel for half its value. The Buckinghams had also departed and Daisy had been out of a job, but she had soon found work with Mary Ann Anderson who was a rough, tough woman who, earlier in the year, had been arrested for running an unlicensed grog shop and disorderly house. Chained to a log outside the police station, a common punishment due to the lack of prison buildings, she had impressed even the hardest of men with the range of her invective.

Bart was not happy that his Daisy should be working for Mary Ann, or Bull Pup as she was nicknamed, after the dog that was always at her side, but in that terrible winter it had been a matter of survival. Arriving outside the clap-board building, Bart took off his hat and went inside. The fumes of stale alcohol caught him in the back of his throat, hitting his empty stomach and making him retch, although he quickly covered his mouth with his hand as Bull Pup emerged from a back room with a look on her face that would have scared a lesser man. Then, to Bart's surprise, she grinned.

'Well, if it isn't young Bart. I thought you was the law come to arrest a poor woman for trying to earn an honest living.'

'Is Daisy about, Miss Mary Ann?'

'We was busy last night.' Nudging Bart in the ribs, Mary Ann gave him a knowing wink. 'She's a working girl and don't you forget it. If you go tiring her out you'll have Bull Pup to answer to.'

Biting back an angry retort, Bart gritted his teeth. The meaningful leer on Mary Ann's face made him want to punch her in the mouth, anything to wipe that smile off her face; but for all her foul language and toughness, she was still a woman and he'd never hit a woman, not yet anyway.

Mary Ann jerked her head in the direction of the door to the back of the building. 'Go on then. I'll not charge you this time, young fellah, but I ain't running a charitable institution here.'

Bart grunted a reply, fisting his hands but

keeping them close by his sides, as he headed for the rooms where Mary Ann's girls entertained their clients. Anger roiled in his stomach, cold and bitter as gall, making his mouth dry; his heartbeat quickened, sending the blood drumming in his ears. The thought of another man laying hands on Daisy made him physically sick and a red mist blurred his vision. Barging into her room without knocking, Bart came to a halt by the bed where Daisy lay sleeping, her golden hair tumbled about her face and her red lips parted slightly as though she were having a pleasant dream. The room smelt of stale sweat and cheap grog; it was a tart's room and his beloved Daisy was a common whore. Looking down on her as she slept, jumbled visions clouded Bart's mind of unwashed, uncouth men using her lovely body for their pleasure. Fuelled by hatred for these unknown violators, Bart's heart was filled with murder and his soul racked with anguish. In sleep she looked like an angel, innocent, young and vulnerable. Choked by a rasping sob, Bart fell to his knees by the bedside, buried his face in his hands and wept.

'Bart?'

He felt Daisy move beneath the covers but he could not lift his head. Her arms were about him and she was murmuring his name over and over again.

'Bart, Bartie dear, what's wrong with you? Speak to me.'

Ashamed of his weakness and of his inability to control that dark river of rage that had almost ruined his life, Bart wrapped his arms around Daisy's waist and laid his head against her breast.

Rocking him in her arms like a baby, Daisy stroked his hair back from his forehead. 'There, there, love. I dunno what brought this on but everything's going to be all right.'

'I – I'm sorry,' Bart mumbled, hiccuping and pulling away from her to rub his eyes on the back of his hand. 'I'm sorry, Daisy.'

'So you should be, you bad boy. You've made the front of me nightgown all wet,' Daisy said, kissing him on the forehead.

Her tender but puzzled smile and the sight of her breasts outlined by the damp cotton of her nightgown filled Bart with love and a surge of desire that sent thrills through his body, but at the same time made him feel ashamed. He was little better than the men who paid for her affections; his lust for her body was as great a sin as theirs, for hadn't he heard this often enough in the lengthy Sunday sermons that Uncle Enoch had forced him to endure? He loved her with all his heart, but without money he could not protect her or take her away from this degrading way of life. What sort of a man was he to have left his own sister, a mere child, to the mercies of a miserly old hypocrite like Enoch? What sort of useless creature was he that could not find gold even when others were stumbling over nuggets that made their fortune overnight?

'Oh, Bartie, love. Don't take on so,' Daisy whispered, in between kisses. 'Come to Daisy, she'll make it right for you.'

Unable to resist her lips or reject the only comfort that Daisy had in her power to give him, Bart climbed onto the bed beside her, closing his eyes and allowing her gentle hands to undo his clothes. 'I love you, Daisy. I want to take you away from this rotten place.'

'You will, dear,' Daisy whispered, nipping the lobe of Bart's ear while her hands caressed his body. 'You will, Bart. But not until later.'

He was drowsing in Daisy's arms, physically sated and happy, but was dragged back to reality by someone thumping on the door.

'Daisy, wake up in there. You got a customer.' Mary Ann's voice had a steel edge to it that must be obeyed.

Daisy wriggled from Bart's arms, and climbed out of bed. 'You got to go, love. I'll see you later.'

'No!' The word was wrenched from Bart's throat in a cry of pain. 'No, I won't let you. You can't go with another man. You're mine, Daisy.'

She dragged her wrap around her shoulders,

eyeing him coldly. 'Keep your voice down. I got a job to do.'

'Bugger that,' Bart cried, scrambling out of bed and grabbing her by the shoulders. 'You got to give it up, girl. It's not for the likes of you.'

'Likes of me? Don't talk soft, Bart. You know what I am, what I got to do to earn a living. Stop acting like a fool.'

'A fool! Yes, I must be a fool to love you like I do.' Bart struggled to control his temper. 'It's got to stop, Daisy. I can't let you sell yourself like a common harlot.'

Her eyes narrowed and flashed with anger. 'But I am a common harlot. You knew that when you asked me to marry you.'

'Don't say that.' Pressing his hands against his temples, Bart felt his self-control slipping into an abyss. 'Don't ever say that. I want to marry you, I do.'

She faced him, hands on hips, allowing her wrap to fall open, and revealing her curvaceous body, still glistening with a silky sheen from their lovemaking. 'Then do it. Marry me or get out of my life. I'm a whore, remember, and I don't do it for free.'

The rage that had been simmering in Bart's belly exploded into a firestorm at her taunting words and something seemed to snap inside his head. He lashed out with his fist, knocking Daisy to the floor where she lay in a crumpled heap.

For a moment, Bart stared at her inert figure, not fully understanding how she had come to lie there at his feet. Dazed and shaking from head to foot, the full horror of what he had done hit him in the stomach like a punch from a bare-knuckle fighter. He fell to his knees and cradled Daisy's head in his arms. His tears fell on her upturned face, mingling with the blood from her cut lip which had already swollen to twice its size. 'Daisy, Daisy, please forgive me. I never meant to hurt you. Daisy.'

Without warning, or maybe he had simply not heard her knocking, the door burst open and Mary Ann stood there with her dog snarling at her side and a burly miner standing behind her. Before he knew what had hit him, Bart was thrown bodily out into the street.

'And if you put a foot inside my place, I'll have you horsewhipped, you cowardly bastard,' Mary Ann roared, tossing his felt hat into the street after him. 'Keep away from her, d'you hear me? You'll keep away from me too, if you value your skin.'

Nursing his bruised jaw, Bart got slowly to his feet, swaying dizzily. Mary Ann and the miner had disappeared back into the building; the business of the town was going on around him with no one taking the slightest bit of notice of his plight. He picked up his hat and dusted himself down, still dazed and hardly able to believe what he had just done. Shame burned in his soul and, although he longed to find Daisy and beg her forgiveness, Bart knew that he could not face her even to apologise. Giving way to his vile temper, he had sunk to the lowest point in his life and if she hated him, then it was what he deserved. There was only one thing he wanted at this moment and that was rum, dark sweet rum that would blot out pain and thought. Slowly, limping slightly where he had landed awkwardly on his left leg, Bart made his way to the nearest grog shop and ordered a drink.

The stench of horse dung and urine-soaked straw made Bart catch his breath and retch. Opening his eyes, he looked up into the liquid eyes of a horse tethered in its stall. The horse whinnied and pawed the ground close to Bart's head and the sound reverberated in his eardrums like the booted feet of a marching army; the light hurt his eyes and jagged shafts of pain seemed to be splitting his skull. He raised himself on his elbow, and his fuddled brain slowly came to the conclusion that he was lying on a heap of straw in a stable. He had no idea how he came to be here, what time of day or night it was, or who had dumped him here in the first place. Sitting up and groaning as demons with picks hammered inside his head, past events began to seep back into his stupefied mind. Daisy!

'Oh God, what have I done,' Bart groaned, licking his dry lips with a tongue that felt too large for his mouth. Getting to his feet, he staggered out into the stable yard, shielding his eyes from the harsh light of the spring sunshine. He felt sick and weak and he couldn't remember the last time that food had passed his lips, but somehow he managed to get to the pump and stuck his head beneath an icy torrent of water. When he had slaked his thirst, Bart stood, shivering in the deserted stable yard. Judging by the height of the sun in the sky it was early morning and the town was just waking up.

Daisy, he must find Daisy and beg her forgiveness. He would go down on his bended knees and promise her anything if she would just tell him he was forgiven. Catching sight of his own reflection in the grubby glass panes of the stable window, Bart ran his hand through his tousled hair. The wild-eyed fellow staring back at him was not the image he wanted to present to Daisy. He needed a bath, a shave and some hot food in his belly before he even began to feel human again. He touched his waistcoat pocket, and heaved a sigh of relief on finding the pouch of gold dust. He had an overwhelming desire to find the honest fellow who had delivered his drink-sodden body to the safety of the stables last night without first robbing him of his only means of sustenance. But first things must come first, and Bart slowly made his way out into Buckingham Street and headed for the bathhouse.

Two hours later, clean-shaven, sober and well fed, Bart entered Mary Ann's establishment, dragging his hat off his head and looking about nervously, half expecting to be forcibly ejected before he could speak up for himself.

'So you've turned up again, eh?' Mary Ann leaned across the bar, glowering at him.

'Hear me out, lady,' Bart said, twisting his hat in his hands. 'I come to beg Daisy's pardon and yours too, for behaving like a hooligan and a brute.'

'Nicely said, mister, but you're too late. She's packed up and gone.'

'Gone?' If Mary Ann had hit him with a bar stool, Bart would not have been more shocked or knocked off balance. 'No, she can't have gone. We was engaged to be married.'

'Seems to me she's had a lucky escape then. Get on your way, fellow, or do I have to throw you out?' Lifting up the hatch, Mary Ann strode out from behind the bar counter.

Backing away, Bart held up his hands in a gesture of submission. 'I'm going. Just tell me where to find my Daisy and I'll never bother you no more.'

'I'll tell you, but it won't do you no good. Daisy was leaving today anyway. She's gone to

Riverton to help Rosie Hayes look after her new baby.'

Still slightly fuddled by last night's excess of alcohol, Bart stared at Mary Ann as if she were speaking a foreign language. 'Why would she do that? She never mentioned it to me.'

'Maybe you never give her a chance,' she said, curling her lip. 'Maybe you was too interested in satisfying your carnal desires to care what Daisy thought or did. You're all the same, you men.'

'I got to find her. I got to get her back.'

'Get a hold of yourself, fellah. You go chasing after Daisy now and she'll spit in your eye. And I wouldn't fancy your chances if Bully sees what you done to her. Now get out of here before I lose me temper. You've cost me a good worker and I'll not forget that, so if you know what's good for you, you'll keep out of me way from now on.'

Although Bart's first instinct was to set off for Riverton and bring Daisy back, forcibly if necessary, Mary Ann's words had hit their mark. He had brought this situation about with his own ungovernable temper and, if he wanted to win Daisy, then he would have to prove to her that he had changed. During the long trek up the mountainside to his hut, moving slowly under the burden of provisions, Bart's anger and fear at the thought of losing Daisy for ever slowly crystallised into a single-minded determination to make himself worthy of her. As he reached the hut, Bart stood for a moment, looking at the site with critical detachment. With Tate's help he had picked this spot in a sheltered gully, just high enough above the Arrow to avoid being swept away when it was in full spate but close enough to allow easy access for the daily drudgery of panning for gold. Across the river, the Arrow Face rose steeply beneath its thick blanket of native bush. At his back, the foothills of the Crown Range climbed less steeply but to a greater height. This was not a bad place, Bart decided. Here he would build a stone cabin, with a chimney and a sturdy roof that would withstand the heavy snows of winter. He would make a home fit for Daisy, with a brass bed and a rocking chair so that she could sit by the fire in the dark evenings, and they could plan their future. He would tell Daisy about London and above all, he would tell her about Eliza and his ambition to return home a wealthy man. He would rescue Eliza from that old bugger Enoch, and he would see that his little sister married a man of standing, not a waterman or a stevedore, but a bloke with learning and a respectable trade or profession.

Staring up into the clear azure sky, Bart took a deep breath of the crystal air and closed his eyes. 'God, if you are up there, I swear I'll mend me ways. I'll not let my women down again, but I need your help, not for myself you understand, but for my Daisy and my Liza. Help me to help them, God. If you can spare a moment, that is.'

Realising that he had spoken out loud as his voice reverberated across the gorge, coming back in a mocking echo, Bart grunted, feeling his cheeks redden even though there was nothing but an eagle soaring overhead who might have heard his mumbled prayer. He scurried into his hut and dragged the door across the entrance.

It was not easy building a cabin large enough for a man and wife to live together and Bart was unskilled, although getting better with practice. In the day he waded in the river, panning for gold, or if the weather was too inclement then he began tunnelling into the mountainside. He had noted how other miners did their work, digging a little each day and shoring up their work with timbers, but it was a slow process and he found only minute amounts of gold. In the summer evenings, after a supper of damper or porridge and tea, with the occasional treat of a bit of boiled bacon, Bart set about gathering rocks and extending his hut, starting first with a chimney. His first attempt collapsed in a particularly bad storm, but he began again next day, learning from his mistakes in construction, and by the end of the summer he had succeeded in making a working chimney. By mid-autumn, he had completed the outer shell of his cabin, and before the onset of winter he had saved enough money to buy timber and to hire a packhorse to bring it up the gorge, thus enabling him to construct a sturdy roof.

During all this time, Bart had continued to find small amounts of gold, either dust or tiny nuggets little bigger than a grain of rice, but having saved his hoard he raised enough cash to keep him in food during the worst of the winter storms. In the times when it was too dangerous to work in the swollen waters of the Arrow, he worked on the inside of his cabin, pounding the dirt floor until it was hard and dry as cement. He used planks left over from the roof to make a bed big enough for both him and Daisy. The brass bed would have to wait until later. Not for a minute had Bart allowed himself to think that this might all have been in vain. For almost a year, he had clung to the belief that Daisy truly loved him and that all he had to do was to prove to her that he had changed. Every stone in this cabin, every plank and every shingle was a testament to his love for her; once she had seen the home he had built, she would know that he was sincere and she would marry him.

Bart had intended to wait until spring but now the cabin was finished he knew he could wait no longer and he must set off to find Daisy and bring her home. Packing a few things in a canvas bag, he set off for Arrowtown, his boots crunching on the thick frosting of snow. Although he had hoarded his money, buying only the barest necessities, he had invested in a pair of good, if second-hand, boots and a waxed linen coat lined with felt to keep out the intense cold. He arrived in Arrowtown in the early afternoon, and went straight to the refurbished Prince of Wales Hotel where he ordered a steak dinner and a pint of beer.

'Haven't seen you in here before, mate,' the barman said, drawing a pint from a barrel and handing it to Bart.

'That's because I ain't been in here for a while,' Bart said, not particularly wanting to chat for he was out of the way of conversing with people, but he needed information and where better to get it than in Bully's former place of residence. 'I knew the chap what used to own this place.'

Wiping spilt beer from the counter, the barman gave Bart an appraising glance. 'Friend of Bully's was you?'

'Not exactly, but I did know him and his wife. I heard they'd gone to live in Riverton.'

'You're behind the times, mate. The word is that they left there to join Rosie's brother, Conrad, in Carey's Bay near Port Chalmers. Are you thinking of paying them a visit?'

'None of your business,' Bart said, picking up his glass and moving away from the bar to a table. He could hear the barman muttering something uncomplimentary under his breath, but he didn't care. He would have his dinner and then he would set off, walking to Port Chalmers. He'd done it once before, and he could do it again.

It was not a pleasant journey. Bart soon decided that only a fool or a man desperately in love would have undertaken such a long and arduous trek in the middle of winter, but he refused to be beaten by the weather, frostbite or sheer physical exhaustion. The journey took him almost twice as long as it had when he and Tate first walked to Fox Camp, and it was the nearing the end of August by the time Bart reached Port Chalmers. Exhausted and with little money left, Bart found a cheap lodging house near the harbour. It was late in the evening, and after a supper of mutton stew, his first hot meal in a month, Bart fell onto the mattress allocated him in a room shared by several other fellow travellers. He sank into a deep, dreamless sleep.

Next morning, filled with hope and determination, he found his way to the public baths, and set about getting clean and tidy. When he found Daisy he wanted to make a good impression. By midday, Bart was clean-shaven, bathed and had managed to get his underclothes and shirt laundered and, if not dry, at least not soaking wet as they had been on some of the rainier days of his long journey. With hope in his heart, he set off to find the offices of the local newspaper. Enquiring at the front desk, he was uncomfortably aware of a change in the man's expression when he enquired about the Hayes family. 'You're a stranger in these parts then, mister?'

'I am,' Bart agreed, 'but I am a friend of the family.'

'Then I'm afraid it's bad news I have to give you, my friend. There was a tragic accident at sea just a couple of weeks ago. Captain Hayes managed to save himself, but his wife and baby were drowned, along with one of Mrs Hayes's brothers and the nursemaid, whose name escapes me at present. Are you all right, mate?'

Unable to speak for the choking sensation in his throat, Bart stumbled from the building and only saved himself from falling by clinging to a lamppost. As he swayed on his feet like a drunken man, passers-by crossed the street to avoid him. If he had taken care of Daisy she would still be alive. It was his fault that she had drowned; he had killed her as surely as if he had pointed a pistol at her beautiful head. Stumbling along the street, Bart had no idea what he was going to do, but he needed to get to Carey's Bay and to see the house where she had been living with the Hayes family. He had no idea what he would do when he got there; he was simply following his instinct like a migrating bird.

It was late afternoon and the winter night was closing in on the Otago Peninsula by the time he arrived outside the gates of the Buckinghams' house. Carey's Bay was a small community and it had not been difficult to gain directions from the townsfolk. Standing in the street, Bart looked up at the building, lost in the desolation of his thoughts as he tried to imagine Daisy's last days spent in this place. The sound of hooves on the road behind him made Bart move aside as a man drew his horse to a halt and dismounted, casually flinging the reins over the picket fence. He cast Bart a curious look. 'Can I help you, sir?' The man was well dressed and spoke in a beautifully modulated voice, as if he were an actor addressing an audience.

'I don't think so.' Shaking his head, Bart vaguely remembered seeing him at the Provincial Hotel in Arrowtown. If this man was a member of the Buckingham family, then he must say something; make some appropriate remark. Out of practice at dealing with people, Bart cleared his throat. 'I'm sorry for your loss, sir.'

'You knew my sister?'

'I met her once or twice in Arrowtown. I was going to marry Daisy, the maid what was drowned alongside Mrs Hayes and her baby.'

Buckingham paused, staring at Bart. 'You've

been misinformed, sir. It was Mary Crowley who sadly passed away. Daisy is our parlour maid and I'm glad to say she's alive and well and in the house as we speak.'

For the second time that day, Bart felt the world spin about his head as if he were about to faint, and he clutched the fence for support. 'Daisy's alive?'

'Come with me.' Placing his hand beneath Bart's arm, Buckingham led him through the gate and up the path to the house where he rapped on the door.

It opened and Daisy stood in doorway holding a kerosene lamp. With her pale golden hair shining like a halo, she looked to Bart like an angel from heaven. For a moment she stared at him, wide-eyed and with her lips moving silently in shock.

Buckingham pushed Bart forward. 'I think you know this fellow, Daisy.'

'Bart!' Daisy's voice broke on a sob as he swept her up in his arms.

'Well, it seems that good has come out of bad,' Buckingham said, relieving Daisy of the lamp before it fell to the ground and was smashed. 'I'll hang up my own coat and hat then, shall I, Daisy?'

Bart and Daisy were married in Port Chalmers two days later, with Conrad Buckingham giving the bride away and Betsey, the cook, and Jakes, the handyman, as witnesses. Conrad paid for the hire of a bullock cart to take them back to Arrowtown, insisting that it was his wedding present to the newly married couple. As soon as the brief ceremony ended, Bart and Daisy set off for home. If the journey was arduous and beset by flooded roads, wheels sinking in mud up to the axles and even a late snowstorm or two, Bart was oblivious of everything except the delight of having Daisy all to himself. Nights spent curled up with his bride on the hard boards of the cart, with rain beating a tattoo on the tarpaulin overhead, were as blissful to him as sleeping in a featherbed in the grandest hotel he could imagine. Daisy was everything that he remembered and even more: he was a man deeply in love and, for once in his life, Bart was totally happy. When they arrived in Arrowtown, they left the bullock cart to be rehired for the return trip to Port Chalmers, and set off on foot for the cabin.

The winter snows melted, sending icy water tumbling down the mountainsides and swelling the Arrow River into a foaming torrent, scouring the riverbed with dislodged rocks and gravel. As he climbed out of bed, Bart was careful not to disturb Daisy, but he could not resist dropping the lightest of kisses on her slightly parted lips and on her swollen belly. He covered her tenderly with the eiderdown that he had purchased with the last of his money. Nothing was too good for Daisy; she must be cared for and cosseted during the months to come while their baby grew in her womb. Bart couldn't help smiling at the thought of his son, or maybe it would be a girl, a perfect blend of Daisy and Eliza for him to love and cherish. It was cold in the cabin, the fire having died down to ashes in the night, and Bart dressed quickly, pulling on his boots and tying the laces. He would fetch water and then light the fire, so that the room was warm for Daisy when she awakened. He would have tea brewed so that she had something to ease the morning sickness that had been bothering her lately. As he plucked his jacket from the back of the chair, a folded sheet of paper fell to the floor. He retrieved it and put the letter he had written to Eliza on the table: it had taken days to compose. Daisy had helped him put his feelings into words and had corrected his poor spelling. In it he had told Eliza about their life, about the child they were expecting and how he was certain that his luck was about to change. Soon they would be rich and he would bring his wife and baby home to England. All would be well; he knew it in his bones.

Shrugging on his jacket, Bart picked up his hat and, jamming it on his head, he let himself quietly out of the cabin. Half blinded by the brilliance of the early morning sunshine, he collected the wooden bucket that he used for toting water from the river and set off down the bank, slipping and sliding on the mud. The sound of the rushing torrent filled his ears and the spray sparkled in the sunlight, forming rainbows across the water.

The river was in full spate and, as Bart made his way to the edge, he paused for a moment, his breath taken away by the power and beauty of nature. Then, just as the rainbow pierced the surface of the water, Bart saw something gleaming on the riverbed. Blinking hard, he thought at first it was simply a trick of the light, a refraction of sunbeams on wet gravel. His heart seemed to miss a beat and then it began to race; he was not sure whether the pounding in his ears was the drumming of his own pulse or the roaring tumult of the river. Wading into the icy waters Bart felt the powerful surge of the current beating against his legs as it swept everything in its path; he knew what he was doing was dangerous but he was not going to give up this, his first real chance of riches. Moving in and out of his vision beneath the swirling mass of gravel and water was the largest gold nugget that he had ever seen. Plunging down beneath the torrent, Bart's fingers clawed at the gold as he attempted to prise it from the mud that held it fast. When his lungs were close to bursting, he came up for air, shaking the water from his hair and eyes. Then he dived down again digging frantically, oblivious of the pain from his cut fingers and torn nails. Coming up once again, he filled his lungs with air and then lunged with all his strength; the lump of gold, twice as big as his fist, came away in his hands just as a wall of water hit him in the back, knocking him off his feet. Bart kicked out, but his boots were full of water and his sodden clothes weighed him down. The river was hurling him from rock to rock, taking him up to the surface like a cork and then sucking him down into its green depths. Above him, Bart could see daylight and he clutched his gold to his chest. He could see Eliza and Daisy smiling down at him through the ripples. He had not let them down after all. He was a rich man.

Chapter Eleven

As Eliza turned the key in the lock, she paused before opening the chandlery door and looked up at the name above the shop front. Illuminated by the first tentative rays of morning sunlight, the weathered gold letters seemed to wink at her, starting her day on a cheery note. *E. Bragg, Ship Chandler.* Once that title had belonged to Enoch, and the store had been a terrible place, but during the last six years she had made it her own. It had not been easy, and there had been many times when Eliza had felt like giving up; none more so than in the dark days after she had learned of Bart's death. It had seemed to her then that cruel fate had robbed her of all those she loved most in the world. In the initial shock of bereavement, she had been tempted to hurl herself into the Thames, seeking relief from the swirling waters that would blot out grief and reunite her with Bart and her dad. But, in the depths of her despair, when even the love of her adopted family and Davy could not reach her, Eliza had discovered something in her deepest self: a core of stubbornness and the will to survive. Bart would not have wanted her to give in; she would keep going for his sake and for the sake of his child.

With dogged determination, she had set about learning the trade of the ship chandler. In the beginning, she had made enemies, especially amongst the merchants and mill owners who had been Uncle Enoch's church-going cronies. They had kicked up a fuss when Arnold had gone to collect their outstanding debts; they had bullied, threatened and cajoled but eventually, thanks to his lowering brow and iron fists, they had paid up. After that, Eliza had never allowed credit to anyone. She had tried to deal fairly with suppliers and customers alike and sometimes she had been swindled, cheated and defrauded, but it had all added to her learning and understanding of the business. She had become a familiar figure at auction sales, warehouses and trade exhibitions. She had learned how to cut a deal with men twice her age and she had done all this with Arnold at her side.

'Morning, Miss Eliza.'

Eliza turned with a cheery wave to acknowledge Jiggins, the rope maker, on his way to work near Limehouse Dock. This early in the morning, the docks and the river had a freshly washed look about them. The people of the night had gone to ground, and the air was cool and untainted by the stench that would gradually rise above the city in the heat of the day. Letting herself into the shop, Eliza took off her bonnet and shawl and laid them neatly on a shelf behind the counter. She peered into the mirror tucked in between a stack of ledgers and she patted her hair into place, tucking in a few wayward strands that refused to be confined in the chignon at the back of her head. She adjusted the high neck of her grey dress, touching the mourning brooch that contained a lock of her mother's hair, a habit that she had almost unconsciously adopted. The brooch was her link to the past, to the people whom she had loved and lost; the simple act of touching it seemed to bring her closer to them.

Satisfied that she looked neat, tidy and businesslike, Eliza set about inspecting the shelves and making sure that they were fully stocked before Arnold and Millie arrived. She had deliveries for Arnold to do that morning with the help of Millie, who was now sixteen, and an able assistant, keen to learn the chandlery trade. Ted still worked in the sail loft, although he seemed to Eliza to have aged suddenly and he left a great deal of the work to Davy, who was now a fully qualified sailmaker in his own right. He had chosen to stay on and work with Ted rather than seek employment elsewhere. Although she did not want to admit it, Eliza knew in her heart that Davy's apparent lack of ambition was down to her. They had been close friends for as long as she could remember, and that was the trouble; Davy might have other ideas but she had always thought about him as a brother and even more so since Bart's tragic death. It had taken five months for the letter to reach her. At first she had been overjoyed to receive a letter from him, informing her of his marriage to Daisy and the child that they were expecting. It was a letter full of love and hope, but the tear-stained postscript had been written by Daisy after Bart's body had been dragged from the river. She related how his battered body had been found a couple of miles downstream, entangled in a mass of weed. Even in death, he had appeared to be smiling as he clutched the large gold nugget in his stiff fingers. Daisy had ended the letter abruptly at that point.

Eliza had written back immediately, begging Daisy to come to London as soon as she was able, but she had never received a reply to her letter; she did not even know if Daisy had been safely delivered of her child. All she could do was hope that somewhere, on the far side of the world, Bart's son or daughter was now a thriving, happy five-year-old. This made her even more determined to make a success of the business so that she would have something worthwhile to leave to Bart's child. Eliza had decided long ago that she would never marry, and therefore would never have children of her own. With Freddie gone, she had no interest in the young men who had tried to find favour with her. She knew that she would never, could never, love anyone as she loved Freddie. The worst of it was that she did not even know if he was alive or dead: many convicts did not survive the long voyage out to Australia and who knew what privations he might have suffered if he had ever reached the penal colony. If he had survived, then he had probably forgotten all about her; she had been little more than a child when he was sentenced, and he could have had no idea what passions had burned in her young heart. If still alive, he would be a man in his prime and might even have taken a wife. Eliza had long since given up hope of ever seeing Freddie again, but that had not prevented him from haunting her dreams. She was now considered to be a young woman of property; there had been would-be suitors, both young and old, but she had dismissed them without a second thought.

Opening the order book, Eliza sighed, not knowing quite what had brought about this melancholy host of memories and ghosts from the past. She must write up the delivery notes that she would pass on to Millie, who in turn would supervise Arnold loading up the wagon with the goods. Although he could neither read nor write, he had the ability to memorise the contents of each crate, sack and barrel, but Millie would accompany him on his rounds, checking off the items on the bill of lading to make sure that a dishonest quartermaster or mate didn't cheat them.

Eliza looked up as the doorbell jangled and she smiled as Millie and Davy entered the shop. Davy held the door, allowing Millie to pass, and she was laughing at something he had said. With her bonnet slipping off her head and the sunlight striking golden lights in her dark blonde hair, Millie bobbed a mock curtsey.

'Thank you, sir.'

'Don't mention it, ma'am.' Bowing from the waist, Davy grinned. 'You're a cheeky little monkey, Miss Turner. Best get to work.'

Millie's smile faded and a shadow passed across her face as if a cloud had momentarily blotted out the sun. Eliza stifled a sympathetic sigh; she could only guess at what Millie was feeling, but it was painfully obvious that her childish hero-worship for Davy had deepened into something much more adult. Davy, on the other hand, seemed completely oblivious of Millie's feelings, treating her in much the same way as he treated his sister Mary. Why, Eliza thought, was love so complicated? She might have locked her own heart away in a protective shell inside her breast, but that did not stop her feeling desperately sorry for Millie's unrequited love for Davy. Perhaps it had been a mistake, allowing her to work in the shop? Maybe it would have been better if she had found her a place in service like Mary, who worked as a parlour maid for a silk merchant's family in Islington. Eliza closed the order book and handed it to Millie with what she hoped was a cheerful smile. 'Best make a start on this as soon as Arnold arrives.'

'I told you she'd forget what day this is,' Davy said, nudging Millie in the ribs. 'I win.'

Still smiling, but puzzled, Eliza looked from one to the other. 'Win what? What have I forgotten?'

Millie kissed her on the cheek. 'It's your birthday, silly. You're so busy with your business that you've even forgotten what day it is. You're twenty today, Liza. Really, really grown-up. Happy birthday.'

From behind his back, Davy produced a slightly wilted bunch of jewel-bright asters. 'Happy birthday, Liza. Here, best put these in water. They've come all the way from Ilford, picked fresh this morning so the coster told me.'

'Ta. They're lovely.' Eliza buried her face in the spice-scented petals, and for no apparent reason, she felt tears welling up in her eyes.

'Give them to me and I'll put them in water.' Millie held out her hand. 'They'll brighten up the counter a treat.'

Eliza swallowed hard, shaking her head. 'It's all right, dear. I'll see to them. You'd better open up the back door for Arnold. He should be loading up the wagon and you need to check the goods or he'll be sure to leave something behind.'

'Work, work, work,' Millie called cheerfully, as she made her way to the back of the store. 'Can't you ever take a day off?'

Eliza turned away to search for a suitable container for the flowers but Davy caught her by the hand, holding it and looking into her eyes with a frown wrinkling his forehead. 'She's right, Liza. You never take a day off. You work too hard, girl.'

'And who would run the shop if I wasn't here?' She went to pull her hand away but Davy held it in a firm grasp.

'There's more to life than making money. When did you last have a bit of fun, Liza? Come to think of it, I can't remember the last time I saw you laugh.'

'Don't talk soft. What's got into you today?' Eliza jerked her hand free and turned on her heel, walking to the back of the shop where she found a slightly battered tin jug. 'Keep an eye on the shop for a minute, will you, Davy? While I fetch some water from the pump.' Suddenly she needed to get out of the store and away from the spectres of the past that haunted every nook and cranny. It was stiflingly hot in the yard, the stinking, fly-ridden heat of August that wrapped itself around the city in a suffocating hug.

Arnold had almost finished hefting the goods onto a hired wagon. He touched his cap and grinned when he saw her, but he carried on with his work. Millie was leaning over a large barrel with the order book spread out before her; she looked up, chewing the tip of her pen. 'You could be nicer to Davy, you know.'

Eliza tut-tutted as the water gushed from the pump, splashing her full skirt. 'I dunno what you mean.'

'He got up at crack of dawn to walk to market and get them flowers just for you. And he's hired a private room at Paddy's Goose tonight. It's supposed to be a surprise party and he's been saving up for months to pay for it. If you don't turn up, Liza, I'll never speak to you again. I mean it.'

With cold water overflowing from the jug and spilling onto her boots, Eliza stared at Millie, momentarily stunned by this angry outburst. Such heated words, and the tone in which they were delivered, were as shocking as hearing a tiger's roar coming from the mouth of a kitten. 'I don't want no fuss,' she said, shaking out her damp skirts. 'I'm not much of a one for parties.'

'No, you go around with a long face, or else you got your head stuck in a ledger or studying

255

the shipping news and thinking of business. You never think that there's others what might like to have some fun, or give you a bit of a laugh. You treats poor Davy like he don't matter, when you must know that he – he loves you with all his big, stupid heart.' Bursting into tears, Millie threw the pen onto the ground and ran sobbing into the storeroom.

'What's up with her?' Arnold stood in the gateway, scratching his head and frowning. 'Have I done wrong, missis?'

'No, no, not you, Arnold. It's me. I'm afraid I've upset her.'

'You never said you wasn't coming to the party?' Arnold stopped short, clamping his hand across his mouth. 'Bugger it! I wasn't supposed to tell.'

'Never mind, I know all about the surprise party. Just go on the delivery.' Picking up the book that Millie had abandoned, Eliza took out the copy of the ship's order and handed it to Arnold. 'You can do this one on your own, Arnold. I'm sure I can trust you.'

He stared down at the piece of paper and a slow smile spread across his face. 'Don't worry, missis,' he said, tapping his forehead. 'I got it all up here.' Chuckling to himself, he shambled out of the yard and climbed up onto the wagon.

Eliza hurried back into the shop looking for Millie, only to find that Ted had just arrived and was ranting at his two young apprentices for being late. Dippy Dan stood in the doorway, sucking his thumb and shaking with fear, even though the tirade was not directed at him personally. Glancing at the clock on the wall, Eliza saw that they were on time, but it was no use trying to argue with Ted in one of his strange moods. Of late he had been subject to sudden, violent tempers that came seemingly from nowhere and left him angry and shaking for some time after. She had put these attacks down to his fears that steam engines were taking the place of sail, and might soon put him out of business. In the evenings, after supper, Ted often sat with his pipe clenched between his teeth, staring into the middle distance, or went out for long walks on his own, returning long after Millie and Eliza had put Dolly to bed. Then, of course, there was Dolly's gradual slide into a fantasy world where the entire royal family were her bosom friends. Her delusions were child-like and harmless and she appeared to be happy in her world inhabited by imaginary companions, but Ted was deeply upset by her ramblings and had little or no patience with her. He blamed the medicine that Freddie had prescribed, and on which she had become totally dependent. Eliza had tried to wean her gradually off the laudanum-based elixir, but without it Dolly became frantic, complaining of stomach cramps, cold sweats and terrifying nightmares.

All this flashed through Eliza's mind as she saw Ted's lined face contort with pain. He had a grey tinge to his skin, and his eyes were bulging from his head with a wild, unfocused look. He shook his fist at the two boys, who scrambled up the ladder into the sail loft. 'Get on up there. I'll deal with you later. And you, you stupid bugger, Dippy. I dunno why I keep you on, you useless good-for-nothing.'

Dan lumbered after them, shivering and muttering to himself as he climbed the ladder.

Eliza set the jug of water on the counter. 'Don't get yourself so upset, Dad.'

'Them young beggars, idle sods the pair of them. I've a mind to give them a good thrashing.'

She laid her hand on his shoulder. 'Don't carry on like this. They're just boys and they're not late, at least not more than a couple of minutes.'

Ted turned on her, his normally mild countenance twisted into an angry scowl. 'Are you arguing with me, miss? Haven't I taught you nothing in all the years you've been under me roof?'

Eliza thought for a moment he was going to strike her; she modified her tone. 'I'm not arguing, I'm just suggesting that you calm down a bit.'

The slap echoed around the empty shop,

bringing Davy sliding down the ladder, and Millie popped up from behind a set of shelves, wide-eyed and trembling.

Clasping her hand to her cheek, Eliza stared in disbelief at Ted. Never, in all the years she had been in his care, had he ever raised his voice to her in this way, let alone struck her.

'Liza, are you all right?' Pushing Ted aside, Davy took Eliza by the shoulders, tipping her head back so that he could examine her cheek. He turned on Ted in a fury. 'What the bleeding hell d'you think you're doing, old man? There was no need for that.'

'Don't shout at him,' Millie cried, rushing forward to support Ted's swaying figure. 'Can't you see he's been took poorly?'

Eliza hurried to help Millie as she guided Ted to a chair. He slumped down, holding his head in his hands and trembling as if he were having some kind of seizure. Before Eliza could stop him, Davy had picked up the jug of water and tipped it over his head.

The effect was instantaneous and Ted stared up at him, with a look of utter confusion on his face. 'What happened?'

'You took a swim, you old bugger,' Davy said angrily. 'After you'd slapped Eliza in the face. What the hell got into you, I'd like to know.'

'Don't,' Eliza said. 'I don't think he knew what he was doing.'

Ted jumped to his feet, glaring at them all in turn. 'What's up with you all? You're talking rubbish, boy. I'd never hit Liza.'

Eliza bit her lip. Fear knotted her stomach as she exchanged worried glances with Davy. 'It's all right, Dad,' she said, making a huge effort to sound calm. 'It was nothing, you mustn't worry about it.'

'I'm not worried. I'm fine. It's you lot who are out of order.' Stomping past them with an irascible shake of his head, Ted made for the ladder to the sail loft.

Millie began to cry softly, covering her face with her hands. 'What's wrong with everyone today? It should be a nice day for Liza's birthday but it's all spoiled.'

'No, of course it isn't,' Eliza said, with a conviction that she did not feel. Something was terribly wrong with Ted, but it was no use burdening Millie with her worries. 'Maybe we'll have a bit of a party tonight, after work. How about that?'

'Now why didn't I think of that?' Ruffling Millie's hair, Davy smiled at Eliza. 'Seems like a good idea to me, though. Cheer up, nipper.'

Millie turned and ran behind one of the stands of shelves.

'What did I say?'

'Oh Davy, you treat her like a kid.'

'She is a kid.'

Ted's voice from above put a stop to any argument that might have developed. 'Get up here, Davy. I'm not paying you to stand around chatting.'

'I tell you, Liza. The old man's going mad and I can't stand much more of it. If he don't stop treating me like I was still an apprentice, I'm going to sign on for a sea voyage.'

The last thing that Eliza felt like was a party in the White Swan, or Paddy's Goose as it was known by the locals. On a normal day she would have stayed on at the chandlery long after everyone else had left. This was her quiet time when she could count the day's takings and lock them away in the iron box that Enoch had kept hidden beneath the counter. Having done that and entered everything in the ledger, she always checked that all the doors were locked and that all the lamps and candles had been extinguished. But today had been unlike any other day and Davy had insisted that she left early, even though the apprentices and Dippy Dan were still finishing off a bit of work in the sail loft. He had persuaded her that the lads were quite capable of locking the door on their way out and that Dan, although he was not the sharpest knife in the box, could be relied upon to stay there and ensure that everything was left as it should be. Reluctantly, Eliza had allowed Davy to walk her home.

One way or another, it had been a thoroughly upsetting day from start to finish and the thought of a party in the pub was more depressing than exciting. But Millie and Davy had their hearts set on celebrating her birthday and how could she explain to them that it was at this time of year when she missed Bart and Freddie the most. How could she tell any of them that it was on her birthday that she felt the loss of her mother and father all the more keenly? Even though Dolly and Ted had been the best of surrogate parents, and she loved Millie with all her heart, they were not blood relations. If she were to tell the truth, she would have liked to be quiet this evening instead of the centre of attention: sometimes, just occasionally, it would be nice to have some time to herself, when she could think and remember her lost loved ones without everyone fussing round and trying to cheer her up.

At home in Hemp Yard, everyone seemed determined that she would have a splendid time and even Dolly had seemed to rally a little. Ada, who now came round every day to help take care of Dolly, had dressed her in her best print gown and had even managed to tame her cloud of white hair into a knot at the back of her head, although stray wisps kept popping out, giving her head the appearance of a dandelion clock. She chattered excitedly, making little sense, and Eliza automatically agreed with everything that she said; it was easier than trying to bring her confused mind back into the real world.

Millie had put on her best dress and tied ribbons in her hair; her cheeks were flushed and her eyes sparkling with excitement. She kept running to the window every time there was the rumble of a cart in the street outside or the sound of hobnails on cobbles.

'Four white horses,' Dolly said, looking up expectantly. 'Are they bringing me carriage now, Eliza?'

'There's no carriage, Mum,' Millie said, casting an anxious glance at Eliza.

'But we are going to the palace, aren't we?' Dolly's bottom lip wobbled as if she were about to cry. 'We are going to see the queen?'

'That's right, we're going to see the queen,' Eliza said, wrapping Dolly in her shawl.

'What's that about the queen?' Ted came downstairs, struggling with his collar stud. 'What's she on about now? Help me, Liza. I can't do up this damn stud.'

Dolly rocked backwards and forwards in her chair, pointing her finger at Ted and giggling. 'He can't go to the palace looking like that. The queen won't let him in. Pussycat, pussycat where have you been? I've been to London to look at the queen.'

'If you can't say something sensible, woman, keep your stupid remarks to yourself.'

'Don't,' Eliza said, attempting to fix the collar onto the stud. 'You know she can't help it, Dad.'

Dolly smiled up at them and began to sing the nursery rhyme in a tuneless falsetto. Ted turned his back on her, glaring at Eliza. 'She's gone barmy and I can't stand it. Where's my Dolly gone? I don't know that mad woman sitting there.'

'Hush, now. She'll hear you.' Somehow Eliza managed to secure the stud even though Ted was jerking his head this way and that. She cast a beseeching glance at Millie. 'Go outside and see if they're coming.'

Millie nodded. She opened the door and peered out. 'I can see them,' she cried excitedly. 'It's Davy and Pete, and they've got a handcart.'

'What's the point of taking Dolly to the pub? She doesn't even know what day it is.' Pushing past Millie, Ted paused in the doorway. 'I'm going on ahead to make sure we can get her into the back room before any of my mates sees her in that state.'

An involuntary sigh escaped from Eliza's lips as she watched him walk out of the small house that had once been such a happy home. She had never felt less like celebrating anything in her whole life, but Millie was obviously looking forward to the party and she didn't want to spoil it for her.

'Is the carriage coming?' Dolly demanded. 'Are there four white horses and a footman with gold braid?'

'Yes, Mum,' Eliza said hastily, seeing Dolly's bottom lip starting to quiver. 'It's just as you wanted. Let me help you up. Give us a hand, Millie.'

Somehow, they managed to get Dolly onto her feet just as Davy and Pete arrived.

Davy walked past Millie without a sideways glance and he flashed an appreciative smile at Eliza. 'You look good enough to eat, girl. Are you ready for the off?'

'We're all set.' She could have shaken him for not noticing that Millie had made a special effort with her appearance. Even across the room Eliza could sense the hurt and disappointment radiating from her.

'You look nice too, Millie,' Pete said, grinning sheepishly and shifting from foot to foot.

Resisting the temptation to hug him, Eliza smiled. She had always liked Davy's brother Pete, who at seventeen was a good-natured, gangly youth, with arms that seemed too long for his body so that his hands and wrists poked out like bundles of sticks from jacket sleeves that were several inches too short.

'Some people wouldn't notice if I was in me birthday suit,' Millie said, scowling at Davy.

'Course we would,' Davy said, tweaking one

of her hair ribbons. 'You'd look like a skinned rabbit.'

'I don't like coney fur,' Dolly said, swaying on her feet as Millie and Eliza tried to hold her up. 'Fetch me ermine wrap, Millie. I don't want to wear this old crocheted shawl. I got to look me best for her majesty.'

'Let me have her,' Davy said, scooping Dolly up in his arms. 'Come along, Aunt Dolly, we got your conveyance waiting outside.'

'I won't go unless I got four white horses,' Dolly protested, smacking the side of his head with her hand. 'And where's the footman with gold braid?'

'I'm here, missis,' Pete said grinning.

'You're not a footman. You ain't got no gold braid.' Twisting round in Davy's arms, Dolly held her hand out to Eliza. 'I need me medicine, Liza. Give us a drop or I'll wet meself.'

'Best do as she says,' Davy said, jerking his head at the brown medicine bottle on the mantelshelf.

Eliza hesitated. The doctor had insisted that they must cut down on Dolly's medication; he had said that she was becoming addicted to laudanum, and it was making her illness worse instead of better.

'For God's sake, give it her,' Davy hissed. 'You know she'll do it if you don't give her a dose.'

Before Eliza could say anything, Millie had

266

taken the bottle from the shelf. 'Here, Liza. Give her some quick. We don't want to spoil your party and we can't leave her here on her own.'

Dolly had begun to kick and wail and there was nothing Eliza could do but uncork the bottle and hold it to Dolly's lips. She drank thirstily, grabbing the bottle so that Eliza had to struggle to get it away from her greedy mouth. 'She shouldn't have that much,' Eliza said, shaking her head. 'It's sending her doolally tap.'

The effect of the laudanum was almost immediate and Dolly's mouth curved in a beatific smile as her head lolled against Davy's shoulder. 'Tell the queen I'll be there in two ticks,' she murmured, closing her eyes.

'Get her on the cart while she's off with the fairies,' Pete said, holding the door open. 'She'll never know it weren't the coach and four but Greasy Harry's handcart what he uses to take the pig carcasses from Smithfield to his sausage factory.'

With Dolly slumped on the cart like a November effigy or a guy, Davy pushed and Pete pulled from the front; Eliza and Millie followed on behind as they made their way to Paddy's Goose in Shadwell High Street. In the private room at the back of the pub, Ted was sitting on one side of the fireplace smoking a pipe and drinking a pint of beer while he chatted to Jiggins. Ada was attempting to control the younger boys, Eddie, Artie and Sammy, who were chasing each other round and round and in and out of the tables, while Ruth and Mary sat primly sipping their drinks, and obviously considering themselves too grown-up for such goings-on. Only Janet was missing but she was now married and living in Plaistow with her husband and baby. Being heavily pregnant with her second child, she had declined the invitation, but had sent a basket of apples by way of a present.

'That was kind of Janet,' Eliza said, having admired the gift.

'She sent it special, seeing as how she remembered you liked apples,' Ada said proudly.

Taking one, Millie bit into the rosy apple. 'And her Len happens to be a porter at Covent Garden market. I bet he pinched these when no one was looking.'

'Don't be unkind,' Eliza whispered, trying not to laugh. It was well known that Len was on the mean side of thrifty, but she would not hurt Ada's feeling for the world.

Having settled Dolly in a chair well away from his boisterous brothers, Davy made his way across the room to Eliza. 'Happy birthday, Liza.' Slipping his hand inside his jacket, he pulled a small package from his breast pocket. 'It ain't much but I'm sick of the sight of that mourning brooch. I thought it was time you had something a bit more cheery.' Taking her hand, he closed her fingers around the crinkled brown paper.

'Ta, but you shouldn't have.'

'Well, open it then.'

Teasing the paper apart, Eliza stared down at the brooch, a lover's knot made of twisted gold wire. 'It's lovely. But it's real gold; you shouldn't have wasted your money on me, Davy.'

Davy frowned. 'It's my money and I saved up a whole year for that, Liza. Put it on; let me see you wearing it.'

With her fingers touching the mourning brooch, Eliza looked up into Davy's expectant face. She knew that he meant well, but he could not possibly understand what this brooch meant to her. To refrain from wearing it would be like casting her memories aside, and she couldn't do it. She was about to pin the lover's knot just below her collarbone when Davy stopped her. 'Not there,' he said, making a move to unpin the mourning brooch. 'Take that miserable thing off.'

Eliza slapped his hand away. 'No.'

'What's the matter?' Millie was at her side, looking anxiously from one to the other. 'What have you done, Davy?'

Shrugging, Davy turned away from them. 'Nothing. She's just being bloody silly.'

Ada grasped him by the arm. 'Don't, Davy. Don't spoil her day.'

'I need a drink,' Davy said, making for the door. 'I'll be in the taproom. Seems I'm not wanted here.'

Eliza opened her mouth to protest but no words came. With her hand covering the brooch at her throat, she felt tears stinging the back of her eyes. Davy did not understand her at all: in this room full of people, she had never felt so alone. Even Millie was staring at her with a hostile expression in her eyes, a resentful look that spoke more than words. Ada was holding her arm, patting it and trying to soothe her feelings by telling her that Davy was a good boy and he meant well.

A sudden sharp pain in the palm of her hand made Eliza uncurl her tense fingers and look down. A bead of scarlet blood oozed from the spot where the pin of the lover's knot had pierced her skin. Before she had time to wipe it away, the door to the taproom opened and Davy burst in, followed by Pete. The expression on their faces caused a sudden hush in the room and even the small boys paused in their wild game.

'Fire,' shouted Davy. 'The chandlery and the sail loft are on fire.'

Chapter Twelve

The air was thick with acrid smoke billowing from the building and belching in great clouds from the broken windows. Burning pitch, paint and paraffin filled the air with noxious fumes. The explosive power of the fire had shattered the windowpanes and shards of glass covered the street like jagged hailstones. With her lungs bursting and her muscles screaming from the effort, Eliza worked in the human chain, handing bucket after bucket of water to Davy as it came along the line that stretched down to the quay wall. Her eyes watered from the stinging effects of the smoke, but there was no time to feel pain or to acknowledge physical discomfort; the fire must be put out at all costs or the whole row of warehouses and shipping offices would be razed to the ground.

'Take a rest, Liza,' Davy said, peering at her anxiously over his shoulder as she handed him an overflowing bucket. 'This is man's work.'

'It's my business that's going up in flames,' Eliza said, shoving the bucket into his hands. 'Never mind me.'

At the front of the chain she could hear Ted's voice ringing out loud and clear directing the operation and controlling the crowd of onlookers that had collected to watch the spectacle. All the men in the pub had turned out to help put out the blaze, and above the roar of the inferno there was the sound of horses' hooves as the owners of the neighbouring premises arrived. Word had spread quickly in this close-knit community and now everyone, from the boy apprentices to the owner of the warehouse adjoining the chandlery, had rolled up their sleeves and joined together to battle the fire. With its bell jangling the horse-drawn wagon of the fire brigade, K division, clattered onto the cobbles and the firemen went into their well-practised drill.

'Stand back,' Ted roared, spreading out his arms and urging the crowd to move away. 'It's going to go at any minute.'

The ground beneath Eliza's feet began to shake. A low rumbling sound evolved into a mighty explosion of tumbling masonry as the walls collapsed and the roof caved in, sending up a choking fog of dust, sparks and flying debris. Eliza's knees buckled beneath her as a wave of dizziness swept over her. She would have crumpled to the ground if a strong pair of arms had not dragged her clear of the danger and continued to support her. All around them there was a moment of stunned silence; buckets of water fell from nerveless hands, spewing the muddy water from the Thames onto the cobbles where it hissed and evaporated in the intense heat. Then pandemonium broke loose all around them as the human chain dispersed, men and woman running for cover as bits of brick and mortar hailed down on them.

As she fought for breath in the thick cloud of dust and smoke, Eliza realised that she was being held in the arms of a complete stranger.

'Are you all right?'

The voice that penetrated her consciousness was deep and pleasant and the accent was that of an educated gentleman. The hand that was chafing hers was soft and smooth as a lady's. With a huge effort, Eliza fought off the feeling of nausea and faintness that was threatening to engulf her. Murmuring her thanks, she drew herself upright, peering into the flaming abyss that had once been her home and her livelihood. 'It's gone – all gone.'

'Let me take you home. It's not safe here.'

'Who are you?' Rubbing her eyes with the back of her hand, Eliza squinted through the pall of smoke at the man who, minutes ago, had simply been part of the anonymous chain of people trying to save the building. In the fiery glow of the flames she saw that he was tall, thin and as sooty as a chimney sweep. Then, as she fully regained her senses, the identity of the stranger did not seem to matter. 'Davy, where's Davy?' Turning away, Eliza scanned the faces in the crowd milling around her. 'Davy, where are you?'

'Liza, I'm here.' Davy's familiar figure pushed through the crowd and he swept her up in a hug that lifted her feet from the ground. 'Thank God. I thought you was buried underneath that mass of bricks.'

'No, I'm fine, thanks to this gent.' Eliza turned to her rescuer, but he was nowhere to be seen. 'He's gone.'

'Never mind that now. Let's get you home.' Davy took her by the hand and began pushing his way through the crowd.

'Bad do, Davy,' Jiggins said, slapping him on the back. 'But at least we saved the rest of the street.'

'Wait.' Eliza came to a halt, refusing to budge. 'I can't just leave it like this. I might be able to salvage something from the store.'

'It's nothing but ashes, love. It's all gone, including the sail loft and everything in it. There's nothing we can do tonight.'

Staring into the glowing embers with tongues of flame licking round the fallen beams, Eliza shook her head. 'I've lost everything. Everything.'

'Don't think about it now.'

'They all turned out to help,' Eliza said, gazing

round at the familiar faces in the crowd as they began to disperse. The scarecrow-like figures, blackened, wet and with their clothes singed and torn, were slowly ambling off to their respective homes. Even in their exhausted, dirty state, most of them managed a wave or a weary smile of sympathy as they filed past her.

'If you need anything, feel free to call on me.' A portly man with his face beaded with sweat was shrugging on his jacket. Eliza recognised him as Aaron Miller, the corn merchant who owned a large warehouse in Pennington Street and a fleet of ships. Although she had never dealt with him direct, she had supplied his company with much of their chandlery requirements. Deeply touched that such an important man should have come to her aid, it was all she could do to acknowledge his kind words. In spite of her distress, Eliza could only wonder at the spirit of the people who had turned out to help quench the fire regardless of their own safety. The human chain had been manned by shopkeepers, costermongers, dockers, bootblacks and even gentlemen, like the young man who had probably saved her life and then disappeared into the darkness without even revealing his identity. They had nothing in common except the East End spirit that always seemed to come alive in times of crisis. Old grudges were forgotten, gang wars set aside and the dark river gave up its waters to save life instead of taking it away.

'Come on, Liza,' Davy said, placing his arm round her shoulders. 'We won't let this beat us. Let's go home.'

'Yes, I suppose so.' Eliza allowed him to lead her away from the smouldering building with the firemen still in attendance dousing the embers to prevent the fire rekindling. 'We left Dolly in the pub. We must fetch her; she'll be scared to death.'

Davy gave her shoulders a comforting hug. 'Mum and Millie will have looked after her.'

'Yes, of course,' Eliza said, rubbing her eyes. Now that the danger was past, the whole scene was taking on a nightmarish quality. 'We'd best find Ted. He was a proper hero tonight. Just like his old self.'

'I expect he's gone back to the pub. He'd be worried about Dolly.'

'Yes, that's it, he'll have gone to fetch Dolly home.' Exhaustion was catching up with her and Eliza allowed Davy to help her over the rubble.

A sudden shout from one of the firemen brought them to a halt.

'A body. Over here.'

'Ted!' His name was wrenched from her throat as an icy hand clutched Eliza's heart: she knew, without even looking over her shoulder, that it was Ted. He had been at the forefront of the firefighting regardless of his own safety, protecting the business that had been the major part of his life for almost half a century. She had heard his voice sounding firm and decisive just like the old Ted when he had taken her from Uncle Enoch's cruel clutches. It was only latterly that he had become ill-tempered, impatient and unreasonable; but for all his moodiness she had still loved him. Now, some primitive animal instinct told her that it was Ted lying there beneath the ruins of his life's work. 'Ted.' Her voice broke on a sob as she struggled to free herself from Davy's restraining hand.

'Don't go there,' Davy said, holding her tightly. 'It might not be him.'

But she had broken free and was running and stumbling over the debris.

A fireman barred her way. 'It ain't a fit sight, miss.'

'I think it's me – me dad.' Choking on a sob, Eliza fell down on her knees. A hand and arm stuck out of the mound of charred wood and bricks and in the red glow of the embers, Eliza saw the outline of a balding head and just the top of a torso. His starched collar had burst open and stuck out at right angles. Very gently, Eliza laid it back into place. 'He always had trouble with that bloody collar stud.'

*

277

Next day, after a night when she had barely slept, and despite Davy's insistence that she should stay at home, Eliza went to the corner of Old Gravel Lane and Wapping Street to examine the ruins, and to see for herself if anything could be salvaged from the fire. A gang of workmen were shovelling debris into horse-drawn carts and had almost cleared the thoroughfare. A sickening smell of burning lingered in a pall over what remained of the building and, although the flames had been doused, spirals of smoke rose in plumes from the blackened timbers. Eliza could see nothing but desolation and it was obvious that the flames had consumed everything in their path. She turned at the sound of footsteps behind her and saw Arnold shambling towards her, holding his cap in his hands.

'Terrible thing, missis. Terrible.'

'Everything has gone, Arnold. We've lost everything.'

'Have you looked?'

'Of course I haven't looked.' Instantly regretting her snappy retort, Eliza moderated her tone. 'I don't think anything could withstand all that heat.'

Arnold's face set in a stubborn, child-like expression. 'Won't know if you don't look, missis.'

'Very well.' Hitching her skirt above her ankles, Eliza picked her way over the debris. She knew that nothing but action would satisfy Arnold when he was in one of his mulish moods. Besides which, he could be right, there might be something they could save from the wreckage. She could hear him lumbering along behind her, stumbling over fallen masonry. She ignored the warning shouts from the workmen that the building was dangerous and there could be pockets of fire still smouldering.

'Wait there, missis,' Arnold said, lifting Eliza off her feet as though she were a rag doll and setting her down on the flagstone that had once been the doorstep. Eliza was not about to argue. The stench of the charred remains filled her nostrils, and amongst the rubble pools of water hissed and bubbled with steam. It was like the vision of hell that the vicar had described in his long sermons when Eliza was a child. If this was Uncle Enoch's revenge, then it was complete.

'Look here.' Arnold raised one large hand, beckoning to Eliza. 'I reckon I found something. Best mind your step though, missis.'

Stepping carefully, Eliza made her way to where the counter had once been but was now a blackened mass of wood and brick. Arnold kicked at something with the toe of his boot and, hearing the metallic ring, Eliza's spirits lifted. If it was the iron box that contained a week's takings, then all might not be completely lost.

'Can you pick it up, Arnold?'

Grunting, Arnold scrabbled amongst the bricks and roof tiles and, after a good deal of swearing and with sweat pouring down his face, he managed to heft the box onto a fallen rafter. Eliza's hands shook as she unhooked the bunch of keys from the chatelaine at her waist. The gold sovereigns inside it might have melted with the heat but, as the lid ground on its rusty hinges and fell open, she saw that the coins were untouched. Tears of relief sprang to her eyes as she picked up a handful of gold, copper and silver.

'Best tuck it away safe,' Arnold said, glancing anxiously over his shoulder. 'There's men no better than sewer rats what takes advantage of this sort of mishap to loot and steal.'

'You're right,' Eliza said, taking off her shawl. She tipped the coins into its folds and knotted the material into a bundle. It was not a fortune, but at least it would pay for Ted's funeral, and help to keep the family fed until she could find work. She raised her head to thank Arnold but he had already moved away, climbing over debris to get to the yard at the back of the building. Tucking the bundle under her arm, Eliza followed him. The back door had gone but the lintel was still standing and it seemed unreal to stand beneath it looking out into the back yard. Arnold was stomping around, kicking over bits of roof timber and with his boots crunching broken tiles. He turned to Eliza with a triumphant grin on his face.

'This lot ain't been touched. There's barrels of pitch, kedges, anchor chains and all sorts here. You ain't lost all your stock.'

'And nowhere to sell it,' Eliza said, looking around and frowning. 'You're right though, Arnold. This stuff isn't worth a fortune but it would be a start.'

'It will all get pinched if it's left out here.' Arnold kicked at a barrel as if to emphasise his words.

'Then it must be stored somewhere.' A gleam of hope flickered in Eliza's breast. With the money in the cash box and what remained of the stock in the yard, she might just have a chance to rebuild the business. The fire might have destroyed the fabric of the building but she was not going to admit defeat.

'Hey, Miss Bragg.'

A voice from the alley outside the yard dragged Eliza back to reality and she looked up to see Joe Bullen striding towards them dragging his son by the ear. Stepping over the broken fence, Joe shoved Dippy Dan forward. 'Dan's got something to tell you, miss.'

Hanging his head, Dan stared down at his feet. 'It were me, miss.'

'I don't understand.' Eliza raised her eyes to Joe's harsh face. 'What's wrong with him, Mr Bullen?'

'He done it, miss. He knocked the paraffin lamp over and then the stupid bugger run off without telling no one. I've already leathered him with me belt, but you can hand him over to the coppers. I've washed me hands of the witless little sod.'

Dan began to whimper and his father cuffed him on the side of his head. 'I've done me duty by the poor fool for twenty years. Now he's on his own. Do what you like with him.' With one last malevolent glance at his son, Joe stormed off towards the docks where he worked as a labourer.

'It were me. They'll lock me up in prison.' Dan's sobs grew louder and his whole body shook. 'I never meant no harm, but the flames was so pretty – all blue and yellow – I couldn't do nothing but watch. Then the fire began to spread and I run. I run and run and I hid in the cupboard under the stairs at home, until me dad found me.'

Arnold laid his big hand on Dippy's shoulder. 'There, there, cully. Don't take on.'

Somehow Eliza could not find it in her to be angry with Dan. It would be like blaming a small child who knew no better, even though he had been responsible for the disaster that had not only robbed her of her business but had taken Ted from them in a terrible accident. There was no point in assigning blame: it had happened

and the future must be faced. Above all, she had
Dolly and Millie to care for. There were funeral
arrangements to be made, and she must find a
temporary home for what was left of the stock.
Arnold was staring helplessly at her, waiting for
her instructions, and Dippy Dan was sobbing on
his shoulder like a baby. Squaring her shoulders,
Eliza made an effort to sound calm. 'Arnold, I
want you to look after Dan. There's no need to
mention what happened to anyone. What's done
is done. I've got things to see to, but I want you
to stay here and keep an eye on this stuff. Stay
here until I come back, d'you understand?'

'Yes, missis.' Arnold's eyes gleamed with relief
and he patted Dan on the back. 'Did you hear
what the missis said, boy? You and me is going
to guard this lot until she comes back. Now stop
piping your eye and we'll set about tidying up.'

With a vague plan formulating in her mind,
Eliza went out through the alley to Old Gravel
Lane. She stopped when she saw Davy walking
briskly along the street towards her. As he drew
nearer she could see that his face was drawn and
a worried frown creased his brow.

'You shouldn't be here, Liza. You ought to be
at home with Dolly. This ain't no place for you.'

'You got no right to tell me what to do. At least
I'm doing something.'

Davy's face crumpled into a look of near
despair. 'What can I do? The business is gone,

and Ted's lying in the dead house along with those they pulled out of the river in the drag.'

Eliza winced; if he had slapped her in the face it could not have hurt more. It was true, last night the police had taken Ted's body to the dead house to await the coroner's arrival and the issuing of a death certificate. She had not dared to think about his poor broken body lying there with only the bloated corpses from the Thames to keep him company in the long night vigil. Trying to make Dolly understand what had happened had been heartbreaking and, even then, Eliza was not sure that she fully comprehended the fact that her beloved husband was dead. In the end Eliza had given her a hefty dose of laudanum and Dolly's screaming hysterics had gradually quietened down, but then her mind had begun to ramble and she appeared to be talking to Ted as though he were sitting in his chair by the range. Millie had helped Eliza get Dolly up the stairs to her bed and then she too had collapsed in floods of tears. It had taken Eliza a long time to calm and comfort her. It had been a dreadful night and one that she knew she would never forget.

Now Davy was standing there, telling her what to do and looking as though the world was about to come to an end. Her stretched nerves snapped into a burst of temper. 'Stop feeling sorry for yourself for one thing and, for heaven's sake, take that miserable look off your face.'

Davy stared at her, his eyes wide with shock. 'Liza.'

'Don't Liza me. Get off your backside and do something useful, or do I have to do the thinking for everyone round here?' Eliza turned away from him but Davy caught her by the wrist.

'Here, take this. It's what I went round to your house to give you but Millie told me where you'd gone.' He pressed an iron key into Eliza's palm.

'What's this?'

'You'll need Enoch's house now, either to sell it or rent it out to a family what can pay the going rate. We've lived off your charity for the last five years, Liza. Even me dad agrees that we can't go on doing it.'

'But . . . this is silly.' Eliza stared down at the key in her hand and then raised her eyes slowly to Davy's face. 'No, I don't want this. We'll manage, Davy. Somehow we will manage and I won't see your mum and the nippers put out on the street.'

'I can't live off a woman. I can't do it.'

The bleak expression in Davy's eyes went straight to Eliza's heart. Taking his hand, she closed his fingers over the key. 'Don't talk like that, Davy. This is me, Liza, your good friend. We're like family and families take care of each other.'

Davy shook his head. 'I don't know what to say.'

'We'll talk about it later. Right now I'm going to see the vicar about Ted's funeral and then I've got a bit of business to do.'

'What business? What are you going to do?'

In spite of everything, Eliza smiled. The urgency of his voice and the anxious look in his eyes made him look like a frightened schoolboy, and she suddenly felt old enough to be his mother. 'Nothing bad, I promise you.' She thrust the bundle of money into his hands. 'I managed to save this from the fire. Take care of it for me until I get home, there's a good boy.'

Without waiting to see his reaction, Eliza walked off in the direction of St Peter's church. There was enough money to give Ted a good send-off, which was the least she could do for the man who had been a second father to her. It was unthinkable to let the parish bury Ted in a pauper's grave, even if it meant that they went without necessities for a while. An hour later, having made the necessary arrangements with the vicar and the undertaker, Eliza stood outside the warehouse in Pennington Street that ran alongside the London Dock. A cooper was hammering a cask on the quay wall, the cranes clanked and their chains rattled as they flew up and down. The thunder of empty casks rolling on the stones and the splash of ropes hitting water were all familiar sounds to Eliza as she stared up at the four-storey brick warehouses with their impressive stone plinths. The air was pungent with the smell of tobacco, tar and rum mingled with the sickly stench from bins filled with horns and hides. Bracing her shoulders, Eliza walked into the outer office and asked to see Mr Miller.

After waiting for what seemed like hours but was probably only half an hour, Eliza was shown into a wainscoted office.

'Miss Bragg to see you, Mr Miller.' The clerk bowed out of the office, closing the door behind him.

The young man seated behind the desk stopped writing and raised his head. A look of recognition lit his face and he stood up, smiling. 'Miss Bragg, we meet again.' Moving quickly around the large mahogany desk, he held out a chair for Eliza and the scent of expensive cologne and bay rum brought back vividly the awful events of last evening. She sat down suddenly as her knees gave way beneath her. Although his face had been disguised with a mask of soot, she would recognise that voice anywhere.

'You're the bloke who saved me when the wall come tumbling down.'

'I only did what any man would have done in similar circumstances. If I'd realised what a lovely young lady I'd plucked from the jaws of death, I might not have left so quickly, Miss Bragg.'

His flippant tone was making Eliza feel distinctly uncomfortable. His expensive clothes and his self-assured manner were those of a gentleman, and she felt at a definite disadvantage in the shabby mourning gown that she had snatched from the cupboard early this morning. She had not given it a second thought then, but now she was acutely aware that it was old-fashioned, the black dye had faded into green-tinged streaks and it smelled strongly of mothballs. Clasping her hands tightly in her lap, Eliza angled her head. He was young and arrogant, totally self-assured and yet there was something about him that was not unattractive. But she had come here on a mission, and she was not going to allow him to intimidate or patronise her. 'My business is with Mr Aaron Miller what owns the warehouse.'

'I'm Brandon Miller. My father is at a meeting in the City but I'm sure I can be of assistance, especially when it involves a beautiful lady in distress.'

Eliza studied his face. She was used to dealing with men in the hard world of commerce, but she was finding it difficult to categorise Brandon Miller. 'Thank you, but I'd rather speak to your father. He knows me.'

A flicker of annoyance momentarily wiped the

urbane smile from Brandon's face. 'My dear young woman, I've spent four years studying ancient Greece at Oxford and I'm more than capable of handling a small matter like this.'

Eliza tossed her head. 'I'm sure that will be very useful if you deal with a lot of old Greeks, but we gets all sorts of foreign sailors coming ashore. You'd have done better to learn to parley French or Italian in my opinion.'

Brandon's eyes opened wide and then he threw back his head and laughed. 'My God, Miss Bragg, you're a one to be sure.'

Rising to her feet, Eliza gave him a frosty look. 'I can see I'm wasting your time. I'll come back another day when Mr Aaron is in the office.'

He motioned her to sit down. 'No, please. Tell me what you came for.'

'My business is with the organ grinder, not the monkey.'

Brandon's laughter echoed round the oak-panelled room. 'I've been called lots of things in my life, but never a monkey.'

'The show is over, Mr Miller. I'm going.'

His smiled faded and he leapt to his feet. 'I'm sorry. I've obviously caused you some unintentional offence. You must forgive me, Miss Bragg, but I'm not used to dealing with young ladies in business.'

Eliza hesitated, undecided whether to make a

dignified exit or to plead her case. Asking for help did not come easily.

He came round the desk and held out a chair. 'Please sit down and tell me why you came.'

She hesitated. He was too young, too good-looking and too full of himself for her liking. She was used to dealing with down-to-earth sea captains, quartermasters, rope makers and merchants. She had come prepared to speak to Aaron Miller, who might be a wealthy corn merchant and ship owner, but had the common touch. He was well known in the London Docks, where he conducted his business in person rather than through a series of managers. His son was another matter. He had obviously been raised as a gentleman, but his arrogant attitude irritated Eliza. She decided that it did not sit well on a man of business, and she steeled herself to resist his undeniable charms.

Brandon motioned her once again to be seated and Eliza stared at his fingers gripping the back of the chair. Last night those hands had pulled her to safety and held her; she remembered their touch with a shiver that was not altogether unpleasant. 'I come to see your dad. It's a business matter. I ain't looking for charity.'

'I can assure you that I never thought any such thing. If my father promised you assistance, then I'm sure he would trust me to give you any help and advice that you need.'

There was nothing for it, Eliza decided. The situation was desperate and she needed to store what was left of her stock in a secure place before nightfall. She sat down and, taking a deep breath, she launched into her appeal. 'I need a place to store the stock in my yard that escaped the fire, and a horse and cart to shift it.'

Brandon perched on the edge of his desk. 'That shouldn't be a problem.'

'And I want to rebuild the chandlery with the sail loft above it.'

'Now that's another matter. To rebuild would cost a lot of money.'

'I know that, but I had a deal in mind that might benefit us both.'

'A deal?' Brandon slapped his hand on his knee, chuckling. 'You are a remarkable young woman, Miss Bragg.'

There he was, patronising her again: the conceited, toffee-nosed young puppy. Eliza clenched her hands in her lap, digging her fingernails into her palms to stop the hot retort that sprang to her lips. Forcing herself to sound calm, although she couldn't quite prevent a tremor in her voice, she looked him in the eyes. 'If your company will lend me the money to rebuild and restock, then I'll guarantee to supply your dad's ships at a rate that he won't get nowhere else in London.'

He did not reply at once. He raised himself

from the desk and walked over to the window, where he stood staring out while he appeared to be considering her offer. Eliza hardly dared to breathe, willing him to speak and put her out of her misery. With difficulty, she held her tongue.

He turned slowly, eyeing her with a wary expression. 'This is a most unusual situation. Over what period would you repay the loan?'

'I couldn't hope to repay nothing for the first year. Then, when I'd got the business going properly, I thought we could work out a suitable arrangement regarding repayment and interest.'

Brandon's lips twitched. 'But until then you would supply our ships with chandlery at a reasonable rate?'

'If it's so funny, then perhaps I'm wasting your time.'

'Forgive me, Miss Bragg, but yours is a most unusual request. Tell me how you came to be involved in what is normally a man's world?'

'I was raised in the chandlery. I might not have had the advantage of a public school education, but I grew up in the East End and I know what's what.'

'I'm sure you do, and you are extremely good-looking as well, which must be an advantage.'

'Look, mister. You can save the flowery talk for your upper-class ladies. I'm offering you a good deal and I don't give a damn whether or not you think I'm pretty. I need an answer, yes or no.' For a moment, Eliza thought she had gone too far. Brandon was eyeing her with a mixture of respect and a flicker of irritation. It was easy to imagine that he was used to getting his own way, especially from those who he considered were the under class. Well, she was no one's lackey and if she failed to get financial backing from the Millers then she would go elsewhere. Folding her arms across her chest, Eliza waited for his answer.

'I can let you have storage space and the necessary transport, but as to the loan, I'll have to speak to my father about that.' Brandon went to his desk, sat down and wrote something on a sheet of paper.

'Of course.' Eliza fought to keep the note of sheer relief from her voice. She was glad that he had his head bent over the document so that he could not see that, now the ordeal was over, she was trembling.

'There. This gives instructions to my foreman to allot you a suitable space in the warehouse, where you may store your goods until such time as you are able to retrieve them. It also gives permission for the use of one of our drays and a driver.' Brandon handed the note to Eliza but snatched it away before she could take it, holding it just out of her reach. 'A smile would be nice, Miss Bragg.'

'If I was a man would you ask me to smile?'

A spark of genuine amusement replaced the teasing glint in Brandon's dark eyes. 'If you were a man we wouldn't be having this conversation.'

Torn between wanting to grab the note from his hands, the desire to wipe the grin off his face and the need to save her business, Eliza somehow managed to sketch her lips into a smile.

'There, that didn't hurt much, did it?' Brandon handed her the note.

'Thank you.' Clutching the piece of paper in her hand, Eliza rose from her seat with as much dignity as she could muster. She was about to leave the room when the door opened and Aaron entered the office.

'Miss Eliza. My clerk told me that you had asked to see me. I was so sorry to hear about poor old Ted. He was a good man and a craftsman; he'll be sorely missed.'

'Miss Bragg came to us for help, Father,' Brandon said smoothly. 'She has a business proposition for us, but I've told her that the decision rests with you.'

'Well, my dear. Last night I offered you my assistance and Aaron Miller doesn't go back on his word. Come to my office, the pair of you, and we'll discuss it over a glass of Madeira, or a cup of coffee if you'd prefer it, Eliza.'

Two hours later, Eliza arrived back at the chandlery seated on the cart beside the driver.

Her elation at reaching an agreement with Aaron was tempered with disappointment. He had agreed to lend her the money to rebuild the property, but only to the height of one storey. Without Ted as sailmaker and with the increasing number of steamships coming into use, he could not, he had said, as a man of business, warrant the expenditure on a sail loft that might soon be outdated and unprofitable. Eliza's heart sank as she saw Davy standing in the yard talking to Arnold. They had parted on a row this morning and now she was the bearer of bad news; it would seem that she had not tried on his behalf and that was just not true. She had done everything but beg Aaron to extend the loan to cover a second storey and sail loft, but he had been adamant. As the driver drew the horse to a halt, Davy came towards her with a conciliatory grin on his face and this only made Eliza feel worse. Dear Davy, always so kind and good-natured and now she was going to have to dash his hopes of taking over the business; it seemed dreadfully unfair. She held out her arms and allowed him to lift her down from the cart.

'I'm sorry.' They spoke the words in chorus and then laughed.

'No, I'm sorry,' Eliza said, smiling up at him. 'I was short-tempered. It was my fault.'

'I was being pig-headed as usual and I should have had more thought for you, Liza. After all you'd been through.' He took something out of his pocket and held his hand out to her. 'Ma found this on the floor in the pub.'

The gold brooch glinted in his palm and Eliza picked it up with a gasp of relief. 'I thought it was lost for ever.'

'And you'll wear it for me?'

'I will, Davy. When the mourning period for Ted is over. I will wear it. I promise.'

'Ahem,' the driver coughed.

'I'm sorry to keep you waiting, mister.' Eliza gave the driver an apologetic smile as she slipped the brooch into her pocket. 'Arnold, Dan.' She waved her hand to attract their attention. 'You can load the goods on the cart. It's going to a safe place until we can reopen the shop.'

Dan gave a whoop of joy, and Arnold managed a lopsided grin as they began hefting the barrels onto their shoulders.

'How did you get him and his wagon?' Davy demanded. 'And where've you been all this time, Liza?'

Taking him by the arm, Eliza moved aside to let Arnold and Dan get on with the work of loading the cart. 'We need to talk, Davy. I've got some good news, but I'm afraid I've got some bad news too.'

Chapter Thirteen

'There's only one thing for it now, Liza,' Davy said, walking slowly by her side as they made their way back to Hemp Yard. 'I'll have to find a shipmaster what'll take me on as sailmaker.'

'Oh, Davy, I'm so sorry.' Eliza tucked her hand in the crook of his arm. 'I tried me hardest to make Mr Miller see that it would be in his best interest to build a sail loft above the shop, but he wouldn't have it.'

'I know you did, and I love you all the more for it, Liza.'

'Don't say that. I've told you before, I ain't interested in romance.'

'You might feel different if it was that Brandon Miller chap showing an interest in you.'

'Don't talk soft.' With an exasperated sigh, Eliza pulled her hand away and was immediately sorry for her impatient gesture. She moderated her tone, trying to make a joke of it. 'What would I want with a lairy cove like him? He's so full of his own self-importance and his blooming Oxford education, learning about old Greek things. I got no patience with his sort.'

'Bleeding hell!' Davy was not listening to her and he stopped short, pointing his finger at two figures in front of them, one supporting the other as they weaved drunkenly from side to side in the street. Carters and draymen shouted streams of invective as the pair narrowly escaped being run down. 'It's me dad,' Davy said, breaking into a run.

Picking up her skirts, Eliza followed him. She reached them just as Davy hooked his father's arm round his shoulders.

'Do you know this man?' The well-dressed, bearded gentleman, who had been attempting to guide Arthur's drunken steps, turned his head to stare at Davy.

'It's me dad, sir. Where did you find him?'

'In Gutter Alley, dead to the world. A pitiful sight.'

'Pitiful, my eye. He's a disgrace. It would have served him right if you'd left him there and let the rats gnaw off his finger ends.'

'That's not a very Christian attitude, young man.'

'Maybe not, sir. But we've had to live with his drunkenness for as long as I can remember. I've watched me mum scrimp and save to feed us nippers with no help from him, the old bugger.'

'Come on, Davy,' Eliza said, tugging at his sleeve. 'Whatever he's done wrong, he needs a bit of help now. We'd best get him home.'

Arthur's legs buckled at the knees and his feet shot out in different directions. Davy and the bearded stranger staggered beneath his weight as they worked together to keep him from falling to the ground.

'If you don't mind me asking, sir,' Davy said breathlessly, 'who the devil are you?'

'I'm William Booth, my boy,' he said, relinquishing his hold on Arthur to put his top hat straight. 'I am a minister in the Methodist Church. My good wife, Catherine, and I run the East End Christian Mission in an attempt to save poor souls like your father.'

'No hope there, sir,' Davy said, hoisting Arthur over his shoulder in a fireman's lift. 'I'll take him on now; we're not far from home. I thank you for your trouble.'

William pulled a card from his breast pocket and handed it to Eliza. 'When this good man sobers up, send him round to my mission. We can help him.'

'Where's me new mate Willum?' Arthur demanded in a slurred voice as he hung over Davy's shoulder. 'Are we in Australia? You're all upside down.'

'God bless you, old chap,' William said, bending double to peer into Arthur's florid face. 'I hope to see you in the mission.'

'That'll be the day.' Davy walked off, staggering beneath Arthur's considerable weight.

'He don't mean to be rude, sir,' Eliza said, embarrassed by Davy's rudeness. After all, the gent had only been trying to help.

William smiled down at her. 'No need to apologise, my dear. But it would be of benefit both to Arthur and his family if he were to attend.'

She watched him walk away with the feeling that here was a great and a good man. Somehow all her troubles seemed trivial in the face of such a splendid spirit. Davy was halfway down the street and she had to run to catch up with him.

'Damned creeping Jesus,' he said, hefting Arthur higher on his shoulder. 'He should mind his own business. I'm going to take the old soak home.'

She knew better than to argue with Davy when he was angry. 'You do that, Davy. And be sure to tell Ada that she can have the house for as long as she wants it. There's no question of rent until you gets yourself fixed up with a ship.'

'At least Pete's still got his job in the brewery.' Davy shot her a resigned glance beneath his furrowed brows. 'I know the old lady will want to pay you something, but if you could cut the rent down a bit, I'd be more than grateful. I'll pay you back as soon as I can. I promise I will.'

'Don't even think about repayment. Friends and family help each other in times of need. You'd do the same for me.'

For a moment, Eliza thought she saw a tear sparkle in the corner of Davy's eye, but he turned away too quickly for her to be certain. She stood, watching him tote his human burden until he disappeared round the corner of Green Bank into Bird Street, then, with a heartfelt sigh, she made her way home to Hemp Yard. She would have to break the news gently to Millie that Davy would be going away to sea, and she must prepare Dolly for Ted's funeral: she didn't know which task was going to be the harder.

After the funeral, when everything had been paid for, including a modest wake held at Paddy's Goose, Eliza counted out the remainder of the money from the cash box. With strict economy, they might be able to live until Christmas, but without any income from the shop, and only half the rent from the property in Bird Street, it was going to be difficult.

Millie had moped about for a day or two after being told that Davy was looking for a shipmaster to take him on, and then without saying a word to Eliza she went out early one morning, returning late in the evening. By this time, Eliza was sick with worry, and she was about to send Davy out looking for her when Millie came breezing through the door, looking very pleased with herself. Eliza's initial outburst of anger was tempered with relief and then concern when she saw Millie's dishevelled and exhausted state. She would not listen to explanations until Millie had supped a bowl of bread and milk.

After she had eaten, Millie admitted that she had walked all the way to Covent Garden Market and had joined the women grubbing about amongst the flower stalls, picking up stray and broken blooms. The street flower sellers were a close-knit group who resented strangers encroaching on their territory, but they had seemed to take her youth into account and had not chased her off. The West End was their favoured place for setting up their pitches, and Millie had trudged all the way to the City where she had sold her nosegays on the steps of St Paul's. She pressed five pennies into Eliza's hand and blushed to the roots of her hair when Davy picked her up and kissed her on both cheeks.

Two weeks later, and after many hours of footslogging around the docks and wharves, Davy had found a captain of a tea clipper bound for India who was only too pleased to take him on as a sailmaker. It was a tearful farewell. Eliza wept silently, trying to put a brave face on things, but Millie hung around his neck, sobbing as if her heart would break.

Davy disentangled her arms and kissed her on the tip of her nose, smiling down into her tear-drenched blue eyes. 'Goodbye, nipper. Be good for Liza. She's going to need all your help.'

'You treat me like a kid,' Millie said, scowling.

Davy tugged at her tumbled curls. 'Don't never grow up. Stay just as you are, young Millie. I wouldn't change a single thing about you.'

'You don't understand nothing.' Millie's voice broke on a sob. She pushed past him and raced up the stairs. The whole house shook as she slammed the door of the room she shared with Eliza.

'What did I say?' Davy turned to Eliza with a baffled look.

She could not betray a confidence. 'Don't worry. She'll get over it.'

'Are you going somewhere then, Davy dear?' Dolly had been drowsing under the influence of laudanum, but the slamming of the door had awakened her with a start. She stared at Davy with a bemused frown. 'Are you going up West? Can I come with you?'

Eliza tucked a crocheted blanket around her. 'Not today, Mum. Maybe tomorrow.'

'Oh, but I want to go up West today.' Dolly's lips trembled and her eyes misted with tears. 'I need me medicine, Liza. I feel one of my turns coming on.'

'It's too soon, Mum. You had some not an hour ago.'

'I'm shaking all over. I'm having one of me turns.'

'Best go, Davy,' Eliza said, reaching for the bottle of laudanum.

'I'll wait outside.' Davy blew a kiss to Dolly and hurried out into the street.

As soon as Dolly was settled, Eliza followed him. He was leaning against the wall, waiting for her. He smiled and held out his arms. 'I'll miss you, girl.'

It seemed the most natural thing in the world to walk into his outstretched arms. Eliza smiled up into his face, realising just how much she would miss him. She had always taken Davy's presence for granted, but now he was really leaving: going away for months, maybe even years. He held her close and kissed her long and hard on the lips. 'I'll take the memory of that with me, girl.'

'Oh, Davy.' Eliza choked back tears as she saw the naked emotion in his eyes. She couldn't send him away thinking that she didn't care for him. It was a dangerous life at sea. What if he never came back? What if he were to disappear from her life like Bart and Freddie? She slipped her arms around his neck and closing her eyes she pulled his head down until their lips met. With the thought of their parting clamping like a cold hand on her heart, she gave herself up to the sensuous delight of being held in a man's arms and tasting the sweetness of her first real kiss. Something awakened inside her that was a need long denied, a heat and desire that was alien and frightening, but equally wonderful. Even as her body revelled in its first experience of sexual arousal, a small voice inside her head told her that this was wrong and she was cheating Davy by allowing it to happen. She tore her mouth free, pushing him away with the flat of her hands. This was all wrong – Davy was like a brother to her. For a mad, mad moment she had allowed herself to imagine that it was Freddie who held her in his arms, crushing her body against his, devouring her lips, touching her mind and soul and setting her pulses racing. She saw the hurt in Davy's eyes and she turned her head away with a laugh that sounded, even to her own ears, more like a sob. 'Get on with you, Davy. You'll have me crying too in a moment. Best go now. Best go.' When he did not answer, Eliza shot him an anxious glance beneath her lashes. She would remember that stark look for as long as she lived.

Silently, Davy picked up his ditty bag and strode off towards the docks.

'Oh, Davy,' Eliza whispered. 'I am so sorry.' But he was too far away to hear her. Unable to face going back into the house, she decided to walk as far as the chandlery: she needed to see how the work was progressing, and it would take her mind off the tumult of emotions that raged in her breast. She would not think about love and loss now; she would concentrate on the one solid thing in her life – the shop that was her rock, and her livelihood.

She would have liked to have had a say in the rebuilding of the store, but Aaron held the purse strings and he had given Brandon the task of overseeing the project. Brandon was at the site every day, giving orders and generally making himself unpopular. Eliza knew that the men disliked him and sniggered about his blatant lack of knowledge of the practical side of building, but at least he kept them from slacking. There was just one condition that she had insisted on before she signed the contract, and that was to have Arnold and Dippy Dan hired as labourers. She could not see faithful Arnold and his invalid mother go hungry. They had taken Dan in after his father had abandoned him, and now Arnold cared for the poor, slow-witted boy as if he were his own son.

Eliza paused on the corner of Old Gravel Lane, her problems momentarily eased by the sight of four bricklayers working on the beginnings of the new walls. It was early September, and, although the fierce heat had gone out of the sun, it was still warm and pleasant and above all dry, so that the work could progress at a pleasing rate. She could see Arnold's bare torso, glistening with sweat as he mixed cement, and Dan was helping him, or maybe hindering him. She smiled at the sight of the unlikely pair working together. Arnold seemed to have endless patience with Dan and made use of his muscle power, if not his brains. As she crossed the street, she looked up at the sound of an approaching horse's hooves. Her heart sank as she saw Brandon riding towards her. As usual, he was impeccably dressed from his gleaming leather boots to the points of his starched shirt collar. As he drew his chestnut stallion to a halt beside her, he lifted a gloved hand to doff his top hat. 'Miss Bragg. Good morning.'

Even more conscious of her faded, outdated mourning dress and shabby bonnet, Eliza bobbed a curtsey. 'Good morning, Mr Miller.' She was about to walk on, but he dismounted and leading his horse by its reins he fell into step beside her.

'It won't be long now and you'll have your emporium ready for business.'

'Yes, the builders seem to be doing a splendid job.'

'Only because I keep them at it. Turn your back on these fellows and they'll not only slack, but they'll sell off materials and find no end of different ways to cheat their employer. They need a firm hand, Miss Bragg, just like a thoroughbred Arab stallion.'

'Or a woman?' Eliza shot him a sideways glance. She had vowed that she would not antagonise him, but somehow the words always seemed to escape from her lips before she could stop them.

Brandon stopped, eyeing her suspiciously, and then he laughed. 'I wouldn't have the nerve to say that to a spirited woman such as yourself.'

'But you think it nevertheless?' Somehow she couldn't stop needling him. He was so cocksure of himself that Eliza wanted to prick the bubble of his self-esteem, but it seemed that she had failed again as everything she said appeared to amuse him. It was so frustrating that she would have liked to knock his top hat to the ground and stamp on it.

'Here, boy!' Brandon waved at Dan. 'Hold my horse.'

Dan looked up at Arnold, who nodded his assent.

'Handle him carefully, boy,' Brandon said, handing over the reins. 'Walk him up and down and have a care. That nag cost me a fortune at Tattersalls.'

As Dan led the horse up the street, Eliza turned to Brandon with an exasperated sigh. 'Don't you never stop boasting about your blooming money?'

A pained expression muddied his dark eyes. 'That isn't fair. I was just stating a point.'

'You was boasting. You can't forget that your dad is rich, but it doesn't make you better than the rest of us, Brandon Miller.'

His frown dissolved into a smile. 'You called me Brandon. That's the first time I've heard you use my Christian name, Eliza. I may call you Eliza, mayn't I?'

Shrugging her shoulders, Eliza stepped over the threshold into what would be the main shop area of the chandlery. 'Call me what you like, Mr Miller. But I'd prefer to keep our business dealings formal.'

'Don't be like that, my dear. We got off on the wrong foot, but I'd like us to be friends as well as business partners.'

She turned to give him a cool look. 'Why? Why would you want to be friends with a common girl like me? You've made it pretty plain what you think of the lower orders, so why bother to pretend?'

'I'm hurt. No, I'm more than hurt that you think of me as a – a snob. I have standards it's true, but I would never look down on a beautiful and clever young woman such as yourself.'

'There you go again,' Eliza said, shaking her head. 'You can't help it, can you? Patronising, pompous and too big for your breeches.'

'There, you do like me. Admit it, Eliza. You find me irresistible.'

She was about to retaliate, when she saw a twinkle in his eyes. The humour behind his banter was not lost on Eliza and she managed a smile. 'I suppose you're not all that bad really.'

'So we can be friends as well as business colleagues?'

'Maybe, but only if you stop treating me like an empty-headed butterfly-brain.'

With an exaggerated gesture, Brandon crossed his heart. 'I will, but only on the condition that you accept my father's invitation to our home for dinner on Friday evening.'

'Oh, I don't know about that. I don't go out much.'

'Then you should. A pretty young – I mean a businesswoman such as yourself ought to get out socially. You would meet merchants, traders and ship owners who would be useful contacts in the commercial world.'

She had nothing to wear that was suitable for such a grand occasion. Eliza shook her head. 'No. I'd like to, but I can't.'

'Of course you can. I'll send our carriage to pick you up at seven-thirty on Friday evening. I'm sure you wouldn't want to disappointment my father, now would you?'

Ada poured tea into a chipped china cup for which there was no saucer. 'That's only four days away, Liza. A dinner party with a lot of toffs. I wouldn't fancy that.'

'It's business, Ada,' Eliza said, taking the cup of tea and staring into the clear straw-coloured liquid. She knew very well how precious the much-used tea leaves were, but she had not wanted to offend Ada by refusing her hospitality.

'All the same,' Ada said, easing herself onto one of the hard wooden chairs. 'You can't go to a gaff like that if you ain't got the proper duds.'

'I know, and I can't afford to buy nothing new, not even from the pawnbrokers or second-hand from Lumber Court down St Giles way.'

'Huh,' Ada said, sipping her tea. 'All you'd get there is fleas and lice. No, we got to think of something else. I feel so bad that I can't pay you the full rent, Liza. I'll have to wait until next month afore I can get my allotment from the shipping company and Arthur's still not working.'

'He's on the drink again?'

'No. He's always down the mission run by that Mr Booth these days. Mary and Millie encouraged him to go; the two of them was convinced that Mr Booth could get him off the booze.'

'And did he?'

'Yes, dear. He's not touched a drop for two weeks, but now he spends all his time at prayer meetings asking the Lord for help. I ain't sure what's worse. Neither way brings in any money.'

'But you have enough to feed the family?'

'We're managing. Eddie earns a few coppers as a shoeblack, though I'd rather he attended the ragged school with Artie and Sammy. Then Mary brings us some leftovers from the kitchen at the big house in Islington; that is when she gets her afternoon off.' Ada paused, and her tired eyes lit up as if she had had a wonderful idea. 'I know, we'll ask Mary. It's her half day tomorrow and she might be able to help you do up one of your old frocks, Liza. She's been promoted to lady's maid. The poor girl what had the job went down with smallpox on a visit home, and that was her done for. So Mary got the job. They say it's an ill wind, don't they? Anyway, I'll send her round to see you as soon as she comes home.'

As Eliza walked home to Hemp Yard, she felt as if a big, black cloud was hanging over her, even though the sun was still shining and the heat reflecting up from the cobblestones. She doubted whether Mary would be able to help, although she hadn't liked to say as much to Ada. She was not certain if anyone could help her out of this particular situation; she could plead illness or a sick headache, but if she did so then she would miss an opportunity to make her mark amongst the very people who would help her resurrect the business. It was at times like this that Eliza missed Bart the most. She tried not to dwell on what might have been if he had lived, but, in truth, she could not entirely believe that he was dead. In her heart, she hoped that one day he would turn up on the doorstep, grinning and telling her that reports of his untimely demise had been a terrible mistake. Then there was Freddie. It was too painful to let her thoughts dwell on what might have happened to him.

She arrived home, not in the best of spirits. Millie was sitting on a stool beside Dolly, reading to her from the Bible, although Dolly had her eyes closed and seemed to be fast asleep. Millie looked up and smiled. 'I got home early, Liza. Sold all me flowers and made threepence. We'll have boiled bacon and pease pudding for dinner tonight.'

'Threepence! You did well,' Eliza said, taking off her bonnet. 'But I don't like to think of you walking all the way to Covent Garden and back each day, let alone sitting outside St Paul's in all weathers.'

'It ain't so bad, Liza. I don't mind and at least it's a good pitch. Sitting at the bottom of the steps I can hear the organ playing and watch the people going in and out. They're a bit more generous when they come out from a holy place.'

'It's still not right that you should have to sell flowers on street corners.'

'The Lord helps them what helps themselves,' Millie said, smiling. 'Mr Booth said that at one of the Christian Mission meetings. I've learnt all sorts of things there, and I get comfort from praying for Davy's safe return.'

'That's another thing. I know you took Mr

Little to the mission because you care for Davy and his family, but it ain't right for you to associate with all them topers and drug addicts.'

'You worry too much, Liza. I like singing hymns and Catherine, Mrs Booth, is thinking of starting a soup kitchen for the poor. She says I can help her and it stops me thinking about Davy all the time.'

Eliza felt the colour rise to her cheeks as she remembered the hunger of Davy's kiss and her unexpected response. What could have possessed her to encourage him when she loved Davy only as a brother? She tried to think of something comforting to say, but Dolly stirred in her chair and opened her eyes, staring at Eliza. 'Why are you dressed all in black like a crow, Liza?'

'I'm in mourning for Ted.' Eliza went to Dolly's side and held her hand. 'Don't you remember?'

'No dear, Ted's working in the sail loft.' Dolly gave her the sunniest of smiles. 'You must be thinking of someone else. Ted will be home in a while and he'll get my supper.'

'Yes, Mum, of course he will.'

'Is it time for me medicine, Liza?'

Exchanging worried glances with Millie, Eliza shook her head. 'Not yet.'

Dolly shivered. 'I think it is. Go and fetch Ted, tell him I want me medicine. If you can't find Ted then get that nice man, Dr Freddie, he'll make me up a bottle of the elixir. He knows how to make me feel better.'

Eliza patted her hand. 'Don't fret, Mum. I'll get you some medicine.' She went to the mantelshelf and took down the brown glass bottle. It was empty.

'I know what you're going to say,' Millie said, shaking her head. 'But we got to wean her off that stuff, it's bad for her. Drugs come direct from the devil, that's what Mr Booth says. Drugs and drink are both as bad as each other.'

Eliza slipped the bottle into her pocket. Sometimes she could happily go down to the mission and strangle Mr Booth. He seemed to have both Millie and Arthur permanently in his thrall. She couldn't argue with the sense of what he was preaching, but then he didn't have to live with Dolly, whose mind wandered at the best of times, and whose only relief came from a small, brown medicine bottle. She reached for Ted's tobacco tin where she kept the money set aside for housekeeping. Shaking the pennies out into her hand, she repressed a sigh; the money was disappearing at an alarming rate. Dolly's constant need for laudanum was not only worrying but it was also expensive. Eliza stared at the coins in her hand, reluctant to spend any of it on a drug that was stealing what was left of Dolly's mind, but painfully aware of the results if she were to deprive her of her one comfort. 'There's nothing for it, Millie. You know what we'll go through tonight if she don't get her laudanum and I can't face it.'

Millie hesitated for a moment and then she held out her hand. 'Give me the bottle. I'll do it, but I don't like it.'

'I don't like it either, but we can't let her suffer.'

'I'll go to the apothecary's on the way back from the pie shop,' Millie said, jingling the pennies in her hand. 'I'm blooming starving.'

When she had gone, Eliza considered lighting the fire in the range in order to boil a kettle of water for tea, but she abandoned the idea. What little coal was left must be hoarded against the approach of autumn and bad weather. Their financial situation was dire and, whether she wanted to or not, she must attend the dinner party given by Aaron Miller. She would need all the help she could muster to get the business going before the onset of winter.

Late on Friday afternoon, Mary arrived at the house carrying a bolster case that looked as though it were about to burst its seams. She thrust it into Eliza's arms with a nervous smile.

'I can't stay, Liza. Mrs Wilkins will skin me alive if she finds out I've left the house without her permission.'

'Ta, Mary. I can't thank you enough for this.'

Eliza looked inside with a gasp of pleasure. 'What a lovely colour, and it's real silk too.'

Millie leapt up from her seat at the table to help her extricate the shimmering folds of the evening gown. To Eliza's astonishment, there seemed to be yards and yards of whisper-soft pink silk, trimmed with cobwebs of fine lace. 'It's the most beautiful thing I've ever seen, but it's too good. I daren't wear this, Mary.'

'You'd better, since I risked me neck to borrow this for you. Luckily, Miss Cynthia is away in Hertfordshire staying with her grandparents and not expected back for a week. Just don't spill anything on it, Liza. And don't let no one near you with sticky fingers or I'll be dead meat.'

'Stop saying that,' Millie said, frowning. 'She's nervous enough already. You got to stay a bit, Mary, and put Liza's hair up for her because I don't know how to do it and you do.'

Mary bit her lip, glancing at the clock on the mantelshelf. 'Well, I suppose I could stay for half an hour. Sit down then, Liza. Let's see what I can do for you.'

At precisely seven-thirty, the Millers' coachman knocked on the door to escort Eliza to the carriage that was waiting in the main street, Hemp Yard being too narrow to allow anything longer than a donkey cart to turn around. As she walked behind the coachman, she could see faces

317

peering at her through grimy windows. Others stood in their doorways, watching her open-mouthed. Tomorrow she would be the talk of the yard, and tongues would be wagging; the gossips would be wondering how a poor girl could afford such a gown. She could almost hear them suggesting that she was no better than she should be; all done up like a dog's dinner and going off in a private carriage. They would say there was a man at the back of it, a fancy man with money. She held her head high, concentrating on subduing the writhing snakes in her stomach. Tonight she had to make a good impression. As Eliza stepped into the Millers' carriage, she had never felt so frightened or alone.

By the time they reached the imposing frontage of the Millers' Queen Anne mansion, she was in two minds whether or not to plead sickness and return home. The coachman opened the door, pulled down the step and offered her his arm. She could still make her excuses. But it was too late – a liveried footman had opened the front door and Aaron was coming towards her, smiling and holding out both hands. 'My dear Miss Eliza, you look absolutely stunning.'

She didn't know whether to shake his hand or bob a curtsey. In the end she did both. 'It was kind of you to invite me, Mr Miller.'

'Come and meet my wife.' Aaron led her into the marble entrance hall, which seemed as large at St Paul's Cathedral to her bemused eyes. He took her into a reception room crowded with people who were all staring at her, smiling and nodding. A sea of strangers, Eliza thought, in which she might sink without trace if she were not very careful. Brandon was standing beside a woman who seemed to be the hostess and, Eliza reasoned, must be his mother. He was smiling at her, but there was a teasing glint in his eyes that made her spine stiffen and brought her chin up. She bobbed a curtsey to Mrs Miller, who seemed small and inconspicuous beside her tall, elegantly dressed son.

'Anne, this is Miss Eliza Bragg, the young woman who owns the chandlery.' Aaron turned to Eliza. 'Miss Eliza, my wife Anne.'

Anne looked Eliza up and down and her lips smiled but her eyes were cold. 'How do you do, Miss Bragg. Welcome to our home.'

'Thank you, ma'am.'

'Brandon, do your duty,' Anne said, tapping him on the arm with her furled fan. 'Introduce Miss Bragg to the rest of our guests.'

As Brandon offered her his arm, Eliza knew that she had not made a good impression on his tight-lipped mother. But the appreciative sparkle in Brandon's eyes told her that the combined efforts of Millie and Mary had not been in vain.

They had tugged at the laces on her stays until she could barely draw a breath, but she could probably boast the smallest waist in the room. Her neck felt as though it would snap beneath the weight of her hair elaborately coiffed into a pale golden coronet on the top of her head, skilfully threaded with beads and silk flowers by Mary. She could not look down without blushing at the expanse of bare bosom revealed by the low-cut gown, but Brandon and the other gentlemen were obviously relishing the sight.

'You look good enough to eat, Eliza,' Brandon whispered in her ear as he guided her across the red carpet towards a prosperous-looking man seated with his overdressed, bejewelled wife. 'Smile at the old buffers and they'll be falling over themselves to give you trade discounts and put business your way.'

By the time they had done the full circle of the room, Eliza felt that her smile had set in concrete on her face. Brandon had done nearly all the talking, speaking for her and squeezing her arm when he wanted her to make the appropriate response; she was beginning to feel like a ventriloquist's doll.

'You did well, Eliza,' he said, taking a glass of sherry from a tray proffered by a servant and handing it to her. 'The men will be eating out of your pretty little hand.'

'Maybe, but the women all hate me.' Eliza

gulped a mouthful of the wine and felt the unaccustomed alcohol shoot straight to her head. She had not eaten all day and she had never drunk anything stronger than port and lemon or small beer.

'Steady on,' Brandon said, raising an eyebrow and grinning. 'You'll get squiffy if you carry on like that.'

'I shouldn't have come. They all think I'm a tart.'

'They're not used to women in business, especially young and beautiful women like you, Eliza. Don't judge them too harshly, and use your looks and charm to your advantage.'

Sipping her drink a little more slowly, Eliza stared up at him over the rim of the glass. 'How come you know so much all of a sudden?'

'All right, I may not be an expert in building and shipping, but I did learn something at university and that was how to mix with the upper classes as well as the people in trade, like us. Be confident, Eliza. Think of yourself as just as good, if not better than these people and they'll love you for it. Let them see that you're unsure of yourself and they'll walk all over you.'

'How am I supposed to be nice to them when they stare at me boobies?' Eliza said, fanning herself vigorously as she caught the lecherous glance of a middle-aged tobacco merchant seated on the opposite side of the room next to his snooty-looking wife.

'Come now, you can't blame him. Just remember he charters a fleet of ships to import tobacco. You need men like Brigham Stone to put business your way and get you back on your feet.'

Casting a covert glance at the toad-like Stone, Eliza shuddered. 'I think he wants to get me off me feet, Brandon, and flat on me back.'

Brandon's laugh echoed round the ornate high ceiling and there was a momentary lull in the conversation as all heads turned towards them.

'Won't you share the joke, Brandon?' Aaron's voice broke the silence.

Brandon opened his mouth to reply and Eliza stamped on his foot. Her soft satin slipper, also borrowed from Miss Cynthia, could not have made much impact on his leather shoe, but it surprised him enough to hold his tongue. Luckily for Eliza, the butler announced that dinner was served and the assembled company rose to their feet. She would not have been surprised if they had stampeded into the dining room bellowing like a herd of hungry bullocks, but they lined up in pairs and, to her dismay, Brigham Stone offered her his arm. She looked to Brandon to save her, but he nodded as if telling her that she must accept, and he escorted Mrs Stone into the dining room.

If Eliza had thought things were difficult earlier, she was horrified to see the mahogany dining table, stretching, it seemed, for miles, glittering with silver and crystal and an alarming array of cutlery at each place setting. She was seated between Brigham Stone, who kept leaning over and speaking to her with his eyes wandering to the swell of her breasts, and on the other side a short, fat man with a fuzz of white hair sprouting in tufts from a shining bald pate. He had been introduced as Silas Granger, a manufacturer of brass instruments, and he was trying to talk to her, quite sensibly, about stocking her store with his chronometers, sextants and compasses. When the first course was served, Eliza was relieved to find that it was soup, but which spoon should she use? Watching out of the corner of her eye, she saw Mr Granger lift the rounded spoon on the outside right of his cutlery. Swallowing a mouthful of red wine, Eliza picked up her spoon, but the maid was offering her a bread roll and she almost knocked her wine over as she reached out to take the bread. It was a nightmare, and as course replaced course, Eliza ate very little, sipping her wine and trying to copy the table manners of the other guests.

By the time dessert arrived, she was feeling quite tipsy and her head was swimming. She was fed up with Brigham's suggestive remarks, and he kept touching her thigh beneath the table-cloth. Finally, when his fingers moved insistently towards the top of her leg, Eliza could stand it no longer and she stuck her fork in his offending hand. Brigham let out a yelp of pain, jerking his arm away and spilling Eliza's glass of red wine down the front of her frock. Stunned with shock, Eliza watched the blood-red liquid trickle down between her breasts, staining the pink silk as if he had stabbed her in the heart.

Chapter Fourteen

There was a moment of horrified silence as Eliza rose slowly to her feet, staring at the fingers of crimson wine creeping down the bodice of her borrowed gown. Then everyone started talking at once, offering sympathy and advice on how best to remove wine stains from silk. Brigham's face glowed ruby-red and he made an ineffectual attempt to dab at her bodice with his table napkin, but Eliza seized him by the wrist, gripping it tightly in her clawed fingers. 'This was your fault, mister,' she hissed, through clenched teeth.

Brigham shot a nervous glance at his wife who was sitting opposite him, visibly bristling. His mouth wobbled into a parody of a smile but his eyes were codfish-cold as he turned on Eliza. 'You stabbed me in the hand, you little bitch.'

'My dear Miss Bragg,' Brandon said, getting hastily to his feet. 'What an unfortunate mishap.' He signalled to the butler who was hovering near the serving table. 'Mason, send for my mother's maid. I'm sure she will know how best to limit the damage to Miss Bragg's gown.'

Eliza nodded her thanks, forcing a smile. She dug her fingernails into Brigham's fat wrist. 'You'll pay for a new gown, or I'll tell your missis just what your wandering hand was doing beneath the tablecloth.'

His pale grey eyes bulged from their sockets. 'All right, all right. Keep your voice down.'

'You're a real gent.' Eliza released his arm. She glanced round at the concerned diners, raising her voice. 'It weren't your fault that I spilt me wine, Mr Stone. But I call it more than generous to offer to replace me frock.' Despite the fact that she was trembling from head to foot, she bobbed a curtsey to her host and hostess. 'It's been lovely, but as you can see I really need to go home and get out of these wet duds. So if you'll all kindly excuse me.'

'Must you leave so soon?' Brandon had made his way round the table and was standing at her side. 'I'm certain that my mother would be only too happy to loan you something dry to wear.'

Anne Miller sucked in her cheeks. 'Of course,' she said, in a strangled voice.

'Ta, but I wouldn't want to put you to so much trouble.' As she left the table, Eliza leaned towards Brigham whose colour had drained from his face leaving him with a sickly pallor. 'I'm holding you to it. I'll be round at your place in the morning to collect.'

He stared at her with narrowed eyes, lowering

his voice so that only she could hear. 'That won't be necessary. I'll send my man round to the chandlery first thing in the morning. Be there.'

'Don't worry, I will.' Tucking her hand through Brandon's proffered arm, Eliza allowed him to lead her from the dining room. She could hear the babble of voices rising above the sound of shuffling movements as the gentlemen, having risen from their seats as she left the table, sat down again. Knowing that she was the main topic of conversation, Eliza felt her cheeks burning but she held her head high, biting her lip to keep back tears of humiliation.

As they walked through the anteroom and out into the spacious entrance hall, Brandon shot Eliza a worried glance. 'Won't you change your mind, Eliza? It seems a pity to spoil the evening just because of a trifling accident.'

Trifling! Eliza bit back the sharp retort that rose to her lips. Did this spoilt young man not realise how desperate a situation had been caused by this trifling accident? No, she thought bitterly, of course he did not. He had been brought up in a world so dissimilar from her own that, although they were separated only by a few mean streets, they might as well have been raised on different planets. Mary had risked her job to borrow this gown, and if her employers discovered what she had done, then she would be cast off without a reference or, even worse, might find herself up in front of the beak for stealing. And all this was the fault of one lecherous old man who couldn't keep his hands to himself. Eliza had enough experience of the world to know that men like Brigham Stone treated women as playthings, objects of lust but entirely disposable. They didn't believe that women had brains and if they did encounter a female who admitted to thinking about anything other than frills and furbelows, they labelled them as bluestockings, a disgrace to their sex and unnatural. It had been a terrible mistake, she thought miserably; she should have refused the invitation in the first place. Casting a sideways glance at Brandon, she saw to her disgust that he was staring at the sticky snail-trail of wine on her breasts as if he would like to lick it off with his tongue. There was a hot, unfocused look in his eyes that she had seen on many occasions when men had propositioned her. If only she were a man, she would punch Brandon on his aquiline nose. But she was not a man and she could not afford to insult the Millers and so she smiled. 'No, ta. I must go home.'

'Then I'll send for the carriage.'

'I can walk. It ain't far.' If she stayed a minute longer, Eliza was afraid that she would lose her tenuous grip on self-control and she would disgrace herself by crying.

Brandon's dark eyebrows knotted together over the top of his nose and he shook his head vehemently. 'No. It's not safe for a young woman to walk these streets at night. I won't hear of it. You'll go in our carriage and I won't take no for an answer.'

Before she could reply, he had barked an order at the footman who was standing to attention in the vestibule. The servant hurried outside to summon the carriage and Eliza shivered as a cool breeze wafted in through the open door. She had come as she was, not having a suitable wrap or a half-decent shawl, and now she was feeling distinctly chilly with goose pimples popping out all over her bare arms.

'You're cold,' Brandon said, placing an arm around her shoulders.

'Only a bit.'

With a swift movement, Brandon twisted her round and kissed her on the lips. It was a brief salute, and he drew back almost instantly with an apologetic smile dancing in his eyes, but his arms still held her. 'Forgive me, Miss Bragg. I'm afraid I gave in to temptation.'

A polite cough from the footman made Brandon release her.

'The carriage is outside, sir.'

Eliza stepped away from him. She was trembling with affront and anger. How dare he kiss her on the mouth like a common tart! If only Bart were here, he wouldn't stand for a man's taking advantage of his sister. But then if Bart were here, she wouldn't have to go begging for money from wealthy merchants. Brandon's swift embrace had only added to the disastrous events of the evening. She had made a scene at dinner, and the borrowed gown was ruined. Things could hardly get much worse.

'Let's get you into the carriage, my dear,' Brandon said smoothly and without any apparent embarrassment. 'I'd see you home myself, but Father and I have some important business to discuss with the gentlemen after the ladies have retired to the withdrawing room.'

He offered her his arm, moving so close to her that she could smell the bay rum pomade that slicked his hair to his well-shaped head, and the faint scent of cigar smoke that clung to his evening suit. It brought back the dreadful memories of the night of the fire when he had dragged her clear of the collapsing wall: that fatal night that had changed her life. She held her head high and suffered Brandon to lead her to the waiting carriage.

He helped her into the vehicle, momentarily holding on to her hand and raising it to his lips. 'We must do this again and soon, my dear. I think you and I could do extremely well together.' With a disarming smile, he stepped back to allow the footman to close the carriage door.

She could have cried, although this time it was

with pure relief. The evening had been a complete disaster, but at least she was now on her way home. She might not have the physical power to fight off the unwanted attentions of men, but there were other weapons at her disposal and a sharp tongue was one of them. As the coachman urged the horses forward, Eliza leaned out of the window staring pointedly at Brandon's shirtfront, which was stained with a blush of pink where he had held her close to his chest. 'Oh dear,' she said, curving her lips in a smile and fluttering her eyelashes. 'I'm afraid the wine has ruined your nice white shirt, Mr Miller. What will your mother make of that, I wonder?' She had the satisfaction of seeing the smile wiped from his face as he glanced down at his stained shirtfront. As she sank back against the leather squabs, Eliza felt a bubble of hysterical laughter rise in her throat.

The carriage sped through the dark streets and she was dimly aware of the coachman shouting at revellers, who either were too drunk to be aware of the danger of flying hooves and carriage wheels, or were deliberately baiting the driver of an expensive equipage. The crack of a whip and the exchange of abuse were just background noise as Eliza struggled to imagine how she would break the news to Mary that the gown was ruined. Although she was well aware of the dangers of driving down Ratcliff Highway at night, even in a closed carriage, she pushed the thought to the back of her mind. It was not uncommon for coachmen to be dragged from their vehicles and clubbed to the ground, the occupants robbed and sometimes murdered and the horses stolen. But it seemed that Aaron Miller's coachman was well equipped and, at one point, when the horses were forced to a halt whinnying and neighing with fright, Eliza heard the sharp report of a pistol shot and then the coach lurched forward, moving at a spanking pace. As they reached the narrow entrance to Hemp Yard, the coachman drew the horses to a halt. He barked instructions to a couple of street urchins to hold the horses while he saw the young lady to her door.

'You can't be too careful, miss,' the coachman said as he helped her down onto the cobble-stones. 'This here place is beyond the law and young ladies like yourself shouldn't be out alone at night. I wouldn't let me own daughters do it and you shouldn't neither.'

Too tired and emotional to argue, Eliza allowed him to escort her to the front door. He waited while she turned the key in the lock. 'Thank you,' Eliza said, smiling. 'You was kind, mister.'

'Hawkins, miss. And it weren't nothing.' He tipped his hat and went off into the darkness.

Eliza went inside and closed the door. She had

hoped that Millie would be in bed, but she was seated at the kitchen table reading a book in the guttering light of a single candle. She looked up with a surprised expression. 'You're home early, Liza. Did you have a good time?'

'It was business. I didn't expect to enjoy myself.' Reluctantly, Eliza moved into the circle of candlelight. 'I had a bit of a mishap, Millie.'

Millie's eyes opened wide and her hand flew to her mouth. 'You're bleeding.'

'No, I'm not. It's a wine stain. Red wine got spilt down me front.' Eliza pulled out a chair and sank down onto the hard wooden seat. 'I dunno what I'm going to do about it. I made the old bugger promise to pay for it, but that's not going to help Mary.' Now that she was safe at home, the whole horror of the evening crowded in on her and tears flowed down her cheeks. With a cry of distress, Millie flung her arms round her and they clung to each other sobbing.

Eliza found that having let go, she couldn't stop: she was crying for the ruined gown, for letting Mary down so badly, for Bart's death in a foreign land, for Freddie's transportation to Australia, for Ted who had been like a father to her; for her lost youth and unfulfilled dreams. At last, exhausted by the tempest of tears, she gulped and sniffed, patting Millie's back as if she were a baby. 'There, there, don't take on so. I –

I'm sure we can find a way out of this. Things will look better in the morning.'

Next morning, leaving Millie still asleep and looking touchingly young and vulnerable with her face tear-stained, and her curls matted around her forehead, Eliza got up early. She crept downstairs to the back yard where she held her head under the pump, allowing the cool water to wash away the traces of last night's storm of emotion. Drying her hair on a scrap of towelling, she went into the living room and dressed herself in her plain, grey gown. She was about to take the mourning brooch from the mantelshelf but she hesitated, running the tips of her fingers over the glass dome and the silver mount. The pale lock of plaited hair lying on a bed of silk was now as faded as the daguerreotype of her mother, who had lived for so long in her imagination but was now just a ghostly image on a piece of tin. With one last tender touch of her finger, Eliza left the brooch where it was. The time for grieving was past and she must face up to the future on her own. Sentiment must be set aside and she must not show herself to the world as a vulnerable young woman: if she was to succeed in a society run by men like Brigham Stone and Brandon Miller then she must use her brains and never let them spot her weaknesses. Brushing her hair vigorously, Eliza scraped it back from her face in a severe style, securing the bulk of it in a snood at the nape of her neck. She had never thought herself particularly pretty, and she was mystified why men seemed to find her attractive, but that only led to trouble. She intended to appear mature and businesslike when she met Brigham Stone's man at the chandlery. He would probably try to haggle and do her down as to the amount of money to recompense for the ruined gown, but Mary's job was at stake here. Eliza had no clear idea how they would repair the damage before young Miss Cynthia Wilkins arrived home from Hertfordshire, but she would think about that later.

She let herself quietly out of the house and headed in the direction of Old Gravel Lane. A cool easterly breeze tugged at her shawl and played with the ribbons on her bonnet. A pale, buttery sun was struggling to pierce the early morning autumn mist, and from the river Eliza could hear the muted moan of foghorns. Wrapping her shawl more tightly around her body, Eliza quickened her pace until she reached the chandlery. Standing on the opposite side of the street, she felt a buzz of excitement at the sight of the walls rising from the ashes. The front door and shop window were already in place, but unglazed, and the carpenters were chipping and sawing at rafters and beams for the roof. She could just see the top of Arnold's head and no doubt Dippy Dan was near at hand helping him in whatever task they were doing at the moment. At this rate the store would be finished well before Christmas and she would be back in business. The mere thought of regaining control over her life made her spine tingle and her pulses race.

The moment of elation passed as Eliza remembered the reason why she had come to the building site so early in the morning. She paced up and down for what seemed like an hour and was beginning to think that Brigham had either forgotten his promise or had reneged on it, when she heard the clip-clop of horses' hooves and the rumble of carriage wheels on the cobblestones. Turning her head, she saw a private carriage rounding the corner of Old Gravel Lane and the coachman drew the horses to a halt outside the chandlery. Her heart sank as Brigham Stone himself stepped out onto the pavement, a cigar clenched between his teeth and an uncompromising expression on his face.

'Miss Eliza.' Brigham strolled across the road to stand in front of her.

He was too close for comfort and Eliza instinctively took a step backwards but she met his stern gaze, looking him in the eye and hoping that she appeared more confident than she was feeling. 'Good morning, Mr Stone.'

'You've caused me a lot of bother, miss.' Brigham glared at her, chewing on his cigar. 'I don't usually deal with petty extortionists myself but when they're young and pretty, I make an exception.'

Eliza felt her hackles rise; she didn't like the tone of his voice or the lecherous gleam in his eyes. Making a great effort, she managed to control her desire to slap his fat face. 'I don't want nothing but a fair recompense for the damage you caused last night, mister.'

Moving the cigar from one side of his mouth to the other, Brigham gave a derisive snort. 'You may have looked like a young lady last night, but this morning you look like a drab and you talk like a guttersnipe. Don't think you can compete with men of business, my dear. The only place that you'd be of interest to me is naked and in my bed.'

'Don't you dare speak to me like that. I've run my business successfully for the last few years without having to crawl to men like you.'

'Hoity-toity!' Brigham spat his cigar butt onto the pavement, grinding it into the ground with the heel of his boot. 'But I like a bit of spirit in my women.' He slipped his hand into his inside breast pocket and pulled out a leather pouch from which he extracted two golden sovereigns. 'Here, this will pay for a new gown.'

Eliza held out her hand to receive the money

but even as Brigham offered it to her, he closed his fingers over the coins. 'But I expect something in return.'

'What?' Eliza heard her voice crack with anxiety and she realised that she must have shouted when she saw Arnold's worried face peering through the window of the chandlery. She lowered her voice. 'What do you mean? You promised me.'

Brigham's eyes narrowed and he pushed his face close to hers. 'You tried to blackmail me, you little bitch.'

'Anything wrong, missis?' Arnold vaulted through the open window and was loping across the road towards them, balancing his ungainly gait by flailing his arms in a fair imitation of a windmill.

Eliza held up her hand. She would like nothing better than for Arnold to rip Brigham Stone into little pieces but that would not serve. 'It's all right, Arnold. We was just discussing business.'

Fisting his hands, Arnold let them drop to his sides, glowering at Brigham. 'If you say so, miss.'

'Best get back to work,' Eliza said, making a huge effort to sound calm. She lowered her voice. 'Don't threaten me, Mr Stone. I can still go to your missis and snitch on you, so don't think I wouldn't do it.'

'And I can tell Aaron Miller that you are a cheating little trollop who doesn't deserve financial backing. If my friend Aaron were to demand repayment of his loan now you would be in Queer Street, my dear.'

Eliza held out her hand. 'I only want what's due to me.'

'I admire brass neck,' Brigham said, dropping the coins into her palm and closing her fingers over the money. 'But I think you're wasting your obvious natural talents in trying to do a man's work.'

The implication of his words was obvious, and Eliza tried to pull her hand away but he gripped it with surprising strength, making her wince with pain. 'Let go of me, you're hurting.' She attempted to prise his fingers open with her free hand, but this only seemed to amuse him. For a moment she thought she was going to have to cry out to Arnold for help, but the sound of horses' hooves diverted Brigham's attention. His expression changed from amused contempt to one of annoyance. He dropped Eliza's hand as if her flesh had burnt his fingers. She looked over her shoulder and saw that it was Brandon who was almost upon them.

He drew his horse to a halt beside them, and he dismounted with an ominous scowl contorting his handsome features. 'What's going on, Stone?'

'Nothing to concern you, Brandon. Keep out of my affairs.'

'Miss Bragg is my concern. We're business

partners in case you hadn't realised it, so her welfare is of great interest to me.'

Eliza stamped her foot. 'Will you two stop talking about me as if I ain't here?'

There was a moment of silence as they stared at her in surprise. She could see that Brigham's mouth was working, like a landed salmon gasping for breath on the quay wall, but she ignored him, turning her attention to Brandon. 'Mr Stone and me was discussing a business matter and now it's settled. I'll bid you both good day, gentlemen. I got better things to do than stand round arguing with the likes of you.' She stalked off with her head held high, curbing the desire to break into a run. Her heart was thundering away inside her chest like a runaway horse and, although she heard Brandon calling after her and begging her to stop, she ignored his pleas, praying inwardly that he would not follow her.

At the point where Old Gravel Lane dissected Green Bank and King Street, she could not resist the temptation to glance over her shoulder and she saw Brigham and Brandon exchanging words. Judging by their aggressive stance, it was clear that they were not chatting about the weather, and, despite her agitated state, Eliza chuckled at the sight of them facing each other like a pair of angry turkeycocks. With the gold sovereigns clasped tightly in her hand she headed home, but Brigham's savage words kept repeating in her brain. 'You may have looked like a young lady last night, but this morning you look like a drab and you talk like a guttersnipe.' It was true that she spoke the cockney dialect, as did all the ordinary folk in this part of London, but last night when she was with the more gentrified merchants and their wives, Eliza had realised that the social gap between them was vast, if not unbridgeable. She might put on fine clothes and have the looks of a lady, but when she opened her mouth she knew that she immediately placed herself firmly in the lower social class. As she opened the door to the house in Hemp Yard, Eliza couldn't help comparing it with the fine mansion owned by Aaron Miller. She knew now that if she wanted to be taken seriously by the likes of the Millers, Brigham Stone and Silas Granger, then simply knowing her trade was not enough; she would have to learn to speak and act like a lady.

'Oh, Liza, where have you been?' Millie came rushing towards her as soon as Eliza opened the front door. 'Dolly's out of her head and rambling even worse than usual and there's no laudanum left in the bottle. I can't calm her down and I couldn't go to the market to buy me flowers because I daren't leave her. Thank goodness you've come home.'

From upstairs, Eliza could hear Dolly wailing

and sobbing. She was calling for her mother and for Ted in a piteous, child-like voice. Uncurling her fingers, Eliza stared down at the gold coins that had left red indentations in the palm of her hand. All the gold in the world would not bring back Ted and Bart, nor could it cure the madness that was slowly taking Dolly away from them.

'Please, Liza,' Millie entreated, with tears running down her cheeks. 'Do something. You got to do something to help her.'

Eliza nodded wordlessly and going to the mantelshelf she took a penny from the tin and handed it to Millie. 'Run to the apothecary shop and get a penn'orth of laudanum. We can't let her go on like this or she'll do herself harm.'

Millie hesitated. 'But Catherine Booth says we shouldn't give her drugs. They'll destroy her.'

'The brain fever is destroying her. Either way we'll lose her in the end and I'd rather she went happy than in a dreadful state.' Wiping Millie's tears away with the tips of her fingers, Eliza kissed her on the forehead. 'Go on, love. I dunno what else we can do for her.'

Millie nodded and sniffed. 'I'm going, but what about the dress that Mary borrowed from Miss Cynthia? What'll we do about that, Liza?'

'I'll take it back to Mary and see if we can sort something out. Now, please, get the stuff for Dolly before she brings the whole street in.'

*

It was well past midday by the time Eliza arrived at the silk merchant's house in Islington, a mid-terrace Georgian house in a square that had once been select but was beginning to look a little run-down and seedy. She glanced up at the soot-blackened façade, hoping that no one in the family had seen her arrive carrying a sus-piciously fat bolster case. The tall, small-paned windows stared blindly back at her and there was no sign of movement behind them. With a sigh of relief, Eliza hurried down the area steps to the tradesmen's entrance. A skinny child, who could not have been more than eight or nine, opened the door, staring blankly at her.

'I've come to see Mary Little,' Eliza said firmly. 'Can I come in?'

'Dunno.'

'Then perhaps you could ask inside?'

The girl disappeared into the depths of the kitchen and a waft of steamy air laced with the smell of boiling beef and onions caught Eliza in the face making her catch her breath. Moments later, Mary came hurrying into the narrow passage and her face lit with a smile. 'Eliza. You've brought it back. Come inside.'

'Mary, there was a bit of an accident.' Pulling back the bolster cover, Eliza uncovered the wine stain. 'I'm so sorry. But I got enough money to make the damage good.'

'Oh Gawd!' Mary's pale skin blanched to

ashen. 'What'll I do? Miss Cynthia is coming home in three days' time.'

Eliza opened her mouth to suggest that a good dressmaker might be able to fashion a copy, but someone was coming down the area steps and she hid the bolster case behind her back just as Arthur arrived in the doorway. He pushed past her without seeming to notice her presence.

'Dad! You was told not to come here again.' Mary barred the way as he headed for the kitchen. 'Cook said she'd take a ladle to your skull if you come begging again.'

'Come now, daughter. I'm on a mission for God, collecting food for the poor.'

Eliza laid her hand on his sleeve. 'Mr Little, maybe this isn't the best time or place.'

Arthur peered at her and then his lined faced cracked into a smile. 'Gawd's strewth, Eliza. I hardly recognised you.'

'You don't recognise no one, Dad,' Mary said. 'You was so sozzled all the time that you hardly knew your own family.'

'It's true,' Arthur said, dragging off his cap and clutching it to his chest. 'I was a sinner and a drunkard, but now I've seen the light and I'm working for the Lord.'

'Dad, if you go in there and start begging for food, cook will take it out on me and I'll lose me job.'

'The Lord will provide,' Arthur said, lifting Mary out of his way.

'He won't find me another job if I loses this one.' Mary cast a beseeching look at Eliza. 'Say something, Liza.'

'Mr Little. I'm sure you wouldn't want to get Mary into trouble.'

Arthur stared at her beneath lowered eyebrows. 'No, of course not.'

'Then, with respect, Mr Little, why don't you try another house? One with a more Christian attitude to the poor and needy.' Eliza dropped the bundle on the floor and slipped her hand through Arthur's arm.

'That's right, Dad. You won't get nothing from cook, she's a mean old so-and-so.' Mary lowered her voice. 'And she's a Catholic.'

'But I was promised some boiled beef and carrots,' Arthur protested as Mary and Eliza urged him towards the outer door. 'And some taters.'

'And a slap with a ladle too, don't forget,' Mary said, pushing him out into the area. 'Dad, if you go back to the mission now, I promise to come round this evening and help with the soup kitchen, and whatever else Catherine has for me to do. Just go now, please.'

Arthur shook his head. 'Mr Booth said the path of righteousness wouldn't be easy. Now I got an ungrateful child telling me what to do.'

'Consider it a test of your faith, Dad.'

Arthur went up the steps grumbling, with Mary pushing him from behind. Eliza snatched up the bolster case and followed them. At the top he paused, refusing to go any further. He fell to his knees and began praying in a booming voice that echoed round the square.

Eliza held her breath. They were already attracting unwanted attention from passers-by. If anyone from the house came out to see what the noise was all about, they would be discovered in possession of Miss Cynthia's ruined gown. Then there would be real trouble.

Chapter Fifteen

'Please go away, Dad,' Mary begged. 'Try another house in the square if you must, but please keep away from the Wilkins family or I'll lose me job. After all, it's not as if you're bringing any money into our house, is it? Mum has to depend on us kids to keep food on the table.'

'Ungrateful child!' Arthur's voice boomed out across the square, sending a host of sparrows chattering up into the trees. 'How sharper than a serpent's tooth it is to have a thankless child.'

Eliza laid her hand on his arm, speaking in what she hoped was a soothing voice. 'Is that from the Bible, Mr Little?'

Arthur beamed at her. 'Shakespeare, my dear Eliza. King Lear if I remember right. I was an educated man until the drink done for me. I was destined to be a lawyer's clerk, but I got into bad company and bad habits and I had to find menial work on the river. But now I've seen the light and I'm joining the army of God along with Mr Booth. I repent of my sins. I am a changed man.' Striding off down the street, Arthur announced his conversion to passers-by and the world at large, getting some very funny looks, so Eliza thought. She was relieved when he disappeared down the area steps of a house on the other side of the square.

'Oh my Gawd,' Mary said with feeling. 'I think I preferred the old man when he was swipey. At least you knew where you was then.'

'Never mind that, Mary, we're still in trouble,' Eliza said. 'Do you know a good dressmaker who could make a copy of Miss Cynthia's gown?'

'The dress! I'd almost forgotten, what with the old man going on and on about God and such. As it happens I was going to the dressmaker this morning to collect a couple of Miss Cynthia's gowns that had to have the seams let out. The greedy cow never stops eating and she'll end up as fat as her mother if she ain't careful.'

'Never mind Miss Cynthia. Where is this person?'

'She lives quite near. I dunno what she'll say about the wine stains, though. We might have to grease her palm a bit to keep her mouth shut.'

Half an hour later they were in the dressmaker's squalid basement room. Mrs Dunne squinted at the damage through a spiral of tobacco smoke rising from a clay pipe clamped between her teeth. The room was dark with just a chink of light from the top of the barred window, and

348

smoke hung in wreaths around the beams. Eliza wondered how much Mrs Dunne could see in this poor light and, with sparks of lighted tobacco erupting from the bowl of the pipe, it seemed like a miracle that she had not set the house afire, or at the very least burnt holes in her work.

Mrs Dunne shook her head, grinding her teeth on the stem of the pipe. 'Ruined!'

'Yes, we know that,' Eliza said, making an effort to curb her impatience. 'But can you do anything in three days? It's a matter of great urgency.'

Mrs Dunne gave her a sideways glance, her small eyes gleaming. 'And what if Miss Cynthia was to find out? I daresay there'd be a bit of a fuss.'

'Yes, a bit of a fuss,' agreed Mary. 'I'd lose me job and worse. Can you do anything, missis?'

'I might, but it would cost you.'

'I can pay,' Eliza said, fingering the coins in her pocket. 'How much did you have in mind?'

Taking the pipe from her mouth and drawing air through her teeth with a hissing sound, Mrs Dunne gave Eliza a sly look. 'How much you got, dearie?'

'Tell me first what you can do.'

'Me? I can do anything with a needle and thread. A true professional I am. And, as it happens, I made this gown for Miss Cynthia and there's a bit of the same silk left that might just make a new bodice.'

Mary shot her a suspicious glance. 'You crafty old mare, I bet you charged Mrs Wilkins for the full yardage.'

'Perks of the trade, dearie,' Mrs Dunne replied, seemingly unbothered. 'I couldn't do the job for less than two guineas.'

'Too much,' Eliza said, shaking her head. 'Fifteen shillings and that's being generous.'

'Fifteen shillings? Come on, dearie, have a heart. I'm a poor widow woman trying to make an honest living.'

'Yes, and you diddled Mrs Wilkins out of the price of a couple of yards of silk, so the material ain't going to cost you nothing.'

Mrs Dunne shrugged her shoulders. 'It's me expertise you're paying for. One pound fifteen and that's my last offer.'

Eliza picked up the ruined dress, taking a step towards the door. 'I'm sure I can find another dressmaker to do it for less.'

'Ah, but not one with the exact matching piece of silk and the skilful hands to make it right. After all, Mr Wilkins, being a silk merchant, he's going to know the difference between good and shoddy material.' Mrs Dunne picked up her pipe and sucked on it. Angling her head, she stared pointedly at Eliza's shabby dress. 'Tell you what. You seem like a young woman what's got her head screwed on right, even if you do look like a ragbag. Give us one pound fifteen and I'll throw in a dress and shawl what was made, and paid for, but the young lady went and died of smallpox and had no need of said garments. She was about your size, before she passed away, that is.'

Before Eliza could answer, Mrs Dunne hobbled over to a bed in the corner of the room that was piled with garments, and after rummaging around for a while she pulled out a dress and a shawl. 'Here, you can try this on and see if it fits, but I got a good eye and I can tell you for nothing that it will look as if it was made for you.'

Fingering the fine poplin, Eliza felt a sensual shiver run down her spine. The deep, ultramarine colour was rich and vibrant, quite unlike anything she had ever possessed in her life. The high collar, bell-shaped sleeves and skirt cunningly drawn flat over the stomach and full at the back was made in the latest fashion. A gown like this would have cost all of one pound ten, more than a week's wages for a working man, and it would be just the right garment to wear when she wanted to make an impression on cynical businessmen.

'She died of the smallpox,' Mary whispered in her ear. 'Don't touch it, Liza.'

'Would I risk catching the foul disease?' demanded Mrs Dunne, knocking the bowl of her pipe on the sole of her boot and scattering ash on the flagstones. 'No, the poor lady never had it on her back, not after the final fitting, and she was as fit as a fiddle then.'

Eliza stared at the garment, struggling with her conscience. The dress was too elegant for a girl from Hemp Yard: with money so short, every penny counted. She ought to haggle and get a cheaper rate for repairing Miss Cynthia's gown, never mind treating herself to such an extravagance. She closed her eyes, holding the fabric to her cheek and imagining how she would look wearing such a fine gown. 'All right,' she whispered. 'I'll take it.'

'And the shawl?' Mrs Dunne held up a cobweb of finely crocheted, silvery-blue wool. 'It'd match your eyes.'

Nodding her head, Eliza held out her hand but Mrs Dunne whipped the shawl away, holding it behind her back. 'Another half-crown for the shawl.'

'But we agreed on one pound fifteen shillings for both.' Biting back tears of disappointment, Eliza shook her head. 'Keep the shawl then.'

'It's a lovely piece of work and would finish off the outfit a treat. I'm robbing meself but give us an extra shilling and it's yours.' Mrs Dunne stroked the soft woollen material as if it were a small kitten. 'Just an extra shilling, that's all.'

The temptation was too great and Eliza snatched it from her. 'All right, I'll take it.'

With her new gown and shawl wrapped in a piece of butter muslin, Eliza followed Mary up the area steps to street level.

'I got to get these duds back to the house,' Mary said, peering over the top of her bundle. 'Tell Millie I expects I'll see her at the mission tonight. It's not my idea of a high old time but then I ain't as good a person as she is. Anyway, I promised the old man I'd go, so I'd better turn up.'

Eliza frowned. 'I think she's spending too much time with those drug addicts and boozers. She should be mixing with people of her own age.'

'She misses Davy. She misses him an awful lot but she knows he's sweet on you, Liza. It's hard for her.'

'She's only sixteen; she'll change her mind half a dozen times before she meets the man she'll settle down with.'

Mary shook her head. 'I don't think so. As to the mission, why don't you come tonight and see for yourself? I'm sure you'd like Mrs Booth, she's a real lady.'

'Maybe, I'll think about it.'

Having said goodbye, Eliza set off for Hemp Yard with Mary's words still echoing in her

353

mind. She had been so quick to pass Millie's feelings for Davy off as an adolescent infatuation, but she remembered only too well the intensity of her feelings for Freddie when she had been a similar age: feelings that surfaced all too often and had not abated with the passage of time or enforced separation. Sometimes it was almost possible to imagine that she had put all that behind her, but the mere glimpse of a man with hair the colour of burnished bronze, the scent of cinnamon and sassafras, or a certain tone of voice could bring the emotions flooding back. The acute pain had passed but all the memories lingered on, playing over and over in her brain like the strains of a sad, sweet song. Even though she might never see Freddie again, Eliza knew that she would never forget him. She made up her mind to be more sympathetic to Millie's feelings for Davy.

Hugging the precious bundle to her breast, Eliza hurried homeward, trying to imagine what she would look like in such an elegant gown. Her visit to the Millers' opulent mansion had opened her eyes to a whole new world of wealth and luxury and, for the first time in her life, she was conscious of her own humble circumstances. Aaron had been kind and had treated her with respect, unlike his son, who seemed to think that she did not mind being slobbered over without a by your leave. Well, she did mind. She had been shocked and offended by his action, but Eliza could not quite forget the sensation that his kiss had aroused in her breast. It was Brigham Stone's cruel words that still rankled; he had called her a cheating little trollop and he had said that she spoke like a guttersnipe. He had propositioned her, even though he had made it clear that she was beneath him in every way. Eliza strode through the streets of Islington, heading south towards Wapping with her head held high. She would show those men who thought she was cheap and inferior. She would become a lady of business, and she would learn to dress and speak properly so that she could deal with the likes of Brigham Stone and Aaron Miller on equal terms. When she had her chandlery up and running again she would make a tidy profit. She would be successful and earn the respect of all the men who had looked on her as a slip of a girl with little brain and no determination. She would work hard to make a good life, not only for herself, but also for Dolly and Millie, and she would see that no harm came to Ada and the nippers while Davy was away at sea.

Eliza was tired by the time she reached Hemp Yard; her feet were sore and she could feel blisters popping up on her heels where her boots had rubbed. She paused for a moment, with her hand on the latch, glancing over her shoulder at the narrow street festooned with lines of washing. This was home, her place of safety, and inside the house were the people she loved. She was instantly ashamed of wanting more. She opened the door and went inside. Dolly was fast asleep in her chair and Ada was kneeling by the range, attempting to coax flames from a couple of lumps of coal.

Eliza set her bundle down on the table. 'Where's Millie?'

Ada looked up and her face creased into deep crevices of worry. 'What happened at the Wilkins's house? Did Mary get into trouble?'

'No need to worry, we got it sorted out.' Eliza paused, frowning. 'But why are you here, Ada? I left Millie to look after Dolly.'

Ada scrambled to her feet. 'I come round earlier to see if I was needed today. Millie was fretting about losing a day's money, so I said I'd stay with Dolly while she went off to the market.'

Dolly opened her eyes and sat bolt upright. 'Is that you, Ted?'

'She's had one of her bad days,' Ada whispered. 'Keeps asking for Ted and getting upset when he don't come. I give her a spoonful of laudanum, but it seems the more she has, the more she wants.'

'It's all right, Ada,' Eliza said, taking off her bonnet and shawl and laying them on a chair. 'You go on home and I'll see to her.'

'I'll do that, ducks. And thanks for sorting things out for my Mary.'

'It was nothing, really.' Eliza couldn't look Ada in the eye as her tender conscience gave her a mighty jab. She had put Mary's job in jeopardy, and she had purchased a gown for herself at a price that would have fed the Little family for a week. She longed to rush upstairs and try it on, but respect for Ada made her hold back. She doubted if Ada had ever owned a garment or a pair of boots that had not come second-hand from a dolly shop or a market stall.

'Well, don't look so glum, Liza,' Ada said with a weary smile. 'I'm sure you done your best.'

'Is that you, Liza?' Dolly reached for her spectacles. 'It is you. What have you got there?'

Eliza shook her head. 'Just an old dress, Mum.'

'Let's see it then.' Ada's eyes brightened. 'It's time you had something decent to wear, Liza.'

Reluctantly, Eliza pulled the dress from the butter muslin wrapping and held it up for them to see.

'I had a dress that colour once,' Dolly said, sighing. 'Ted says it makes me eyes look like cornflowers.'

'It's beautiful.' Ada clasped her hands together, her eyes shining. 'Go and put it on, Liza. Let's see how you look in it.'

'And fetch my blue gown too,' Dolly said, giggling. 'I'll dress up for Ted when he comes back from work. He likes me in blue, with ribbons in me hair. I were dressed like that when he took me to tea at Buckingham Palace. Her majesty said I looked a real treat, she did.'

Eliza hesitated, but Ada gave her an encouraging smile.

'Don't mind her, ducks. I'll keep her company while you try on that lovely dress.'

Minutes later, Eliza came slowly down the stairs, treading carefully so that she did not trip over the hem of the gown, which was several inches too long, but otherwise fitted perfectly.

Ada held up her hands and although she was smiling, her eyes were misted with tears. 'You look so beautiful, Liza. I could cry at the sight of you.'

'Here, take it off,' Dolly said, removing her specs and throwing them on the floor. 'That's my dress, Eliza. The one I wore to tea at the palace. Did I ever tell you about that? We had jam sandwiches and seed cake. Strawberry jam it were and I can still taste it. There's a stain on the skirt, you can't miss it.'

'I'd better go up and change,' Eliza said, gathering up the voluminous skirts. 'I'm just upsetting her all over again.'

'Tell me about her majesty,' Ada said, going to sit beside Dolly and taking hold of her hand. 'What did she say to you then, Dolly?'

Eliza made for the stairs but the sound of the

front door being flung open made her spin around in time to see Millie stagger into the living room and collapse on the nearest chair. Ragged skeins of blood ran from her nose and there were livid scratches on both cheeks. Her shawl was torn almost in two and her blouse was ripped from shoulder to waist, exposing the swell of her firm young breasts above her stays.

'Millie, what happened?' Forgetting all about her new gown, Eliza rushed over to her, tripping over the long skirts in her hurry. She put her arms round Millie's trembling shoulders and hugged her. 'There, there, don't cry, love.'

Ada leapt to her feet, covering her mouth with her hands. 'Who done that to you?'

'It were the flower women. They ganged up on me when I tried to set up a pitch at the bottom of the steps outside St Paul's.'

Dolly let out a wail and began to sob, rocking backwards and forwards in her chair.

'That's terrible,' Eliza said, stroking Millie's hair back from her face. 'Why did they do such a dreadful thing?'

'They was a new lot that I hadn't seen afore. They said I was queering their pitch. Said I didn't belong there. Told me to push off and not to come back. They stamped all me flowers into the ground and I'd not sold a one. I'm s-sorry, Liza.'

'It wasn't your fault, dear. I should never have let you go in the first place.'

'I'll fetch a cold compress for your nose,' Ada said, hurrying into the scullery.

Dolly stopped crying, and leaned forward peering at Millie. 'Is she coughing up blood? Has the young woman got consumption, Liza?'

'It's Millie. She's had a little accident. There's nothing to worry about.'

'Give her a dose of my medicine. It always works wonders for me, dear.' Dolly leaned back in her chair and closed her eyes. 'It works wonders.'

Ada hurried back into the room clutching a wet rag, which she applied to Millie's nose. 'Hold that there, ducks. It looks worse than it is.'

'Does it hurt much?' Eliza asked anxiously, but before Mary could answer there was a loud rapping on the front door.

'Someone's in a hurry,' Ada muttered.

'I'll go.' Eliza hurried to open the door and found herself face to face with Brandon Miller.

'Good grief. What happened here?' Brandon peered over her shoulder.

'I can't speak to you now,' Eliza said, barring his way. 'I'm sorry but this ain't a convenient time. You can't come in.'

She barely came up to his shoulder and her attempt to stop him viewing the scene failed miserably. Taking off his top hat, Brandon tucked it under his arm. 'I need to talk to you, Eliza. Of course, I can shout through the letterbox, but the whole street is watching us even now.'

Reluctantly, she stood aside. 'Come in if you must.'

'I've had more enthusiastic welcomes,' Brandon said, stepping over the threshold. 'Aren't you going to introduce me, Eliza?'

'Mr Miller, this ain't your mum's front parlour, and if you had any sense at all you'd see that we got a difficult situation here.'

Brandon glanced at Millie, raising an eyebrow. 'You look as if you've come to grief, Miss – er . . .'

'Millie Turner,' Millie murmured, holding the rag to her nose.

Eliza didn't like the way Brandon's gaze wandered to Millie's exposed breasts and, snatching up her shawl, she draped it over her. 'She's been done over by them bleeding flower women outside St Paul's. How them wicked doxies got the nerve to sell flowers outside a holy place I'll never know, but Millie's fallen foul of them and this is what they've done to her.'

Brandon shook his head, frowning. 'What could a girl like this have done to provoke such a cruel act?'

'Life's like that round here, Mr Miller. Maybe people don't behave like that in Oxford, but this is the East End and times are hard for poor folk.' Firmly placing herself between Brandon and

Millie, Eliza met his bemused gaze with a defiant lift of her chin.

'I'm beginning to realise that, Eliza.'

Dolly opened her eyes and stared at Brandon. 'Is that Prince Albert come to visit us?'

'Of course he ain't the prince,' Ada said, hurrying to her side. 'The poor prince died a few years back. You remember it, Dolly. And her majesty's been in mourning ever since, that's why she don't invite you to the palace no more.'

'That's true,' Dolly said, nodding her head. 'So if you ain't Albert, who are you, young man?'

'Is that woman completely off her head?' demanded Brandon, raising an eyebrow. 'I say, Eliza, you never told me you lived in a madhouse.'

'That woman, as you call her, took me in as a child and cared for me like a mother,' Eliza hissed, taking him by the arm and pulling him towards the door. 'I'll thank you not to come here and insult Dolly. She's a sick woman.'

'My dear Eliza, I'm sorry if I offended you yet again. I've obviously called at a bad time.'

'Tell the rude young man to go back to the palace,' Dolly said, wagging her finger at Brandon. 'I'd expect the Prince of Wales to have more respect for an old woman. Tell him to ask his mother to send me an invite soon. I got a terrible longing for a slice of seed cake.'

Ada patted her hand. 'We'll send the message,

Dolly. But her majesty's got lots of other things to attend to. Ain't that right, your highness?'

Brandon was staring at Ada and Dolly as if he was watching a Punch and Judy show and Eliza nudged him in the ribs. 'You'll do that, won't you, Prince Edward?'

'God above, this really is a madhouse,' Brandon said, opening the front door. 'I'd best be going.'

Eliza followed him out into the street. 'You haven't said why you come.'

'I came,' Brandon said, with heavy emphasis on the words, 'I came to invite you to attend a meeting at the office tomorrow morning at half-past nine. My father wants to discuss business with you.'

'I'll be there.'

Brandon paused, looking Eliza up and down until she felt the blood rushing to her cheeks. 'Didn't your mother ever tell you it's rude to stare, Mr Miller?'

'It's Brandon, as well you know.' He took her hand in his, looking deeply into her eyes. 'One day, my dear, I mean to take you away from this hellhole. I'd like to set you up in a style worthy of your looks and undoubted talents.'

The hot look in his eyes was matched by the seductive tone in his voice, and his meaning was all too clear. The sound of Eliza's hand slapping Brandon's face echoed from house to house in the narrow street. Red weals striped his cheek, but Eliza was unrepentant. 'Talk to me like that again and I'll tell your father what an ungentlemanly rat he has for a son.' Eliza went inside the house and slammed the door. Tending Millie was uppermost in her mind now; whatever Aaron Miller had to say to her paled in comparison to the hurt that Millie had endured, and all for the sake of a few coppers.

Next morning, wearing her new gown on which she had worked last evening, taking up the hem with minute stitches so that it now just grazed the tips of her toes, Eliza arrived early at the offices of Miller and Son. This time there was no question of having to sit in the waiting room, and she was shown straight into the oak-panelled boardroom where portraits of Aaron and Anne Miller stared down at her from a lofty height. As the clerk closed the door on her, Eliza stood for a moment, taking in the grandeur of the room and staring in wonder at the polished mahogany table that was long enough to seat twelve men on either side. At its head, and presumably for Aaron himself, was a chair that looked to Eliza like a carved mahogany throne, its seat padded with crimson velvet. Pale autumn sunlight filtered through stained-glass windows, reflecting prisms of colour onto the highly polished surface of the table. Eliza was just catching her breath at this magnificence when Brandon made an entrance. He came straight up to her, took her hand and kissed it. 'I apologise for my behaviour yesterday, Eliza. It was unforgivable.'

'It was.'

'Nevertheless, I hope you will forgive me.' Brandon's eyes twinkled, and his mouth curved in a rueful smile that was hard to resist.

Eliza snatched her hand free but she nodded in assent. 'I will, as long as you promise not to speak to me like that again or make cruel jokes about Dolly.'

'Cross my heart and hope to die, painfully and slowly in the torture chamber at the Tower if I renege on my promise.' Brandon made a big show of crossing his heart and the golden glints danced in his dark eyes, making it almost impossible for Eliza to hold on to her anger.

She struggled with the temptation to smile. 'And you'd deserve it too.'

'I agree entirely.'

The door opened and Aaron came towards them with a purposeful look on his craggy face. His dark eyes were like Brandon's in size and shape, but the expression in them was shrewd, calculating, and as he looked at Eliza she was certain that he could read her thoughts. His lips smiled but his eyes were hard. 'Brandon, I want a word with Miss Eliza in private.'

Brandon's eyes widened as if this was the last thing he was expecting. 'But, Father . . .'

'In private, I said.'

'Yes, Father.'

As Brandon left the boardroom, Eliza had a vision of him as a puppy having had a scolding from its master and retreating with its tail between its legs, but the stern look on Aaron's face subdued any desire she might have had to giggle.

'Sit down, Miss Eliza.' Aaron took his seat in the chair at the head of the table. 'Please.'

Eliza pulled out a chair and sat down. Something was wrong: was he angry with her for leaving the dinner party so early? She folded her hands tightly in her lap and raised her chin to look Aaron in the eyes. 'If you've got anything to say, Mr Miller, I'd rather you come straight out with it.'

'That's how I always do business, Eliza.' Aaron leaned his elbows on the table, steepling his fingers and fixing her with a basilisk stare. 'My good friend Brigham Stone tells me that you went to him, behind my back, offering to supply his ships at a better rate than the one which you and I agreed. He said that when he refused you propositioned him, offering him your favours in return for his business.'

Shocked by this cruel injustice, Eliza gasped. She felt as though the air had been sucked from her lungs; she was shaking from head to foot, but somehow she managed to retain eye contact. 'That,' she said, in as firm a voice as she could manage, 'is a wicked lie.'

For a moment, although it felt like a lifetime to Eliza, Aaron held her gaze. Eliza stared back, not daring to breathe. She wanted to scream and shout that Brigham was a lying cheat and a would-be seducer of young women, but she held her tongue.

At last, a slow smile curved Aaron's lips and his eyes twinkled. 'I thought as much, but I wanted to hear it from you.'

Drawing a deep breath, Eliza felt dizzy, elated and angry all at the same time. 'Then why put me through all this if you didn't believe him in the first place?'

'I'm a good enough judge of men to know when someone, even an old friend and colleague like Brigham, is telling me a pack of lies. I was testing your mettle, my dear, and I wasn't disappointed. Most young women when falsely accused would have resorted to screaming hysterics and protestations of innocence. You kept your head and outfaced me. Not many people can do that.'

'Well, now you've had your game with me, Mr Miller, I think I'll be going.' Eliza rose to her feet and was about to leave when Aaron motioned her to sit down.

'I have something to say to you that is just between the two of us.'

She hesitated for a moment, but there was too much at stake to allow mere pride to get in the way. She sat down. 'Well?'

'Have you wondered why I am investing heavily in the chandlery, Eliza?'

'I thought that was your business. I'd have been a fool to turn down such an offer.'

Leaning back in his seat, Aaron spoke slowly, never taking his gaze from her face. 'The night of the fire might have been the first time I ever spoke to you, but I've watched you growing up. I would have liked to have had more to do with your upbringing, but Enoch refused to allow me anywhere near you.'

'I don't understand.'

Aaron smiled. 'How could you understand? The reality is that I knew your mother before she met your father.'

The truth struck Eliza like a thunderbolt. 'You was in love with her?'

'I was in love with her. When I first laid eyes on Lucy, I thought she was the most beautiful girl I had ever seen. She was everything I could have wanted in a woman.'

The mention of her mother's name cut straight to Eliza's heart, and her hand automatically went to touch the brooch at the neck of her bodice. For a while she had replaced it with the delicate lover's knot that Davy had given her, but when dressing this morning she had opted for the mourning brooch, perhaps as a talisman; she had not given it any thought until this moment. 'I – I don't know nothing about her, except what Bart told me. He said she was always smiling; she had golden hair and smelled of violets. But I don't understand how you knew her. I mean you're a rich man and my dad was just a waterman.'

'I wasn't always rich. Lucy's father owned the granary where I worked as a clerk. I'll never forget the first time I met your mother. It was a bitterly cold day in January, and she came into the office like a breath of spring sunshine. Her hair was just like yours, a shining golden halo, and her ringlets bobbed every time she moved her lovely head. She had the bluest eyes I've ever seen and they were always laughing. I fell in love with her there and then.'

'And did she love you?'

Aaron's face contorted with pain. 'Yes, she did. To my amazement, the dear girl returned my feelings. I adored her, but I was near penniless, a humble employee, and I hadn't anything to offer her.'

'So did you just give up without a fight?'

'No, I did not. I begged her to run away with me and she agreed. But your grandfather, Harry Henderson, discovered our secret. He sacked me and he sent Lucy to live in the country with an old aunt.'

'Didn't you try to see her?'

'I had to find work. I couldn't support myself, let alone a wife, if I was not earning. I was well in with the warehouse manager and he bore a grudge against your grandfather. He took me on again, but this time only as a common labourer. The next thing I knew, Lucy was married and completely out of my reach.'

Eliza was silent for a moment, trying to work things out in her head. 'But,' she said slowly, 'if my grandfather disapproved of someone like you, why would he let her marry a mere waterman?'

'I wasn't in his confidence.' Aaron lowered his gaze, staring at his fingers as they drummed out a nervous tattoo on the desk. 'Old man Henderson cut Lucy off without a penny. He wouldn't have anything to do with her after she married, even though she was his only child.'

'Didn't her mother try to stop him treating her so bad?'

'Lucy's mother died giving birth to her.' He raised his eyes to her face with a twisted smile. 'It's ironic, Eliza, but history seems to have repeated itself. My beautiful Lucy died in childbirth, God rest her soul. I was tempted to make myself known to you after Enoch died, but I could see that you were managing quite well on your own, and so I simply kept an eye on you and even put a bit of business your way. Maybe I should have come forward earlier, but I think it was my pride that stopped me. It took a fire to bring us together, Eliza.'

'I can't take it all in,' Eliza said, getting to her feet and pacing the floor. 'It's not the picture of her that I had in me head.'

'Your mother was a flesh and blood woman, Eliza. I did love her and I believe I could have made her happy, if only Harry had given me a chance to prove myself.'

'So how did you do it then?' Eliza came to a halt in front of the desk. 'How did you get to be so rich?

Aaron threw back his head and laughed. 'Practical to the last, Eliza. Well, I'll tell you; I hated the way old man Henderson had treated Lucy. As I said before, I managed to get work back at Henderson's warehouse and I set about learning the business from the bottom upwards. When Harry grew too old and feeble to cope any more, I became the manager of the business. I paid myself handsomely and I invested my money. With some luck, and a bit of good judgement, I made a lot of money on the stock market and I bought first one ship and then another. By the time the old man died I was rich enough to buy the granary and the warehouse. The rest you know.'

Eliza stared at him, struggling to comprehend the full implication of his words. Uncle Enoch had always led her to believe that her mother was a woman of no consequence, from a poor background. It was a shock to realise that, had it not been for following her heart, her mother would have inherited a large part of the business that now belonged to Aaron Miller.

'I'm sorry, Eliza,' Aaron said softly. 'This has been a bit of a shock for you.'

She clasped her hands together to stop them trembling. In the echoing, church-like silence of the boardroom, she felt suddenly so close to her mother that she could almost have reached out and touched her. Despite the worldlier picture that Aaron had painted of her, Eliza could not dispel the angelic image that she had cherished for so long in her heart. She raised her eyes to the stained-glass windows, and for a brief moment she thought she saw her mother's face smiling at her through the shimmering dust motes dancing in the sunbeams. The faint creaking of Aaron's chair brought her abruptly back to reality, and she turned her head to see that he was watching her with a guarded expression in his dark eyes. 'I knew so little of my mother. You've given me a lot to think about.'

'I understand.' Aaron reached behind his chair and tugged on a bell pull. 'I'll get Brandon to escort you home.'

'No, please. I'd rather be alone.'

'It's not safe . . .'

'Mr Miller, I've grown up in Wapping. I can look after myself, ta.'

Aaron rose to his feet, holding out his hand. 'You do understand why I want to help you, don't you, Eliza? I loved your mother and I know she would have been proud of you.'

Staring at his workmanlike hand, with its square-tipped fingers, Eliza laid her own small hand in his and, looking up into his face, she managed a wobbly smile. This man had known and loved her mother; he was the only person alive who could bring her close to the young woman who, in giving birth to her, had sacrificed her own life. Eliza curled her fingers round Aaron's. 'I understand.'

Outside in the street, Eliza drew a deep breath. Her thoughts were confused by a multitude of conflicting emotions and she needed to be alone. Brandon had been reluctant to allow her to walk home unaccompanied, and was frankly curious as to why his father had wanted to see her, but Eliza had not enlightened him. She had refused his offer to escort her home, or to allow him to send for the coach. She needed to walk, to give herself time to think about Aaron's revelations, which were surprising and shocking, but had brought her dead mother a little closer. She could relate only too well to her mother's agony of grief, having lost the man she truly loved. She could only hope that her mother had found some happiness with her father.

As she neared the solid normality of the chandlery, Eliza could see the builders raising the roof trusses with Arnold and Dan, as usual, working side by side. She stopped for a moment, taking comfort from the sturdy brick walls of the new building that would soon be her place of business. Then she realised that someone else was standing on the pavement, no more than a few yards from her.

For the second time that morning, Eliza received a shock that caused her heart to miss a beat and the world to stand still. She would have recognised that straight profile beneath a silk top hat anywhere. He appeared taller than she remembered; his skin was tanned to the colour of teak, but he didn't look a day older than when she had last seen him six years ago. Clutching her hand to her throat, Eliza opened her mouth to call his name but no sound came.

Chapter Sixteen

'Freddie?' His name was wrenched from her lips in an involuntary cry. But was it really Freddie, or a complete stranger who reminded her of him? Was her imagination playing tricks on her? Eliza took a step forward and then stopped.

He turned his head slowly to look at her. His eyes were in deep shadow beneath the brim of his top hat. He was dressed like a gentleman of means, in a coat that was cut to the latest fashion, checked trousers and highly polished leather ankle boots. It seemed to Eliza that everything was happening in slow motion. For a frozen moment in time, it seemed to her that the world had stopped spinning: she held her breath. The hammering of the carpenters beating nails into wood resounded like a drum roll announcing a momentous event.

He was walking towards her so slowly that he might have been wading through the deep, dark waters of the Thames. 'Freddie?'

He was so near now that they could have reached out and touched fingers. A smile of recognition curved his generous lips and, taking off his hat, he tossed it high in the air with a whoop of delight. 'Eliza! By God, it's my little Liza.' He caught the hat in one hand and set it on the back of his head, taking her by the shoulders and staring at her in amazement. 'You've grown up, Liza. I can hardly believe it's you.'

'Oh, F-Freddie.' Tears gushed from Eliza's eyes as if a dam had suddenly burst.

He wrapped his arms around her, holding her close to his chest. 'There, there, dear girl. There's no need for tears. I've come home.'

'Here, you. Leave her be!'

Arnold's angry voice and the sound of his booted feet on the cobbles made Freddie release his hold on Eliza and he put her behind him. 'Hold on, fellah. I'm a friend.'

'You ain't much of a pal to make her cry like that,' Arnold roared, grabbing Freddie by the collar.

'No, Arnold, no,' Eliza cried, in between laughter and tears. She stepped between them, holding Arnold off with the flat of her hands. 'This is Dr Freddie Prince, you remember him. He used to lodge with Beattie.'

Arnold's black brows knotted over the bridge of his nose. 'I remembers him all right. He was the one what got poor Beattie in the family way.'

'If that were true, then I would be thoroughly ashamed of myself,' Freddie said, his smile fading. 'In any event, I would have supported

Beattie and her child if it hadn't been for circumstances beyond my control.'

Arnold fisted his hands, waving them in front of Freddie's face like two large York hams. 'Don't you use none of your fancy words on me, you – you crocusser. You left Miss Eliza and Beattie to face the world on their own, but they don't need you now.'

'Please go back to your work, there's a good chap.' Eliza gave him a gentle shove, but his huge bulk remained as static as a stone colossus. 'Please, Arnold, do as I ask. There's no need to worry about me.'

He glowered at Freddie as if he would like to give him a good pasting, and then shrugged his shoulders. 'All right, but you call me if he gets too familiar. I knows his sort.' He shambled off, hawking and spitting on the road as if to underline his point.

'He's right though,' Freddie said ruefully. 'I'm all the things he said I was, and an ex-convict into the bargain. But I'm back now and I truly mean to make it up to you and to Beattie.'

Eliza managed a watery smile. 'You never did nothing wrong to me. As for Beattie, I saw her baby and, unless your dad was a Chinaman, there's no possibility that you was its father.'

'I knew that I could not have been the father, but it's a relief to have it confirmed.' Pulling a large silk handkerchief from his pocket, Freddie handed it to Eliza. 'Dry your eyes, my dear.'

In spite of everything, Eliza found herself chuckling. Happiness was welling up inside her. Freddie had come home. He was here beside her and she wanted to dance up and down and shout for joy. All the suppressed emotion, the longing and the uncertainty as to whether her feelings for him had simply been puppy love had vanished in that first moment of recognition. She buried her face in the soft silk of his handkerchief, and inhaled the scent of him that was so heart-rendingly familiar.

'Let me have a proper look at you.' Taking her by the shoulders, Freddie held her until she lowered the handkerchief and looked him in the face. As he wiped away the last of her tears with the tips of his fingers, a tender smile played on Freddie's lips. 'You've grown into a beautiful young lady, Liza. You were little more than a child when I was sent off to the penal colony, and now just look at you.'

There was no mistaking the admiration in his eyes, and Eliza's heightened senses detected something more. She had seen that flicker of appreciation before; a certain look that men gave her, confirming that she was no longer a child. She lifted her face, longing for him to kiss her on the lips in the way that Brandon had kissed her, but as she glanced up at him beneath her lashes, her heart went cold.

Freddie dropped his hands to his sides with a shadow clouding his eyes, and the moment was lost. Perhaps it had never happened. Eliza searched his face for the answer, but his expression was controlled and unreadable.

'Well now, my dear Eliza. We've six years to catch up on.' Freddie jerked his head in the direction of the chandlery. 'I can see that a lot has happened while I've been away.'

A cold east wind blew down the street, hurling bits of straw and sawdust into the air. Eliza shivered; the sun was still shining from a translucent blue sky with tiny puffballs of clouds tossed around like playful lambs, but she felt chilled to the bone. He took her hand and tucked it into the crook of his arm. 'You're shivering, Liza. Let's find somewhere nice and warm where we can talk.'

Seated by Freddie's side in a chophouse near Execution Dock, Eliza toyed with a large helping of steak pudding, which normally would have been a real treat, but now her appetite seemed to have deserted her. Freddie, however, ate his with relish and he encouraged her to talk, listening sympathetically while she related the events of the past years, ending with Aaron's offer to rebuild the chandlery and his startling revelations concerning her mother.

'My poor Eliza,' Freddie said, wiping his

mouth on a table napkin. 'You've been through so much and I wasn't there to help you.'

She forced her lips into a smile. 'It weren't your fault. You didn't choose to go off to Australia.'

'That is true. But in a way it's been the making of me, Eliza.'

'It certainly looks that way. I thought you was transported for seven years, and here you are large as life and dressed like a toff. Did you escape from the penal colony?'

Freddie leaned back in his chair and a lazy smile lit his face. 'I'm a free man, Liza. It's a long story, but in the end I earned an absolute pardon.'

She rested her elbows on the table, cupping her chin in her hands. 'Tell me about it.'

'You really wouldn't want to know all the sordid details, but suffice it to say that my limited medical skills came in very useful, especially when I first arrived in the colony. I tended the sick to the best of my ability and, having successfully treated the governor of Swan River colony for extremely painful boils, I was granted a ticket of leave. Eventually I found myself in the Northern Territories and I headed for the goldfields, where I set myself up as a doctor, treating the miners for everything from the pox to typhoid, bites from venomous snakes and spiders to broken bones. I can't say I struck gold myself, but they paid me handsomely in gold dust and even small nuggets. One of the unfortunates that I couldn't save had struck it rich and, with no one in the world to mourn him, he left his hoard to me. When I got my pardon, I made my way to Sydney and booked passage on a ship heading for New Zealand. I stayed there for a while, and then I took another vessel bound for London.'

'Well, I never did.' Eliza could hardly bear to take her eyes off Freddie's animated countenance. He had made his story sound like a great adventure, although she knew he wasn't telling her the worst of his experiences. She longed to reach out and touch the laughter lines that radiated from the corners of his eyes, and to smooth the twin furrows between his eyebrows caused by harsh sunlight in the outback. But she did none of these things and she sat back in her chair, clasping her hands on the table in front of her. 'There must be so much more you haven't told me, Freddie.'

'All in good time, my love.'

'But you won't go away again, will you?'

'I'm here to stay, Liza. And I wasn't wasting my time entirely in the penal colony. I had access to the governor's library and I spent my evenings studying medical books.'

'So you're a proper doctor now?'

'Not exactly, but I know a lot more than I did when I was peddling my elixirs door to door.'

'Will you do that again?'

Freddie shook his head. 'No, I've bought a property and I intend to set up a clinic in the East End. Pay my debt to society by treating the poor and sick.'

'Oh, Freddie, that's so wonderful.'

'Hold on, Liza, you'll have me thinking I'm a saint in a minute and I promise you I'm far from that. I'll treat a few City bankers and merchants on the side.' Freddie tapped the side of his nose and winked. 'For a huge fee, of course.'

A bubble of laughter rose in Eliza's throat and she found herself laughing, really laughing for the first time since he had gone away.

'That's better,' he said, with a nod of approval. 'This is the Liza I remember most, not the sad-faced, serious young woman I met on the corner of Old Gravel Lane a couple of hours ago.' Reaching across the table, he took Eliza's hand in his and held it, looking deeply into her eyes. 'I know you've had a hard time, my love, but Freddie's here now. Here to stay, and I have a surprise for you.'

'You have?' Eliza wondered how many shocks one person could take in a day. 'What sort of surprise?'

Freddie leapt to his feet. 'Come with me. This news is too good to deliver in a chophouse.' He grabbed her by the hand and pulled her to her feet.

'Where are we going?' Eliza demanded, as he led her through the closely packed tables towards the street door. 'Why can't you tell me here?'

'It's not too far to walk,' Freddie said, plucking his top hat from the stand and opening the door. 'A stroll will bring the colour back to your cheeks. Just wait until you see what I've brought back from the Antipodes. You'll get the surprise of your young life.'

Young life, thought Eliza, struggling to keep up with him. He still talks as though he's my father. There might be nine or ten years between us, but if it makes no difference to me, why should he care? Just a short while ago she thought Freddie had seen her as a grown woman, but now he was talking to her as if she were still a child.

'Keep up, Eliza,' Freddie said, striding along and towing her behind him like a wayward toddler. 'Chop-chop.'

She was out of breath and gasping for air by the time Freddie stopped outside a house over-looking the river at the end of Dark House Street. Squashed tightly between a tea warehouse and a tavern, the five-storey, double-fronted edifice, with a crumbling Georgian portico and grimy stucco, looked oddly out of place and sadly neglected, like an ageing courtesan propped in the corner of a bar and about to tumble off her stool.

A painful stitch made Eliza clutch her side. 'Who lives here?'

'I do,' Freddie said proudly, taking a large iron mortice key from his coat pocket and unlocking the front door. Sweeping off his hat, he stood aside to usher Eliza into the entrance hall. 'Welcome to my home. This crumbling pile of bricks and mortar will eventually be Dr Freddie Prince's clinic for the poor and needy.'

Eliza stepped inside, wrinkling her nose at the pervading smell of damp rot and mildew. Spiders' webs hung in festoons from the cornices and the floorboards were so caked with dried mud and dirt that it could have passed for a stable. A staircase rose from the centre of the square hall, dividing on a mezzanine lit by an arched window and winging elegantly up in two curves to a galleried landing. 'You own this house?'

'Every last cracked brick and worm-eaten timber, my dear. What do you think?'

'It's a bit of a mess.'

'But it has potential, Eliza.' Freddie surveyed his property with a blissful expression on his face. 'A bit of a clean and a lick of paint and it will be a palace fit for a queen.'

Eliza opened her mouth to say that it was probably only the dirt that was holding the whole thing together, when a woman appeared through a doorway at the back of the hall. For a moment, Eliza thought she must be a servant or someone hired to do the cleaning, but the woman came towards them, smiling and holding her arms out to Freddie. As she drew closer, Eliza could see that she was quite young, and pretty in a blowsy sort of way. She was dressed in a yellow watered-silk gown trimmed with black braid and cut daringly low to reveal a generous bosom, rather too much of it in Eliza's opinion, and her waist was impossibly small. Her corsets must have been killing her!

'So you found her then, Freddie, my love.' She wrapped her arms around Freddie's neck and kissed him on the lips.

'I found her, Daisy. Although she's grown into such a fine young lady that it took me a few moments to realise that it was indeed my little Eliza.'

Daisy released him, turning to Eliza with a smile fixed on her face and eyes narrowed like a duellist looking down the barrel of a pistol. 'She's not the child you described.'

Freddie chuckled and slipped his arm around Eliza's shoulders, giving her a hug. 'Not too grown up, I hope.'

'Aren't you going to introduce us, Freddie?' Eliza met Daisy's hostile stare with what she hoped was a cool look and a sinking heart.

'My dear girl, of course. But there is someone else I want you to meet as well. Go and fetch him, Daisy. Let's do this properly.'

'Anything you say, Freddie darling.' With a coquettish smile, Daisy sashayed off with her silver-blonde ringlets bobbing and her hooped skirts swaying. 'Tommy,' she called. 'Tommy, where are you?' She opened a door across the hall and disappeared inside.

Eliza shot a puzzled glance at Freddie, but he just smiled and nodded. Suddenly she wanted to slap him. Was this awful woman his wife or his mistress? If so, why hadn't he thought to warn her? Her instinct was to slam out of the house never to return, but she forced herself to stand still and, hopefully, to appear calm.

From inside the room she could hear Daisy's voice. 'There you are, Tommy. Oh, you bad boy! I told you not to play with them cockroaches, nasty dirty things.'

'She's a fine woman really,' Freddie whispered in Eliza's ear. 'You'll like her when you get to know her.'

Eliza bit back the sharp retort that she already hated the common, brassy trollop. She recognised the type as soon as she had set eyes on Daisy, dyed blonde hair, breasts like pillows and ready to oblige any man with a few bob in his pocket; it was Beattie Larkin all over again.

Daisy reappeared dragging a small boy by the

hand. Judging by the tears welling up in his large brown eyes and the red weals on the side of his face, Daisy had fetched him a clout for playing with bugs. As they stopped in front of Eliza, the boy plugged his thumb in his mouth, staring up at her.

There was something disturbingly familiar in those large, pansy-brown eyes, something about the mutinous lift of that small chin – a look – an instinctive feeling. Eliza had to stop herself from scooping Tommy up in her arms and cuddling him.

'Liza, I want you to meet Daisy Bragg, Bart's widow, and this fine young fellow is Tommy, your brother's son.'

For a moment Eliza thought she was going to faint. The ceiling and the floor seemed to be spinning in a vortex around her, and if Freddie had not supported her, she might have fallen. She could hear his voice but the words made no sense at all. It was Daisy's shrill tones that penetrated her consciousness.

'Poor thing, she's gone quite pale, Freddie. Go and fetch some sal volatile or something from your medicine bag.'

'Of course, you're right, Daisy. You always were a practical woman.' Freddie helped Eliza to the staircase and sat her down on the bottom step. 'Sit down for a while, Liza. Daisy will look after you.'

The thought of being looked after by Daisy acted quicker than a burning feather wafted under her nose. Eliza lifted her head. 'I'm all right. It was a shock and I've had plenty of those today.'

'Course she has, you great booby,' Daisy said, slapping Freddie on the arm. 'I dunno, men! Why don't you make yourself useful, Freddie? Go and tell that stupid girl, Sukey, to make us a nice cup of tea. I'm sure that would do Eliza more good than a sniff of smelling salts.'

Freddie's face crumpled with consternation as he bent over Eliza. 'I'm a clumsy dolt, Liza. I should have broken the news more gently.'

'It's all right, Freddie. Really it is. I'm fine now.'

'Best give it a minute or two or we'll have you swooning all over the place,' Daisy said, preventing Eliza from rising with a firm pressure on her shoulders. 'Freddie, tea!'

'Yes, general!' Winking at Eliza, Freddie gave Daisy a mock salute and strolled off into the dim recesses of the house.

'Now then, dearie,' Daisy said, her smile fading. 'I can see you don't approve of me, but that's your problem, not mine. Me and Freddie are very close and I won't let no one come between us. Do you get my meaning?'

'Mama.' Tommy tugged at Daisy's hand.

She looked down at him with an impatient tut-tutting sound. 'Hush, Tommy. Mama's talking to your Aunt Eliza.'

'I don't know you,' Tommy said, glaring at Eliza.

Daisy patted him on the head. 'Of course you don't, love. But you will get to know your auntie very well, and when you're a big boy she'll show you how to run the shop that by rights belongs to you.' Daisy kept her gaze fixed on Eliza's face. 'That's right, isn't it, Eliza? If my Bart had lived then he would have inherited the business, so when Enoch dies it should go to Bart's son.'

'Enoch died several years ago. The shop belongs to me now, but I'll see that Tommy gets his fair share.' Wrapping her arms around his small body, Eliza gave him a hug. 'I'm your auntie and I hope we'll be very good friends, Tommy.'

'You talk funny,' he said, eyeing her warily. 'Everybody here talks funny. I want to go back home.'

'This is home now,' Daisy said, prising him from Eliza's arms. 'Go and play with your bricks while I have a little chat with your auntie.'

Tommy's bottom lip stuck out and his eyes filled with tears. 'Don't want to play with bricks. I'm hungry.'

'Then go and ask Sukey to make you some bread and milk. Freddie's in the kitchen, you can tell him to hurry up with the tea. Off you go, there's a good boy.' Clapping her hands together, Daisy shooed him off in the direction of the kitchen.

'He's a fine boy,' Eliza said, watching him trot off on sturdy little legs, with a lump in her throat and a surge of love threatening to overwhelm her. 'Bart would have been so proud of him.'

'And Bart would want Tommy to inherit the business.'

'Is that the only reason you brought the boy all the way to England?' Eliza demanded, rising to her feet. 'You told me in your one and only letter that Bart had found gold. Surely you don't need money?'

Daisy shrugged her shoulders. 'It's all gone. I bought a hotel in Arrowtown but it weren't easy running it with a child to raise, so I sold up and went to live in Wellington where I bought a pub. I got in with a gambling man who robbed me blind, drank all me profits and then buggered off, leaving me with a pile of debts. I was desperate, and then one day Freddie come into the bar and we got talking, as you do. He'd seen me name above the pub door and he says, I knew a family called Bragg back in Wapping. Wapping, says I, why that's where me dear departed hubby come from. That's how it come about, and when Freddie says he's booked a passage to England, then I think, why not? Uncle Enoch can't be as black-hearted as Bart said, and even if he was, then I can get round most men if I put me mind to it.'

'Then it's a pity you won't have a chance to find out, isn't it?'

Daisy pushed her face close to Eliza's. 'Look, dearie, don't get clever with me. I've had to fight for survival ever since I was ten. You cross swords with me and you'll come off the worse.'

'I'm not scared of you and you ain't the only one what's had to struggle.'

Daisy drew back a little way, her voluptuous breasts flushed pink and threatening to burst from her bodice as she drew a deep breath. 'Get on the wrong side of me and you'll be sorry. You may be my sister-in-law, but get in my way and I'll make mincemeat out of you, girl.'

Eliza glared at her, wondering how Bart had managed to fall in love with such a scheming slut. But just thinking of Bart was enough to make her bite back a bitter retort; whatever Daisy's faults, he had loved this woman and she was the mother of his child. Eliza held up her hands. 'I don't want to fight with you, Daisy.'

'Just as well,' Daisy said, tossing her head so that her ringlets bobbed up and down and her gold earrings jiggled. 'You'd be the loser, I can tell you.'

'Answer me one question, honestly.'

Daisy's lip curled. 'Honestly? That's asking a bit much.'

'Tell me what Freddie is to you. Are you just using him because he's got a bit of money or do you love him?'

'I love him, of course. At least that's what he believes and I intend to keep it that way.'

'That's so cruel and unfair. He's a good, kind man and I won't let you use him this way.'

'I thought as much.' Arms akimbo, Daisy squared up to Eliza. 'You're sweet on him yourself. I seen the way you look at him, and I'm warning you to keep your hands off Freddie. If you so much as flutter your eyelashes at him I'll take Tommy back to New Zealand and you'll never see him again.'

A knot of fear twisted in Eliza's stomach. In spite of the fact that she had only known of Tommy's existence for less than an hour, he already held a place in her heart. He was Bart in miniature and he must be loved and protected; she was ready to fight. 'Take him away and you won't get a penny from the chandlery.'

'Oh, don't worry, dearie. I'll go to the law and stake Tommy's claim as rightful heir to Enoch Bragg's business. Keep me sweet and we'll get along fine, but keep your hands off my man.'

'I don't want Freddie,' Eliza said, tossing her head. 'I got a gentleman friend and we're stepping out together. He's young, rich and handsome and his father owns a big warehouse and half a dozen ships. Freddie's too old for me, and I simply ain't interested in him.'

'What's this, girls? Are you fighting over me?' Freddie's voice echoed off the high ceiling in mocking tones, but Eliza was quick to hear something else in his voice. She turned her head to meet his gaze, and she knew by the hurt look in his eyes that he had overheard her last words. It was too late to take them back; if she weakened now, admitting that she had lied, she knew for certain that Daisy would carry out her threat and she would never see Tommy again.

'Freddie, darling, isn't that good news?' Daisy pushed past Eliza and threw her arms around Freddie, smiling up into his face. 'Little Liza has a fellah.'

'Yes, I heard what she said.'

Eliza shivered at the harsh tone of his voice and the look of cold indifference that turned his eyes to the colour of the Thames in winter. She had been pushed into a ridiculous lie by Daisy's cunning and she knew that she was trapped. If she tried to fight Bart's widow she would lose her nephew and Freddie too. Somehow she managed to force her lips into a smile. 'It's getting late. I'd best go home.'

'Aren't you going to tell us his name, Eliza?' Freddie demanded, in a cold, clipped voice. 'I'd like to meet this paragon of virtue.'

'Yes, do tell us, dear,' Daisy said, flashing a knowing wink at Freddie. 'If he's real, that is.'

Eliza knew she was being manoeuvred into a corner and her one thought was to escape from this crumbling mansion: the stinking, vice-ridden streets outside seemed far less dangerous than being in the presence of a jealous woman like Daisy. 'I really must go.' She made for the front door but Freddie was there before her.

Daisy stamped her foot. 'Let her go, Freddie.'

Ignoring Daisy, he caught Eliza by the wrist and held her with an iron grip. 'You haven't answered my question, Liza. You mean a great deal to me, so I feel entitled to know the name of the man who has captured your young heart.'

Chapter Seventeen

'Brandon Miller. His name is name is Brandon Miller, and now I really must go.'

'And who is Brandon Miller?' Freddie leaned his shoulders against the door, barring her exit.

'His father is Aaron Miller. He's one of the richest men in Wapping. I told you about him, Freddie. He's the bloke what offered to help me when the chandlery burned down.'

Freddie stared at her for a moment, then his serious expression dissolved into the smile that she had always loved. 'Well, that's not so bad. At least he's a gentleman, Liza. If you like him then I'm happy for you.'

'Freddie!' Daisy said with an impatient toss of her head. 'We've got things to do, my dear. I'm sure Eliza is eager to get home.'

'That's as maybe, but I won't allow her to walk home on her own.' Freddie went to retrieve his hat and gloves from a side table. He stuck the top hat on his head at a jaunty angle. 'I won't be long.'

'But we was going to the warehouse to choose furniture. Doesn't our home mean nothing to you, Freddie?' Daisy moved towards him, pouting and swaying her hips.

'It's all right; don't worry about me,' Eliza said, wrenching the door open. 'I can take care of myself.'

'Nonsense. I wouldn't forgive myself if anything happened to you.' He paused briefly, to brush Daisy's restraining hand off his arm. 'You can go to the warehouse, Daisy. I'm sure I'll like whatever you choose.' He followed Eliza into the street, closing the door and cutting off Daisy's stream of protests.

Eliza quickened her pace. 'There's no need to upset her by taking me home.'

'There's every need.' Freddie lengthened his strides to keep up with her. 'You're too young and vulnerable to walk these streets in safety. Anything could happen to you.'

'Freddie, I have to do business around the docks. I've been doing it for the last six years.'

'Look at yourself, Liza.' Freddie drew her to a standstill in front of a tavern window. He twisted her round, holding her by the shoulders, so that she was faced with her own reflection. 'Take a good look. You're no longer the little girl who used to accompany me on my rounds. I don't think much of your gentleman friend if he allows you to wander round the docks on your own.'

The touch of his hands on her shoulders was light, but the heat from his fingers seemed to sear

396

through the layers of woollen shawl and the thin poplin of Eliza's gown. For a delightful moment she allowed herself to lean against his well-muscled body and she closed her eyes, breathing in the scent of the man she had known and loved for so many years. But he was not for her. He already had a woman. She must accept that fact and live with it. Opening her eyes, she twisted free from his grasp. 'Brandon looks after me. He does. And I usually take Arnold with me when I go about my business.'

'It's not the sort of business I would have chosen for you, Liza.'

'But it wasn't your choice, was it? You're not my father, Freddie.'

If she had slapped his face, he could not have looked more shocked. But he seemed to collect himself quickly and he released her with a rueful smile. 'Of course not. I'm sorry, Eliza. I can't quite get used to the idea that you're all grown up now.'

'Well, I am.'

He raised her hand to his lips and kissed it. 'Are we still friends?'

Her heart was thudding against her ribs and she could feel the blood rushing to her cheeks, but somehow Eliza managed a smile. 'Of course we are.' She linked her arm in his and they walked on.

By the time they drew near the chandlery they

were almost back on their old terms, but Eliza was aware of a slight constraint that had crept into Freddie's manner since she'd mentioned Brandon's name. Although she longed to confess that she lied about her relationship with him, she could not bring herself to tell Freddie the truth. Admitting a childish fabrication like that would only convince him further that she was too young to be taken seriously. Her thoughts were jumbled and her nerves were shredded after a day that had provided almost more shocks and surprises than it was possible to bear. Her see-sawing emotions had taken her to the heights of happiness and the depths of despair, but Eliza's natural optimism made her cling to the good things that had happened to her today. She had learned startling facts about the mother that she had never known, she had found her dearest Freddie, and she had met Bart's son. She banished thoughts of Daisy and her proprietorial attitude to Freddie from her mind. She would worry about that later.

Freddie stopped outside the chandlery, pointing to the roof trusses that stood out in the gathering dusk like the skeleton of a beached whale. 'Why is there no upper floor? There isn't room for the sail loft.'

'Mr Miller would only put up the money for one storey, Freddie. He said that sail would soon be a thing of the past, what with the new steam engines and such. I wasn't in a position to argue with him.'

'That must have been hard on young Davy. I always thought he would take over from Ted when he retired.'

'I'm sure he would have, but for the fire. There wasn't much choice but for him to follow his trade at sea.'

'You must miss him.'

Eliza met Freddie's questioning gaze with a smile. 'I do, but not half as much as poor Millie. She loves him dearly, but he still thinks of her as a child. That's very hard to bear.'

'I think Davy has eyes for one girl only, Liza.' Freddie squeezed her hand.

'Nonsense, that was just puppy love. We was never anything but good friends. Come on, Freddie, it's getting cold and Ada will be wanting to get home to her own family.' She curled her fingers around his hand, and they walked on at a brisk pace, into the sepia-tinted dusk.

Hemp Yard was too poor an area to have benefited from gaslights, and it was in almost complete darkness, except for the odd ghostly glimmer of a candle mirrored in the few windowpanes that were not stuffed with paper and rags. Bats careered about overhead and starlings chattered noisily as they came in to roost. Eliza hesitated outside the door. 'Before we go in, I have to warn you that you'll find Dolly sadly changed. Sometimes she's not quite in her right mind and the only thing that calms her is a dose of laudanum.'

'You mean she's addicted to the stuff?'

'I'm afraid she is. She had come to rely on the tonic that you made up for her and I tried to make it myself, but it didn't work unless I added more and more laudanum.'

'I am so sorry, Liza. If I had known I was going to be transported to the other side of the world I would never have started Dolly on that path. It was only supposed to be a temporary measure.'

'I know and you mustn't blame yourself. It's a sickness of the mind that makes her as she is, and the laudanum is the only thing that seems to help.'

'I'd like to see her.'

'She may not know you.' Eliza opened the door. As she stepped inside, the sight of Brandon standing with his back to the range wrenched a gasp of surprise from her lips.

'Eliza! I had to see you.' He came to meet her with his hands outstretched, but his smile faltered as he saw Freddie. 'Who is this?'

Freddie was so close behind her that she could feel his muscles tense, and Brandon had his chin stuck out like a bull terrier about to attack. Eliza's nerves were stretched to snapping point, but somehow she managed to keep calm. 'Brandon, I want you to meet an old friend of mine. Dr Freddie Prince.'

'How do you do, sir?'

Freddie eyed him up and down. 'So you are Brandon Miller.'

It was more a challenge than a statement, and Eliza stared from one to the other with a growing feeling of annoyance. They were squaring up to each other as if they meant to fight, but neither of them had the right to argue over her. She was about to say so, but Brandon spoke first. 'And what exactly is your interest in Eliza?'

'I'd say it was none of your business, Mr Miller.'

'Anything to do with Eliza is my business, Dr Prince.'

'Stop this, both of you.' Eliza had suffered enough of this stupidity. She stepped in between them. 'Isn't it enough to know that Freddie is probably my oldest friend, Brandon? He doesn't have to explain himself.'

'You don't need to defend me, my dear.' Freddie was smiling, but there was a hint of steel in his eyes. 'As Eliza said, we're old friends. I've known her since she was a child.'

'So where were you when she needed you?' Brandon's lip curled and his voice was filled with contempt. 'I didn't see you rushing forward to help her when the chandlery was razed to the ground. A fine friend you are.'

'Had I been in the country I would have come to her aid, but I was sentenced for a crime that I did not commit and transported to a penal colony in Australia. I've served my time and now I'm a free man.'

'A convict!' Brandon's tone was acid spiked with ice.

'Actually, I'm a medical man and I intend to practise my profession in my recently acquired establishment in Wapping Wall. If you have need of a doctor, Mr Miller, then feel free to call on me. My rates are very reasonable.'

'Please stop,' Eliza said angrily. 'There is no call for either of you to behave like this.'

'There's every need, my dear Liza,' Freddie said stiffly. 'If this young man is your intended, then he is entitled to know who and what I am. I would do the same in his shoes.'

'I appreciate your candour.' Brandon clicked his heels together in a mock salute. 'Now if you wouldn't mind leaving us, I have a lot to say to Eliza.'

She shook her head. 'I'm sure it can wait.'

'It cannot. I came to speak to you and I won't leave until I've had my say.'

'This is my house, Brandon. I'll thank you not to forget it. Freddie was kind enough to escort me home and he wants to see Dolly.'

Brandon gave a derisive snort. 'That woman is out of her mind. She threatened to wet herself if

402

your maid didn't take her out to the privy. In my opinion she should be locked away.'

'And your opinion counts, does it?' Freddie said coldly. 'Dolly is suffering from an illness, but she is certainly not mad. She is a kind and lovely lady and deserves our respect.'

Eliza could have kissed him, but she managed to contain her feelings. She was about to show Brandon the door, when a splintering crash from the direction of the scullery and a cry for help from Ada put everything else out of her mind. She ran to her aid, closely followed by Freddie. Dolly seemed to be having some kind of fit and Ada was attempting to lift her from the ground where she had fallen.

'Leave her to me,' Freddie said, lifting Dolly with effortless strength. He carried her into the living room and set her gently down in her chair, holding her until the spasms passed and she opened her eyes.

'Are you all right?' Eliza went down on her knees, brushing strands of wiry grey hair back from Dolly's forehead.

'She was took ill on the privy,' Ada said, straightening her apron that had somehow got itself tangled round her neck. 'We was stuck in there for half an hour or more. I'd have thought he'd have come to see if he could help instead of loitering about in here,' she added, glaring at Brandon. 'Useless toff.'

'I didn't come here to be insulted,' Brandon said, snatching up his hat and gloves.

'So where do you usually go then?' Ada's lip curled with contempt.

As her overwrought nerves threatened to turn into hysteria, Eliza could not look at Freddie. Even though he said nothing, she knew that he was laughing at Ada's sarcastic remark.

Brandon rammed his hat on his head, glowering at Ada. 'I'll choose to ignore that piece of impudence.' His expression changed subtly as he turned to Eliza. 'Will you see me to the door, my dear? I have something to say to you.'

Dolly groaned. 'I need a dose of me medicine.'

'A nice hot cup of tea is what she needs,' Ada said, bustling over to the range and picking up the kettle.

Brandon wrenched the street door open, pausing on the threshold. 'Eliza, a moment of your time, please.'

'Shut the door, there's a terrible draught,' Dolly said in a quite reasonable voice. 'Where's me specs? I can't see a thing. Me head aches something rotten.'

Eliza looked to Freddie for help. 'Shall I give her a dose of laudanum?'

'I think a cup of tea would do her more good,' Freddie said. 'If you'd be so kind, Mrs Little.'

'It's Ada to you, doctor. I'm so glad you're back. We really need you here. Not like some people who think they're too good for the likes of us.' Ada aimed her last remark at Brandon and, turning her back on him, she stomped off into the scullery carrying the steaming kettle.

'I'm leaving,' Brandon said crossly. 'I'll speak to you later, Eliza.'

'Shut the blooming door.' Dolly took her spectacles from Freddie, who had found them on the floor, and she hooked them on the tip of her nose, peering at Brandon. 'I don't know you, do I?'

'It's Brandon, Mum,' Eliza said, stroking her gnarled hand. 'You know Brandon.'

Dolly shook her head. 'Never heard of him.'

Brandon hovered in the doorway, seeming unwilling to leave but equally reluctant to stay. 'The woman is insane and probably dangerous. She ought to be in an asylum.'

'Don't be silly,' Eliza snapped. 'Of course she isn't dangerous. Dolly is just a bit confused.'

'Tell him that toffs shouldn't come to Hemp Yard, Eliza. Tell him there's sorts round here what would cut his throat for his bootlaces, let alone a pair of fine leather boots like those.'

'I'm leaving now, Eliza,' Brandon said stiffly. 'But I'll be back later this evening and I'll take you out to supper so that we can have a private conversation.'

Her first instinct was to tell him to go and boil his head, but she knew that Freddie was staring at her. 'I'd love to, Brandon. But I'm so very tired. I can't go out tonight.'

'Then I'll take you out tomorrow evening. Be ready at seven-thirty and wear something presentable. I don't dine in cheap taverns and chophouses.' Brandon shot a darkling look at Freddie, and walked out into the darkness.

'Masterful, ain't he?' Freddie said, chuckling. 'How did you stumble across a flash cove like him, Liza?'

'Brandon is a gentleman. He was educated at public school and then Oxford. Without him and his father I couldn't hope to rebuild the chandlery.'

'Be wary of his sort.'

Eliza was saved from replying by Ada coming in with a tray of tea. 'There, just what the doctor ordered,' she said, chuckling at her own joke and setting the tray down on the table. She glanced down at Dolly, who was sitting upright in her chair but with her eyes closed. 'She looks more peaceful now. Thank God you come back to look after her, doctor. You've been missed, I can tell you.'

'Have I?' Freddie shot Eliza a quizzical look. 'Everyone seems to have managed perfectly well without me.'

Eliza shrugged her shoulders and went to pour the tea.

'You don't know the half of it,' Ada said,

plucking her shawl from the back of a chair. 'Eliza's worked so hard to look after all of us. What with my Arthur drinking himself stupid in the old days; then he went and got religion, and now he spends all his time at the mission. If it weren't for Eliza, me and me kids would be out on the streets.'

'Is that so?'

'It is too. She could have sold Mr Enoch's house or rented it out for the going rate, but no, she wouldn't do that. Eliza's let us live there at a peppercorn rent. I can't tell you what it's meant to me to have a proper roof over me head.' Ada wrapped her shawl around her shoulders, casting a grateful smile in Eliza's direction. 'She's a good girl and that's a fact. Now I'd best stop gabbing and go home to get supper for the boys.'

'Mind how you go, Ada,' Eliza said. 'And thanks for looking after Dolly. I know she can be a bit of a trial.'

'Never you mind that, ducks. I'd do anything for you, you knows that.'

'Dr Freddie!' Dolly opened her eyes and gazed up at Freddie with a look of genuine recognition and a pleased smile. 'Hello, ducks. Nice of you to call round. Will you stay and have a cup of tea with me?'

'She recognises you! Oh, Freddie, she recognises you.' Eliza clasped her hands together, trying not to cry. 'Maybe she's getting better.'

'It's a miracle,' Ada said, wiping her eyes on her apron. 'A blooming miracle. She's been off in loony-land for so long that sometimes she don't even know Millie or Liza, let alone me.'

Freddie took Dolly's hand in his, smiling down at her. 'How are you, Dolly? You don't look a day older, my dear.'

She slapped him on the wrist. 'Don't talk daft, boy. I saw you yesterday when you brought me my medicine. Anyone would think you'd been away for years. Ada, where's that tea? I'm parched.'

Ada picked up a cup that Eliza had filled with tea and she took it to Dolly. 'There now, drink your tea and I'll see you in the morning.'

'Ta,' Dolly said, taking the cup in both hands and peering at Ada over the top of her spectacles. 'Who are you, ducks? Do I know you?'

An hour later, when Freddie had left the house, promising to return next day with a medicine for Dolly that would gradually lessen her need for laudanum, Eliza came downstairs having put Dolly to bed. She was bone tired and every muscle in her body ached. She glanced at the clock on the mantelshelf and saw that it was almost eight o'clock and Millie had not yet returned. She had supposed that she must be at the mission with Arthur and the Booths, but it was getting late and now she was beginning to worry. There was a pan of vegetable broth on the hob, but Eliza had no appetite. She made another pot of tea, reusing the leaves from the last brew, and sat by the glowing embers of the fire, sipping weak tea and going over the events of the day in her head. She was, she realised, too tired and numbed to feel any great emotion at the revelation that Aaron had known and loved her mother; too tired even to experience the pain of discovering that Freddie had taken a mistress who was her dead brother's widow. There was, Eliza thought, one bright shining star in the whole murky firmament and that was Tommy, Bart's son.

She was sitting and dreaming up ways of getting to know her young nephew when the door opened and Millie came in on a gust of smoke-laden night air. Her cheeks were pink from exertion and she looked pleased with herself. Eliza jumped to her feet, tiredness forgotten in her relief on seeing Millie safe and sound. She hugged her and then shook her. 'Where have you been, you bad girl? I was worried sick.'

'I can look after meself,' Millie said, twirling free from Eliza's grasp and giggling. 'I've been working, if you must know, Liza. I've got a job and it don't entail grubbing for a few pence selling flowers in the street. And I'm starving.' Tossing her shawl onto a chair, Millie went to the range and lifted the lid off the black iron saucepan, sniffing appreciatively. 'Ada makes the best soup in London. Want some?'

Eliza sat down again as a wave of exhaustion washed over her; she shook her head. 'No, ta. Tell me about this job. You haven't done nothing silly, have you?'

'Of course not.' Millie danced off into the scullery.

Eliza could hear her moving about the room, the sound of a knife hacking through bread, the clatter of crockery and the jingle of cutlery. Millie reappeared carrying a tray and set it down on the table. 'It was Brandon's idea.'

'Brandon!' Eliza jerked upright in her chair, her tiredness forgotten. 'What's he got to do with you?'

'He come round this afternoon, looking for you. He asked me how I was and I said I was fine now, thanks very much.'

'Never mind all that. Please get to the point.'

Millie ladled soup into a bowl and went to sit at the table, picking up her spoon. 'I told him I was looking for work and he said he might be able to help.'

'Help? How?' Eliza could feel her heart thumping wildly inside her chest. She had seen the look in Brandon's eyes when Millie had come home after being attacked by the street flower sellers. It would have been obvious to anyone that the sight of firm young flesh had aroused him. Brandon was a sensual man, used to getting his own way with women of a certain class. The memory of his kiss still lingered; Eliza had only to close her eyes to recall the hardness of his body pressed against hers. She had to drag her thoughts back to the present and concentrate on what Millie was saying.

'Brandon said if I was to go to his home, ask for the housekeeper and tell her that he had sent me, then she would find me employment. So I did and she give me a job as a chambermaid. That's why I'm so late.'

'A chambermaid! Oh, Millie, there wasn't no need for you to go into service.' Eliza rose to her feet. She went to sit at the table opposite Millie, who was unconcernedly dipping chunks of bread into her soup. 'The roof is being raised on the chandlery and it will be up and running before Christmas. We can work together, love, just as we did before.'

Millie popped a piece of bread in her mouth, munched and swallowed. 'I'll leave the Millers then, and come and work for you. Don't look so serious, Liza. It will be all right, I promise you. Brandon is such a good bloke – if I wasn't sweet on Davy, I think I could quite fancy Brandon, but then he is only interested in you. It's the story of my life.'

Somehow, Eliza managed to keep a straight face as Millie gave a world-weary sigh and then attacked her dinner with the appetite of a healthy sixteen-year-old. She could do nothing about Millie's unrequited love for Davy, but she could put a stop to any ideas that Brandon might have with regard to seducing a young chambermaid. She would make her feelings on that point very clear to him over dinner tomorrow, but for now there was Millie to consider, and as Eliza watched her enjoying her food, she felt a rush of protective love. No one, neither man nor woman, was going to hurt her little sister. Millie was just as much part of her family as little Tommy, and she loved them both.

'What's up?' demanded Millie, pausing with the spoon halfway to her mouth.

'I've had the most incredible day,' Eliza said, smiling. 'I'm not sure where to begin.'

Next morning, Millie was up before dawn to start her first full day working for the Millers. Although it was usual for housemaids to live in, Millie said that the housekeeper had been agreeable to her residing at home, providing that she arrived punctually for work, and did not complain if her duties kept her at the house until late. It was not a happy thought that Millie would be wandering the streets of Wapping late at night, but Eliza kept her peace, determined to speak to Brandon that evening. Hopefully, the Millers' housekeeper could be persuaded to find

Millie a bed and allow her to stay in the house on the nights when she was working late.

Dolly was still sleeping peacefully, worn out by the excitement of the previous evening. Although Eliza usually went out every morning to inspect the building work, she had stayed at home today with the excuse of helping Ada, who was out in the back yard, doing the washing. Eliza had convinced herself that she was not waiting in to see Freddie; she was staying in because she was needed here. The weather was mild for late October, but the water in the washtub cooled rapidly and had to be topped up with the kettle from the hob. Eliza did the fetching and carrying, using it as an excuse to look out of the front window to see if Freddie was coming. When there was no one in sight apart from the bare-footed children who were too young to go to school or to send out on the streets selling bootlaces or matches, and the rangy mongrel curs that scavenged for scraps in the gutters, she tried not to feel too disappointed. Freddie had promised that he would bring some fresh medication for Dolly, and she was certain that he wouldn't let her down.

But as the morning went on, Eliza began to worry. It could be that Daisy had stopped him; maybe she had insisted that he went with her to the furniture warehouse. She left the window with a sigh, and, having tucked the crocheted blanket around Dolly who was now dozing peacefully in her chair, Eliza picked up the kettle and went out into the yard.

By the time the washing was mangled and hanging damply on the rope line stretched in zigzags across the yard, Eliza had given up hope of seeing Freddie. She left Ada pegging out the last of the bed sheets in a mist of steam that was pungent with the smell of carbolic soap. In the living room, Eliza had taken down the tin from the mantelshelf and was counting the coppers. Despite her thrifty housekeeping, there was just enough money left to keep them in bread and tea for a week. They had not eaten meat for a month, and had been living mainly on vegetable soup or boiled potatoes. It would be at least a month before she was back in business and able to support her family. Millie had been so happy to have found work, but servants were usually paid quarterly, and that would come too late to be of any help. She stared at the coppers in her hand, aware that her options were limited. Aaron held the purse strings, paying for the building materials as well as the wages of the builders. He had already advanced her money and it would be difficult to ask for more. It was a hard truth to acknowledge, but Eliza suspected that she had sold her soul to the Millers and it would take her a lifetime to repay them. She was reaching up to put the tin back on the shelf when the front door burst open, making her jump. The tin flew out of her hands, spilling its contents on the floor.

'I'm sorry, Liza. I didn't knock for fear of disturbing Dolly.' Freddie went down on his knees beside her as she searched for the coins.

'There should be more,' Eliza said frantically, scrambling over the flagstones. 'There should be another penny.'

He sat back on his haunches. 'Steady on, love. One penny isn't going to break the bank.'

'Freddie, you don't understand.' Crawling on her hands and knees, Eliza went under the table, pushing the chairs aside in search of the lost coin.

'Are things so bad then, Liza?' He rose to his feet, brushing dust from the knees of his trousers.

Eliza went to stand up and banged her head on the table. 'Ouch! That hurt.' She stood up, rubbing her sore head. 'I can't lie to you, Freddie. This is all the money I have in the world and it's got to last until Christmas.'

Chapter Eighteen

'My dear girl, is that all?' Freddie was smiling as he peeled off his gloves, one finger at a time.

As she watched him, Eliza could only think that the cost of a pair of fine kid gloves such as those would keep them for weeks. 'I'm serious, Freddie. I have tenpence left to keep us in food, coal and candles. I don't know how I'm going to manage until I get the business going again and Millie gets her wages from the Millers.'

'I wasn't laughing at you, Liza. All I meant was, why didn't you tell me before?' Freddie slipped his hand into his inside breast pocket and drew out a pouch bulging with coins. 'I'm not a wealthy man, poppet, but I'm not poor. How much do you need?'

'I – I can't take your money.'

He tipped the contents of the pouch onto the table and counted out five pounds in crowns, florins, shillings and sixpences. 'There, that should do for the time being. If you need more, you only have to ask.'

Eliza eyed the money, biting her lip. 'I won't be able to repay you for a very long time.'

'If you talk like that you'll make me angry.' Freddie laid his hands on her shoulders, holding her gently, but firmly. 'Look at me, Liza.'

She raised her eyes reluctantly. 'I'm sorry. I only meant . . .'

'I know what you meant.' His lips curved into a rueful smile. 'Are you forgetting that I'm old enough to be a quite senior member of your family, my dear? As such I'm entitled to help you without any question of putting you in my debt.'

'Oh, Freddie.' Eliza bit her lip, bitterly regretting the words that he had overheard when she was battling verbally with Daisy. 'I was cross and I didn't mean it to sound like it did.'

'There, there, think nothing of it.' Freddie turned away abruptly, apparently intent on the task of stowing the remaining coins in the pouch. 'If I can make things easier for you, then I will.'

Eliza wiped her eyes on the back of her hand; she had grown accustomed to hiding her innermost feelings for fear of showing weakness in the harsh commercial world. Freddie's kindness and generosity was almost overwhelming. She gulped and sniffed. 'Th-thank you.'

He took a handkerchief from his pocket and handed it to her. 'Dry your eyes, poppet, or Ada will be hitting me over the head with a saucepan for upsetting you.'

Eliza laughed in spite of herself. 'You are such a fool, Freddie.'

'I am, and I know it.'

For a brief moment, their fingers touched and a tingling sensation like pins and needles shot up her arm, sending thrills down her spine. She turned her head away, hoping that he had not seen the hot colour rise to her cheeks. 'You promised to bring Dolly some medicine.'

'I did, and I have.' Freddie put his hand in his coat pocket and produced a brown medicine bottle. 'When she asks for laudanum, give her a teaspoonful of this. There is laudanum in it, but only in a small dose, which I'll reduce further every time I make a fresh mixture. It will take time, Liza, but it should gradually reduce her dependency on the drug.'

'Will she be cured of the brain fever?'

'I'm afraid not, poppet.'

Eliza took the bottle, fingering it and feeling the glass still warm from being held in his hand. 'Thank you for this, and for the money. I will repay it, in time.'

Before Freddie could answer, Ada came in from the scullery, her normally pale cheeks flushed from a combination of cold air and exertion. 'Are you two deaf or something? Dolly's been calling out for ages. I heard her clear out in the yard, and I'm sure the whole street could hear her too.'

'I'll go to her,' Eliza said, with a guilty start; she had been so involved with Freddie, and the complicated feelings that he aroused in her, that she had heard nothing apart from the beating of her own heart.

'Don't bother, I'm going.' Ada was already halfway up the stairs, grumbling as she went.

'I really didn't hear her. Poor Dolly, she'll think I deserted her.'

'She'll have forgotten all about it before she gets to the bottom of the stairs. And I've got a surprise in store for her.'

'You have? What is it?'

'How long is it since Dolly left this house?'

Eliza shook her head. 'I don't know, a year, maybe two.'

'I thought as much. She needs to get out and about. As I'm setting up in practice, I've bought a dog cart, and an old nag to pull it, so that I can go out and about town with speed and safety. You and Dolly can be the first to ride in it.'

'A dog cart?' Eliza ran to the window, peering out. 'Where is it? Are you teasing me, Freddie?'

'I paid a lad to hold the horse while I came to see you. Let's hope he hasn't taken it for a spin, though I doubt if old Nugget could make it further than Limehouse without collapsing between the shafts.'

An hour later, Freddie drew Nugget to a halt outside his residence in Dark House Street.

'Are you sure this will be all right with Daisy?'

Eliza asked, as he helped her down from the cart.

'She's gone to the furniture warehouse to spend my money. That will keep her occupied for the best part of the day. Now do you want to see young Tommy or not?'

'Of course I do.'

'Here, this isn't the palace,' Dolly said, peering out from beneath a pile of rugs that Freddie had thoughtfully provided. 'I thought we was going to have dinner with the queen and young Edward, the cheeky little sod. You may think I don't remember nothing, but I know he was at our house last night. Told him to shut the door, I did.'

'So you did, Dolly.' Freddie lifted her in his arms and carried her to the front door, which Sukey held open with a disapproving look on her peaky face.

'Mistress won't like it, sir.'

'Mistress won't know unless you tell her, and I suggest that you keep quiet, Sukey. Bringers of bad news usually get a clout round the ear for their pains.'

Sukey scuttled off in the direction of the kitchen and Freddie carried Dolly into the front parlour, setting her down on the only chair in the room. 'There, Dolly, you sit by the fire and I'll tell her majesty that you're here.'

'I can't see too well without me specs. But it seems a bit bare for a palace. Where's the gold and silver and the footmen? It wasn't like this when I last come to dinner.'

'I'll send the maid in with a glass of Madeira and a slice of cake,' Freddie said, tucking a rug around Dolly's knees. 'Rest there, Dolly, and we'll be back in a minute.'

'It wasn't like this in my day.' Dolly leaned back in the chair, closing her eyes. 'But a glass of Madeira wine would be nice and I got a real fancy for a slice of seed cake.'

As they left the room, Eliza caught Freddie by the sleeve. 'Oughtn't we to tell her the truth? I don't think all this pretence about the palace is good for her.'

'Humour her, poppet. Just for the time being, let her live in her dream world. There are worse places to be.'

'I suppose so.'

'Put your trust in an old crocusser, my love.'

Responding to the irrepressible twinkle in his eyes, Eliza laughed out loud.

'It's so good to hear you laugh again,' Freddie said, caressing her cheek with the tip of his forefinger. 'You've shouldered a burden that would have been too heavy for most men, let alone a young girl.'

The magic moment dissipated with his last words. The pleasure that Eliza had felt and the tenderness of his touch were all as nothing if Freddie still saw her as a mere child. She bit back harsh words; she wanted to shout out loud that she was a grown woman with a woman's emotions and needs, but being in the house that Freddie shared with Daisy made it impossible for her to speak out. Her knees were shaking and Eliza felt as though the dark waters of the Thames were closing over her head. She was drowning. 'Where's Tommy?' She saw a lifeline and made a grab for it. 'You promised that I could see him.'

'Of course.' Freddie's tone was suddenly neutral. 'I'll take you to him.'

He led the way to a room at the back of the house that had been set up as a nursery with a truckle bed in one corner, a table and two chairs and a large, gaudily painted rocking horse that looked as though it had been stolen from a merry-go-round at a fair. A fire blazed in the hearth, the coals glowing orange and black, with flames roaring up the chimney like a tiger caged behind the bars of a nursery fireguard. Tommy was sitting on the bare floorboards, playing with a set of coloured wooden bricks. He looked up with an oddly adult expression on his small face as Freddie entered the room, closely followed by Eliza.

'Tommy, my boy. Look who's come to see you.'

'Hello, Tommy. Do you remember me? I'm your Auntie Liza.' Eliza went down on her knees in front of him, and she picked up a couple of bricks. 'What were you building?'

'It fell down,' Tommy said, looking past Eliza to Freddie. 'Where's my mama?'

'She'll be home soon, old chap. Your Auntie Liza will keep you company while I go and see to the horse.' Freddie left the room, closing the door behind him.

She sat back on her haunches watching Tommy as he began to pile the bricks one on top of the other. He seemed so self-contained but Eliza sensed his feeling of isolation. She remembered only too well her own childhood, and the hours spent alone at night in the unfriendly confines of the sail loft while Bart was out working on the river. Her heart went out to the boy; he resembled Bart so closely that it almost hurt to look at him. She wanted above everything to be able to get to know Tommy and to love him, but she did not know how to begin. It pained her to realise that she had no idea how to talk to him, or break into the private little world that he seemed to have built for himself. She tried to think of something to say that would amuse him, but her inability to do so only underlined her lack of experience in dealing with children. Eliza took a deep breath, and tried again. 'So, Tommy, what was it before it fell down?'

'A boat.'

'Do you like boats?'

'We come to London on a boat. A big boat.'

'So you did. If your mama will let you, I could take you to the docks to see some big boats.'

For a moment a glimmer of interest lit his eyes, and then it faded. 'I got to stay indoors. Mama said I must.'

'Well, I'm sure we could fix something. And I know that your mama would want you to come and see my store, where I sell things to do with boats. You'd like that, wouldn't you?'

Tommy pushed a pile of bricks towards her. 'Build a boat now.'

For all her efforts, Eliza soon found she was hopeless at building with wooden blocks, and Tommy was eyeing her attempts with masculine contempt. She tried to make a joke of her feeble efforts, but he refused to respond and she was rapidly coming to the conclusion that he simply didn't like her. By the time Freddie returned from the stables, Eliza was almost at her wits' end and she cast him a desperate but silent plea for help.

'Not going too well?' Freddie helped her to her feet, adding in a low voice, 'Give the boy time.'

'She don't know how to build a boat,' Tommy said, leaping up and tucking his small hand into Freddie's. 'She's a girl and girls are no good at anything.'

Freddie winked at Eliza over the top of Tommy's head. 'Oh, I wouldn't say that, old chap.'

'It's true that I'm not much good with building blocks,' Eliza said, smiling ruefully. 'But perhaps I'll get better with practice.'

Tommy tugged Freddie's hand. 'I'm hungry.'

With a mighty swing, Freddie hefted him onto his shoulders. 'And I've persuaded Sukey to lay out a picnic luncheon in the parlour. Although,' he added, turning to Eliza, 'she's not the best cook in the world so I wouldn't get your hopes up too high. Mind your head on the lintel, Tommy.'

Eliza followed them out of the nursery and down the hall to the parlour, where Dolly was dozing in front of the fire, an empty wine glass still clutched in her hand. She opened her eyes as they entered the room, and, as Freddie set Tommy down on the floor, she sat bolt upright, peering short-sightedly at him with her silver hair sticking out from her head in a crown of corkscrew curls.

'Are you the queen?' demanded Tommy, eyeing Dolly with an unblinking stare.

She glowered for a moment and then gave him a gap-toothed smile. 'That's right, ducks. I'm the queen and who might you be, young man?'

'Tommy Bragg.'

'I like you, Tommy Bragg. You may sit beside me and tell me a story.'

'Grown-ups tell children stories.'

'I'm the queen and you have to do like I say.'

Tommy seemed to consider this for a moment and then he went to sit on the floor beside Dolly. 'Are you hungry, queen?'

Dolly put her head on one side, considering. 'I could do with another slice of that seed cake.'

'I'll get it for you,' Tommy said, making a move to get to his feet.

'Stay where you are, boy.' Dolly pointed a bony finger at Eliza. 'That's what servants are for.'

'Well,' Eliza said, exchanging amused glances with Freddie. 'It's amazing. I couldn't get through to him at all and yet Dolly can.'

'Then we'd best play the game,' Freddie said, picking up a knife and handing it to Eliza. 'Cut a slice of seed cake for her majesty, serving wench.'

'If I'm the servant then what are you, Freddie?'

Freddie pulled a face. 'How about court jester?'

They ate their food sitting on the floor, with Dolly reigning supreme from her throne and regaling Tommy with stories about picnics with Eastern potentates and foreign royalty in the grounds of Buckingham Palace. Eliza nibbled a slice of the pork pie that Sukey had provided. She was so happy to be sitting close to Freddie that she did not even complain when Tommy accidentally dropped his portion on her skirt, leaving a greasy stain.

As the sky darkened outside, hurling rain at

the windows, the shadows in the corners of the room deepened, and they were marooned on an island of flickering firelight. She was as close to Freddie as she could be without actually touching him and nothing seemed to exist outside that enchanted circle of light; Eliza felt warm and safe for the first time in years. She closed her eyes and allowed her senses to soar with happiness. The fire snapped and crackled, making music with the pitter-patter of the raindrops against the window glass. Dolly's high-pitched voice mingled with Tommy's childish laughter, echoing off the high ceiling, and creating the impression that there was a party in progress.

The spell was broken abruptly when Daisy burst in upon them, bringing with her a gust of cold, damp air. 'Well, you all look cosy, I'm sure.'

Tommy leapt to his feet and ran over to her, throwing his arms around her waist. 'Mama, mama, we've had such a good game. She's the queen and I'm the prince.' He pointed to Dolly who had risen to her feet with her paper crown hanging tipsily over one ear.

'That's nice, dear,' Daisy said, casting a stony glance in Freddie's direction. 'Just look at you, Tommy. You've got jam all over your clean shirt.'

'Don't scold the boy, Daisy.' Freddie raised himself from the floor, holding his hand out to help Eliza to her feet.

Eliza could see by the expression on her face that this simple gesture had not gone down well with Daisy. She longed to fly to Tommy's defence, but she held her tongue knowing that it would only make things worse.

Daisy shot a furious glance at Freddie. 'Tommy is my son and don't you forget it, Freddie Prince.'

'Mama.' Tommy tugged at her sleeve. 'We've had a picnic on the floor.'

'Go and find Sukey. Tell her I want a cup of tea and some bread and cheese.'

'But I want to stay and play with the queen,' Tommy said, stamping his foot. 'It's not fair.'

'Do as I say or I'll box your ears.' Daisy made her hands into fists and Tommy fled from the room. She turned on Freddie, her eyes flashing with anger. 'This is all your fault, Freddie. Bringing a mad woman into the house and filling the boy's head with nonsense.'

Dolly collapsed onto her chair. 'Liza. What's going on? Who is that woman and why is she shouting at my poor Albert?'

Eliza hurried to her side. 'It's all right, Mum. Don't get upset.'

'I was the queen,' Dolly said, clutching Eliza's hand. 'And then she come in shouting and I don't know who I am. Tell her to go away.'

'There, there, calm down, dear.' Eliza stroked Dolly's hair, carefully removing the paper crown. She cast an anxious glance at Freddie.

He turned to Daisy, speaking quietly but firmly. 'We'll talk about this later.'

'Don't take that tone with me.'

Freddie shrugged his shoulders. He went to the table and poured a measure from the medicine bottle into Dolly's wine glass. 'Here, Liza, let her sip this.'

Eliza held it to Dolly's trembling lips. 'Drink this, love. You'll soon be right as rain.'

Daisy lowered her voice just a little. 'I don't want Tommy's head filled with stupid stories that will give him nightmares. That woman is out of her head.'

'Come now, Daisy,' Freddie said mildly. 'Where's the harm in the boy having a bit of fun?'

'Fun? He makes up enough stories as it is without you encouraging him. And why did you bring her here when you knew I was going to be out?' Daisy shook her finger at Eliza, raising her voice. 'What's your game, missy?'

'I just wanted to see Tommy. I didn't mean to stay so late.'

Daisy made a move towards Eliza, but Freddie caught her by the wrist. 'My dear, don't blame Eliza. It was my fault and, as usual, I didn't stop to think. I knew she wanted to see the boy. I should have spoken to you first, but you know how I am.'

Daisy frowned up at him and then she smiled,

giving his cheek a playful slap. 'I do know you, you big bad boy.' She kissed the imprints of her fingers on his cheek and turned to Eliza with a tight-lipped smile that did not reach her eyes. 'I don't mind you seeing Tommy, Eliza, but I'd rather you did it when I'm here.'

'Yes, of course,' Eliza said hastily. 'I do understand. Now I really must get Dolly home. I have to go out this evening and I need to get her settled.'

'I'll bet you've got that nice gent to take you out.' Daisy's expression changed subtly, and she leaned her head against Freddie's shoulder. 'Aren't you the crafty one?'

'You're not going to accept Brandon Miller's invitation to supper, are you?' Freddie's voice was edged with steel.

'He's taking me out to discuss business.'

'I don't like it. You shouldn't go out with him, not without a chaperone. It's not right.'

'Don't listen to him, my dear,' Daisy said, her face wreathed in a sunny smile. 'He's an old spoilsport. You go out and have a good time.'

'It's business, not pleasure.' Eliza stared down at her crumpled skirts with a feeling of dismay. This was her only good frock and Brandon had told her to wear something suitable. The grease stain caused by Tommy's slice of pie had spread down the front of her skirt and it would be almost impossible to remove. She shook her head. 'Maybe I won't go after all.'

'I can guess at your problem – you got nothing to wear.' Daisy seized Eliza by the hand, dragging her towards the door. 'We'll soon fix that, and you'll be the belle of the ball, so to speak. Freddie, fetch the cart and be ready to take them home.'

Daisy raced across the hall and up the sweeping staircase to her room on the first floor. She kept a tight grip on Eliza's hand, giving her no option other than to follow in her wake. In the half-light, Eliza saw an unmade bed, with tumbled pillows and coverlet. In her mind's eye she saw Daisy and Freddie, coupling in just the same way as she had seen him with Beattie. With a sick feeling in her stomach, Eliza turned away.

Daisy waded through piles of clothes that lay scattered about the floor like fallen leaves in autumn. 'I can't wait for the furniture to arrive,' she said, pulling garments at random from an overflowing cabin trunk. 'I'm sick of living in a mess. Here, this one might fit you. I was thinner in those days.' Daisy held up a shimmering gown of scarlet satin, trimmed with black velvet bows and fringed braid. 'Bart always liked me in this. He'd approve, I'm sure.'

'Oh, I dunno.' Eliza stared at the garish garment, struggling to find a tactful way of refusing. 'It's beautiful, but I think it's a bit too grand for me.'

'Stuff and nonsense.' Daisy held the gown

against Eliza. 'It's perfect. You want to impress the rich bloke, don't you?'

'Like I said, it's business.'

Daisy thrust the gown into Eliza's arms with a knowing grin. 'I was in that sort of business, ducks. I was a professional afore I met your brother. There ain't nothing you can tell me about twisting men round me little finger. You wear that frock tonight and he'll give you anything you want.'

'Why are you doing this for me, Daisy?'

'Well, it's not because I'm your affectionate sister-in-law. Although I did love Bart, in me own way; so don't run away with the idea that I was just using him.'

Eliza shook her head. 'No, I promise you. I never thought such a thing.'

'Let's be honest with each other, Liza. It's a tough life for a widow woman, especially when she's got a kid in tow. I thought I'd got Freddie where I wanted him, until I saw him with you, and now I'm not so sure. Seeing you hitched to another bloke is the only way I can see clear to getting you out of me hair. Is that plain enough?'

'It's clear, but you're so wrong. Freddie still thinks of me as a kid. He's not interested in me. Not in the way you think.'

Daisy's eyes narrowed. 'That's as maybe, but at least we got things straight. You keep your hands off my man, and I'll let you see Tommy. I want fair shares of the business for my son, or else I'll take the case to the law, and you'll end up with nothing. Do you understand?'

Eliza drew herself up to her full height. 'I would always treat Bart's son fair. You got no need to worry on that score.'

'Then we'll get along fine,' Daisy said, smiling. 'I ain't a hard woman, Liza. But I am tough. I've had to fight for everything I got. As I see things, there ain't no reason why we can't be friends, so long as you understands the rules.'

Freddie was about to leave the house in Hemp Yard, but he paused on the doorstep, turning to Eliza with a frown puckering his brow. 'You will take care, won't you, Liza? Don't let that fellow take advantage of you.'

'There's no need to worry about me. I can take care of myself.' She wanted to cry, but Eliza managed a tight little laugh.

Freddie appeared unconvinced. 'I mean it. Make certain he escorts you home, but don't ask him in. Keep the conversation strictly to business, and if he starts to flirt with you – put him in his place.'

'Goodbye, Freddie.' Eliza closed the door on him and her smile faded. She was not looking forward to her evening with Brandon, but the future of her business depended upon him. The bricks and mortar might be in place, but she still needed to buy stock for the chandlery. Without the Millers' backing, it would be impossible. She glanced at the clock on the mantelshelf: in just one hour he would be calling for her and Millie was not home yet, even though she had promised to ask the housekeeper if she could be let off early. Eliza snatched up her shawl and wrapped it around her shoulders. There was only one solution, and that was to see if either Ada or Mary could keep an eye on Dolly until Millie returned. Letting herself out into the cold night with frost beginning to settle on the cobblestones, Eliza hurried to the house in Bird Street.

A gust of steamy air laced with the odour of carbolic soap belched out into the street as Ada opened the door. The sound of childish shrieks and splashing emanated from the living room and Eliza realised that she had interrupted bath night. 'Oh, dear,' she said apologetically. 'I was going to ask you to come and sit with Dolly for a bit, but it seems like a bad time.'

'I would come,' Ada said, wiping her hands on her apron. 'You know I would, but I daren't leave the boys on their own. They'd either drown each other, burn the house down or flood it.'

'Could Mary do it, just until Millie gets in?'

'I'm sorry, ducks. It is her night off but she's gone with her dad to one of them mission meetings. They've taken to going round the pubs preaching on the evils of the demon drink. Time was when you couldn't get my Arthur out of the boozer. Now he's in them trying to reform the punters. I dunno what the world is coming to.'

'Don't worry. I'll manage.' Wrapping her shawl more tightly around her head, Eliza ran all the way home.

She found Dolly sleeping peacefully and heaved a sigh of relief. But a quick check on the time made her realise that she had just half an hour to get ready. She went into her bedroom to try on the borrowed gown. Daisy had spoken the truth when she said she had been much slimmer when the dress was made for her. Even so, Eliza's firm young breasts were no match for Daisy's generous bosom and the neckline plunged so low that it left little to the imagination. She rifled through her things and found a fichu that had belonged to Dolly in the days when such items of clothing were fashionable. She draped it round her bare shoulders and tucked it into the top of her stays. Feeling more confident, she put up her hair, fastening it with combs, and went downstairs to await Brandon's arrival. She paced the floor with a mounting degree of nervousness.

He arrived on time, looking quite breathtakingly handsome in his top hat, tails and flowing opera cloak lined with scarlet satin. His appreciative glance both comforted and disconcerted Eliza and she sought vainly for an excuse not to accompany him.

'Are you ready, Eliza?'

'Not quite – I mean – I ought to wait for Millie to come home. I can't leave Dolly on her own.'

'The girl is on her way. I made certain that the housekeeper let her off on time.' Brandon stepped inside the house and picked up her shawl. 'You really ought to have a mantle, my dear. It's quite chilly outside.' He glanced at the empty grate, raising an eyebrow. 'And not much warmer inside.'

'I don't feel the cold,' Eliza countered, not wanting to admit that she did not possess a mantle, and the unlit fire was a necessary economy. 'I'm ready, but I really should wait for Millie.'

'You worry too much, Eliza. What harm could come to the old lady in the next half-hour or so?' Brandon smiled, proffering his arm. 'My carriage awaits.'

She hesitated for a moment. 'I'm coming, but first I must ask our neighbour to listen out for Dolly, just in case she wakes before Millie gets home.'

When they arrived outside the Ship and Turtle in Leadenhall Street, Eliza's back was aching from being held stiffly erect in an attempt to prevent the motion of the carriage from throwing her against Brandon. She stifled a sigh of relief as the coachman opened the door and let down the steps. She smiled as she recognised Hawkins, the coachman who had shown her kindness when he had driven her from Pennington Street to the chandlery. But before she could acknowledge him, Brandon had leapt out and helped her from the carriage, issuing a curt instruction to Hawkins to walk the horses and then wait until they were ready to return home. Eliza felt sorry for the poor man having to huddle beneath his many-caped greatcoat on such a cold night. The pair of matched greys were snorting and steam rose in great clouds from their hides: they really ought to be in a nice warm stable, she thought, accepting Brandon's arm and wondering whether he possessed even the smallest amount of conscience. But he showed no sign of caring for the comfort of his servant or his animals, and he led her into the fuggy interior of the pub. The tempting aroma of food was laced with the fumes of strong spirits, together with the malty smell of ale, and the air was thick with tobacco smoke. A waiter came hurrying towards them and, judging by the welcome Brandon received, it was obvious to Eliza that he was an old and valued customer. The bar was crowded and all the tables occupied, but the waiter led them up a narrow staircase to a private room on the first floor. As he bowed out, Eliza caught a knowing gleam in his eye and she had to curb the desire to run after him. Slowly, without taking his eyes off Eliza, Brandon placed his opera hat on the side table and then peeled off his gloves. With a theatrical flourish, he discarded his cloak.

'Let me take your shawl, Eliza.' His hands rested a little too long on her shoulders for comfort and his eyes wandered from her face to the fichu, which had slipped just a little.

Adjusting the gauzy material, she moved away on the pretext of examining the table that was set for two, with starched white linen and brightly polished silver cutlery sparkling in the candlelight.

Brandon made no attempt to follow her. He went to a side table where he filled two glasses with wine from a decanter. He handed one to Eliza. 'Let's have a toast, my dear.'

Wishing that she were anywhere but here, she took the glass from him. The ruby-red claret brought back memories of the dinner party at the Millers' house when Brigham had caused her to spill her wine, ruining the gown that belonged to Miss Cynthia. In a detached part of her mind, she thought that an accidental spill this evening would barely leave a mark on Daisy's scarlet dress.

'Here's to you, Eliza. The prettiest girl in London. And here's to our cordial relationship, both personal and in business.' Brandon raised his glass and drank deeply.

She could feel the blood rushing to her cheeks, but she held his gaze and sipped her drink, trying not to wrinkle her nose at the oaky flavour of blackcurrants and plums, with a bit of vinegar thrown in. Why toffs made such a fuss over wine, she couldn't think. She would have liked to ask for some lemonade to make it sweeter, but Brandon was rolling the tart liquid round in his mouth as if it tasted like honey drizzled from a honeycomb. Eliza raised her glass. 'To a successful business partnership,' she said, deliberately ignoring the inference to anything more personal.

Brandon took his glass and the decanter to the table, and setting them down on the snowy cloth he pulled out a chair. 'Take a seat, my dear. You must be famished.'

She sat down and Brandon took a seat opposite her. He reached out to tug at a bell pull. 'I took the liberty of ordering when I booked the table. Their turtle soup is superb, and I thought you might like to try the roast pheasant. We'll think about dessert later.'

In the deep shadows she could just make out a divan covered with plump cushions. Brandon was busy topping up her glass with wine, and Eliza had the uncomfortable feeling that it was she who was going to be the dessert. But if that was Brandon's plan, he gave no hint of it in his conversation. Over the turtle soup, which was actually very good, he kept her entertained with stories of his escapades at Oxford. The roast pheasant was delicious but extremely rich, and Eliza couldn't help thinking that this meal would have fed them all at home for a week at least. Brandon ate with relish, drinking deeply, and sent for another bottle of claret even before the soup bowls were removed from the table. Eliza drank very little; she must keep a clear head and not be lulled into a false sense of security by his undeniable charm and wit. Every time she tried to raise the subject of restocking and reopening the chandlery, Brandon managed to steer the conversation away to some other topic. He was, she had to admit, an amusing companion and he seemed intent only on giving her pleasure. As she studied his handsome, animated counten-ance, Eliza found herself gradually becoming hypnotised by his beautifully modulated voice. If it weren't considered the done thing to talk about business over dinner, then she would just have to follow his lead and be patient.

By the time the covers were removed, Eliza was feeling more relaxed.

'May I take your order for dessert, sir?' The waiter hovered respectfully by the table.

'I'll ring for you when we're ready,' Brandon said, with a dismissive wave of his hand.

The waiter bowed out of the room and Eliza's nerves began to jangle as the mood was broken.

'I – I'm not very hungry,' she said, pleating her table napkin with fidgety fingers. 'It's getting late and I really ought to go home.'

Brandon's dark eyes seemed fathomless in the dim light. He rose slowly to his feet, swaying almost imperceptibly. 'Come now, Eliza. You don't want to spoil a perfect evening by running away early.'

She pushed back her chair and stood up, dropping her napkin on the floor. 'I'm quite tired, Brandon. It's been a long day.'

He was at her side before she had a chance to make for the door. 'Don't be a silly little goose. I'm not going to hurt you.' He drew her into a close embrace.

'Let go of me.' Eliza tried to push him away, but he held her in an iron grip.

'One kiss, my dear. Just a little kiss.'

His breath was hot on her cheek and his lips found hers in a kiss that was laced with wine and desire. With one arm clamped round her waist, he tweaked the fichu from her shoulders, and a swift tug at her bodice exposed her breasts to his groping fingers. Eliza struggled and attempted to kick his shins but was hampered by the hoops that supported the full skirts of her gown. With a sound that was halfway between a groan and a growl, Brandon lifted her off her feet and carried her to the divan. He threw her down amongst the cushions. Before she had a chance to clamber to her feet, he was on her, kissing her roughly and without tenderness, almost as though he was trying to devour her. Eliza struggled and scratched at him with her nails, but the weight of his body was crushing the air from her lungs so that when he released her lips she could only utter a faint cry for help.

'Shut up, you fool,' Brandon snarled. He thrust his hand under her voluminous skirts, pushing, prodding and seeking the seat of his desire between her legs. 'You've been asking for it all evening, and now you're going to get it.'

The pain was too much for Eliza, and in desperation she brought up her knees and rolled off the divan with Brandon tumbling after her. She tried to crawl away but he grabbed her by one of her ankles, dragging her back across the polished floorboards.

She opened her mouth and screamed for all she was worth. Kicking out with her free foot she caught him a hefty blow on the face that made him yelp with pain. She seized her chance, scrambled to her feet and ran to the door. She was tugging at the handle as he got up, swearing and holding his face. 'You little bitch.'

For a moment, she thought the door was locked, but then to her intense relief it opened and Eliza stumbled into the corridor. She raced down the stairs into the crowded bar room. Coming to an abrupt halt, with her hair tumbling about her shoulders and her bodice open to the waist, she crossed her arms over her naked breasts. There was a sudden hush in the bar. Brandon was so close to her that she could feel his hot breath on the back of her neck. Her eyes sought a way of escape through the crowded bar room but a tall figure emerged from the smoke and gloom, dressed in black from head to toe. Holding a Bible before him like a shield, he pointed his finger at Brandon. 'You lecherous, fornicating sinner. You'll be damned to hell for your drunken debauchery.'

Chapter Nineteen

Arthur Little strode across the floor, barging between the tables and unseating a couple of drunken customers on the way. He stopped when he reached Eliza, and his bushy eyebrows almost disappeared into his hairline as a look of recognition dawned in his eyes. 'Eliza?'

'Oh, Mr Little. I ain't never been so glad to see no one in me whole life.' Eliza would have flung her arms around him, but that would have exposed her nakedness. She stood, shivering, as a murmur of voices rippled round the bar, rising to a crescendo of hoots and laughter. Glancing over her shoulder, she saw Brandon glaring at Arthur, his face white with fury.

'Get out of here, you sanctimonious old fool. What right have you to come into a public house canting and raving like a lunatic? This lady is with me. So mind your own bloody business.'

'That's right, mister. You give her one for me.' A purple-nosed man raised his tankard, and then slurped a mouthful, spilling most of the ale down his neck.

A roar of laughter accompanied his action and

Brandon made a dive for Eliza, but she dodged behind Arthur and found Mary, wide-eyed and staring at her in disbelief. 'Liza? What's happened to you?'

'Oh, Mary. Thank God you come.'

Mary slipped off her shawl and wrapped it around Eliza's bare shoulders. 'Let's get out of here, Liza. Leave it to Dad; he'll sort the bugger out.'

By this time the pub was in complete uproar with the crowd jeering and cheering. Arthur stood firm, with his Bible clutched to his chest. Brandon was raving alternately at Arthur and at the punters, who appeared to be egging him on. Eliza and Mary slipped outside unnoticed.

'What was you doing in there?' Mary demanded, shivering. 'Who was that man?'

Eliza shook her head. 'I w-want to g-go home.'

'You can't walk all the way to Wapping in that state. Just look at you, Liza. You look like a Billingsgate doxy.' Mary glanced nervously over her shoulder as a carriage rumbled towards them drawn by two grey horses.

Hawkins drew them to a halt and leaned down from his box. 'Gawd's strewth, young miss. What's he done to you?'

'Please, Mr Hawkins. Will you take us home?' Eliza cast him an imploring glance. 'I know you might get into trouble, but you've got daughters of your own, you told me so.'

He hesitated for a moment, glancing at the closed pub door and then back at his restive horses. Hawkins nodded. 'I can always say one of the horses lost a shoe and I had to find a farrier, which wouldn't be an easy task at this time of night and in this part of town. Hop in, young ladies.'

The next morning Eliza got up early, and, leaving Millie to light the fire and make Dolly's breakfast of tea and toast, she went first to the chandlery to inspect the builders' progress. Although she had slept badly, and was still burning with shame and humiliation after Brandon's failed attempt at seduction, she was determined not to allow his despicable behaviour to prey on her mind. She fully intended to go to the offices of Miller and Son and tell Brandon exactly what she thought of him. She would go to Aaron, if necessary, but she would not let his son think that he could treat her like a common slut.

On the corner of Old Gravel Lane, Arnold and Dan were surveying the newly constructed roof and munching thick slices of bread and dripping. Arnold turned his head at the sound of Eliza's heels click-clacking on the frosty pavement, and his face split into a broad grin. 'Morning, miss. The roof's finished and the inside is all but done. We're almost back in business.'

Some of Eliza's gloom lifted and she managed

to force her lips into a smile. 'That's wonderful.'

'Will you let me stay on and help?' Dan asked anxiously. 'I'm a good worker, ain't I, Basher? I done real good. He'll tell you so.'

Eliza nodded. 'I'm sure we can find you something to do, Dan. And first of all you can show me round the inside.'

Arnold flashed her a grateful smile. 'The boy's been worriting hisself sick, thinking you wouldn't have no need of him now.'

'We'll need all the help we can get to set the store up as it was.' Eliza picked up her skirts. 'Come with me, Arnold. You too, Dan. I want to see if the carpenters have finished putting up the shelves and building the stands.'

Everything inside the new shop was to Eliza's liking, except for the fact that there was no sail loft. It seemed odd to be in a one-storey building, and she knew she would miss having Davy working up above her while she was serving in the chandlery. But her first concern was to fill the shelves with new stock and start trading. Then she would be able to pay off the Millers and regain control over her life. Brandon would never again have the chance to take advantage of her.

After she had inspected everything, and had consulted with the foreman to find out when the work would be finally completed, Eliza left Arnold and Dan sweeping up wood shavings and she set off for Pennington Street. First of all, she wanted to thank Hawkins, who had risked his job to bring herself and Mary safely home. She found him sitting outside the stables, warming his hands against a brazier filled with glowing coals. She went straight up to him, holding out her hand. 'I come to thank you for what you done last night.'

He stood up, rubbing his grimy mitts against his greatcoat before taking Eliza's hand and giving it a squeeze. 'That's all right, miss.'

'But did you get into trouble? Please tell me if you did.'

'When I got back I found that Mr Brandon had been drowning his sorrows, so to speak. He never even noticed I'd gone. Him and the religious gent what was preaching against the evils of drink was the best of pals. Laughing and joking together they was, and both as drunk as lords.'

She thanked him again and walked on towards the offices of Miller and Son. Her anger at Brandon was now fuelled by the knowledge that he had got Arthur drunk, undoing all the good work done by Mr Booth and his wife at the mission. She marched into the outer office, by-passing the anxious clerk, and headed straight for Brandon's door. She went in without knocking.

Brandon was slumped over his desk with his head resting on his arms. He looked up, staring at her with bleary, bloodshot eyes.

'I want a few words with you, mister,' Eliza said, standing before him, arms akimbo, ready for a fight.

'Not now, please. I'm a sick man.'

'You deserve to have a bad head and I hope it hurts like a dozen navvies with pickaxes hammering inside your worthless skull.'

Closing his eyes, Brandon raised his hands to clutch his forehead. 'It does. And worse.'

'Good.' Eliza reached across the desk and pulled his hands away from his face. 'Now you listen to me, Mr Brandon Miller. You said it was going to be a business meeting. You never said it was going to be funny business.'

Brandon's mouth twisted into a smile and then he winced. 'Don't make me laugh, Eliza. It hurts.'

She slapped his cheek with the flat of her hand. 'And I hope that hurt too. You are a despicable, lying cheat. You treated me like a common whore and you got poor Arthur drunk. That man had given up the booze until you tempted him.'

'You little bitch.' Brandon clutched his cheek, staring up at her in disbelief. He got slowly to his feet, swaying slightly. 'You'd better watch your manners, miss.'

'Or what?' Eliza demanded, facing him squarely.

'Or I'll foreclose on your loan and you'll lose your livelihood. You'll be glad then of men like

Brigham Stone when they offer you money for your services.'

Eliza raised her hand to strike him again, but Brandon caught her by the wrist. 'You came from the gutter, Eliza. I can send you straight back to it. So don't cross me, my dear.'

Although his words struck her like cold steel, Eliza met his eyes without blinking. 'We'll see what your father has to say about that.'

A fleeting expression of doubt flickered in Brandon's eyes. 'Leave my father out of this. You're dealing with me now.'

Eliza broke free of his grasp. 'The higher a monkey climbs,' she said, repeating something she had once overheard when a group of sailors were chatting together in the shop, 'the more you can see of his arse!'

The look of shock on Brandon's face would have been laughable, if Eliza had been in the mood for mirth, but her whole future and that of her family was wavering in the balance. She turned on her heel and stormed out of the room, slamming the door behind her. She headed straight for Aaron's office, almost colliding with him as he was about to leave. He eyed her in some surprise. 'My dear Eliza. Whatever is the matter?'

She could hear Brandon's footsteps approaching and she clutched Aaron's arm. 'I need to speak with you, sir. In private.'

Aaron frowned. 'I'm in a hurry. Won't it wait?'

'No, sir. I need to speak to you now.'

'Then you'd better come into my office.'

Aaron held the door for her and was about to close it when Brandon pushed past him. 'This concerns me, Father.'

'Very well, but I haven't got all day.' Aaron sighed audibly and went to sit behind his desk.

'I don't want him here,' Eliza protested, jerking her head in Brandon's direction. 'What I have to say is for your ears only, Mr Miller.'

'I'm a busy man and I don't want to listen to tales of petty squabbles.'

Elbowing Eliza out of the way, Brandon leaned his hands on the desk. 'Father, I'm sorry to say that we were mistaken in our assessment of Miss Bragg's character.'

She stared at him, momentarily lost for words.

'Explain yourself, Brandon.' Aaron sat back in his chair, folding his arms and staring from one to the other.

'That's not right,' Eliza cried, finding her voice, although it sounded high-pitched and strange even to her own ears. 'He tried to force hisself on me, Mr Miller. He took me to dinner in a pub with a private room . . .'

'So that we could discuss business,' Brandon interjected smoothly. 'The rebuilding of the chandlery is complete and I wanted to find out when Eliza intended to purchase the stock. Then

I discovered that she had used the funds we issued for her own purposes and she was demanding more.'

Unable to believe her ears, Eliza gripped the back of a chair. 'That's a lie.'

'And, Father, she offered me certain favours if I were to agree to her demands.'

Aaron sat forward, leaning his elbows on the desk and staring at Eliza. 'Is this true?'

'No, sir. It's a pack of lies. He tried to have his way with me and I only just managed to get away. If Arthur Little and Mary hadn't come into the pub preaching against the evils of drink, I – I can't bear to think what might have happened.' Eliza broke off on a sob as tears of anger flowed freely from her eyes.

'See how she protests and cries.' Brandon curled his lip. 'She's nothing more than a common whore and an actress to boot.'

'Take that back,' Eliza cried, fisting her hand. 'I'm neither of them things and you never give me the money to buy stock.'

Brandon caught her by the wrist. 'See how she does it, sir? She fooled us both into thinking she was a sweet and innocent young thing, but she's just a scheming hussy.'

'I gave you the benefit of the doubt on a previous occasion, Eliza.' Aaron's eyes were bleak as he stood up slowly. 'I trusted you, Eliza. I thought you were so like your mother, but I can see now that I was wrong.'

Pushing Brandon aside, she held her hands out to Aaron. 'I've done nothing wrong. I swear to you that I never had any money from Brandon. Not a single penny.'

'She lies, father. Didn't Brigham Stone warn you about her, but you chose to believe Eliza over your old friend?'

'You've struck me to the heart, Eliza,' Aaron said, walking slowly round the desk to face her. 'I treated you like my own daughter and you've betrayed my trust.'

'No, sir. No. I'm telling you, I never done nothing wrong. It's your precious son what's lying.'

'You deceitful trollop,' Brandon said, scowling. 'You're only making matters worse for yourself. Shall I call a constable and have her arrested, Father?'

Aaron shook his head. 'Eliza, the money means nothing to me. If you were in dire need, you only had to ask me and I would have given you anything you wanted. You've hurt me more than I can say. I helped you because of my love for your mother but you've shamed her memory. No!' He held up his hand as Eliza opened her mouth to argue. 'Don't say another word. Brandon, instruct my solicitor to foreclose on the loan.'

'But, sir. The chandlery – it's mine.'

'Not any longer,' Aaron said, walking to the door. 'From this moment on, it belongs to Miller and Son.'

As the door closed on his father, Brandon perched on the desk, eyeing Eliza with a triumphant smile. 'You see what happens when you cross a Miller, Eliza. If you had been obliging you would still own the chandlery.'

She drew herself up to her full height. She was not going to let Brandon see her despair. 'I'd rather starve than let you have your way with me.'

His eyes narrowed and he drew back his head like snake about to strike. 'I'm sure that can be arranged. In fact the cost of rebuilding the shop is greater than the value of the land on which it stands. I shall instruct our solicitor to seize all your assets, including your house.'

'I don't own the house in Hemp Yard. It's rented.'

'But you do own the house in Bird Street. Don't look so surprised, Eliza. I made enquires at the outset of our dealings, just in case things didn't work out as planned.'

Eliza's hand flew to her throat: she was going to be sick or faint. 'You can't do that.'

'My dear girl, I can. And I will send the bailiffs round to your aunt's house too. You could have had everything, but I'll see you end up with nothing. Unless—'

'You don't frighten me,' Eliza lied valiantly. 'There's nothing more you can take off me.'

'No, but I have a fancy for your little sister. I'm sure she'll be more obliging than you, especially when she learns that her job is at stake.'

'You bastard! If you touch a hair off Millie's head, I'll kill you with me own bare hands.'

'I'd enjoy wrestling with you, Eliza. But I think you know who would win.'

'You are an unspeakable rat. No, worse than a rat. I can't think of a word that describes you, Brandon.' Eliza slammed out of the office and ran all the way to the Millers' mansion. She hammered on the door of the servants' entrance, and when a slightly bemused boot boy answered her frantic summons, she pushed past him. After arguing with a kitchen maid and almost coming to blows with the irate cook, Eliza was about to be ejected by a burly footman when the butler came upon the scene.

'I want to see Miss Turner,' Eliza said, pausing in her struggle with the footman. 'Please, mister. It's urgent.'

'Get the creature out of here.' The cook lobbed a soup ladle at Eliza but her aim was somewhat off and it hit the footman in the face. He yelped with pain and brought his hands up to cover his bleeding nose.

Eliza faced up to the butler. 'I'm asking you nicely, mister. Let me see me sister. It's a family matter and I must see her now.'

'Someone fetch Miss Turner.' The butler sniffed, looking down his nose at Eliza. 'I'll have you know, young woman, this is a respectable house and we don't allow such goings on.'

'I ain't budging without Millie.' Eliza folded her arms across her chest.

'If she leaves now then she don't come back.'

She tossed her head. 'No fear of that, mister.'

The sight of Freddie's dog cart being held by a shivering boy at the corner of Hemp Yard made Eliza's heart swell with relief. The barefoot child eyed her suspiciously, and seeing his mottled legs, covered with weeping sores and chilblains, she was moved to put her hand in her pocket. She had precious little money left but this boy's bones were clearly visible beneath skin that had a sickly graveyard pallor. She placed a halfpenny in his hand and told him to go to the baker's shop and buy some bread or a pie. As he scuttled off, Eliza handed the reins to Millie. 'I want a private word with Freddie. I won't be long.'

'I wish you'd tell me what's going on,' Millie said, wrapping her shawl more tightly around her shoulders as rain began to fall from pot-bellied clouds.

'I will, as soon as I've seen Freddie.' Without waiting for a reply, Eliza hurried down the street and let herself into the house.

Dolly was laughing at something Freddie had said and, Eliza thought with a surge of gratitude, she almost looked like her old self. She paused on the threshold, meeting Freddie's enquiring gaze with a wobbly smile. He had been kneeling beside Dolly and he rose slowly to his feet.

'What's the matter?'

His voice held a caress and he looked so achingly familiar and trustworthy that Eliza longed to seek comfort in his arms, but somehow she managed to exert her flagging self-control. 'Freddie, I need to speak to you.'

'Dr Freddie has been telling me all about Australia,' Dolly said, smiling happily. 'He's made me up some special medicine and I feel better already.'

'That's splendid, Mum.'

'We're going there next week. Me and Freddie and your Uncle Ted are going on a ship to Australia and I'm going to see them funny hopping creatures, hankyroos they calls them.' Dolly closed her eyes. 'I'm fair wore out just at the thought of it, and now I'm going to have forty winks. You will tell Ted all about it when he comes in, won't you, ducks?'

'Yes, Mum.' Eliza went over to the table and pulled out a chair. She sat down suddenly as her knees gave way beneath her. 'Freddie, I'm in terrible trouble.'

He sat down beside her and held her hand.

'Take your time, my love. Tell Freddie what's bothering you.'

One look into his sympathetic eyes and the words came gushing from Eliza's mouth in an unstoppable stream. She omitted nothing.

'There's only one thing for it, Liza,' Freddie said, as she finished her story. 'You'll all have to come and live with us in Dark House Street.'

'But we can't do that. What would Daisy say?'

'She's a good-hearted woman when all is said and done. And she is your sister-in-law.'

The flash of relief that Eliza had felt at his offer of a home dissipated like morning mist as reality struck her. Daisy might have a heart as big as Australia thumping away beneath her ample breasts, but she had made it clear that she considered Freddie to be her private property. Eliza stared down at his tanned fingers twined around her small hand and she felt tears sting the back of her eyes. For all his experience of women, Freddie was as naïve as a baby when it came to understanding how the female mind worked. She lowered her eyes and squeezed his hand. 'I don't think that would do at all.'

'Of course it would, my dear. The house is huge and there's plenty of room for all of us.'

'But, Freddie. What about your plans to be a proper doctor? You'll need all your rooms for your clinic.'

'Doctor?' Freddie raised his eyebrows, as if

caught by surprise, and then he chuckled. 'That was yesterday, poppet. I've given up that idea.'

'But you had your heart set on it. You know you did.'

'Circumstances change and a man has to change with them.'

'Is it because of Daisy? Has she made you change your mind?'

Freddie shook his head. 'It has nothing to do with Daisy. I'm considering my options, Liza.'

'So what do you intend to do?'

Freddie seemed about to answer when Dolly stirred, muttered something unintelligible, and then subsided once more into a deep sleep. He jerked his head in her direction. 'I helped put her in that state. I'm not proud of it, and God knows how many other poor souls I've sent in that direction with my nostrums based on laudanum. Doctoring isn't for me – it was a pleasant dream that kept me from going mad in the outback, particularly when I was missing home – and you.'

'But, Freddie . . .'

'You mustn't concern yourself about me, poppet. Don't deny me the opportunity to make up for six long years on the other side of the world, when I could do nothing to help you.'

Leaning her elbows on the table, Eliza rested her head in her hands. Her mind was a jumble of confused thoughts. Brandon's lies and betrayal,

Dolly's illness, Daisy's warning to keep her hands off Freddie: their faces and voices merged into a deafening tumult.

'Is it such a hard decision?' Freddie's voice broke into her thoughts. 'You can trust me, Liza. I won't let any further harm come to you, Dolly or young Millie. I know you think of me as an old man, but I want to look after you, my dear. And you'll be close to Tommy. Millie will be safe from men like Brandon and . . .'

Eliza remembered Millie, standing in the bitter cold, holding the horse. She jumped to her feet. 'I left Millie at the corner of the street. She'll be soaked to the skin and like as not catch a chill.'

Freddie caught her by the hand. 'Will you come with me, or not?'

'Let me go, Freddie.'

He stood up, gripping her hand tightly. 'Tell me that you'll accept my offer.'

She met his unwavering gaze with a hitch in her heart. Living in Freddie's house would be heaven and hell rolled into one. She could still see the rumpled bed in Daisy's room; the bed that she almost certainly shared with Freddie, and where they performed the act that was supposed to be one of love. Eliza remembered all too clearly the stories told her by the unfortunate girls who worked for Mrs Tubbs, the brothel keeper in Old Gravel Lane. Her recent experience with Brandon was muddled up with the memory of that day, years ago, when she had gone to Freddie's room in Anchor Street. She had never been able to forget the spectacle of Beattie's bare buttocks and bouncing breasts as she straddled Freddie on the bed, or the grunts and groans that they had been emitting, like pigs in Smithfield Market. How could she live in a house where he cohabited with another woman? Freddie was the only man she had ever loved – would ever love. Imagining what went on behind closed bedroom doors, with her own brother's widow, would be too much to bear.

'Would it be so terrible to see me every day?' Freddie's voice hardened. 'Or are you secretly in love with that bastard Miller? Is that what has come between us?'

Shocked, Eliza's eyes flew to his face and she recognised genuine pain. She was about to deny his accusation when Millie burst in through the front door, bringing with her a gust of damp air.

'I'm soaking wet and chilled to the bone, Liza. Did you forget I was stuck there holding on to that old nag?' She came to a halt, staring from one to the other. 'What's up?'

Freddie picked up his hat and gloves. 'I've offered you all a home with me, but Eliza is being stubborn.'

'Oh, Liza, no. You can't think of turning down an offer like that. Think of me. Think of Dolly.'

Eliza glanced at Dolly, who was sleeping

peacefully in spite of their raised voices. She met Millie's troubled eyes and she could see Brandon's shadow looming over her. Last of all, she looked round the tiny room that had been her home and her safe haven since Ted had rescued her from the clutches of Uncle Enoch. Wherever she cast her eyes there were mementoes of past and happier times. The china dog that Ted had won for her at a street fair in Spitalfields; the brass clock on the mantelshelf that lost five minutes in every hour; the dog-eared Bible that was the only book in the house and from which Ada read passages to Dolly; the grease stain on the wall shaped like a mushroom, where Millie, years ago, and in a rare fit of temper, had thrown her bread and dripping because she had wanted bread and jam.

Eliza gave a start as Freddie laid his arm around her shoulders. 'I know it's hard for you, Liza. But you haven't got much choice. If you stay here the Millers will send in the bailiffs and take everything.'

'There's so little,' Eliza said, choking on a sob. 'But it all means so much to me.'

'We'll take everything we can pack into the dog cart. Miller can take the chandlery from you, but we'll take legal advice as to the house in Bird Street. We won't let them take that without a fight.'

Millie uttered a strangled cry. 'What will

happen to Ada and the nippers? And what will Davy say when he comes ashore to find his family thrown out into the gutter?'

'We won't let that happen,' Freddie said calmly. 'If the worst comes to the worst, they can come and live in the old servants' quarters in my house. There's plenty of room for all.' He took Eliza by the hand, speaking to her gently. 'Liza, my love, I care about you more than you will ever know. But the choice is yours: what is it going to be?'

Chapter Twenty

She had to get out of the house. Eliza's head was ringing with the sound of Daisy's shrill voice haranguing Freddie for his failures and inconsistencies. She had not forgiven him for reneging on his promise to become a fashionable, if unqualified, practitioner of medicine. Daisy, it seemed to Eliza, had social aspirations far above her station. She never lost the opportunity to nag Freddie for his apparent lack of ambition. Neither had she forgiven Eliza for losing the chandlery that was Tommy's birthright. In fact, Daisy was not a happy woman. She had objected to having Eliza, Millie and Dolly foisted upon her, but she had grudgingly allowed them to have two rooms on the ground floor: one for Dolly with all her possessions arranged around her and the other to be shared by Eliza and Millie. This was a particularly small room at the back of the house, overlooking the stables, and sparsely furnished with two narrow beds and a washstand. Freddie had no say in all this and, when he had asked Eliza if she was happy with the arrangements, she had somehow managed to convince him that she was perfectly content.

The fact that Daisy accepted their presence at all was, as Eliza soon realised, because they were proving useful to her in running the establishment. She had willingly relinquished her role of housekeeper to Eliza, and she had not put forward any objection to the Little family's moving into the basement rooms. In fact she had appeared delighted to have an unpaid servant in Ada, who did most of the cooking. Sukey had been relegated to the position of scullery maid, which had caused a few fights until Eliza was forced to intervene and put her in her place.

Despite her apparent generosity to the Littles, Daisy had been uncompromising when it came to Mille, insisting that she took on the duties of unpaid housemaid. Millie never complained, but there was enough work to keep a small army of servants occupied, and at night she fell into her bed so exhausted that she was asleep as soon as her head touched the pillow. Eliza helped her as much as she could, and she held her tongue, something that she was becoming used to nowadays, but it distressed her to see Millie wearing herself to a shadow with hard work. This state of affairs could not be allowed to drag on for long, but, in the meantime, and until she could think of an alternative, they must make the best of things. At least Daisy seemed to tolerate Dolly, mainly, Eliza thought, because Tommy had taken such a liking to her and they played the royal game together. If she was the housekeeper and Millie the skivvy, then Dolly was the uncrowned queen of the nursery.

After their hurried departure from Hemp Yard, Freddie had enlisted the help of Arnold and Dippy Dan to move everything out of the house, making several journeys with the dog cart until Dolly's bits and pieces of furniture were safely removed to Dark House Street. As Arnold and Dan were now without work, Brandon having made it clear that he wanted nothing to do with them, Freddie's soft heart was touched and he allowed Arnold to bring his aged mother and install her in the loft above the stables. Dan slept on a pile of straw in the stall next to Nugget and both of them seemed happy with the arrangement.

Huddled in the thick folds of an old cloak that had belonged to Daisy, and that she now considered too old-fashioned and shabby for her smart person, Eliza was grateful for its warmth as she walked along the quay wall. It was February, and a cold north wind brought with it spikes of sleet. The gunmetal-grey clouds promised snow later, but Eliza was oblivious of the weather, content simply to be out of the house for a while. She needed time to think and to work out a plan for their removal from Dark House Street.

They had been living in Freddie's house for almost three months now, and although she was earning her keep, Eliza felt that she was living on charity and she hated it. She tried to like Daisy, who for all her faults was neither unkind nor unfeeling, but Eliza could not bear to see her going upstairs at night with Freddie. She had discovered that they had separate rooms, but whether he left his own bed to visit Daisy was an unsolved mystery. Sometimes, in the small hours of the morning when she could not sleep, Eliza was certain that she heard footsteps padding along the corridor directly above her room. Tormented by her own imaginings, she tried desperately to think of a way in which she could get back her business and become independent, but a solution always evaded her.

Freddie had instructed his solicitor to take on the case, but fighting the Millers through the courts would be costly and probably doomed from the outset. Eliza could only hope that the solicitor might find a small loophole in the law that would allow her at least to keep the house in Bird Street. Brandon had taken possession of it, but, so far, nothing had been legally assigned to him. With the dwelling in Dark House Street so full now, Eliza worried that Freddie's generosity was getting in the way of whatever plans he had made to earn a living. She had no idea how much money he had, but she couldn't help feeling that his casual attitude to his dwindling fortune would soon bankrupt him.

A gust of wind snatched the hood from her head, tugging at her hair and tweaking long strands from the combs that held it in place. She paused for a moment, brushing a stray lock from her eyes and staring down into the roiling waters of the Thames, thick and dark as bitter chocolate. It was only mid-afternoon but the winter dusk had already gobbled up the far bank of the river, and the masts of ships loomed high above her, piercing the lowering clouds. It was not the sort of weather to be out in, but Eliza needed time on her own. She had left Tommy playing the royal game with Dolly and, at the thought of him, she found herself smiling.

The one good thing to come out of her enforced stay in Dark House Street was that she had grown close to Bart's son. She had come to know and love Tommy and had slowly won his trust and, she hoped, his affection. Daisy was not a bad mother, but she seemed more interested in striving towards respectability and making a place for herself amongst the wives of City merchants. This entailed going out to tea with her wealthy acquaintances, spending a lot of money on new gowns and bonnets, and taking hackney cabs when she could easily have walked the short distance to their homes.

As Eliza stared down into the turbulent water,

a lamplighter hurried along the quay using his long pole to ignite the gas lamps. They fizzed and popped, flickering inside their glass prisons like trapped sunbeams and making eerie reflections on the water. Eliza shivered as she recalled her childish fantasy that there were dead people beneath the ripples, holding up lanterns to light their way to the afterlife. She walked on, briskly this time, towards a tea clipper that was in the process of being unloaded. As she drew closer to the huge ship, she could just make out the name on its bows and her heart did a bunny hop inside her chest. Keeping well out of the way of the cranes and the men going about their work, she stepped over cables and chains, shielding her eyes against the driving sleet. Then she saw him. Coming down the gangplank with his ditty bag slung over his shoulder. She would have recognised him anywhere.

'Davy. Davy.' She broke into a run, leaping coils of rope and dodging in between oak barrels. He had seen her. Davy dropped his bag on the cobbles and held out his arms. Eliza threw herself into them and clung to him, laughing and crying at the same time. He was holding her so tightly that she could scarcely breathe. He was stroking her hair and he kissed her on the forehead and then the tip of her nose. He smelt of salt water, oiled wool and tea.

'Liza, my little Liza.' Davy's voice cracked with

emotion and then he frowned. 'What the hell are you doing here on your own?'

Eliza wrapped her arms around his waist, looking up into his tanned face. 'I'm not alone any more, Davy. You're here. You're home. I can't tell you how glad I am to see you.'

'Move along, cully. You're in the way.'

A gravelly voice from behind them made Davy turn his head. 'Sorry, mate,' he said, grinning, 'but I haven't seen me girl for six months or more.'

'No, Davy. Don't get me wrong.' Eliza pulled free, realising to her horror that he had mistaken her genuine pleasure on seeing him for something deeper.

He looked down at her and smiled. 'That were a welcome fit for a king. It's almost worth being away for more than half a year to come back to that.' He bent down and picked up his ditty bag. 'Come on, darling, let's go home.'

'Davy, wait.' Eliza laid her hand on his arm. As if it weren't bad enough that she had given him false hope, now she must tell him that his family had lost their home and that they were all living on Freddie's charity. She took a deep breath. 'Davy, I got to tell you something.'

As they walked, arm in arm, Eliza told him everything that had happened since he had left Wapping. It was almost dark by the time they reached Freddie's house and, typical of his disregard for economy, light spilled from all the windows. Sounds of children's voices emanated from the basement area and young Artie was hanging by his breeches from one of the area railings, blue in the face and shouting for help. Davy quickened his pace and lifted his brother to safety. 'It's lucky that spike didn't go right through your bum, you young rascal.'

Artie stared up at him with tear stains leaving trails down his dirty face. 'Davy? Is it really you?'

'It's me all right, young 'un. Now what was you doing playing the fool with rusty iron railings?'

'Trying to see what was going on in the house. They got a fire halfway up the chimney and that kid, Tommy, he has cake to eat every single blooming day.'

Before Davy could answer, the door to the servants' entrance was flung open and Ada stuck her head out. 'Artie, what's going on? Sammy says you'd got yourself stuck through like a joint on a spit. Oh, my Gawd! Davy, is that you up there?'

Davy set Artie on the ground and ran down the area steps to hug his mother. 'It's me all right, duchess. Come home from the sea and mighty glad to be ashore.'

Eliza stood at the top of the steps, ignoring the sleet that had turned to large, feathery snowflakes, mindless of the cold striking up through the thin soles of her boots and smiling at the sight of Ada and Davy hugging each other. Sammy was clinging to Davy's legs and nine-year-old Eddie looked on as if he wanted to join in, but considered himself a bit too grown-up.

'Oh, Davy, Davy,' Ada said, laughing and crying at the same time. 'I can't believe you're home.'

'Well, I am, Ma. Home and not particularly eager to go away again.' Davy glanced over her shoulder. 'Where's the old man?'

'Your dad's gone back to the mission. It's a long story, ducks. I'll explain later.' Ada mopped her eyes on the corner of her apron. 'Here's me going on, like a silly old thing, and you standing out here in the blooming snow. Come inside out of the cold. I've just made a brew of tea and we've got a nice bit of brawn for supper.'

'That'll do a treat, Ma.' Davy hefted Sammy onto his shoulder and as he was about to follow Ada inside he glanced up at Eliza. 'Come on down, Liza.'

She shook her head. 'I must tell everyone that you're home safe and sound.' Sensing that he was about to argue, she blew him a kiss. 'We'll get together later and celebrate.' As the door closed on them, Eliza ran up the steps and let herself into the entrance hall. Her first thought was to find Millie and tell her the good news. But it was Freddie who came to meet her with a look of concern on his face. He helped her off with the cloak that was heavy with melting snow. 'What on earth were you doing walking out alone and in this sort of weather?'

Eliza brushed strands of wet hair back from her forehead. 'Don't scold, Freddie. I just went for a walk, and guess who I met?'

He tossed her cloak onto a chair. 'Someone special I should think, my dear, judging by the flush of your cheeks and the sparkle in your eyes.'

'Davy's come home. Isn't that marvellous?'

Freddie looked away. 'Of course. You must be delighted. I'm happy for you, Liza.'

The bleak note in his voice struck Eliza like a punch in the stomach. She wanted to tell him that he had got it all wrong; that it wasn't for herself that she was pleased, but somehow she could not find the words to express her feelings. She sensed his mood but she could not explain it; she longed to fling her arms around him. She wanted to tell him that she had never loved any man as much as she loved him. But Daisy was coming down the stairs and the moment was lost.

Freddie turned to her, holding out his hand. 'Splendid news, Daisy. Eliza's old sweetheart, Davy Little, has returned from a long sea voyage. We must have a party.'

'No, really,' Eliza protested. 'He's not my—'

'Don't be bashful, dear,' Daisy said, running down the remaining stairs and clutching Freddie's hand. 'I couldn't be happier for you. Freddie's quite right, we must have some rum punch and cake. We'll invite the whole family to join us, although maybe not the old drunkard. Hopefully he'll be serving soup at the mission.'

'You're all heart, Daisy,' Freddie said, giving her hand a squeeze.

'Oh, you flatterer.' Daisy cast him an arch look beneath her eyelashes. Her expression hardened as she turned to Eliza. 'Go and tell Millie to fetch a cake from the bakery and tell Sukey to find the makings for a punch.'

Eliza made a move towards the kitchen: anything was better than seeing Daisy making up to Freddie. But before she had gone two paces, he called out to her.

'Liza, wait.'

She stopped, looking back over her shoulder. 'What is it?'

'We have some important business with my solicitor and I want you to come with me tomorrow morning. I think we may be getting somewhere in our case against the Millers.'

Daisy gave a crow of delight. 'Darling, Freddie. Does that mean my little Tommy will get his inheritance?'

'Let's hope the matter can be settled to everyone's satisfaction.'

Unable to stand being in their presence a moment longer, Eliza hurried to the kitchen where she found Millie on her hands and knees, scrubbing the flagstone floor. Sukey stood by the range, stirring a pan of soup in a half-hearted sort of way, and with such a sullen expression on her face that Eliza wanted to slap her. She felt her temper rise at the sight of Millie working her fingers to the bone, and Sukey getting away with doing as little as possible.

'You can leave that,' Eliza said firmly. 'Mistress wants you to go to the bakery and buy a cake.'

Sukey stuck out her bottom lip. 'But it's snowing. Can't she go?' She pointed the wooden spoon at Millie. 'I got to mind the lamb stew.'

Her temper fraying, Eliza picked up a ladle and brandished it at Sukey. 'Do as you're told, girl. Or I'll report you to the missis.'

Mumbling, Sukey scampered into the scullery, slamming the door behind her.

'Get up, dear,' Eliza said, bending down and taking the scrubbing brush from Millie's swollen and mottled fingers, which looked more like raw pork sausages than a human hand. 'I've got some splendid news, but I think you ought to sit down afore I tells you.'

'What is it? Tell me, Liza.' Millie scrambled to her feet, wiping her hands on her grimy apron.

Eliza motioned her to sit down. 'Davy's come

475

home from sea. He's with Ada and the nippers this moment.'

'Oh!' Millie's eyes rolled upwards and she would have fallen off the chair if Eliza had not grabbed her by the shoulders.

'It's all right,' Eliza said, fanning Millie with her free hand. 'You'll be fine again in a minute.'

With her head bowed, Millie buried her face in her chapped hands. 'It's not all right. I look a sight. I can't see him like this. He'll think I'm a drab.'

'Not if I've got anything to do with it, he won't.' Eliza dragged her to her feet. 'You stop that nonsense, Millie. Come with me and we'll soon have you looking like a proper princess.'

Daisy's scarlet gown fitted Millie as if it had been made for her. Standing back to admire her handiwork, Eliza gave a satisfied sigh. 'You look a treat. Pity we haven't got a proper mirror.'

'There's one in Daisy's room,' Millie said, with a mischievous grin lighting her face.

'Come on then. I'll show you what a pretty girl you are, Millie Turner. And, if I say so myself, I've done your hair up as good as any lady's maid.'

They went upstairs, laughing like naughty schoolgirls. Eliza didn't care whether Daisy approved or not. This was going to be Millie's night of triumph. And if Davy needed a bang on the head with a belaying pin to make him see sense, then that was what he would get. It was fortunate that Daisy was not in her room, and Millie was able to primp before the long mirror and admire the change in her appearance. Eliza stood back, saying nothing, but silently congratulating herself on her efforts. They were about to leave when the door opened and Daisy entered. She stopped short, glaring at them, and then she smiled. 'Well, who would have thought it?'

'We was just going,' Millie said, blushing. 'I ain't never seen meself full-length.'

'Oh, that's all right. I suppose you both want to impress your young men. The handsome sailor for you, Eliza, and his brother Pete for Millie. Suits me down to the ground and never let it be said that Daisy Bragg stood in the way of true love.' Daisy beckoned to Eliza. 'Undo me buttons, there's a dear. I'd ask Freddie but he treats me bedroom like a plague pit. I'll have to get him drunk on rum punch tonight if I want him to have his wicked way with me, and even then he'll probably run a mile. I dunno what's wrong with that man. You'd think he was a bloody monk or something. But maybe tonight my luck will change.' Chuckling, Daisy turned her back so that Eliza could unbutton her gown.

Eliza's fingers shook as she undid the tiny mother-of-pearl buttons. Daisy's words echoed in her head and she could hardly believe that it was true. Had Freddie really tired of Daisy's voluptuous charms? That is, if he had ever enjoyed them at all. Or was Daisy simply saying these things to torment her?

'You can go now.' Daisy whisked away from her, stepping out of the pool of silk. 'Where's your wits, girl? Have you lost them, or are you dreaming of your sweetheart?'

'Don't talk soft,' Eliza retorted, biting her lip. She had been thinking about Freddie and, for a moment, it almost seemed that Daisy could read her mind. She felt herself blushing and was vaguely aware that Millie was tugging at her hand.

'Ta, Daisy,' Millie said hastily. 'Ta for the use of your looking glass. We'll be off then.' She dragged Eliza out of the room, closing the door behind them. 'What's up, Liza? You look like you've seen a ghost.'

'It's nothing. I was just surprised that Daisy was being so nice all of a sudden.'

'She thinks you're sweet on Davy,' Millie said, picking up her skirts as they reached the top of the staircase. 'She thinks that with you out of the way then Freddie will want to marry her. Some chance of that!'

'Freddie isn't interested in me. He still thinks of me as a little girl.'

'Oh, Eliza. Maybe Daisy was right when she

said you'd lost your wits. You are a noodle sometimes.'

'What d'you mean by that?' Eliza demanded, but Millie was already halfway down the sweeping staircase. The sound of voices and laughter was rising up from the entrance hall and Eliza could smell hot rum punch. She reached the wide curve of the staircase in time to hear the gasp of surprise from the assembled party as Millie came into view.

'Well, look at you,' Ada cried, clapping her hands. 'You look like a real princess.'

'What?' Dolly craned her neck from her seat in the middle of the hall where Pete had set her down. 'She can't be a princess. I'm the queen and I don't know her.'

Tommy tapped her on the shoulder. 'She can be in our game, your majesty.'

'It ain't no game, son. I'm queen and I wants a drop of that punch. And a slice of seed cake too.'

Ada hurried over to the table where a cut-glass punchbowl steamed, sending out a spicy fragrance. 'Don't pay no heed to her, ducks. You look good enough to eat.'

'Cake,' Dolly shouted. 'A big piece.'

Millie giggled nervously, covering her hand with her mouth. Eliza could see Davy standing next to Pete and Mary, who had come from Islington on her one half day a month. They were all staring at Millie open-mouthed. Eliza willed

Davy to come forward, and, as if in answer to her summons, he broke away from his family. The look of surprise and admiration on his face as he approached the foot of the stairs was reward for all her labours. He put his hands around Millie's trim waist, lifting her off her feet and holding her for a moment before setting her gently on the ground.

'Well, you're a sight for sore eyes and that's a fact, Millie.'

Eliza clasped her hands together, biting back tears of happiness. Then Davy patted Millie on the head and looked up, holding his hand out to her. 'But you got a way to go before you outshine your big sister.'

Millie's mouth drooped at the corners and teardrops sparkled on her eyelashes. Eliza was tempted to give Davy a good shaking, but somehow she managed to restrain herself. She ran down the remaining stairs and seized him by the arm, standing on tiptoe so that she could whisper in his ear. 'You've hurt her feelings, you big booby. Say something nice to Millie or I'll never speak to you again.'

'What did I do?' Davy stared at her, his eyes widening in surprise. 'I told her she looked nice.'

'Nice! She looks beautiful and it was all for you.'

'She's a kid.'

'No, Davy. She's a grown woman and she loves you.'

If she had hit him with a flagpole, Davy couldn't have looked more stunned. He swallowed hard, glancing over his shoulder at Millie. 'But – I don't understand – surely she knows how I feel about you, Liza?'

Eliza followed his glance and her heart swelled with love as she saw that Freddie had noticed Millie's distress, and he was making her laugh as he ladled punch into a small glass cup. Almost as if he sensed that Eliza was staring at him, Freddie looked up and their eyes met. He smiled and there was both tenderness and understanding in that long glance. Suddenly, it was as though they were the only two people in the room. Everyone else had vanished, time had stopped and there was silence except for the beating of her heart. At the end of a pathway of light, there was Freddie. Eliza could hardly breathe. Then Davy nudged her and the moment was lost.

'She looks all right to me, Liza. I think you've got it all wrong.'

Eliza turned to him with a sigh. 'It's you who's got it wrong. I love you like a brother, Davy. We're friends and always will be, I hope. But I can't promise you more.'

'It's him, isn't it?' Davy scowled at Freddie. 'It was always him.'

'I'm sorry.'

'I've been a fool.'

'No, don't say that. You're a wonderful person and we've been through so much together.' Eliza tucked her hand in the crook of his arm. 'Let's be friends again, Davy. Forget about me and give Millie a chance. She's a sweet girl and she loves you so.'

'You've broke me heart, Liza.'

She squeezed his arm, smiling. 'Come on now, Davy Little. Don't tell me you lived like a monk when you was ashore in foreign parts. I'll bet you broke a few hearts yourself.'

Davy shrugged but the corners of his mouth twitched and an irrepressible twinkle danced in his eyes. 'Not really. I may have flirted a bit, but nothing more.'

She gave him a gentle push. 'A big, handsome bloke like you would set any female heart aflutter. Go now and use your charm on Millie. But I warn you, Davy, if you toy with her affections you'll have me to deal with. And I can be a devil when I'm cross.'

'No, you could never be anything bad, sweetheart.' He bent his head and kissed Eliza on the mouth, smiling into her eyes. 'I ain't one to take no for an answer, Liza. But, for your sake, I'll be sociable.' He strolled across the floor towards Millie and her face lit with an artless smile of delight when she saw him.

Eliza stifled a sigh. She knew that he remained

482

unconvinced: Davy was not one to give in easily. She turned her head to look for Freddie, but the ready smile died on her lips as she saw the hostile expression in his eyes. Her heart sank as she realised that he had seen Davy kiss her and had misinterpreted the passionless salute. Why, she thought miserably, was everything so complicated?

The offices of Bloggs and Burden were situated in a narrow court off the Ratcliff Highway. Not a very salubrious area and one that Eliza would never have ventured into alone, even in broad daylight. Although it was ten o'clock in the morning, there were bodies laid out insensible on the cobblestones, dead drunk from the excesses of the previous night: some of them with congealed blood from knife wounds and others with indigo bruises on their heads, caused by blows from bare knuckles or even cudgels. All of them were most likely robbed clean by thieves and the feral children whose mothers touted for business from shadowy doorways. The stench of privies was mixed with fumes of jigger gin, grog and sangaree, tobacco smoke and the curious smells emanating from opium dens. Eliza clutched Freddie's arm, glancing nervously round as figures more reminiscent of scarecrows than men and women lurched out of shuttered buildings, covering their faces with their hands as if the daylight hurt their eyes.

'This is a terrible place, Freddie,' Eliza said, looking round nervously. 'Couldn't you have found a solicitor nearer to the Inns of Court?'

Freddie patted her hand. 'We're almost there, poppet. You'll understand why we've had to come here when you meet Phineas Bloggs.'

He led the way to a tall, narrow building at the far end of the court. A wild-eyed cat was gnawing on the bones of a dead crow and it snarled at them as they walked past, as if daring them to steal its prey. Eliza shuddered, but worse was to come as they entered the building and she covered her mouth with her hand as the stench of unwashed bodies, urine and rodent droppings made her want to retch. They negotiated the gloomy passage to a room at the very end and Freddie knocked on the door. He went in without waiting for a reply.

In a room so dark that it seemed more like midnight than mid-morning, Eliza peered into the gloom and, in the guttering light of a single candle, she could just make out a table piled high with books and scrolls of paper tied with red tape. Ledgers, dirty cups with flies feasting off the curdled remnants of sour milk, stubs of candles melted into amorphous shapes and a half-eaten meat pie sprouting a small garden of green mould cluttered the top of what appeared to be a kneehole desk. Behind it, squatting on his haunches on a chair, she could just make out a quiff of grey hair sprouting from a balding pate sticking up from behind a copy of *The Times*. A spiral of pipe smoke seemed to be the only thing in the room that moved.

Freddie cleared his throat. 'Good morning, Phineas.'

The newspaper was tossed unceremoniously onto the floor and Phineas squinted at them through a pair of steel-rimmed spectacles perched on the end of his nose. 'Is it? I hadn't noticed.' Leaping up vertically like an excited hobgoblin, Phineas landed on the floor beside them. He held out an ink-stained hand to Eliza. 'You must be the young person of whom we spoke.'

'I'm Eliza Bragg, sir.'

'Of course you are. Take a seat, do.' Phineas pulled up a chair, evicting a large tabby cat with a sweep of his hand. The cat spat at him and arched its back, walking off with an offended flick of its tail. 'Go and catch some rats, you lazy specimen.' Taking a large and rather grubby handkerchief from his pocket, Phineas flicked the seat of the chair. Dust flew up in all directions and he sneezed into the folds of the hanky. 'Do sit down, miss.'

Eliza sat down, stifling a cry of dismay as a small army of fleas fell off the padded arms of the chair onto her hands. Brushing them off, she glanced up at Freddie who had perched on the edge of the desk.

'Don't mind them, miss,' Phineas said, jumping onto his chair behind the desk and assuming a squatting position. 'They're just cat fleas. Don't live on humans, you know.'

'Phineas, can we get down to business?' Freddie brushed a speck of dust, or it could have been a stray flea, from the knee of his checked trousers. 'I've brought Eliza here so that you can explain the situation to her.'

'Precisely so,' Phineas agreed, searching through the pile of documents before him and tossing scrolls, deeds and wills into different corners of the room. 'I have it here somewhere.'

'Phineas has a unique filing system,' Freddie said, winking at Eliza.

'And I can lay my hand on any document at any time. Ah, here it is.' Phineas selected a sheaf of papers. 'I've been in correspondence with Messrs Worboys, Worboys and Grimstone, solicitors to Mr Aaron Miller, with regard to the property on the corner of Old Gravel Lane and Green Bank. Formerly owned by E. Bragg, Ship Chandler.'

'Yes,' Eliza said, nodding. 'That's me.'

'Not according to law, miss.'

'I don't understand.' A convulsive shiver ran down Eliza's spine: Ada would have said that someone had just walked over her grave. She looked up at Freddie for confirmation. He nodded, and her heart sank.

Phineas peered at her over the top of his spectacles. 'If I may be so bold as to ask a lady her age? No, put it another way. You have not yet reached your majority, have you, miss?'

'I'll be twenty-one in August.'

'And therefore any agreements that you made with Mr Miller are not recognised by the law. You were a minor at the time, miss. And a young lady to boot. Put in simple terms, the law does not consider that you are capable of making such decisions or of entering a legal contract without the consent of your guardian.'

Eliza moved to the edge of her seat. 'Yes, but my guardian was dead and my brother also. I inherited the chandlery.'

'The law would say you didn't, miss. The law would say that not only was you too young, but being of the female gender, you could not inherit the business.'

'It can't be true. There was no one else.'

Freddie reached out and laid his hand on her shoulder. 'Don't get upset, Liza, my love. Let Phineas have his say.'

Once again, Phineas vaulted off his chair and began to pace the floor, stepping over piles of documents as if he were in an obstacle race. 'I am in the possession of facts that would never have come to light but for a slight disagreement with Messrs Worboys, Worboys and Grimstone.' He paused to pick up his pipe and light it with the stub of a candle, sending a shower of molten wax down the front of his lapel.

Freddie leaned closer to Eliza, speaking in a low voice. 'Phineas used to be a clerk with Miller's solicitors.'

'And a good servant I was to them too, until the unfortunate incident of the missing funds. But that's another story.' Phineas sucked on his pipe, puffing smoke out of the corners of his mouth. 'Suffice it to say that we parted company, and not on the best of terms. I set up on my own in this rather unfortunate place and Freddie was one of my first clients, although not one of my best successes. Even though I did my utmost, I couldn't save him from the penal colony in Australia.'

'We know all that, Phin,' Freddie said, chuckling. 'Get on with it.'

'All right, I'm getting to the important part. Miss Bragg, I was with the said law firm for a long time. I was there when Mr Aaron Miller went to court to claim paternity of the boy child of a young woman who had come from a good family but had married beneath her.'

The story sounded so painfully familiar that Eliza felt her spine tingle with apprehension. She could hardly breathe and she could barely find the words to ask the fatal question. 'Who – who was she?'

'The young lady, formerly Miss Lucy Henderson, daughter of the late Harold Henderson, corn merchant and warehouse owner, was married to a waterman, Tom Bragg.'

The room began to spin around Eliza in concentric circles. She could have fallen off the chair if Freddie had not caught her in his arms. 'It can't be true. Freddie tell me that he's making it all up.'

Chapter Twenty-one

'I'm afraid there's little doubt about it, my love,' Freddie said gently. 'The paternity suit failed because your mother swore on the Bible that Aaron was not Bart's father, but Phineas had taken a statement from your mother's personal maidservant. She was her confidante and party to the whole, sad affair.'

'I can't believe it,' Eliza said slowly. The idea of her mother as a hot-blooded young woman with carnal desires was so at odds with her vision of an ethereal angelic being that it was shocking beyond belief. 'But if the maid knew who the father was, why didn't she say so in court?'

Phineas shrugged his shoulders. 'Your grandfather, Harry Henderson, was a rich man. He threatened the girl and made her retract her statement. He hated Aaron Miller and wouldn't admit that he had led your poor mother into disgrace, if you'll forgive me for being blunt, miss. Your mother had ruined her chances of marrying into her own class and so old Harry forced her to wed Tom Bragg, a mere waterman, but respectable.'

'How cruel!' Eliza wiped her eyes on the back of her hand. 'How could he do that to his own daughter?'

'Some say as how he never got over it,' Phineas continued, puffing smoke up into the greasy nicotine-stained ceiling. 'Some say as how your grandfather died of a broken heart. Some say as how it was Aaron Miller that arranged for the accident that killed your pa.'

'That's enough, Phineas,' Freddie said sharply. 'That latter is just hearsay and would be inadmissible in court, you know that. It's just gossip.'

Phineas tapped his pipe out on the heel of his shoe. 'I know what I know.'

'But, wait a moment.' Eliza held up her hand as a thought struck her. 'If Aaron wanted to acknowledge Bart, why didn't he contact him when our father died?'

'He had married and had a son and heir. I don't think his wife would have been too happy if Mr Miller had suddenly produced a rival claimant to the family fortune.'

'And your uncle would have had something to say to that too, don't forget.' Freddie reached over and squeezed her hand. 'Isn't that right, Phin?'

'Absolutely correct. Anyway, the long and the short of it is that Miss Eliza ain't entitled to inherit the chandlery, and her verbal contract with Aaron Miller counts for nothing because she was under age.'

Eliza rose to her feet. She felt strangely calm now and almost detached. 'I may not be entitled to anything, but Tommy is. Uncle Enoch would have left the chandlery to Bart, and Tommy is my brother's legitimate son. If what you say is true, Bart was Brandon's half-brother, and if Aaron acknowledged his paternity, then Bart might have had a claim to at least a part of the Miller empire. That would make Tommy an heir too. Isn't that funny?' Eliza started to laugh and found that she could not stop.

'What?' Daisy screeched, her voice rising to a glass-breaking pitch. 'Do you mean to tell me that my Bart was related to that wealthy Miller bloke?'

Eliza shot a reproachful glance in Freddie's direction. She had not wanted to tell anyone yet, let alone Daisy. But, when they arrived home, Daisy had been standing in the entrance hall talking to Davy and Millie; or perhaps talking at them, as they had seemed to Eliza to be unusually silent. Daisy had stopped mid-sentence, turning to glare at Freddie and demanding to know where they had been. Freddie, with his usual good humour, had told her. And then the questions had started. Davy had adopted a proprietorial air, placing his arm around Eliza's shoulders, and demanding to know what gave Freddie the right to act as her guardian. Davy had been so insistent on learning the truth that Freddie had been forced to tell them everything. As the whole sad story came to light there had been a stunned silence, and then everyone had started speaking at once. Eliza was furious with Davy for challenging Freddie and for acting as though he owned her. She resented his interference in her affairs and she told him so in no uncertain terms. Millie shouted at Davy for upsetting Eliza, and Daisy blamed Freddie for everything from the English weather to the recent fall of soot down the chimney in the drawing room that had ruined her new Chinese rug. Freddie looked on, shaking his head.

'Shut up, all of you.' Daisy's strident voice echoed round the hall, bouncing off the crumbling cornices. She stood with her hands on her hips, glaring at each of them in turn. 'What a pack of boobies you are. Can't you see that this is good news for my Tommy? Never mind about your old shop, Liza. From what you've told me, the Millers are worth a fortune and my Tommy would be entitled to a part of it. I'm going to see old man Miller and have it out with him.'

'But, Daisy,' Eliza said, making an effort to sound calm and reasonable, 'you haven't any proof. Aaron would laugh at you.'

'Stuff and nonsense.' Daisy tossed her head. 'You ain't seen me in action yet, my girl. But you will, and before the day is out. Don't take your cloak off, Eliza. I'm going to see Mr Miller right now, and you're coming with me.'

'Oh, no I'm not.'

'Yes,' Daisy said vehemently, 'you are. You may have lost your business, but I'm going to make sure my Tommy gets his rights.'

'You'd be wasting your time. Aaron will never admit that he was Bart's father.'

'We'll see about that.' Daisy turned to Millie with an imperious wave of her hand. 'Go and fetch Tommy. He's playing that silly game with the mad woman. See that he wraps up warm. I don't want him catching a chill, especially now. And you, Eliza, wait there while I get me best bonnet and fur-lined cape, what Freddie bought for me for the sea voyage to England. Davy, go out and find a hackney carriage. I'm going to pay a call on the Millers and I'm going in style.'

Seemingly too stunned to argue, Millie and Davy went off to do her bidding and Daisy rushed upstairs with a flurry of lace-trimmed petticoats. Left alone with Freddie, Eliza turned to him in desperation. 'It will be a disaster. Can't you stop her?'

'You might as well try to stop the tide coming in, my dear. That woman would have made a good general.'

'Then why do you put up with her?' Eliza cried. 'You must really love her, Freddie. Or you would want to wring her neck.'

Freddie's eyes darkened. 'I don't love her. I never have.'

'But you sleep with her.' The words came out before Eliza could stop herself. 'You must care for her just a little bit.'

'No, it never got that far, you must believe me, Liza. I brought her back home because she was the mother of Bart's son, and I knew how much you loved your brother.'

'You did that for me?'

'For you, and for the boy and most of all for myself,' Freddie said, smiling ruefully. 'I don't expect you to understand the feelings of an old reprobate like me.'

'Don't say that. I won't have you say things against yourself, Freddie. You're a good, kind man and I . . .' Eliza bit her lip. She had almost blurted out that she loved him. She turned her head away and was almost relieved to see Daisy running down the stairs trailing her cape behind her.

'Where's that child?' Daisy demanded breathlessly. 'Go and see if he's ready, Eliza.'

Freddie strode to the foot of the stairs. 'Go and fetch him yourself, Daisy. Eliza isn't a servant and I won't have you speak to her like that.'

Daisy paused, looking down at him with her mouth turned down at the corners. 'Freddie!'

'I'm tired of your tears and your tantrums. I've

done everything that you wanted of me, Daisy. I brought you to England and I've given you everything that you wanted in order to keep you happy, and to look after Tommy. You chose to read more into our relationship than there was. Well, here is where the fiction ends. As a matter of honour, I will continue to support you and your boy, but I want you to understand that you are free to go and do as you please.'

'Bah!' Daisy said, curling her lip. 'I've always been free, Freddie Prince. You was useful to me, but now I got me sights set on bigger things. So I'll say ta very much for the roof over our heads. But, cully, I won't be needing it for long. You can trust me to be sure of that.'

Shocked at Daisy's harsh tone, Eliza fought down the desire to rush to Freddie's side. It was no surprise to her that Daisy had been using him, but there was still a nagging doubt in her mind. She clenched her fists, digging her fingernails into her palms to allay the pain of jealousy that shafted through her heart. Daisy might be a lot of things that were not particularly praiseworthy, but she was the sort of woman who could turn a man's head with a flutter of her long eyelashes. She had made Bart fall in love with her; and Freddie – Eliza was not certain, but she suspected that, at the beginning, he too had fallen under her spell.

'Mama.' From the direction of the nursery,

Tommy came running towards them, waving his cap in his hand. 'Millie says we're going for a carriage ride.'

'That's right, ducks,' Daisy said, wrapping her cape around her shoulders with a flourish. 'We're off to make our fortune. Come along, Eliza. If you stand there with your mouth open, you'll be catching flies.'

Outside in the cold, Davy was standing beside a hackney carriage talking to the driver. He handed Daisy in and then lifted Tommy off his feet, tossing him onto the seat and making him laugh. He held his hand out to Eliza. 'Jump in, ducks. I'm coming with you.'

'No, Davy,' Eliza said, climbing nimbly into the carriage without his help. 'Ta, all the same but we've got to do this on our own.'

Davy held the door open, putting his foot on the step. 'I'll come with you, Liza. You didn't really mean what you said the other day, did you?'

Eliza leaned forward. 'Listen to me, Davy. You've got to let me go. I'm your friend and always will be, but I don't love you.'

'You're just saying that.'

'You know me better, I think. I told you before, Davy. You are my dearest friend but I love Freddie, and have done for a long time. You only think you love me and that makes you blind to the person who really does care for you.'

497

Davy's face took on a mulish look. 'You're talking nonsense.'

'You know very well that I'm speaking the truth. The girl what loves you is not a million miles away from here. And you know very well who I mean.' As Davy stepped down from the cab, Eliza leaned out of the window. 'Pennington Street please, cabby.'

Despite his protests that Mr Aaron Miller was busy and would not see them, Daisy sailed past the clerk in the outer office towing Tommy by the hand. Eliza followed them, murmuring an apology to the bemused scribe.

'Where is his office?' Daisy demanded, striding along the corridor and peering at the name-plates. 'Brandon Miller – is that the whoring son?'

Eliza nodded, wishing that Daisy would keep her voice down. She could hear someone moving about in Brandon's office and she hurried on, leading the way to Aaron's inner sanctum. She raised her hand to knock on the door, but Daisy grabbed the handle. 'Manners is out of the window in this case,' she said, thrusting the door open and pushing Tommy in first.

There was nothing Eliza could do but follow her into the room. She tried to close the door but Brandon had come from his office, and he barged in before she could stop him. Aaron rose to his feet, staring at Daisy with a puzzled frown that struck Eliza as being almost comical. 'What the hell is going on?' he roared. 'Who is this woman? And what is she doing here?' He pointed at Eliza, his frown deepening into a scowl. 'I told you to keep away from me. Brandon, send for a constable.'

'Yes, send for a constable,' Daisy said, picking Tommy up and sitting him on the desk in front of Aaron. 'Send for a reporter from the newspaper too. This is a story that will interest the public, I'm sure.'

Brandon grabbed Eliza by the arm. 'What shall I do, Father? Call the constable, or have them thrown out?'

'Throw us out, sonny,' Daisy said, turning on him with a scornful smile. 'Toss your little nephew and his mama out on the street and see where it gets you.'

Brandon's face paled and he turned to Aaron with a look of disbelief. 'Nephew? What is she saying, Father?'

Aaron slammed his hand down on the desk, sending a sheaf of papers fluttering onto the floor. 'Stop this nonsense, woman. If you have something to say, then say it and get out.'

With a suggestive wiggle of her hips, Daisy threw off her cape. 'I'll have me say, Mr Miller. And it's this. My Tommy's father was your son, Bartholomew Bragg. This boy is your grandson.'

The silence that followed this statement seemed to ring in Eliza's ears. There was a cathedral-like hush in the office. She felt Brandon's body tense as he stood close to her.

Aaron stared at Daisy as if she had suddenly sprouted two heads. He looked, Eliza thought with some satisfaction, as though someone had hit him with a mallet. She saw his knuckles whiten as he gripped the edge of his desk. He was breathing heavily and beads of perspiration glistened on his forehead. 'You lying bitch. Don't you dare try to blackmail Aaron Miller.'

Daisy fished inside her purse and brought out a rather tattered sheet of paper, which she tossed onto the desk in front of him. 'There's me marriage lines, Mr Miller. Or should I call you Father-in-law?'

'That's enough of this nonsense,' Brandon said angrily. 'Let me call a constable, Father. The woman is obviously a trickster hired by Eliza to embarrass us.'

'Wait!' Aaron held up his hand.

Eliza made a move towards Tommy, whose bottom lip was quivering ominously, but Brandon caught her by the arm. 'Keep out of this. You've done enough harm already. Just say the word, Father, and I'll throw them out myself.'

'No!' Aaron stared hard at Tommy, and then he laid his hand tentatively on his shoulder. 'Don't cry, boy. This is not your fault.' He glowered at Daisy over the top of Tommy's head. 'But I do blame you, madam. I blame you for bringing the child here, and using him as a pawn in your deceitful game. What do you want? How much do you want?'

'Father, you're not going to stoop to pay off a blackmailer?'

Eliza wrenched her arm free, glaring up at Brandon. 'It's not blackmail, Brandon. What Daisy says is true and if you need further proof, then the court record will show that your father sued for custody of my brother, Bart. He claimed paternity but my mother denied it. Ask him yourself.'

'Father?'

Aaron bowed his head. 'It's true. Bart was your half-brother, Brandon. I knew that he was my son but I couldn't prove it in court. Lucy loved me, but she was in awe of that old tyrant, Harry Henderson, who had threatened to ruin me. She lied to protect me and she sacrificed herself by marrying that common oaf of a waterman. But it all happened long before I met and married your mother. She knows nothing of this.'

'Not yet, she don't,' Daisy said, smirking. 'But if you don't acknowledge my Tommy and give him what is his by rights, then the whole world will know what sort of a man you really are.'

'And you, Eliza?' Aaron walked slowly round his desk as though he were wading through deep water. 'What do you want of me?'

'Nothing. I don't want nothing from you.'

'Not even the return of your little shop on the corner?'

'It were never mine in the first place. You knew that, didn't you?'

'Of course, but I felt I owed it to Lucy's memory to try to look after you. And how did you repay me? By treachery and embezzlement.'

'That's just not true.' Eliza stamped her foot. 'Your son made that up. I never had the money to buy stock. Ask him. Make him tell you the truth.'

'Shut up, Eliza,' Brandon said between clenched teeth. 'He knows what sort of girl you are now. Don't make things worse.'

'What does it matter?' Daisy demanded. 'We're here to settle the business of my son. Not to drag Eliza into it.'

Aaron held up his hand. 'I don't want to listen to this. Be quiet all of you.' He came to a halt in front of Tommy and pulled a handkerchief from his pocket. 'Don't snivel, boy. Wipe your eyes and let me look at you.'

'You be nice to Mama and Aunt Eliza,' Tommy

said, blowing his nose. 'I won't have you shouting at them, old man.'

Aaron stared at him for a moment and then he threw back his head and laughed. 'You're a Miller all right, son.' He ruffled Tommy's hair, declining the return of his hanky. He turned to Daisy and his smile faded. 'I will acknowledge Tommy as my grandson, but don't mistake me for a soft-hearted fool. I'll make you a small allowance, and I'll set up a trust fund for the boy, on the condition that you keep this whole sorry story from my wife.'

Daisy shrugged her shoulders. 'Suits me fine. And I wants a house of me own and the chandlery.'

'The chandlery is out of the question,' Brandon said, pushing past Eliza. 'You gave that to me, Father. Tell her so.'

'I think you have enough here to keep you occupied, Brandon.' Aaron perched on the corner of his desk, next to Tommy. Taking a gold case from his breast pocket he selected a cigar, rolling it between his fingers and sniffing the tobacco with an appreciative smile. 'The boy will inherit the chandlery when he is twenty-one. Until then I think perhaps his aunt should manage the store.' Aaron cast a mocking glance in Eliza's direction. 'How do you fancy working for your own nephew, Eliza? That should make a dent in your pride.'

Eliza held her head high, saying nothing. What was there to say? Bart would have wanted his son to have the business and she could not, in all conscience, object to being designated guardian of Tommy's inheritance. At least she would be able to stop being dependent on Freddie. There was a small room at the back of the rebuilt shop that would serve as living quarters. She could make herself quite comfortable there. Couldn't she?

Aaron clipped the end off the cigar with a small silver instrument, pierced the tip and, taking a vesta from a box on his desk, he struck it, warmed the cigar briefly in its flame and lit it, taking in a mouthful of smoke and exhaling it with a satisfied sigh. Tommy watched this ritual with his mouth open and his eyes round with wonder. Eliza was tempted to push the fat cigar down Aaron's throat and was immediately ashamed of her violent reaction.

Daisy sniffed the smoke like a hound getting the scent of a fox. 'You ain't got one to spare, have you, dearie?'

'Certainly not. I don't approve of women smoking.' Aaron blew a plume of blue smoke into the air above her head.

'Let's go, Daisy,' Eliza said, jerking her head in the direction of the door. She could see that Brandon was getting restive, clenching and unclenching his hands as if he wanted to do someone actual bodily harm.

'That's the first sensible thing you've said.' Brandon strode to the door, flinging it open so that it crashed back against the wainscoting.

'Hold on, dear.' Daisy flashed him a saucy smile and a wink. 'I ain't finished yet.' She turned to Aaron, her smile fading. 'So far so good. Tommy gets the chandlery. Now what about my house?'

With the cigar clamped between his teeth, Aaron managed a wolfish grin. 'That's easy. The house in Bird Street belonged to that old scoundrel, Enoch Bragg. It's yours until the boy reaches his majority. Then he can do what he likes with it.'

Daisy frowned. 'Is it a nice property in a respectable street?'

Aaron's grin widened until Eliza thought that his face would split in two. 'It will suit you perfectly.'

'But, Father . . .' Brandon began and then stopped, biting his lip.

'Go now,' Aaron said, returning to his seat behind the desk. 'Our business is concluded.'

'I need to know how much my allowance will be,' Daisy said, lifting Tommy off the desk and setting him down on the floor. 'I have to support and educate the boy.'

'Don't try my patience. You've got the house

and the chandlery.' Aaron waved his cigar in Eliza's direction. 'And she knows how to run it. It's up to Eliza to supplement your income. Now get out.'

'Come, Thomas,' Daisy said, tossing her head and taking him by the hand. 'We'll leave your bad-tempered old grandpa to smoke his weed in peace. But you ain't heard the last of us, Mr Miller. Come, Eliza.'

'Get out and don't come back,' Brandon hissed, holding the door open.

Eliza met his eyes with an unwavering stare. 'Give me the keys to the chandlery first.'

He closed the door with a thud. 'Come to my office.'

Daisy gave Tommy a push towards Eliza. 'Go with Eliza, ducks,' she said and, tucking her hand through Brandon's arm, she flashed him an arch smile. 'Brandon, dear, we don't have to be enemies, do we? After all, we're family now.'

Eliza placed her arm around Tommy's shoulders, fully expecting Brandon to vent his anger on Daisy. To her astonishment, his grim expression softened and he patted Daisy's hand. 'Well,' he said gruffly, clearing his throat. 'If you put it that way.'

'I do, dear.' Daisy fluttered her eyelashes. 'I'm just a poor widow, all alone in the world except for me little son. I could be ever so grateful to a bloke who would be good to us. You're a man of the world, Brandon, my dear. I think you know what I mean.'

To Eliza's amazement, Brandon actually smiled. Daisy's behaviour was so blatant that Eliza could hardly believe he had fallen for that old trick, but his gaze was fixed on Daisy's generous bosom that had suddenly come into view as her cape slipped, apparently accidentally, from her shoulders. As he went to help her put it back in place, Daisy caught hold of Brandon's hand and allowed it to graze her breast. 'Oh, you bad boy,' she said softly, smiling up into his face. 'I can see I'm going to have trouble with you.'

Eliza took Tommy by the hand and hurried on to Brandon's office. There was no need for the boy to see his mother acting the whore, and yet, in her heart, she could not blame Daisy, who was securing her future in the only way she knew. Eliza could almost forgive her for using Freddie, especially now that it was obviously so much in the past that Daisy had probably forgotten his name. She took Tommy into the office and she did not have long to wait until Daisy and Brandon came in arm in arm.

There was a suspicious lip-shaped pink patch on Brandon's cheek. Eliza had always suspected that Daisy's cherry lips and pink cheeks were due to the application of rouge, and now she was certain. She held out her hand to Brandon. 'The key to the chandlery, if you please.'

He went to his desk and opened a drawer. Taking out a small bunch of keys, he tossed it to Eliza. 'Don't think you've won, Eliza. Let's see you stock the shop without any help from me.'

She opened her mouth to reply but a meaningful glance from Daisy made her change her mind. Still clinging to Brandon's arm, Daisy gave it a squeeze. 'We won't fall out over little details like that, Brandon dear. Why don't we send Eliza and Tommy home in the hackney, and you take me to view the house in Bird Street? I'd feel so much safer on the arm of a strong fellow like you.'

'I have work to do, Mrs Bragg.'

'It's Daisy. And I'm sure you could squeeze me in somewhere. I gets scared in strange houses, especially going up them dark stairs to the bedrooms. I take it that the place is furnished? If you get my meaning.'

Brandon obviously did. He seized another set of keys from the drawer and put them in his pocket. 'Of course. If you put it that way, Daisy. How can I refuse?'

Arriving back in Dark House Street, Eliza helped Tommy down from the hackney cab. He headed for the gate in the area railings. 'Where are you going, Tommy?'

He paused at the top of the steps. 'I'm going to play with Artie and Sam. And Ada gives me cake.'

Eliza smiled. 'What would we do without Ada? All right, dear. You go and play with the boys. I'm going inside to tell Uncle Freddie the good news.'

Tommy shot her a puzzled glance. 'About Mama's new man?'

'Well, er, not exactly. I meant about your good fortune in finding your new grandpa.'

'Oh, him.' Tommy shrugged his small shoulders and ran helter-skelter down the area steps.

Eliza paid the cabby and went indoors to look for Freddie. Attracted by the sound of voices, she went into the drawing room. As usual, Dolly was dozing in her chair by the fire, and Millie and Mary were sitting at the table poring over a rather dog-eared copy of *The Young Ladies' Journal*. Millie looked up and smiled. 'Liza, come and look. It says here that crinolines are out of fashion and that a thing called a bustle is going to be the latest craze.'

'We'll all have huge bums,' Mary giggled. 'Miss Cynthia's got old Ma Dunne to make her up a gown like this one. She looks just like one of them pouter pigeons in it, but she thinks that she looks just topping, and she's thrown out all her old gowns, even the one what we went to so much trouble to get fixed. Ain't that a laugh, Eliza?'

The thought of Miss Cynthia discarding the gown that had cost her so much grief and expense made Eliza want to go round to the house in Islington and give the young lady a piece of her mind. She managed a weak smile. 'Did she ever wear that pink gown again?'

'Not her. She never even took it from the clothes press. Some people have got more money than sense.' Mary bent her head over the magazine. 'What do you think of this one, Millie? I should love to wear something like this when I finds a bloke to marry me.'

Millie nodded her head, but she was looking at Eliza and not at the magazine. 'Have you seen Davy yet?'

'No. I was looking for Freddie.'

'I dunno what you said to Davy, but he come indoors looking really grumpy and Freddie took him into the parlour. They've been there ever since.' Millie's smile faded. 'Is everything all right, Liza? What happened with old man Miller?'

'Daisy was amazing. She made the old man admit that Bart was his son and then she turned on the charm with Brandon.'

'She's a hussy,' Mary said, pulling a face.

'Oh, Mary, don't be such a prude,' Millie said, casting Eliza an anxious glance. 'She don't mean it, Liza. Daisy's not so bad when you gets to know her.'

Mary tossed her head. 'She's still a doxy.'

'Girls! Don't squabble.' Torn between irritation and amusement, Eliza wagged her finger at Mary. 'Didn't Mr Booth warn you about the dangers of making judgements on others?'

'I expect so. I do try to act like a Christian, but being good don't come that easy, Liza,' Mary said, blushing and hanging her head. 'Me dad is always preaching at us, but I can still see him as he was when he was boozed up. Now he spends all his time going round pubs and spouting about the evils of drink, while Mum and the nippers lives on Freddie's charity. I don't think I knows what's good and what isn't.'

Millie placed her arm around Mary's shoulders, giving her a hug. 'You are a good girl. Look how hard you work and yet you gives nearly all your wages to your ma. If that ain't good, then I don't know what is.'

Leaving them to comfort each other, Eliza slipped out of the room, closing the door behind her. She made her way to the morning parlour at the back of the house. This part of the building was the most dilapidated of all and most of the rooms were unfurnished and swathed in cobwebs. Not for the first time, she wondered what had possessed Freddie to buy such a large and crumbling mansion, especially since he had given up his plans to become a medical man. It was bitterly cold in the passage and she was glad that she had not discarded her cloak in the relative warmth of the drawing room. The winter dusk had fallen early and it was almost too dark to see her way, but a glimmer of light beneath the parlour door guided her footsteps. She went in without knocking and found Freddie and Davy seated on either side of the fireplace, with only the feeble glow of the embers to light the room.

Freddie got to his feet, smiling and holding out his hand. 'Liza, my dear. You look perished. Come and sit by the fire.'

Davy gave her a reproachful look and said nothing. Appearing not to notice, Freddie took a spill from the jar on the mantelshelf and held it against the glowing lump of coal. He went round the room lighting candles. 'There, that's better. Now we can see each other.'

Eliza huddled in the warm spot where Freddie had just vacated his chair, casting an apprehensive glance at Davy. It hurt her deeply to think that their friendship was in jeopardy. 'Davy?'

Normally, he would have responded with a smile but his expression was carefully guarded and he stood up, ignoring her and addressing himself to Freddie. 'I'll give you my answer when I've had time to think about it.' He left the room without a backward glance. Eliza watched him go with a lump in her throat and unshed tears stinging her eyes.

Freddie drew up a chair beside her and sat down, taking her hand in his. 'He's a good chap, Liza. He loves you and he's taking your rejection badly, as any man would who had lived off dreams.'

A feeling of lassitude was claiming Eliza as the warmth of the fire soothed her chilled bones. She allowed her cloak to slip from her shoulders. Freddie was so close to her that she could have laid her head against his shoulder, but this was not the time to seek comfort for herself. She had to break the news that Daisy had already found another man. She curled her cold fingers around Freddie's warm hand and she lifted it to her cheek. The old, familiar feeling of coming home to a safe haven enveloped her like a fur rug. 'He'll forget all about me when he goes back to sea.'

'We had a long talk and he told me that he has no intention of going away again. He intends to stay at home and support his mother and brothers.'

Eliza turned her head to look at him. 'He only went to sea because he couldn't find work ashore.'

'And I think I've come up with the ideal solution.' Freddie kissed her hand, smiling into her eyes. 'Something that will suit us all.'

Eliza drew away from him. Her senses, which were so attuned to Freddie's every mood and whim, warned her that he was about to embark on one of his great and glorious schemes. 'Freddie, what it is? What have you done?'

Chapter Twenty-two

Freddie clasped both her hands and his eyes were alive with enthusiasm. 'My dear, I've been racking my brains to think of a way to look after you and to keep you safe. I know that young Davy is sound and reliable and I've offered him a business partnership. That's what he went away to consider.'

'What?' Eliza stared at him, barely able to believe her ears. 'What sort of partnership?'

'I've got this huge house so close to the river that you could spit out of the window and hit a barge. What does that suggest to you, Liza?'

'That you've gone mad?'

'Close, but not quite right,' Freddie said, chuckling. 'I've decided to turn the top floor into a sail loft.' He jumped to his feet, pacing the floor and gesticulating with his hands. 'It's an enormous space, or it will be if we knock down a few partition walls. I've got the capital to set up the venture and young Davy has the expertise. His family are already settled in the basement, quite happily it seems, and dear Ada is a much better cook than Sukey could ever hope to be.'

'But would it pay? Aaron Miller seems to think that steam will take over and sailing ships will be a thing of the past.'

'That will happen in time, my pet, but there will be a demand for good sailmakers for a long while yet. And I don't intend to let it stop there.'

'No?' Eliza said faintly, as she watched Freddie pacing the floor as he warmed to his theme.

'No, indeed. You lost your business to that old scoundrel Miller. We'll start up our own chandlery here, on the ground floor. It's big enough, and we couldn't be in a better position, overlooking the river and close to the wharves and docks.'

'But, Freddie . . .'

He came to a halt in front of her. 'Think about it, Liza. I'm giving you back your independence, my love. You've had such a hard time and all I want is your happiness.'

In the grip of a multitude of turbulent emotions, Eliza stared up at him. She didn't know if she wanted to throw her arms around him or to slap him. He was grinning at her like an excited schoolboy, waiting for her approval. She knew very well that to condemn his scheme out of hand would cut him to the quick. 'Oh, Freddie, what can I say?'

He seized her hands, pulling her to her feet. 'Don't say anything yet. Think about it and you'll see that it's a wonderful plan.'

516

They were so close that Eliza could feel the heat from his body and inhale the achingly familiar scent of him: she had only to stand on tiptoe to kiss his lips. If she slid her arms around his neck, she could hold him close and tell him how clever he had been. She raised her face, half closing her eyes. He must kiss her now. If he did, he would realise that she was no longer a child but a full-grown woman.

'Well, sweetheart, don't keep me in suspense,' Freddie said, smiling cheerfully and seemingly quite unaware of the passion he had aroused in her breast. 'It's a good idea, you must see that. And it will give you and Davy time to get to know each other again. If you see him as a man and not just a childhood friend . . .'

Eliza pushed him away with all her might. 'You bloody fool, Freddie Prince. You stupid, bloody fool.' Picking up her skirts, she ran from the room.

'Liza, I don't understand. Don't run away from me.'

Freddie's voice behind her only made Eliza run faster. Tears were flowing freely down her cheeks as all the pent-up emotions of the day converged on her in a storm of weeping. How stupid could Freddie be? How could he try to bring her together with Davy, when the only man she had ever wanted was himself? She could hear his footsteps pounding on the flagstones behind her. He was not hampered by hoops and petticoats and he was gaining on her. Eliza ran past the downstairs room that she shared with Millie, heading instinctively for the staircase. Freddie was close behind her, begging her to stop but she carried on, desperate to get away from the pain of loving him. Daisy's room was at the top of the stairs and the door was open. Eliza ran inside and shut the door. Leaning against it, sobbing and gasping for breath, she turned the key in the lock.

'Liza, let me in.'

The sound of his voice made her knees tremble. Unable to speak, Eliza shook her head.

He hammered on the door. 'Liza, dear girl, I don't know what I've done to upset you so. Please let me in.'

'G-go away.'

'No, not until you tell me what's wrong.'

'P-please g-go away. I'm all right, really I am.'

'Eliza.' Freddie's voice deepened as he rattled the handle. 'Let me in. If you don't, I'll break the door down.'

Wiping her eyes on her sleeve, she unlocked the door and moved away. The last thing she wanted was for Freddie's shout to bring Davy running to her aid. 'C-come in.'

Freddie burst into the room. 'What in hell's name is wrong?'

She shook her head, biting her lip. She must not cry again. She must not.

'Darling girl.' Freddie took her gently by the shoulders. 'You can tell me anything; you know that. Haven't I always been more like an elder brother to you, or maybe a rather young uncle?'

The tears that threatened to spill out of her eyes seemed to dry up in an instant. White-hot fury consumed Eliza so that she was shaking all over. She brushed Freddie's hand away with an angry cry. 'Yes, and that's the trouble.'

'Liza?'

'You're not my brother or even a damned uncle, and I never thought of you as such.' Eliza moved closer to him, glaring up into his face with her hands clenched. 'I love you, you stupid dolt. I've always loved you.' She beat her fists against his chest, pummelling him harder with each word. 'I love you.'

For a moment that seemed to expand into eternity, Freddie met her angry stare with a look of bafflement. 'You love me?'

She looked away, biting her lip. She had never meant it to happen this way. Wasn't it always the man who declared his passion for the woman in penny novelettes? Now he would think she was cheap or silly, or both.

'Liza, my own darling.' Freddie lifted her chin with his finger, forcing her to look him in the face. 'Are you sure? I mean, I'm not at all the sort of man that I would have picked for you, had I been your – er – older relation.'

'I don't care about all that. You're not old and I don't think you'll ever be old, Freddie Prince. Not if you live to be a hundred.'

'My darling girl, I was a convicted felon, transported to a penal colony on the other side of the world. I've done many things that I'm not proud of. How could a sweet and wonderful girl like you love someone like me?'

The tender yet diffident look in his eyes meant more to Eliza than a million words. She slipped her arms around his neck, linking her hands and pulling his head down so that their lips were almost touching. 'As easily and naturally as breathing in and out all day.'

'I don't deserve you, Eliza.'

'But do you love me, Freddie?'

'With all my heart, all my soul and all my life, my dearest, dearest Eliza.'

She closed her eyes, giving herself up to the sweet sensation of their first kiss. She had waited for this moment for so long, imagining how it would feel to be held in Freddie's arms: how it would feel to be kissed by the only man she had ever loved. And she was not disappointed. Their bodies seemed to melt into one being as he kissed her with slow caresses of his lips that grew more intense and demanding as she responded eagerly, hungrily and greedily, wanting more and more. Her ears were filled with music; her senses were soaring towards the skies and her heart was pumping wildly, sending fire to every part of her body. She had come alive, as if being awakened from a long sleep.

When at last they drew away to gasp for air, Eliza sighed with ecstasy. 'Do you believe me now?'

Freddie smiled into her eyes, tracing the outline of her full lips with the tip of his index finger. 'Oh, I believe you, my darling. And I love you more than you could ever imagine possible.'

Eliza turned her head to look at Daisy's unmade bed. 'Then take me, Freddie. Make love to me as you made love to her.'

His smile faded into a troubled frown. 'Don't say things like that, Liza. Don't even think it. I was telling the truth when I said I had never been Daisy's lover.'

'I don't care. I want you to make love to me more than I've ever wanted anything. I may be a wanton and no better than Daisy, but I can prove to you that I'm a grown woman.'

Freddie's furrowed brow smoothed and his eyes crinkled at the corners. He dropped a butterfly kiss on Eliza's pursed lips. 'You are a woman, my love. You don't need to prove anything to me. And when I do make love to you it will be with the blessing of the church and in our own bed.'

Eliza's heart gave a hitch inside her chest. 'Are you proposing to me, Freddie Prince?'

He kissed her again. 'Don't be forward, Eliza Bragg. You wait until I've got a ring and can do the whole thing properly.'

'I want the world to know that we love each other, Freddie.'

'All in good time. But it would be wise to wait until everything in the house is resolved.'

It must be kept secret, this wonderful love that filled Eliza's heart and soul with such joy that she wanted to dance and sing. She wanted to run out into the foggy street and proclaim it to the passers-by. She wanted to climb down the slimy stone steps to the foreshore, wade through the stinking, slimy mud and detritus and give her joyous news to the river. The dark waters would carry the message into the swirling depths that had swallowed up her father so many years ago. He would be able to rest more peacefully now, knowing that his only surviving child was happy in love. But Freddie was adamant that they must keep their happiness to themselves, just for a little while longer, until Daisy had moved into the house in Bird Street, and to give Davy time to reach a decision about the sail loft. Eliza had wanted to disagree, but wrapped in Freddie's arms, in the twilight gloom of the bedroom, she listened to his voice and felt his heart beat to the same rhythm as her own. She was so happy that it hurt.

'Now, darling,' Freddie said gently. 'Tell me what happened in Miller's office. How did he take the news that he was Tommy's grandfather?'

When she had finished relating the events of the afternoon, Eliza glanced anxiously up into Freddie's face for signs of distress at Daisy's fickle behaviour. She could have cried with relief when he threw back his head and laughed. 'The minx! Well, good for Daisy. She's a survivor. And at least the boy will have a future. But there's one thing, Liza.' Freddie's expression hardened. 'I won't have you working in the chandlery for Miller or even for Tommy. The business I intend to start here will be ours, although I certainly don't expect you to slave away in the shop.'

Eliza snuggled up to him, taking his hand and placing it on her belly. 'I will be too busy having our babies, Freddie.'

He chuckled. 'You forward girl, have you no shame?'

She smiled up into his eyes. 'None at all. Kiss me again, Freddie.'

In the days that followed, Eliza found it almost impossible to keep silent. She lived for the quiet moments that she snatched alone with Freddie when everyone else in the house was going about their daily business. Daisy had enrolled Tommy at a dame school not too far from Bird Street, but, as usual, Dolly and Tommy shared nursery teatime. They ate their meal of bread and jam, cakes and tea, playing the royal game and picnicking on the floor by the fire. Eliza was amazed that they never tired of the game, although she suspected that in Dolly's dreamland she really was the queen and young Tommy the prince. Not that it mattered much, as long as Dolly was happy. Occasionally she surfaced into the real world, but these brief excursions into reality only upset her, particularly when she remembered that Ted was no longer with her. Freddie had gradually weaned her onto a minimal dose of laudanum and she passed her days halfway between sleeping and waking, pleasantly muzzy and quite content. Eliza had no idea how much her mental state would deteriorate in the future, but at least it was a slow and painless process.

A week had gone by and still Davy had not given Freddie an answer. It was early evening and Dolly had been tucked up in bed by Ada. Daisy had not yet returned from Bird Street, where she went daily to supervise the work of redecorating the house. At least, that was her excuse. Eliza suspected that she was meeting Brandon on the sly, but she kept her thoughts to herself. Millie had put Tommy to bed, and she said that he had been so tired that he had fallen asleep while she was reading him a bedtime story. Now everyone, except Daisy, had gathered for supper in the kitchen, as they did on these winter nights when the dining room was too cold to bear, and the chimney smoked, filling the air with smuts that floated down like black snowflakes.

Ada served them soup from a large iron saucepan on the range and hot bread from the oven. Freddie took his seat at the head of the table and Eliza sat at the opposite end, trying hard not to look at him for fear of giving away their secret. She felt that her face was set in a permanent smile and she was bursting to tell Millie, but Davy had taken a seat beside her and he looked anything but happy. Millie kept glancing at him with a worried frown puckering her brow, but she said nothing. Only Ada seemed impervious to the atmosphere in the room and she ladled soup into bowls, keeping up a constant flow of conversation and seemingly not bothered by the lack of response.

Eliza took a mouthful of vegetable broth, but she could hardly swallow. She nibbled a piece of bread and it almost choked her. Glancing at Freddie, she met his gaze and her heart did a somersault inside her chest. The look in his eyes sent thrills down her spine and she felt her cheeks burning as she stared down at her plate.

'What are you grinning at, Liza?' Davy demanded crossly. 'I don't know why you look so pleased with yourself.'

Millie laid her hand on his arm. 'Leave her be, Davy.'

'I – I wasn't grinning,' Eliza said, breaking her bread into tiny crumbs. 'I mean . . .' She sent a mute plea for help to Freddie.

He cleared his throat with a loud harrumph. 'Davy. Have you – er – thought about my proposition?'

'What's this then?' Ada had been about to take the saucepan into her room to feed the boys and Mary, who had stayed for supper, but she stopped, casting an enquiring look at Davy. 'What's going on, son?'

Davy shrugged his shoulders, chewing on a mouthful of bread, and frowning.

'What is going on?' Millie asked, looking from Freddie to Eliza. 'And where is Daisy? Tommy was really upset that she wasn't there to tuck him in.'

'Well . . .' Eliza began, but Freddie banged his spoon on the table.

'I can see that it's time to set things straight. If you'll sit down for a moment, please, Ada. This concerns you as much as anyone else.' Freddie rose to his feet. 'Davy told me some days ago that he did not want to go back to sea, and I offered him a business partnership. I want to turn the top floor of this house into a sail loft and some of the ground floor rooms into a chandlery.'

'Gawd's strewth!' Ada said, slopping soup from the pan and setting it back down on the range. 'Whatever next?'

'Oh, Davy. That's wonderful,' Millie cried, halfway between tears and laughter.

Davy held up his hand, frowning. 'Hold on. I ain't said I agree to it.'

'But, son, you can't turn down an opportunity like that.' Ada clasped her hands together and her eyes sparkled. 'It would be the answer to all our prayers. Me and the nippers could stay on here, and maybe Pete would give up his job at the brewery to come and help you make sails. It won't matter so much then that your dad has taken up preaching and don't earn a penny for it.'

'And you need never go back to sea,' Millie added. 'We'd be a proper family: all of us together. You can't turn down an offer like that.'

Davy turned to Eliza. 'And what have you got to say about it, Liza? Say the word and I'll stay and gladly accept Freddie's offer.'

She knew that this was the time for complete honesty. Her feelings for Freddie were bubbling so close to the surface that Eliza felt she was about to explode. She rose to her feet and went to stand beside him, clutching his hand. 'I would be more than happy if you said yes, Davy. You see, I've just said the same to Freddie. We're going to be married.'

'You're what?' Daisy's voice cut through the stunned silence like a cheese wire slicing through cheddar. She had entered the kitchen unnoticed in the hubbub. 'Say that again.'

Freddie slipped his arm around Eliza's waist. 'We weren't going to tell you so soon, but seeing as how the truth has come out, yes, I've asked Eliza to marry me and she's made me the happiest man in London. No, the happiest man in the whole world.'

'The truth is,' Eliza said, smiling, 'I asked him.'

'You cunning little bitch,' Daisy hissed through clenched teeth. 'You got me out of the way so that you could make up to my man. Well, I'm telling you, sister-in-law, that I'm not having it. You can't push me out of me own home and you can't take Freddie away from me.'

'That's not fair, Daisy. You was making eyes at Brandon and suggestions that would make a doxy blush, and you've got the house in Bird Street. What more do you want?''

'You planned it that way. You was set on getting Freddie right from the start.' Daisy moved so quickly across the floor that she seemed to be on wheels. She clawed her fingers at Eliza's face and would have torn her flesh if

Freddie had not seen it coming and caught her by the wrist.

'That's enough of that, Daisy. I never made you any promises.'

'Oh dear,' Millie said, covering her mouth with her hands.

Davy helped her to her feet. 'Come on, love. Let's leave them to it. I got a bad taste in me mouth.'

'Son, don't go,' Ada cried, catching him by the sleeve. 'Give Freddie his answer, I'm begging you. For all our sakes.'

Millie sent him a beseeching look. 'Please say you'll stay. I – I need you.'

He frowned. 'I'm glad someone does.'

'What's going on?' Daisy demanded, stamping her foot. 'Bleeding hell, I've only been out of the house for a couple of hours and everything's changed.'

'The business proposition stands,' Freddie said, holding out his hand. 'Shall we shake on it?'

'Please, Davy,' Eliza said. 'Please do. We all need you, and we care about you. We all want you to stay.'

'Well, I don't bloody care,' Daisy said, tugging at the strings of her bonnet and wrenching it off her head. She flung it at Freddie. 'Will you tell me or do I have to scream?'

'Don't scream, for Gawd's sake,' Davy pleaded with a glimmer of humour lighting his eyes. He took Freddie's hand and shook it. 'I accept.'

Daisy opened her mouth and uttered a loud screech.

'All right,' Freddie said hastily. 'With my backing, Davy is going to set up business here, in this house.'

'Oh!' Daisy frowned. 'Well that don't concern me. In fact, none of this concerns me one little bit. She can have you for all I care, Freddie Prince. I never really wanted you anyway, and I'll be taking up residence in my own house in Bird Street as soon as possible. I'll be taking all me furniture, of course.'

'Naturally,' Freddie said agreeably.

'And I'll be taking Sukey with me too.' Daisy glared at each of them in turn, as if daring them to disagree.

Eliza tried not to look too pleased. She would be more than happy to see the back of lazy, sullen Sukey. 'Of course,' she said, nodding in agreement.

Daisy eyed her suspiciously. 'And you'll manage the chandlery until Tommy is old enough to take over? Like Aaron said?'

'I'll help you choose the stock. But you'll have to find someone else to run the shop. I'm going to be busy here.'

'What? But that will cost money.' Daisy frowned, and then she smiled and tossed her head. 'Well, see if I care. Brandon will give me all the help I need.' She glanced at the clock on the wall and her smile faded. 'Oh, lawks! He'll be here any minute and I got to get myself dolled up for a night on the town. He's taking me to a place called the Ship and Turtle. He says their turtle soup is famous and even rich people go there to sample it.' She flounced across the room, pausing in the doorway. 'And don't wait up for me.'

'Wait,' Millie called out anxiously. 'I promised Tommy you would go to the nursery and kiss him goodnight.'

'He'll be asleep by now. I'll see him in the morning. Tell him Mama loves him.' Daisy left the room with a careless wave of her hand.

'Let's hope the kid believes you,' Davy said grimly.

Daisy popped her head round the door. 'I heard that, Davy Little.' She pointed her finger at Ada. 'You. Send Sukey to me right away.'

'Yes'm.' Glowering, Ada picked up the saucepan and stomped out of the kitchen in the direction of the old servants' hall.

'Oh, I nearly forgot,' Daisy said, baring her teeth in a smile. 'Congratulations, Eliza. He says he'll marry you, but I'd keep me legs crossed until I got the ring on me finger, if I was you.'

She closed the door just as Millie pitched a hunk of bread at her, missing her by a fraction of an inch. 'Bitch. Take no notice of her, Liza. She's just a jealous cow.'

'I need some air,' Davy said, making a move towards the door.

'I'll come with you.' Millie slipped her hand through the crook of his arm. 'We'll leave the lovebirds to themselves.'

Davy stared at her for a moment and then he nodded. 'All right, but I was thinking of going to the pub.'

'No matter. I'll go with you.'

'We might get preached at by my dad.'

'I'm a big girl now, Davy. In case you hadn't noticed.'

Eliza held her breath, willing Davy to see Millie for what she was: a loving, sweet-natured girl on the brink of womanhood, who would stand by him no matter what difficulties life had in store for them.

There was a stillness about Davy as he looked into Millie's upturned face and his stern expression melted into a smile. 'You'll need to wrap up warm then, girl. It's bitter outside. Perhaps we'll go for a walk along the river first. I've a fancy to say goodbye to the old ship, seeing as how I won't be sailing on her ever again.'

'I'd like that, Davy.'

As they left the room, Millie glanced over her shoulder, meeting Eliza's gaze with a wink and a smile.

The door closed on them and Freddie jerked Eliza into his arms, claiming her mouth with a kiss. She wrapped her arms around his neck, luxuriating in the sweet sensations that flowed to the core of her being. She had waited so long for Freddie and now it was official, he had told everyone that they were going to be married. She hardly dared to open her eyes in case she discovered that it was all a dream. If it was, then she did not want to wake up.

'I love you, Liza,' Freddie said, kissing her eyelids, the tips of her nose and brushing her lips with a teasing caress. 'Will you do me the honour of becoming my wife?'

Eliza opened her eyes wide. 'You said you wouldn't propose until you'd got me a ring.'

He slipped his hand into his waistcoat pocket and drew out a small box covered in shagreen. 'And I have, my darling. I had to guess at the size, but we can always change it if it doesn't fit or if you don't like diamonds.'

She opened the box and let out a gasp of delight. 'It's beautiful, Freddie.'

He took it from its velvet bed. 'Will you marry me, Eliza?'

'Oh, yes. But I don't want to wait another six years for you.'

'There's no question of that, my darling.' Freddie slipped the ring on her finger and scooped her up in his arms. 'I'll get a special licence tomorrow.' He opened the door with the toe of his boot and strode through the narrow corridors to the entrance hall.

'Freddie,' Eliza said, giggling, as he mounted the stairs. 'What are you thinking of?'

'Of making love to you, Eliza, my dearest. All night long.'

She nuzzled his neck, closing her eyes; dizzy with the scent of him. 'And I thought you were going to be a gentleman.'

'Not tonight, my love. Tonight, and for always, you're mine.'